THE
SPACE
BETWEEN
WORLDS

THE SPACE BETWEEN WORLDS

MICAIAH JOHNSON

NEW YORK

Copyright © 2020 by Micaiah Johnson

Published in the United States by Del Rey, an imprint of Random House, a division of Penguin Random House LLC, New York.

DEL REY is a registered trademark and the CIRCLE colophon is a trademark of Penguin Random House LLC.

ISBN 978-0-593-13505-1

To Grandma Tree
I love you. You made me. Please don't read this
book.

To You
You will always be with me, even if not in the way
either of us once hoped.
There's too much sun where I'm from, I had to give
some away. And so I gave you away.

THE
SPACE
BETWEEN
WORLDS

PART ONE

"In the far reaches of an infinite cosmos, there's a galaxy that looks just like the Milky Way, with a solar system that's the spitting image of ours, with a planet that's a dead ringer for earth, with a house that's indistinguishable from yours, inhabited by someone who looks just like you, who is right now reading this very book and imagining you, in a distant galaxy, just reaching the end of this sentence. And there's not just one such copy. In an infinite universe, there are infinitely many. In some, your doppelgänger is now reading this sentence along with you. In others, he or she has skipped ahead, or feels in need of a snack and has put the book down.

In others, he or she has, well, a less than felicitous disposition and is someone you'd rather not meet in a dark alley."

Brian Greene, *The Hidden Reality*

CHAPTER ONE

When the multiverse was confirmed, the spiritual and scientific communities both counted it as evidence of their validity.

The scientists said, *Look, we told you there were parallel universes.*

And the spiritual said, *See, we've always known there was more than one life.*

\

EVEN WORTHLESS THINGS can become valuable once they become rare. This is the grand lesson of my life.

I'm at the base of a mountain, looking over a landscape I was never meant to see. On this Earth—number 197—I died at three months old. The file only lists respiratory complications as cause of death, but the address on the certificate is the same one-room shack where I spent most of my life, so I can picture the sheet-metal roof, the concrete floor, and the mattress my mother and I shared on so many different Earths. I know I died warm, sleeping, and inhaling honest dirt off my mother's skin.

"Cara, respond. Cara?"

Dell's been calling me, but she's only irritated now and I won't answer until she's *concerned*. Not because I like being difficult—though, there is that—but because her worry over a wasted mission sounds just like worry over me.

Behind me, information is downloading from a stationary port into a mobile one. When it's done, I'll take the mobile back to Earth Zero, our primary Earth, the one the others think of as real. The information I gather is divided up into light data—population, temperature fluctuations, general news—and dark data—what is affecting their stocks that might affect ours, or, if it's a future world, a full listing of where every stock will close on a given day. The existence of the dark data is a big secret, though I don't know why anyone would care. Insider trading doesn't even sound like a crime—not a real one, one with blood.

"Cara . . ."

Still just annoyed. I check the download's progress. Sixty percent.

"Cara, I need you to answer me."

There we go.

"I'm here."

There's a pause while she resets to apathy, but I heard the panic. For a second, she cared.

"You don't always have to leave me waiting."

"And you don't always have to plant me two miles from my download port, but I guess we're both a little petty, eh Dell?"

I can hear her smiling but not smiling from 196 worlds away. I've dodged the physical training for my job since just after my hiring six years ago. She's so uptight, you'd think she'd just report me, but forcing me on these long walks is her answer.

"You're wanted back. There's a file on your desk."

"I already have my pulls for the week."

"Not a pull. A *new* file."

"No, but . . ."

I put my hand against my chest, expecting to feel a divot, some missing chunk of flesh.

I want to tell her it can't be true. I want to tell her I would have known. Instead, I tell her I need an hour and cut the link.

If I have a new world, it means that particular Earth's me isn't using it anymore. I'm dead again, somewhere else, and I didn't feel a thing.

I'm not sure how long I sit, staring out at a horizon that's like mine, but not. The download *ding*s its finish. I could traverse out from here, since there's no one to see me, but I steal a little time exploring the place fate tried to keep from me.

Another me is gone. As I walk into the valley, I'm a little more valuable walking down the mountain than I was walking up.

\

WHEN I WAS young and multiverse was just a theory, I was worthless: the brown girl-child of an addict in one of those wards outside the walls of Wiley City that people don't get out of or go to. But then Adam Bosch, our new Einstein and the founder of the institute that pays me, discovered a way to see into other universes. Of course, humanity couldn't just look. We had to enter. We had to touch and taste and take.

But the universe said no.

The first people sent to explore a parallel Earth came back already dead or twitching and about to die, with more broken bones than whole ones. Some actually did make it through, and survived on the new world just long enough to die from their injuries and have their bodies recalled.

It took a lot of smart people's corpses before they learned that if you're still alive in the world you're trying to enter, you get rejected. You're an anomaly the universe won't allow, and she'll send you back broken in half if she has to. But Bosch's device could resonate only with worlds very similar to our own, so most of the scientists—with their safe, sheltered upbringings in a city that had eliminated childhood mortality and vaccinated most viral illness into extinction—had living doppelgängers on the other worlds.

They needed trash people. Poor black and brown people. People somehow on the "wrong side" of the wall, even though they were the ones who built it. People brought for labor, or come for refuge, or who were here before the first neoliberal surveyed this land and thought to build a paradise. People who'd already thought this was paradise. They needed my people. They needed me.

Of the 380 Earths with which we can resonate, I'm dead in 372. No, 373 now. I'm not a scientist. I'm just what they're stuck with. The higher-ups call us "traversers" on paper. Using ports put in place by the last generation of traversers, we download the region's information and bring it back for greater minds to study. No better than pigeons, which is what they call us, not on paper.

One day, the Eldridge Institute will figure out how to remotely download information across worlds, and I'll be worthless again.

\

BACK ON EARTH Zero, I go straight to my floor after changing into my office clothes. Dell stands out tall in the herd of desks, more than two-thirds of them empty now. Her face is all tight because she's been kept waiting by the only person who ever dares inconvenience her.

"Slumming it, Dell? I thought coming below the sixtieth floor gave you hives."

She smiles, less like she thinks I'm funny and more like she wants to prove she knows how.

"I'll survive."

Of that, I can be sure. Survival is Dell's whole problem. Here, on Earth Zero, she wanted to be a traverser. She was set up for it too: an air force pilot who'd had her eyes on space before the possibility of other worlds opened up. But Dell comes from a good family, one with money a long way back. In some worlds her parents never emigrated from Japan. In some she joined the private sector instead of this government-research-institute hybrid. But she survived in over 98 percent of other worlds, and in most of those she thrived. I've seen three dozen Dells, and all but one wore clothes more expensive than mine.

When I take off my jacket, we both hide our wince. Bruises line my arms in jagged stripes, and those are just the parts she can see.

"It shouldn't be this bad," she says, her eyes moving between quadrants of my body like she's doing hard math.

"It's only because I've been doubling up."

"Which is why I advised against it."

"I need the long weekend."

We've had this conversation five times this week and it always ends right here, where her concern is outweighed by the effort it takes to argue with me. She nods, but the look she gives my arms lasts long enough for me to notice. It's when she notices my noticing that she finally looks away.

Early on, the professionals on the upper stories, scientists like Bosch and watchers like Dell, told me the bruising was from the resistance of an object from one world being forced into another, like the violence of north and south magnets being shoved together. Other traversers, and they are a superstitious lot, told me the pressure we felt had a name, and it was "Nyame." They said her kiss was the price of the journey.

Dell touches the clear screen that's been delivered to me. It looks like a blank sheet of plastic, but once I activate it I'll know the basics of the world that's just been assigned to me. I learned quickly after moving here that the city loves plastic the way my town loves metal. Everything here is plastic. And it's all the same kind. When a plastic thing stops working, they put it down a chute and turn it into another plastic thing, or the same thing but fixed. Plastic here is like water everywhere else; there's never any more or less of it, just the same amount in an endless cycle.

"Do you know what your new world is?" she asks.

"You haven't given it to me yet."

"Can you guess?"

I should say no, because I resent being asked to do parlor tricks, but instead I answer, because I want to impress her.

"One Seventy-Five," I say. "If I had to guess."

I know I'm right by the way she refocuses on me. Like I'm interesting. Like I'm a bug.

"Lucky guess," she says, sliding the screen to me.

"Not really. There's only seven options."

I sit and pull out the drive that contains the payload from my last job. As soon as I plug it in, the dark data will upload to persons unknown and delete itself. I send the light data to the analysts who will interpret and package it for the scientists.

Eldridge thinks we traversers don't know about the first package of intel. Like the organizations responsible for space exploration in the past, Eldridge is technically an independent company, though it's heavily funded by the government of Wiley City. There is an industrial hatch outside the city walls, in the empty strip of desert between here and Ashtown, which brings in resources from other worlds. Taxpayers, government officials, and especially Eldridge's lesser employees are supposed to believe that is how the company supplements the income it gets from research grants. Sure, bringing in resources from another world so we don't have to harm ours is probably worth a mint. But that doesn't add up to tenth-richest-man-in-the-city money, which is what our CEO and founder has.

Because no traverser has ever made a report to enforcement or asked questions, they think they've pulled this elaborate ruse on lower-level employees. But really, we just don't care. A job's a job, and people edging out other people to make money buying and selling something invisible just sounds like rich-people problems.

I look up at Dell, still standing beside me. She's a rich person, but the kind who's always going to be rich. Rich so far back it'd take two generations of fuckups for her family to go broke. There's a lot of this up here in the city. Not new-money rich people, like Adam Bosch, but whole rich families where the wealth is spread out among the members so it doesn't attract attention.

"Something else?"

"Saeed is gone," she says.

"Star? They fired her?" When she nods, I ask, "Did she mess up?"

I hope she did. Starla Saeed is one of the last traversers remaining from before I started. She was born in what they call a civil war but was really just a ruler systematically killing his subjects. When she was twelve she took a journey across the sea that drowned more people than it delivered. She could travel to over two hundred worlds.

If she screwed up, it's just a firing, only interesting because we have the same job and were close once. If she was downsized, she's a canary in the mine.

"One Seventy-Five was the last world only she had access to. When your death on that world registered . . . Why pay two salaries and benefits when they can just put 175 in your rotation?"

What she doesn't say, but thinks: *Why pay a decent salary at all for a glorified courier?*

"One Seventy-Five won't be scheduled for at least a week, but it wouldn't hurt for you to familiarize yourself over your long weekend. And pay attention to the bruising. I want to make sure it's clearing before your next pull."

Again, I can interpret her fear over a wasted asset however I want, and I choose to pretend it's affection. The long look she takes at my arms and chest makes me shiver, and for a second I wonder if I am just pretending. But then she sees my reaction and backs away, nearly running into Jean.

"Ms. Ikari," he says, formally, the way she likes.

"Mr. Sanogo," she says, also formally, the way he doesn't like.

The famous Jean Sanogo has always just been called Jean, or Papa Jean by the papers.

"How is our best girl today?" he asks.

"Stubborn. She's bruising more than usual, tell her to pay attention to it." Dell glares over her shoulder. "She might actually listen to you."

"I assure you, she ignores us both equally," he says, and Dell walks away.

I've finished uploading the information packet under my username, so I log out and log back in with my superior's credentials. I use the stolen access to send a copy of the light data packet to my cuff so I can read through it later.

Jean has pulled over an empty traverser's chair.

"Dell is tense. You need to stop teasing her when you're off-world."

"But then how will she know I like her?" I say.

"You've been flirting with her for five years. She knows." He leans forward, setting down a steaming cup, and adjusts his glasses to look at my progress screen. "Am I witnessing company theft in my name? My wounded heart."

"Come now, old man. It can't really be theft if I'm just reading. You can't steal something that's still there when you've taken it."

"You'll find a large portion of the judicial system here disagrees with you."

I wave my hand. *Judicial* is a Wiley City word if I've ever heard one, and it has no place between us.

Jean knows what I'm doing. Not only was it his idea, but it's his credentials I use to send myself the info. He thinks if I study the figures and look for patterns the way analysts do, I'll be valuable to the company for more than my mortality rate. He thinks I can be more than a traverser, that I can be like him. With the number of desks sitting empty around me, I am desperate to believe he's right.

Jean was in the first group of surviving traversers. Before that, he lived through a rebel army's ten-year border war on the Ivory Coast. As a traverser, he could visit more than 250 Earths. He used to walk the worlds with us, but now he sits in a room and makes the policies surrounding traversing. When he goes out in public, people repeat his famous quote—*I have seen two worlds now and the space between. We are a wonder*—from the moment he landed safely on a new world. They shake his hand and take his picture, but he is quick to remind me that he was once worthless too.

Jean is the one who told me about Nyame, just like he tells every new traverser. It's the name of a goddess where he comes from, one who sits in the dark holding the planets in her palm. He says the first time he traveled to another world, he could feel her hand guiding him. I've never had much use for religion, but I respect him too much to disagree.

"This is 197, yes?" he asks, nodding to the screen showing the info I've just pulled. "The sky scientists were braying over it."

"They're called astronomers, Jean. And yeah, they put a rush on it. They want pictures of some asteroid that's too far away and they didn't want to wait a week for." I try to rotate my arm and wince at the ache.

"They paid a premium to rush a few pictures?" Jean makes a dismissive clucking sound. "Too much money, not enough purpose."

Jean's dislike of astronomers is an occupational hazard, and the dislike is mutual. Those working strictly in the field of space exploration haven't been fond of interuniversal travel, the new frontier that came along and snatched up a chunk of their funding. In return, those who work at Eldridge treat space exploration the way a young male lion looks at an older, sickly male lion—no outright violence, but maybe showing too much excitement in anticipation of the death.

Jean nudges the mug I'm ignoring toward me again. Sighing, I take a sip and barely keep from spitting.

"I was really hoping for coffee," I say, forcing myself to down the dark mixture of vitamin D, zinc, and too many other not-quite-dissolved nutrients.

"Coffee is not what you need," he says in the accent my limited world experience first thought of as French. "Nyame kissed you hard this time."

"With teeth."

"So I see. Dell marked you for observation."

Of course she did. "I've only been scheduling pulls close together so I can take a few days off. I told her that."

"A vacation? I should think staying in place would have more appeal for you."

"Not a vacation. It's . . . it's a family thing."

At the mention of *family* he smiles, which just goes to show what he knows. In the worlds where he survived—where he wasn't a child soldier, where he didn't die trying to stow away into Europe—he did so because of the strength of his father and the bravery of his mother. From the worlds I've studied, his deaths are usually despite their best efforts.

Most of my deaths can be linked directly to my mother.

"Enjoy this time off. Don't do too much studying."

"I'll try."

But not very hard.

I've been staying up too late studying world stats and the company's internal textbooks since he first mentioned the possibility of a promotion to analyst. My mother used to say I was born reaching, which is true. She also used to say it would get me killed, which it hasn't. Not yet, anyway. Not here.

\

BEFORE I HEAD home, I swing by Starla Saeed's place. I'm nearly too late, and I approach her apartment among a stream of people in uniforms moving out boxes of her stuff.

She's standing in the yard, flanked on either side by immigration enforcement. Her eyes are glassy, but clear. She might have been crying earlier, but she's done with it now. She looks strong, defiant, head held high like she hasn't lost everything in the world. I hope I look like that when they come for me.

"Star . . ."

When she turns to me she looks neither surprised nor particularly pleased, but when she looks down at the basket of apples in my hand, she gives a little smirk.

"We're not all Ashtowners, Caramenta," she says. "Some of us have tree fruit in our homelands."

I look down. Most traversers come from the encampments outside of walled cities; I just assumed the other towns were like my wasteland. Starla comes from outside of Ira City in the Middle East, one of the biggest and oldest walled structures nestled in the space between what used to be Iraq and Iran. Maybe the settlements outside of Ira are full of fruit and white bread and everything else Ashtown doesn't have.

A man carrying a box walks too fast, and the sound of glass clinking against glass rings out between us. She watches him like he's dragging her baby by the foot. She looks like she might yell—she's known around the office for her quick temper—but her eyes flick to the enforcement agent standing closest to her and she swallows it down. She's furious, but helpless.

"I just thought you'd like something. I know it's a long flight." I hold out the basket. "You can still resent me, even if you take them."

She smiles again, her mouth wide and full. "I intend to."

She takes the basket, but it's more out of pity than wanting the fruit.

"I'll miss you," I say.

"So look for me," she says. "I'm only missing on a few hundred worlds, and this is just one more. I recommend Earth 83 me. She's my favorite."

A woman in a jumpsuit tells the agents they're done, and the men push Star along. She looks at me over her shoulder.

"Don't waste your time feeling guilty," she says. "It'll be you soon enough."

Over my dead body . . . but that's not what she needs to hear. She needs my absence more than anything. A witness to the shame makes it worse, even if it's a friend. So I nod goodbye, and turn away.

\

THERE ARE INFINITE worlds. Worlds upon worlds into absurdity, which means there are probably worlds where I am a plant or a dolphin or where I never drew breath at all. But we can't see those. Eldridge's machine can read and mimic only frequencies similar to ours, each atom on the planet contributing to the symphony. They say that's why objects like minerals and oil can be brought in easily, but people have to be gone from the world first—their structure is so influenced by their world's unique frequency there's no possibility of a dop. Before we lost 382, there were rumblings of war. I'm not sure how many nuclear bombs it would take to change the song of a place until we can't hear it anymore, but we lost 382 over the course of an hour: a drastic shift making the signal weak, then another, then nothing.

It should scare us more than it does, but they were already an alien territory anyway. That's why the number was the highest. Each number indicates a degree of difference, a slight frequency shift from our own. Earths One through Ten are so similar they are hardly worth visiting. When I pull from there, no more than twice a year, it's just to make sure the intel is still exactly like ours. Three of the worlds in which I still live are in the first ten Earths.

There is something gratifying about going places where I'm dead and touching things I was never even meant to see. In my apartment I keep a collection of things from those places in sealed bags on the wall. I've never catalogued them, but I can identify each item on sight: dirt from the lot where my childhood home would have been in a world where the slums never made it that far; smooth rocks from a river that's been dead on my world for centuries; a jade earring given to me by a girl on another Earth who wanted me to remember her, but who only let me love her at all because she didn't know where I came from. There are hundreds, and when I get back from Earth 175, there will be one more.

The worlds we can reach are similar to ours in atmosphere, flora, and fauna, so most of their viruses already exist here. But just in case, I seal my souvenirs in the bags Eldridge used to use for specimen collection, before they got bored playing biologists and shifted hard to mining and data collection.

I'm staring at my clothes, trying to figure out which to bring. It's hard, living in Wiley while visiting Ashtown. Not a lot of people go between. Sure, Wileyites will visit Ashtown like tourists, and Ashtown kids sometimes get scholarships to Wiley schools, but no one ever tries to *fit* in both places. Wiley City is like the sun, and Ashtown a black hole; it's impossible to hover in between without being torn apart. I've spent my time in the city accumulating the kind of clothes that will make me look like I've never been to Ashtown at all. If I were smart, I'd keep a set of Ashtown clothes for these trips instead of standing out like a mirror in the desert every time I go. But deep down, I don't want to fit in. I don't want to look like I belong there, because one day I want to pretend I never did.

I'm fingering a blouse I can't bring—true black synthetic silk, nothing a former Ruralite holy girl would wear—when my sister calls.

Instead of a greeting, she answers with a grunt of frustration.

"Preparations going that well, huh?" I say, sitting on the bed. Esther is still just a teenager, but the amount of responsibility she's inherited makes her seem older.

"It's fine," she says, voice primly forced. Ruralites aren't allowed to be angry, not at other people, because it would violate their code of endless compassion and understanding.

"Michael still being useless?"

No one tests Esther's faith, or her temper, like her twin brother.

"Cara, you know all people have value and use in the eyes of God. Michael would be a valuable contribution to the dedication . . . if he'd shown up at any of the preparations."

Ah, there it is, Esther's rage—the venom no less potent for all its masking.

"And now we have Cousin Joriah saying he might drop in and—"

I roll off the bed. "Joriah?"

"Yes, you remember. Tall, red hair? He moved out here for a little while when we were young, but then left for the deep wastes as a missionary."

Of course I don't remember. I can't.

"He's based in some small town on the other side of the dead lands now, but Dad thinks he might make the pilgrimage."

She goes on, but I'm not really listening. I reach under my bed, pulling out my box of journals. Esther said when *we* were young, so I pick a journal from not long after Esther's father married my mother. *Caramenta, age 13* is written on its cover. Esther would have been five.

"Hey, I gotta go, but I'll see you soon."

I hit the button on my cuff to disconnect from Esther, then begin searching through the journal. Eventually I find an entry mentioning Joriah moving in, and skim a bit longer until he moves away again, gleaning all I can about him. Apparently he was very funny, though not great at personal hygiene. I find a few more references in later journals, but then it really is time to go. My mother won't yell if I'm late—not like she used to—but she'll cloak herself in this sad, martyred quiet I can't stand. I put the journals back. In them, Cousin Joriah is just called Jori. I whisper both versions of the name so that when I say them out loud later, it won't sound like it's the first time.

I've gotten rid of a lot of things from my past, but I'll always keep the journals. I read them like data from another world, doing research on people who love me. I don't write now. I make lists in my current journal, but that only started as a way for me to practice writing in Eldridge's code, so I'm not sure it counts. In the box under my bed there is one journal for every year, two some years, but I've had the same one for six years now and haven't managed to fill it up. Maybe it's because there's so little I'm sure of these days.

I've been in Wiley City for six years as a resident. In four more, I'll be pronounced citizen. For now, I'm nowhere. I live in Wiley but I'm legally still Ashtown's, and neither has a claim on me that counts. It's a space between worlds, no different from the star-lined darkness I stand in when I traverse. The darkness is worth it, because I know what waits on the other side.

\

REASONS I HAVE DIED:

The emperor of the wasteland wanted to make an example of my mother, and started with me.

One of my mother's boyfriends wanted to cover up what he did to me.

I was born addicted and my lungs didn't develop.

I was born addicted and my brain didn't develop.

I was left alone, and a stranger came along.

The runners came for a neighbor, and I was in the way.

The runners came for my mother, and I was in the way.

The runners came for my mother's boyfriend, and I was in the way.

The runners came for no one, serving nothing at all but chaos and fear, and I was what they found.

Sometimes, I was just forgotten in the shed where she kept me while she worked or spun out, and in the length of her high and the heat of the sun I fell asleep alone and hungry and forever.

REASONS I HAVE LIVED:

I don't know, but there are eight.

CHAPTER TWO

've been driving in the desert for an hour when the truck pulls up too close behind me. I've prepared to be stopped, but deep down I'm still surprised. Getting shaken down by border patrol is only for outsiders, and the man walking up to my car with a greedy silver smile is proof I've made it. His teeth tell me he's one of Nik Nik's lieutenants, the kind of guy I would have been happy to land when I was from here. Like all runners, he smells like dirt and sun. He's tattooed solid up to his jawline, where the ink stops abruptly. The display of vanity strikes me. These days I look for status by reading clothes, haircuts, and high-dollar wrist cuffs, but this too-pretty runner reminds me that I grew up wanting to lick silver teeth.

"Lovely weather for a day trip," he says, like it isn't the same ninety degrees with a hot-wind kicker it always is out here.

"Not taking a day trip."

I don't know when my posture changed, when my voice dropped, but when I look at him square I want him to recognize me as one of his own almost as much as I don't. I wish I knew him, knew the name his mother called him so I could throw it in his face. Nik Nik's runners all go by mister—Mr. Bones, Mr. Shine—but I'd bet he's an Angelo.

"Toll for lookie-loos from the Wiles is three hundred."

"You mean two-fifty."

"Times are tough."

"I was just here."

"Three hundred."

I reach into my dashboard and take out three hundred, just like last time, though I'm going to try haggling every visit until it works.

He takes the cash with a nobleman's slight bow. "Enjoy your stay in Big Ash."

When he starts to walk away, I clear my throat.

"My receipt."

"Mr. Cheeks," he says. "Tell the next one you're paid up."

MY MOTHER LIVES in a farmhouse in the Rurals where a real farm never was. The Rurals are a part of Ashtown that thinks itself a subdivision, even though the only thing separating it from the concrete stacked pods that make up the rest of the city is a wooden fence and the agreement of people on both sides of that fence. The people in the Rurals are all about charity and piety and religion. The people in downtown Ash are all about anything else.

There aren't many cars out here—even runners usually keep their vehicles on the other side of the fence—and sometimes when I drive out kids run beside me for as long as they can, reaching out to touch the paint. Not today though. Today they're all indoors, sequestered in thankful prayer as they prepare for the dedication ceremony.

My mother's house is in deep, where the gray-white sand begins to turn a natural tan at the edges. The front of the house has been white-washed for the day, the plaster cast of Mary wiped clean. It's Jesus's mother, Mary, not the foot-washing ex-prostitute Mary, which has always struck me as something of a missed opportunity given my mother's background. Mary's head is inclined toward a flute-playing Krishna, who smiles benevolently in the empty way everyone in the Rurals smiles at strangers. And at me. My stepfather generally preaches more from Islam than Hindu, but there isn't really a statue for that.

My mother lets me in, her mouth a line as even and unbending as her principles. Her black hair, 4C hair that I know is twice as wild as my own, is pulled back in a bun so tight it looks straight. Her patterned dress is clean, but washed thin. It bears no scars from mending, so it must be one of her best. I could buy her new dresses. I could keep her in the kind of flash she used to demand from her men before she walked away from the life with a preacher from the dirt. But she won't take anything from me these days, not even a hug.

Her eyes are down. Her eyes are always down, this mostly silent woman who'll wear no skirt higher than her knee and no lip stain darker than a blush. My mother was a woman who had hair feathered whatever color suited her mood and knew how to look men in the eye until they gave her what she wanted.

"You're early," she says. "That's nice."

"I took today off," I say, but she's already turning to lead me inside.

I've seen her a hundred ways—with a shaved head, with hair to her back, with rows of piercings for eyebrows, blind in one eye, pock-marked with no teeth, and even as a still-beautiful matron of the House, who could charge as much as the young because she never used and always took care of herself—but this version is my least favorite. She spends her time passing out pamphlets downtown, shaming the work-ers at the House who took care of me when she didn't, who saved my life enough times to get this version of me to adulthood.

My family's walls are covered with more of the same holiness that's found outside. At least when we were poor she was original, painting murals on the concrete with the same paste she used to dye her hair. Now her walls are grids, family pictures—the old-school static holo-grams that flicker on and off with age—broken up with religious icons.

The more interesting things on the wall—dried animal bones and drawings of creatures with skulls for faces—are from Esther's faiths. My stepfather might love the Bible and the Quran, but my sister gives almost as many sermons as he does these days and she favors less organized religions, some that don't even have a unifying text.

"Joriah wasn't able to make the journey," my mother says, and I exhale a bit of the dread I've been hiding. I won't have to pretend all day then. At least, no more than usual.

She turns away from me. "Company's here," she says.

She won't say *Caramenta*. She's ashamed now to have given her daughter a slum name. My stepfather's name is Daniel. His children are Esther and Michael. My mother was born Mellorie, but those who trick in Ash use *x*'s in their names as an identifier, so she'd been Lorix since before I was born. Here and now, she's just Mel.

My stepfather comes in, his smile wide and genuine. He is blond, like his daughter. It's an advertisement. Real Wileyites have white hair and skin so pale it's a shade off blue. Daniel's hair reminds his congregation that his great-grandfather came here willingly as a missionary from the city, not as a refugee or migrant trying to get into it.

He hugs me easily, with less hesitation than it took my mother to look in my eyes. "You made it. What do you think of the tie? Too on the nose?"

Usually, he wears a tunic like all men from the Rurals, but outsiders are coming and he's attempting to dress like them. His tie is covered in little fish, smiling at one another as they swim in all directions.

"Are you going for holy and approachable, or completely cheesy?"

He fakes thinking about it. "Both?"

"Then it's perfect."

"Thought so," he says, then nods over his shoulder. "Twins are out back."

I see Esther and Michael outside, having the kind of conversation I'm sure only twins have. Esther looks pleading, Michael resolved. Neither seems to be speaking, and yet both have been understood. Michael's black hair would have made him the outsider in the family if Mom and I hadn't shown up. He is nice to me, but not like we're family, not like I am someone he will ever give a nickname or call late at night. The twins don't remember their mother, a woman whose face and past matched theirs far better than my mother's ever will, but I've looked her up. In worlds where their mother lives, my mother never meets Dan and never leaves downtown.

Their conversation picks up again, and the wind carries Esther's raised voice against the window. I turn away, trying to remember the last time I cared about anything enough to scream for it.

I change in my old room, now converted into Esther's office. When she comes in, I take a container from my bag and toss it over my shoulder at her. She smiles as she catches it, running her thumb along the face cream's silver top.

"You shouldn't feed my vanity. It's my worst trait," she says, sitting on the cot that will be my bed tonight.

"That you think vanity is your worst trait is a sign of your vanity."

I put on tights, even though they're thick, black, and hell to wear in the desert, and Esther's eyes fixate on my legs. This last trip has pushed the traversing bruises—unique stripes on either side of my limbs and torso—down my thighs and onto both sides of my calves. That alone wouldn't force me to put on tights, but the garage tattoos on the back of my thighs, a massive eye on each leg, are also exposed.

My mother can never see the tattoos. I've had tattoos removed from my arms, chest, the base of my neck, and behind my ears. I've saved a little at a time to have the rest removed, but I started on the ones in plain view first. The next one I erase will be the largest: the six letters of someone else's name scrawled across my back from shoulder blade to shoulder blade.

"Mom still thinks you never got tattoos before you left Ashtown," she says.

I concentrate on not pausing in my task. "How did that come up?"

"Michael wants a plated tooth. She's been using you as an example, because you're worldly, but you didn't alter your body."

"He wants a runner's tooth?"

"Worse," she says. "He wants onyx, like Nik Nik."

"No." I look up from my tights so she'll know I'm serious. "You can't let him. If runners see him with an emperor's tooth they'll rip it out. It's an insult. If he has to get one, get silver. Silver's safe."

She's looking at me wide-eyed, seeing too much. It's the same way she looked at me when she was twelve. She's probably wondering how a Ruralite girl knows so much about downtown Ash's runners.

"Is that what you two were fighting about?"

She waits a second, deciding whether she's going to let me get away with moving the conversation along, then answers. "We weren't fighting, we were discussing, and no. That was about something else."

My sister tells me everything, so her pause means this is Michael's secret.

"I was good at hiding things from her before I left home," I say, sitting next to her. "That's why Mom never knew."

"And from me. I never saw them either until you came back."

"You were twelve. I could have hidden an eye patch from you then."

We talk for a little while, though mostly I listen. Eventually she looks out the window and stands. I stand, too, but I don't have anywhere to go. This is where we separate. The sun is setting, so she will need to pray. Today, the theme will be gratitude, a litany of thanks from a girl raised in a place with nothing. She will don an apron for tonight's festivities, something her people wear when they interact with the nonreligious, a sign of their willingness to help if asked. And I will wear my dress, a sign that I am not part of the church, just a nonbelieving donor.

But she's taking the face cream with her, just like she does the lip balm and tooth rinses I bring. She wears products from me that change her appearance, and it almost makes up for the fact that she is too fair to ever look like me. When I see her, absent the sunspots of her peers, her teeth shining white in that ever-benevolent smile, I think, *There, there I am*. Because that's what a sister is: a piece of yourself you can finally love, because it's in someone else.

SHOES. I'D FORGOTTEN to bring cheap shoes. I'd grabbed the only dressy pair I owned, black with the distinctive gold line running up the back indicating the brand without saying it. Dell got them for me because she knew I'd embarrass myself at company parties in whatever I owned, and by extension embarrass her, but it doesn't matter that they were a gift. These shoes could buy a month of food for the families out here. When I walk into the new church they click loudly in a crowd of heels too worn down to match the sound. It shames me more than it shames them, but it does shame us both. I make up for it by smiling too much, because my usual aloofness will look like elitism to them.

At the dedication ceremony, senior members of the church speak about how much this new building will mean to the community. I believe it. In my journal there's a picture of the old church. At best, it was a glorified barn. This new building has real walls, the kind that actually keep the heat out instead of just blocking sunlight. And, my stepfather's greatest pride, it has a series of attached rooms, each large enough to give temporary shelter to a family of four. Rural wastelanders eschew formal houses, but on bright days, days when the sun is too close and the atmosphere too thin, even those adept at living rough need more than mud over their heads.

The theme of the night is gratitude, so every speaker thanks God. But the theme for the night is also survival, so they are careful to thank Nik Nik almost as often. I don't know if they're thanking the emperor for a donation, or if they're thanking him for the privilege of having a building without his runners burning it down, but they aren't really grateful, just afraid of what will happen if they don't look it.

Nik Nik is sitting behind me. The Ruralites always save a seat in the back row for him during services, even though he rarely attends. Just as they always save a seat for the House proprietor, even though Exlee has no use for religion. They are both here tonight though: Exlee because standing there looking like the only soft thing in the desert is an excellent advertisement, and Nik Nik because he wants to remind people who bow to God that they must bow to him first. I stare at Exlee, done

up in leather and black glitter, and long for the days when the proprietor knew my name.

After the speeches, my mother serves refreshments from behind a
counter while the rest of my family gives tours of the facility. When I
go to her, she hands me a glass of lemonade like I'm just another donor.
It's her own recipe—hints of honey, the scent of lavender without the
taste. She's not allowed to brag, but when I say it's the best thing she's
ever made she doesn't correct me.

"Did you have to invite everyone?" I ask.

She manages to convey irritation without compromising the be-
nevolence in her face. It's all in the eyes. "He gave. Everyone who gave
is entitled to come."

She has to be respectful, because if you disrespect Nik Nik, he may
want to teach you a lesson. That lesson can be a quadrupled utility bill,
or a house fire set by a smiling runner.

I've never catered to him. But then, I've never been afraid to die,
which has probably been my problem on more than one Earth.

"I don't know why you hate him so much," she says. "It's not as if
he's ever crossed us personally."

I open my mouth to tell her how wrong she is, but she continues,
saving me from making a mistake.

"We left downtown before he even inherited."

Hearing my mother talk about leaving the center of Ash reminds
me where and who I am and which one she is. She doesn't know how
many other hers died in the concrete because of Nik Nik and his even-
worse father . . . but you'd think she could guess.

"You're right. I've never met the emperor. I just don't like the idea
of him."

She stiffens, tapping the lemonade ladle against the bowl.

The sound is too loud in the room, which has suddenly gone silent.
Which means he's here. If I turn around, I'll see the spectacle of Nik
Nik: two tight rows braided just above his left ear, because he is the
third in his line to control Ash; the rest of his hair left down so every-

one who sees him knows he is not a man who works in the wastelands or with machines or at all; and in his mouth, all four incisors plated in synthetic onyx so they shine like black diamonds and, yes the rumors are true, cut just like them too.

And there is a world where in this moment a more reckless and honest me smashes my lemonade glass and cuts his throat with a shard, where I put my hands into his still-warm blood and the thick of it washes away the multitude of shames I carry. But that world and that me are so different from this one I doubt Eldridge would ever be able to resonate with it. I am no longer reckless, and I have never been honest.

I set the glass back down at my mother's station and leave the room to find Esther. I haven't heard Nik Nik's voice in over six years, and I intend to keep it that way.

To bring the night to a close, everyone is gathered outside. Daniel and Esther have each had moments addressing the crowd tonight, but this time it's Michael who steps forward alone. He doesn't speak. He just kneels, checking the wind every so often, until we finally see a faint spark in his hands. By the time he walks back to the crowd the sky is exploding over us. Michael is the son of the Ruralite leader, but he doesn't give sermons. He worships with fire.

The religious are the only ones who use explosive powders anymore. Weapons capable of murdering from a distance were banned after the civil wars, when Nik Senior took power, long before I was born. It feels miraculous to watch the fireworks, louder and brighter than anything Wiley City can ever give me.

Voices murmur through the crowd. This is when Ruralites believe in making confession, when the fire has grabbed God's attention and no mortal ears can hear through the explosion. So I wait, and when the next bloom of gold breaks open into the sky with a scream, I tell my truth.

"I am not Caramenta," I say. "Caramenta is dead."

CARAMENTA DIED SIX years ago on Earth 22, my actual home Earth.

I was born Caralee, but I'd been Caralexx since my seventeenth birthday when I'd finally gotten tired of fighting for scraps in a world that would always be Nik Nik's. Once his dad died and Nik got true power, I put an *x* on my name and became his favorite girl. But he had a jealous streak as wide as his smile. I learned early on he was no different from my mom in handing out punishments for things I'd never done. My real mother—not the wilting silk scrap of a woman on Earth Zero who belongs to Esther, Michael, and Daniel but who will never be mine.

Out on the edge of the wasteland that was still half wet from the mostly dead river, Nik spent the night pretending to drown me. He held my head in the muck, but pulled me back before my lungs were even really burning.

I'd say, *Why'd you stop?*

And he'd say, *Practicing.*

Then he left, and left me alive, like he always did, because he liked me walking back to him tired and blistered. He liked caring for me afterward, as if the damage were done by someone else.

I was in a piece of the wasteland where the Rurals still reach in Earth Zero, face caked in mud that had turned as hard as fired clay under the sun, wishing I had anywhere else to go. That's when I saw the body.

Her eyes had starbursts of red in the white. Her left arm was broken out once and then back in again like a puppet, her shoulders caved forward but her spine bent back. In all my years living rough, I'd never met anyone who could stomach doing that to a person. Hers were the only tracks in the dirt—drag marks, not footprints. She'd pulled herself a little with her good arm, but whatever grace had pushed her had worn off, and a blood tide was crawling from her mouth across the sand.

I crouched down when I should have run away. Maybe I meant to steal what I could. Maybe I needed to see what mark that kind of death left on a human face.

That's when I saw it. The part of the face that wasn't destroyed was mine. The corpse was me, a neater, un-tattooed version of me. I stared at her face, *my* face, and thought it was a joke.

Next I heard the voice, small but not distant. It was saying a name.

I took out the transmitter, grazing an unpierced version of my own ear, and put it in.

". . . menta? Caramenta? Are you there?"

It wasn't that the voice was lovely, but the concern in it was pure and sweet, something I'd never heard before and haven't gotten tired of yet.

"Yes . . . I'm here," I said.

I put on the woman's cuff and it activated, recognizing me as her. The picture on Caramenta's digital ID looked even more like me than her corpse. Her address was in Wiley City. I always wanted to live in Wiley City.

Caramenta, Caramenta, Caramenta. I repeated it so I wouldn't forget.

"Good. Thought we'd lost you on your first day out."

"No. I'm just . . . confused."

An irritated sigh, followed by, "I'm bringing you back. You're not ready. I'll walk you through the return procedure, but just this once. When you get back you'll need to do more than *pretend* to study the manuals."

Maybe it shouldn't have been easy, peeling the clothes off of my own corpse and leaving just enough of my things to identify her as me, but anything is possible once you convince yourself it's necessary. I'm not sorry, and I've never been ashamed.

After I changed into her clothes, Dell pulled me over and I was born into a brand-new world. That was six years ago. Six years since I've heard anyone say my real name. Some days, I can't even remember it.

\

ON SATURDAY I work in the garden with Esther, because it offends me less than accompanying my mother and stepfather while they preach. The ground in Ashtown grows like it's half salt—leftover corruption from the same factories that used to pump soot into the air, giving the town its name—so the "garden" is an abandoned airplane hangar on the edge of my parents' land. There are rows of pots filled with imported soil, and the insulation is better than most houses in this area. The congregation helps with the tending and my stepfather divides the harvest evenly among his parishioners.

Ruralites aren't allowed to gossip, but they are allowed to stare, and those working with us can't help but look at the once-holy daughter of their leader, who went into the city and turned sinner overnight. I stay close to Esther, hiding in the shadow of her belonging. The work clothes I'm wearing stay in the back of my closet until visits like this, so even though it's been years since I bought them they still have that too-new look. Like I am an imposter. And I am. Back in the Wiles, I pass for someone who has known stability and money her whole life. Here, I pass for someone who remembers how to pray and scrape, who would never let the same kind of peppers they've spent weeks nurturing mold forgotten in the back of her fridge. I am always pretending, always wearing costumes but never just clothes.

Esther and I water and check the plants for salt-rot, a parasite carried in on the bodies of flies. It's the only thing that lives in the sludge far to the south that used to be a lake. The environment got too toxic for anything else, but salt-rot survived, jumping from reeds to ground plants to trees, leaving petrified white behind as it leached the nutrients out of its hosts.

On Earth 312 the factories we chased out here are still pumping, and there are no human inhabitants beyond workers who don't leave the airtight facility. In that world, salt-rot continued to evolve after the trees and the flies were dead. In that world it can infect the skin of a human and spread slowly but inevitably until a few years pass and all that's left is a glistening white corpse. They used to call it salt-rot too, but now they call it Lot's Wife and treat it like it's a curse instead of just a virus. I have the tiniest leaf of it in one of my sealed bags in the collection on my wall, and even though Eldridge's specimen bags are guaranteed to contain it, having Lot's Wife in my home is the closest I get to feeling true danger anymore.

I think about that danger as I watch my gloveless stepsister frown at a white leaf before tearing it off and tossing it into the incinerator. On 312, this whole building would be burned, and Esther would be exiled into the wastelands for daring contact with it.

We're supposed to stop to eat, then finish up, but there are two kids watering the other side and Esther walks our lunch over to them. Where Esther's clothes are faded thin but still clean and intact, these children's are crusted and ripped. They've got more in common with me than her, but they've been avoiding my gaze all day.

"We'll just push through and finish up," she says when she comes back from speaking with them. "It's an easy day anyway, and we'll have an early dinner."

She doesn't make excuses, just like she didn't ask before giving my lunch away. When Dan steps down it will be Esther, not Michael, to replace him, and at times like this it's obvious why.

We get home late for dinner, but Michael comes home even later. He plops down loud with his eyes raised. I wonder how long it took him to make noise again, to learn how to lift his eyes. In Caramenta's journals he's a pious boy, as reluctant to be noticed as the rest of his people.

His fingertips are clay red, like all the edgiest Ruralite teens. They dig their fingers into blood-colored rivets in the ground and leave them for as long as they can. The brownish stain on the nails is the closest thing to the black nail polish of downtowners they can get away with.

I'm admiring the ingenuity of his rebellion when he turns it on me.

"Is it true you kill people?"

"Michael!"

He flinches, but doesn't look at my mother. "Jeremiah says traversers actually go to other places to kill people. They laserblast their heads right off."

"You know we don't discuss that . . . business in this house," Daniel says.

That "business" is my job. Or my company, I'm not exactly sure which, but I know it's living, breathing, blasphemy to them. People who don't believe in taking up more space, air, or attention than strictly necessary are unsurprisingly opposed to claiming whole new worlds. They see it as new colonialism, and they're not wrong.

I turn to Michael.

"That's a ridiculous urban legend. Laserblasters don't exist, and even one of Wiley City's stunners would probably get fried if I tried to bring it over." I flex my fingers at him. "I have to use my bare hands."

My mother rolls her eyes, which is close enough to raising her head that I feel accomplished. Esther clears her throat to hide her laugh, and that feels like a victory too.

Michael looks down, considering what I've said. "But do you kill people here? They say that's why we've never seen traversers from other planets. You kill them all."

The company line is we probably have been visited by traversers, and just don't know it. Our traversers have never been caught by another world's surveillance, and other traveling worlds would take all the same precautions. But I don't tell my edgy stepbrother this. I just take a sip from my lemonade, maintaining eye contact long enough to make him shift in his seat.

I heard this theory—that every time a traverser is found on our Earth there's an employee waiting to garrote them and dump their body in a hole—my first week at Eldridge. Other traversers, and there were a lot back then, told the stories whenever we had a second without a watcher present. I was still new, newer even than they thought I was, so I didn't offer an opinion. It wasn't until later, when half of those eager gossips had dropped off and Starla and I were bonded beneath the idea that we'd be the last two standing, that I brought it up.

I asked her if she thought the company killed traversers from other worlds.

She just tilted her head at me.

Eldridge says they've never caught traversers from other worlds, remember?

She was always smart, savvier than me, so her procedural answer was a hint to drop it. It was a company function, after all, but we were alone outside while she smoked something from a green glass pipe that filled my lungs and mouth with the taste of figs each time she exhaled deliberately toward me. It made me bold.

Sure, they say that, but what if . . .

She rolled eyes larger and darker than any I'd seen outside of Ashtown.

What if, what if. So what? A handful of people are killed for trespassing when they're found. And? You still have an apartment. I'm still neck-deep in imported smoke. Maybe they kill people. Maybe they don't. Do you care?

That was when I realized . . . I didn't. I was curious, that was all, but not morally affronted. There might have been people dying, but they seemed inconsequential, against the mention of my city apartment and the promise of citizenship that seemed so close even back then.

Starla wasn't just telling me these hypothetical murdered traversers didn't matter. She was telling me nothing mattered. When I went, she wouldn't riot, wouldn't turn down my pulls to keep me in a job. I wonder if she would have kept inviting me out onto balconies for free smoke if she knew how things would actually shake out—that her selves would keep surviving and mine would die off more and more each year.

After dinner, when my family goes to sleep, I'll pack my things and slip out. Tomorrow is Sunday. They will spend the morning in silent prayer preparing for services I don't even know how to attend. And they will think I'm rusty because I've been gone so long, but soon they'll see I haven't forgotten . . . I just never knew.

Outside of the city the land is cut with a muddy scar that's still a low river in some worlds. This is the place where the dirt on my wall comes from, the place where, under another sun, I watched Caramenta die. I should stop, get out, and acknowledge the loss that no one else ever will. I should, at some point in the last six years, have brought a candle. But I won't.

There's a saying in Ash, mostly downtown, that's been applied to everything from thrones to land to spouses: *It doesn't matter how you got it, if you have it, it's yours.* So I don't mourn the dead girl whose life I live. Just like I don't spare another thought for Starla, whose absence means a bump in my paycheck and nothing else. I just begin the long drive back to the apartment, the city, and everything else I stole. Because it doesn't matter who it used to belong to. It's mine now.

CHAPTER THREE

"You're late," Dell says as I run past her down the hall.

"Obviously," I say back.

I'd love to stay. Forcing Dell into small talk is fun because she's so bad at it with me. It's like she's being asked to communicate with a child or snake—something that is either boring or dangerous, with no in-between. But I'm not just late, I'm late for Jean, so I keep moving.

Every traverser has a more experienced mentor. Because I traverse more than any other employee, I get the honor of having Jean Sanogo himself. No one's ever questioned why my meetings with Jean are weekly while everyone else only checks in monthly. Only Dell ever looks suspicious, but she's classist to the bone so she thinks I need it to survive the pressure of a real job. Jean knows better. He knows growing up under the threat of starvation and homelessness means nothing will ever quite feel like pressure again. He knows even better than I do.

I dated a man a few years back who had never worn an untailored suit or cut his own hair, and who fell fast in love with my durability. He liked the way nothing shook me, not a house fire, not an approaching storm. The way he could count on me to never be afraid was its own aphrodisiac to an only son who'd been raised sheltered and fragile. I liked his fragility, how easily shocked he was, how he never thought to hide it.

His name was Marius and I miss him. But when his family met me, they saw cold where he saw strength. His mother warned him that people who come from Ash have seen so many bodies in the street they don't have feelings anymore, only a survival instinct. He told her I wasn't from *that* Ash. I was from the good, clean, farm-working Rurals. Still, she convinced him he was just a means to an end, a shortcut to security. I thought I cared about him, but I had done precisely that with Nik Nik on my old world, so maybe she was right. I *do* miss Marius, but like I would miss a pet bird—something fragile that trusted me to hold it in my hand, heartbeat against my palm, ribs vulnerable to the whims of fingertips. Maybe it's just the power I miss.

Jean is staring at his screen when I come in.

"Are you just now going over my report?"

"The summary. I've already gone over your analysis." He looks up at me. "Despite the late notice. Three A.M.? This morning?"

"I haven't pulled from that mountain port in a while. I didn't realize we had so much surveillance in that area and I didn't get back from the wasteland until Sunday."

He turns away from his screen. "You forgot to note the discrepancy in population change. Their population loss was holding steady with ours, now it's accelerated."

Four hundred lines of analysis and he would find the one mistake.

"By less than one percent."

"It still goes in the report."

"Analysts neglect significant findings in their reports all the time. I found discrepancies in all of the examples you had me study."

He leans forward, which means he's going to use his dad voice on me even though we've long since established I'm immune.

"Yes, they do, but when the company looks at applying analysts they don't see their skill. They see their credentials, background, and education. The people Eldridge hires have to prove they're unfit despite their background. You'll have to do the opposite, and to do that you need to be infallible where they are flawed."

It takes all the venom out of me, because arguing with him is just arguing against the voice in my head.

"I won't miss it again."

He nods. "When is the next placement test?"

"Six weeks," I say.

"And after that?"

"Six months."

He looks at his screen, then back at me. "That will be too late."

"They're that close?"

I've always known if Eldridge scientists ever figured out a way to remotely retrieve intel I would be out of a job. There is no grace period on the temporary employment visa given to traversers. The moment I'm terminated, the visa dissolves, and I will be escorted out of the city's walls just like Starla. If I can't get hired into a permanent position, if I can't make myself indispensable like Jean, I'll end up back in Ash.

"Bosch is hinting at a big announcement next quarter, something that will increase profits."

"Like cutting payroll."

Jean nods. "It might be something else, and a lot can go wrong even if he's confident, but we can't gamble on their failure," he says. "Can you be ready in six weeks?"

I shrug, but when he narrows his eyes I answer properly. "Yeah. Yes. Yes, I can. I have the hang of the comparison portion, I'm good at writing the actual reports and establishing conclusions. But that stupid memorization section is almost half the score and I can't convince my brain it's important to hold so much useless bullshit."

He types something into his computer. "You're right about your reports; don't leave anything out and you'll be fine. For the next six weeks I'll quiz you on the demographics of each world, starting with the closest by degree to the furthest. The last two weeks before the test date, we'll do a full review of all portions of the test."

"There are three hundred and eighty worlds. You think I can have over sixty worlds studied by next week?"

"There are three hundred and eighty-*two*. Worlds that used to resonate but have gone silent are included on the test too."

"I wasn't even working when 382 went dark!"

"Then you'll get to learn something new. Isn't that exciting?"

"Riveting."

I stand up. It's nine hours until my next pull, which is nine hours that just got earmarked for studying.

"Have you reviewed the file for 175 yet?"

"I haven't had time."

"Make time."

"Why?"

"One Seventy-Five is a future world."

"Why is that a problem?"

I want to ask, *Why does that scare you?* but Jean and I are alike enough that I know he'd never admit to being afraid.

"Because you didn't just die there. You were murdered."

He's too superstitious. He sees future worlds as premonitions. I am not like him or anyone else from outside of Wiley City. I don't have faith in things I can't see. But when he says *murdered,* I get goose bumps.

"I'm sure it's nothing out of the ordinary. I'd be more worried if it were natural causes."

"Cara, if this other you—"

"There is no other me."

It's a stupid thing for a traverser to say, but it's closer to being true for me than it is for anyone else.

"Just look into it."

"I will. I will."

\

WHAT I DON'T tell Jean, what he should already know, is that I've looked up as much information about the me on 175 as I can stand. I know her name is Nelline, and I know she never left Ash. That's how I knew she was the one to die when Dell asked. I don't know how she died for the same reason I couldn't turn around to see where Nik Nik was standing at my family's ceremony: I am too afraid to look. I can't yet process information about, or photos of, Nik Nik. Six years of emotional healing cracks right along old seams when he gets too close. If I open Nelline's last file and find a cause of death linked to him, it will take me back to every time it was me laid out in the dirt looking up. Every time a silver-tipped boot was the last thing I saw for hours.

The section for Nelline's "known associates" was always blank, but I'm sure she was attached to the emperor. She never had the too-thin look of the struggling, which means she had a little security, and there are few enough ways to get it out in the wastelands. I know what I would do if I were her. What I *did* when I was her. The House tried its best by me, but I failed as a sex provider. Don't let anyone ever tell you it doesn't take skill, because it does, and I didn't have it. Maybe the me on 175 was different. Maybe she had something I was missing and could make a real go of it.

But Jean is, as always, right. I need to stop hiding from Nelline's final report. I don't have 175's full world data like I do for Earths I've pulled from, but I've used Jean's credentials to ensure I always have a recent copy of the files from my other selves. It's either a small enough data transfer that he's never noticed, or he just understands and lets me have this. Using my cuff, I bring up the most recent information I got with Jean's login. But the file is nearly empty. No autopsy has been loaded, no pictures of a body, but they must have a body or I wouldn't have gotten the file.

There's only a brief death notice listing her age and naming the cause of death: exsanguination. It's not much, but it's enough for me to picture it.

It won't be a large wound, nothing messy. It's always a small slit across a vein. It would be easy to get help before you die, but the man who kills like this wears a cartridge ring on each middle finger. The one on his left hand thins the blood to water, the one on his right paralyzes extremities but leaves the organs pumping frantically. He inherited the rings from his father, and kills just like Nik Senior did, except he doesn't leave you in a sewage heap or a ditch. He chooses a place where you can see something you love.

The rumor is Nik Nik learned to kill by watching his father, which is why the method is the same, but that the first kill he saw was his beloved older brother Adranik, which is why the location is always kind. Every time I doubt that Nik Nik can truly feel anything at all I remember the way his eyes glazed whenever his brother was mentioned. If nothing else, I know he loved the brother his father killed. Which means he knows what it feels like when a powerful man takes the person you care about most in the world away . . . and still he does it.

The file is incomplete, so I don't know where she was found. But the tox screen and wound description in the notes are familiar enough. There's no mention of it, but I'm sure the small cut is jagged and full of saliva. A perfect match to an obsidian fang.

The first time he used those teeth on me was early in our relationship, our first fight. He'd cut my neck from behind, more a slice with his tooth than a bite. It was a small cut, not even into the artery, but I didn't know that and I'd heard enough stories to believe I was going to die. Especially once he put his fist in my mouth, my teeth stretched to aching against his second and third knuckle. No one my age has ever seen a real gun, but my mother told me my grandfather killed himself with one. In that moment I thought of him, teeth stretched around a metal barrel, and wondered if this death was in my blood.

I waited for the telling spray, the taste they say is bitter and signals that you'll never stop bleeding and you'll never feel again. He left his hand there until my jaw cramped, until the waiting was worse than the ending and I thought about probing the ring for a trigger with my tongue myself, just to have control. Then he pulled his hand away.

"Learn your lesson," he said before walking away.

I didn't. And judging by her cause of death, Earth 175 me hadn't either. Nelline. Her name was Nelline.

Good for you, Nelline.

I hope she died trying to take a piece of something that wasn't hers. I hope she died trying, because my mother always said that was how I was going to go, so her mother probably did too. Was her mother still alive? I poke at Nelline's file, hoping for even a next-of-kin listing, but the information is skeletal even for the basic files I usually download. There's an additional packet of information, but it's earmarked "Medical," which means it's been sent to Dell to compare with my own data. Whether the watchers are sent our dops' medical files for our protection—using the data to become aware of possible health concerns early—or to track the side effects of traversing against a control, none of us are sure. But I do know the files are locked down as confidential, and even logging in as Jean won't let me access them. I need to get them from Dell, and to do that, I'd have to ask her for them, and to do *that,* I'd have to be the kind of person for whom asking for things isn't exactly the same as drinking glass shards. So . . . I'm probably not going to get that file.

To palate cleanse from 175, I pull up 255 me. When I see her fuzzy image I exhale, like always. Earth 255 is my favorite. In the three-dimensional image that pops up, she smiles over her shoulder. It's not posed, just some candid that appeared in their media and so was picked up by our surveillance. She lives in Wiley City, but she wears her hair long and dark and fiercely curly, like she has nothing to lose by looking like an outsider. She's struck the perfect balance of being enough of them to belong, and enough of Ash to be seen as a novelty, a rarity. Valuable.

A Wiley City couple found her when she was four, barefoot and wandering by the main road into the city. So they took her. If my mother had any rights, it would have been a kidnapping, but she was just an independent worker struggling with addiction. If she'd still been attached to the House, the proprietor would have used their power to fight for the child to stay. But you can't work through the House if you use like you need it, so her mother had no support when the couple the papers called saviors abducted her daughter and called it adoption.

Her name is Caralee, too, and her parents let her keep it. They even supported her as she used a portion of her inheritance for outreach to other children in Ashtown.

She got married last month on a balcony on the hundredth floor to a man who is a little rich and a lot in love with her. At least, that's how it looked in the photos the Wiley City press ran. I want to print out her picture and keep it on a wall, like a relative I couldn't be more proud of, but as much as I like knowing she exists, it makes me angry.

I was a climber. When my mother kicked me out as a kid, I would climb onto the roof of our house. 255 was probably just a shit climber, so she walked all the way to the road. That's how fickle fate is. One day you wander instead of climbing, and you end up rich and happy. One day you don't, and you're me. Or you're drained outside like 175. Or you're left bloodied and naked, facedown in the dirt on a world that isn't yours, like the girl whose bed I sleep in.

Fate breaks rough, most of the time.

\

MY PULL TODAY is on Earth 238. It's another rush job, this one being funded by seismologists wanting to know if a recent earthquake was more or less severe on an Earth that hadn't drilled in the area. By this time next month I will hopefully see the number 238 and know the population and time variances from our Earth down to a single death or tenth of a second. But right now I can only remember the practical: that the payload is in a heavy-surveillance country, so I'll need darkness and an obscurer for the cameras, but I died here as a young child, which means I can get out of using a veil if Dell's feeling generous.

I'm not allowed to access the building higher than my level. I have to wait for Dell to send the elevator down. When it doesn't come, I press a button on my cuff to buzz her.

"Rapunzel, Rapunzel," I say into the speaker.

There's a long moment of silence, and then "I'm not a princess" comes over the connection.

"Could have fooled me," I say, but she's already closed the link and sent the elevator.

Dell's prep room is on the eightieth floor, just to the side of the traversing room. I take a second to appreciate the all-glass view. It's an artery floor. Artery floors happen every twenty stories from 40 on, and are as tall as cathedrals. There are walkways on every floor, each lined with trees and gardens lit from the SimuSun panels on the paths above it, but artery floors are so tall real sunlight slips in like a peeking child. Real sunlight as filtered through Wiley City's domed artificial atmosphere, but still.

Dell doesn't know that I know, but she lives on this floor. It's high up for someone with a real job, the same floor Eldridge CEO Adam Bosch lives on, but Dell is an heir. Every day after work she walks out of the office exit on 80, and follows the curves around buildings for six blocks, and then she's home.

I don't live on an artery. Or even close to one. I exit on 40, then take one of the congested escalators down ten stories. I never see the sun, but it's still a good neighborhood. There aren't many bad ones in Wiley City. It was built and is still run by people who care . . . for other Wileyites, anyway. They save all their apathy for the world right outside their walls—for the Rurals, the wasteland, and people like me.

If I were born here, or if I were already made citizen, I wouldn't get kicked out if I lost my job. I'd go to a career center that would give me training to fix the issue that got me fired, then give me listings for a new job. If I lost my job because I was sick or having a nervous breakdown, I'd draw a basic income until I was better. At worst, I'd have to move to a lower level where housing is free, though it's usually reserved for retirees and students. But I'm not a citizen, so unemployment means nothing but a quick banishment.

"Do you miss it?" Dell asks, sneaking up on me the way I usually do to her.

The view isn't even of Ashtown; it's of a random spot in the desert on the other side of the city, but she wouldn't know the difference.

"No," I say. It's the easiest question I've had to answer all day.

I don't think she even cares about the answer. She just likes reminding me where I came from, why I shouldn't know where she lives.

"You don't seem like the kind that thinks deeply about the past,"
she says.

"Because I'm a worker bee and we only think about the job?"

She shrugs. "Maybe."

"Rather be a drone. They get to fuck the queen."

That, she ignores. For some reason seeing her unsettled makes me
brave enough to ask a favor.

"Hey, did you get Nelline's medical records with that last pull?"

She looks at me again, showing a slight curiosity that would probably look like pure confusion on a more open face.

"Nelline?" she asks.

"Me. I mean, the me from 175."

Understanding, she looks away. "That's not really your concern."

I haven't actually asked to see the file, but apparently that's not a
necessary step in her telling me no.

"It's just that Jean thinks . . . I just want to know more about how
she died, or maybe her life before that. If you could just—"

"What good can knowing serve?"

"What harm can come from me seeing the file?"

She takes a breath, then looks me in the eye. "I know you were
killed there, but if you plan on seeking revenge—"

"I'm just curious," I say, though I'm not sure that's it, not all of it
anyway. "Did I try to get revenge over my last hundred murders? I'm
the best in the universe at letting bad shit happen to me."

When the last sentence comes out of my mouth we both make a
sound—her because she's done arguing, and me because it's one of
those truths too true to ever be said out loud.

"It's time we start prep," she says, even though it's early yet.

I bite back a dozen arguments. Asking for access to the file in the
first place cut me. Begging would kill me dead.

Dell has laid out everything I'll need for this pull, little stacks on the
prep table as sensible and organized as her whole life.

The clothes I have to wear today are monochromatic and androgynous. Subconsciously or deliberately, the people in this section of 238 have rebelled against their government's surveillance by refusing to stand out. She turns away when I change, though I stay facing her. Not because I'm daring her to look at me, but because my attempts to be her equal would dissolve if she saw the tattoo on my back.

After I change, she installs the obscurer in the center of my chest, a small square that will disguise my presence from any electronic surveillance. When she reaches for a veil, a web of tape that will cross my face from chin to forehead and cheek to cheek, I stop her.

"I died here when I was four. I don't need that."

The numbers that could get me a permanent position I keep forgetting, but somehow I remember my death age on 373 worlds.

"But you've visited here before. Someone might recognize you and think your presence in the same place is suspicious."

"It's a remote area and the obscurer takes care of drones. No one's seen me in person. Once I encounter someone, I'll start using the veil here. But not before."

All traversers hate the veils. We say it's because they make everything look filmy. And that is the reason *I* dislike them. But the others fear the change. The tape pulls at your skin, changing its shape, then projecting a new image over it. Seeing a different face on yours in an unfamiliar world feels like you've become someone else and will never get back. The more superstitious traversers believe if you die like that, even Nyame in her dark and endless power won't recognize you to bring your heart back to the world where it belongs.

But the practical higher-ups have never heard of Nyame, the unofficial goddess of traversers. If they knew the irrational reason traversers reject the veil, they would force it on us. So we talk about our vision and diminished effectiveness and longer pull times, because these are terms they understand.

Thankfully, Dell bypasses the veil and slips the Misery Syringe into the vest pocket nearest my dominant hand. We never talk about it. If something goes wrong, if I get sent to an Earth where I already exist or if there is a complication with my entry, I am supposed to use the syringe. It will give me two minutes pain free, so I can live long enough to tell Dell what happened. She will recall me, even though the snap of being pulled back so soon will kill me if I'm already badly injured. They say if you time it right, your watcher can pull you before the euphoria wears off. They say you'll never feel a thing.

We walk out of prep and into the traversing room, a huge space with a domed glass roof. The sun is still setting, which means it's not dark on 238 yet and we'll have to wait.

"You'll be going to 175 soon. It's been a while since you've had a new world."

She's stalling, so I stay quiet until she gets to her point.

"Do you ever wonder what sets you apart?"

"You mean why I haven't died?"

She nods, but won't say it.

Why have I survived? Because I am a creature more devious than all the other mes put together. Because I saw myself bleeding out and instead of checking for a pulse, I began collecting her things. I survive the desert like a coyote survives, like all tricksters do.

"Luck, I guess," I say, because the first thing a monster learns is when to lie.

When she steps beside me, the backs of our hands touch. She doesn't react, and I try not to. Soon enough, the sun is winking out and she readies the last step.

"Deep breath," she says, like it's the first time. She injects the serum first into my left wrist and then into my right. Next she kneels, injecting just above each ankle.

It burns, but that's too simple a term. It burns like opening your eyes in the light burns, like being born probably burns. It doesn't feel like my body is responding to a foreign substance, but like the substance is awakening cells usually dormant.

Once the wave has reached every inch of my body, Dell comes with the collar. The serum opens my cells to having their vibrations altered, but it is the collar that will control them, that will send me away and bring me home. It doesn't need to be a collar. I could just carry the marker at the center of the collar and Dell could do a proximity pull for anything in its radius. But Eldridge doesn't trust us not to lose this key to Earth Zero unless it's hanging off of our necks. That, and I think they like reminding us we're pets.

Dell's fingers graze my neck and I shudder with what she thinks is pain. She doesn't know the serum doesn't just open my cells, it hones my senses until all I can think about is how loud the world is and how good she smells.

I climb the ladder of the hatch—a ten-foot-tall metal sphere that gained its name from the hole at the top you use to enter it, and what it looks like when you emerge. Once I secure the door, the hatch is as dark as an empty universe. I'm not allowed to know what material makes up the sphere, but even without its proper name, I would know it anywhere.

Outside, Dell will be putting on headphones and concentrating, like the DJ or safecracker she'll never be. I've always assumed she closes her eyes when she's listening for that corresponding hum, changing the output of the hatch until it matches. Even before Dell has begun the sequence it feels like I'm gone, like the empty space isn't in Earth Zero anymore, isn't anywhere. I stop existing the moment the door is closed, and when Dell enters my coordinates it will feel more like being re-born in the same place than traveling.

The humming in the walls gets louder. Or maybe it's my skin. Doesn't matter. The humming grows until I am the hum, nothing but my own frequency. Dell is adjusting the transmitter, seeking entrance. Science says she's tuning into my destination, but Jean would say she's petitioning a god, adjusting frequencies the way monks hum to access the divine.

I know I am on my way by the sudden feeling of someone else's breath on my neck. Scientists call the pressure along my skin resistance from imperfect frequencies, an atmospheric barrier I have to slide through before I can appear in another world. But Jean calls it Nyame's muzzle, sniffing at me for worth like a wolf determining friend from threat.

Just when my skin begins to bristle, she retreats and I am standing beneath a tree that looks almost familiar. It feels like waking up despite my eyes never closing. I take a moment to orient myself. The tree is familiar because I've landed here before to pull from 238. I visualize my task in detail until I know I won't get confused, won't start believing my real life is a dream and this Earth is my real place.

"Status?" Dell asks, a small voice in my ear. The quality of the audio is like a child's walkie-talkie, and it's the limit of technology that can travel with me.

I let her call me a few more times before I answer.

"Moving," I say, pulling up directions on my cuff.

I make sure the obscurer on my chest is lit and working.

"How far away did you put me?" I ask.

"Oh . . . about two and a half miles."

I ignore the satisfaction in her voice and start walking.

CHAPTER FOUR

By the time I've checked back in with Jean, I'm ready to be in any world that isn't this one. I failed. I got 68 percent on Jean's mock quiz of the first forty Earths. Not a miserable failure, but it might as well be a zero when I don't know how to change it. I read the reports. I wrote the facts over and over again and nothing has helped me retain enough to pass.

Maybe there's something to classism. Maybe eating caviar growing up gives you a bigger brain. Maybe eating dirt poisons your memory.

Or maybe it's just easier to think something is impossible than to try.

Sitting at my desk, I look back over my notes. I know the facts about each world when I see them, but I'm storing them in some part of my mind I can't access when there's a question in front of me and something on the line. It all becomes too important, like I have my own life in my hands, and I choke. I've made a copy of the stat page, but with the info left blank. I'll quiz myself until I get 100 percent, before I move on to memorizing for next week.

"Headache?"

When I look up, Dell's studying me like a map. I've been off observation since the bruising faded, but that doesn't mean she won't put me right back on.

"No, just concentrating."

I usually have time to brace myself before I see her. I didn't think she'd come here more than once in the same month. It's no secret that anything below the fiftieth floor is for traversers, clerks, Maintenance, and other support staff. We're classified as nonspecialists because there was no degree or expert knowledge or developed skill to get us here. With the exception of some of the traversers, we are stunningly expendable.

But she's here now, breathtaking and disapproving, and maybe the latter enhances the former because, like her panic when she says my name off-world, I can convince myself it signals concern.

"What?"

"Are you sure you're not experiencing headaches? Blurred vision?"

"I'll get an aneurism from irritating questions before I get one from traversing."

"Don't treat this lightly. Even the tiniest vibration in the mind is a trauma."

I snort at the princess telling me about trauma. Traversing shakes me, but it's not a *trauma*. The deepest bruises I've gotten world walking are a warm bath next to *trauma*.

"Is that why you're here? To check me for nosebleeds?"

"Your trip to Earth 175 is to be an extended one," she says.

"How extended?"

"You'll need to download from the area's backup ports after your pull."

"How many?"

"Four."

The number is high, but not extraordinary. The main port has the most information, and usually what we see in the backups is just redundant. But sometimes there is a piece of data that never makes it to the main port. If I'm having to do four, Starla must have been fired just before their quarterly clearing.

"Four? So I'll be there an extra forty-eight hours?"

"Seventy-two. There will be a solar event during your pull. You shouldn't be there for that, but we don't know what the conditions will be leading up to it, so we're giving you a buffer."

I nod when I want to shake my head. Seventy-two hours on Earth 175. Three days in a world that murdered me. It makes sense that she's asking about headaches now. Staying that long, the comeback will be rough. If I had a crack, I might shatter.

"You've been given your map of the ports you'll need to hit. The emergency shelters were stocked during the last pull, so your route will include those as well."

I nod. Dell's eyes drift over to the screen with my notes.

"Homework?"

"Punishment," I say. "From Jean."

"He really should know better than to waste his time trying to teach you."

He should, but her saying it out loud hurts. She must see that on my face because she tilts her head with interest, a wave of black hair petting her shoulders as she reacts to my pain like a scientist, not a friend.

"Don't you remember? We spent a week giving you packets and books to prep for your first pull. Once you hit new ground, you forgot everything and we had to restart."

I didn't forget. The one she taught died, and I had to be trained all over again. But I can't say that, so I say, "Going to a different world for the first time isn't enough of an excuse for being a little forgetful?"

"It's not a different world. It's still our world, just with different paths taken."

"Is that how you think of it?"

And if she answers, really answers, we'll have a conversation like equals. Not like royalty bestows thoughts passingly on a commoner, but like two people seeking to understand each other.

She straightens. "It doesn't matter what I think. You're the one who actually goes there."

"But you do live there. I mean, I visit, but I'm not *there*. You're in all of these places, all the time. I can only go because I'm not."

She shrugs, only half listening. I want to tell her I've seen her, just to see if it would make her curious enough to keep talking, but when her hair shifts my eyes snag on a missing bit of green at her ear.

"You've lost an earring." I say it half in awe, because the idea of Dell—careful, perfect Dell—losing anything is incongruous.

She touches the earring in her left ear, then her empty right. She covers it quickly but I see it in her face: despair. I know—though she's never told me—that her grandmother gave her those earrings. This was her paternal grandmother, who never left Japan's walled city when her parents came to this one. She loved her grandmother, because her accent made Dell's name sound like *Dare* and when Dell was a child no one had ever called her daring before.

I don't think Dell would have ever been a pilot had her grandmother not pronounced her name that way. Losing the earring must feel like losing her all over again. That's the trouble with living eighty stories up—sometimes things fall down too far to ever reach again.

"I can help you look, if you—"

But she's already moving away, hiding her eyes from me by looking down at her cuff. She doesn't believe I can help her, but I'm the only one who can.

When I get off work I make the long commute down to my one-bedroom apartment. Somewhere fifty stories up Dell is entering the first floor of what can only be called a mansion this far down. But right now, I have something she needs. I head to my bedroom, my wall of stolen possessions, until I find the bag from Earth 261—the earring from the girl who let me hold her because she didn't know who I was. I take the bag containing the carved jade teardrop off the wall and set it on my nightstand so I won't forget to bring it to her tomorrow. Knowing I can undo the loss she felt today fills me up more than it should. I guess I've been waiting to have something, anything, to offer her.

\

IT WAS AN accident when it happened, with Dell. Two years ago I had a forty-eight-hour on Earth 261, where the border between Ash and Wiley City is just a line on a map. The city was still nicer, and the wasteland was still the wasteland, but Ashtown was actually part of the same territory. The people there could vote and get medical services. In Earth 261, a massive wall doesn't separate the Wiles and Ashtown, it's just a fence, and there are working streetlights on both sides.

I went to the gardens on the eightieth floor to watch young professionals stream in and out of a bar on the corner. I didn't go in; currency is iffy between worlds, and it's a stupid risk to take. I just stayed in the garden, smelling fruit that had already been picked back home.

She came up to *me*. That's important. And maybe I was hoping she would. And maybe I chose that garden because it was near where she lives on Earth Zero. But she was the one who approached, who said, "They're free, you know."

All I did was take the orange from the branch and hold it out to her. After she took it, I said, "Nothing's free," and let her make of that what she would.

And she did.

And the sex was good, though Dell's apartment looked nothing like I had pictured. At first, lying in bed hearing stories about Dell's grandmother that Dell would never tell me herself elated me. But then I got angry. She was only telling me because my Wiley City accent was near perfect, and my pull was close enough to Wiley's sprawl that Earth Zero Dell had dressed me like one of her own. If she knew who I was, where I came from, she'd shut me out as much as my Dell did.

I feel bad, I do. It was a mistake . . . but every time I pull near Wiley City on another Earth, I find myself in that same garden. Just wanting to see her, to see if she'll come up and choose to talk to me again.

Sometimes Dell walks past me.

Mostly, she doesn't.

IF YOU BELIEVE the jokes people in Wiley tell, the not-very-funny jokes whose punch lines never contain genitalia or maiming, office meetings are boring. Harry, one of our more social watchers, recently fired, would nudge me in the elevator on our way up and say, "Once more into the theater, eh?" And I would laugh exactly as loudly as expected.

But secretly, I find the company progress meetings exciting.

Every few months, all Eldridge employees are gathered into a room with a stage that is, yes, very much like a theater. We are given unlimited fresh fruit and baked goods—free—and coffee or juice—also free—and then we settle in and the CEO and founder speaks to us like we're his friends. His opening is always some variation of the first opening I ever heard from the stage: *When I was a boy I used to wonder what it would be like to walk in the stars. Not on them. In the space between. When I was five I'd arrange rocks as models of the solar system and sit among them, turning them over like I could find the secret. I never knew that when I finally got the chance to discover what was out there, I'd be surrounded by such talented, wonderful people.*

I have spoken one-on-one with the man who made traversing possible three times, but the first time was my favorite. Adam Bosch isn't as young as you'd think with everyone always calling him a boy wonder, but he doesn't seem nearly old enough to have changed the world, so maybe that's what they mean. But Wiley City is bad at age anyway. They see a fourteen-year-old runner outside the wall and say, *A suspicious man spotted near the border,* but when a thirty-three-year-old Wiley-ite murders his girlfriend it's *Good boy goes bad.*

The first time I met Adam, Dell was lecturing me in the hatch room. I was fresh on Earth Zero, nervous that any second I'd be found out, and nervous that my incompetence would get me fired before I was.

"Go easy, Ikari," he said, appearing like a ghost, an angel, a magician. "We were all new once."

He was kind to me. He's always been kind to me. That day he was wearing the same outfit he wears every year in the annual press releases. The white shirt and wide-legged black pants that news outlets mock, and yet he refuses to change. If he were from Ash, I'd say he wears them because the mockery is a challenge and he can't be seen backing down. But he's not. He's just one of those scatterbrained geniuses who doesn't think about appearances.

Still, his clothes were the reason I couldn't stop staring at him. They're simple; no one else would find them striking, but that shirt was so white and those pants were so impractical, and there was magic in their very existence for a girl from a place with more dirt than air and as many scorpions as flies. No one could wear those clothes outside of the city, and when I laid eyes on him it was impossible to think of him as a scientist, to think of him as anything but magic.

He walked past Dell straight to me. He looked down at the apple in his fingers like he'd forgotten it was there, then he held it out to me. Another thing that means nothing in the city, but the ground in Ash is barren and the warehouses only hold fruit that can be stacked to make the most of the space—berries in rows, or grapes crawling up the wall behind them. Mostly, we just have vegetables.

When I took the apple with near lust he said, "You're from Ash-town, aren't you?"

It sounded more like curiosity than judgment, so I nodded but was quick to add, "I'm from the Rurals."

Then he looked at me. It was the first time he met my face and it made me realize he'd been looking just to the left of my eyes the whole time.

"Are you?" he said.

And for some reason I wanted to tell him the truth. That I wasn't faithful, or worthy. That I was a liar from the concrete that everyone feared. It felt like he already knew. So I shrugged and looked down, which is the closest I've ever come to telling someone the truth before or since.

"It doesn't matter. You're doing great. We're all rooting for you," he said before he walked away. Dell resumed lecturing me after that, but the words rolled right off.

That last part turned out to be a lie, but I don't hold it against him. I'm not sure I could ever hold anything against Adam Bosch. Caramenta kept the letter offering her employment in a keepsake box I haven't bothered to throw away. Every time I reread it, I trace his hand-signed name at the bottom, and I feel the same deliverance and grati-tude she must have felt. I could never be attracted to him, not the way I want Dell like my next breath. But I feel about Adam Bosch the way people in the Rurals feel about Moses or my stepfather.

When the lights dim for the meeting, my stomach drops. Adam Bosch is excited and it makes the air a little excited too. He's talking about impending breakthroughs, and while he doesn't name the proj-ect, we all know it's remote downloads. The analysts are celebrating because the technology is so close he can promise it is months, not years, off. And sure, they're excited because now data retrieval will be instantaneous and not monthly. But they're also excited because tra-versers will be gone. And what are pigeons but an infestation, at the end of the day?

Instead of the pride I usually feel to be part of a real company in the city, I just feel ashamed, the weight of my 68-percent score hanging over my head like an ax.

The last part of Adam's speech is cryptic. He's hinting at some com-ing change that will transform the nature of the company. Everyone else is excited. We are all keenly aware of how much of our funding relies upon the city, and if some new product can make us independent so we're no longer reliant on a government's annual budget, I should be cheering for it. But I've already stopped listening. Whatever it is, I probably won't be around when it happens anyway.

After we're dismissed, I grab an armful of free food to go with the rations I've already brought from home. I'm going to 319 today, and I always take extra when I go there.

Dell doesn't quite meet my eyes as she readies me, just like everyone looked away from me in the hall. I'm Eldridge's dead girl walking.

I grab my backpack after she loads me up and sighs.

"Are you smuggling extra food again?" she asks. "I saw you shoving danishes in there."

"Consider it my severance package."

"Cara . . ."

"What? Are you going to tell me my job's not on its way out? There were maybe six traversers in there, Dell. Six. For the whole sector. They're scaling us back."

"Them. They're scaling them back. You're more valuable than all the rest. You'll outlast them all."

"The last of a species still dies, Dell. Just a matter of time."

"It will be okay."

Such a Wiley thing to say. Such a Wiley thing to even get to believe.

"How? Will you make it okay? Take me in when I get my slip? Marry me when my residency is void?"

Her breath comes up short at that, like I said something offensive. And it must be, to her. I want to remember this, this borderline disgust at the idea of me, but for some reason I can never keep it long enough to stop wanting her. I reach into my pocket and pull out the Eldridge sample bag containing her earring. Not the one she lost, but its other-world cousin so she'll never know the difference.

"I found this on my way home yesterday."

She snatches it like a child and holds it to her chest. The reaction is rare and human, and I let myself stare, because it's the closest I'll ever get to her holding me like that on this world. She looks up, and catches me staring.

There's a moment between us. It's like a snap into focus where all at once she *sees* me, she finally understands that all my flirting is just hiding in plain sight, just being so obvious she'd never guess she is the one thing on this world that I know and all I want. But then it happens. She looks, for just that first moment, afraid.

The universe is brimming with stars and life, but there is a section of sky that is utterly dead and empty. They call it a *cold spot,* a *supervoid,* and they say it got that way because two parallel universes got too close to touching. That's us. That's me and Dell. We coexist, parallel but never touching, and if one of us goes too far, if I ever get too close, the

Eridanus Void opens between us. We both withdraw and leave a cold darkness in the space where we almost touched that three suns couldn't light.

"I tried to sell it, but I guess it's worthless without the other one."

She half smiles, but it's really a negative smile. It's the saddest thing I've ever seen.

"Of course," she says. "And I suppose it is in an Eldridge specimen bag because . . . ?"

"What? Like you've never snuck office supplies home? I told you. Severance package."

I start climbing the ladder into the hatch before she can say anything else, because if I stare at her much longer, this woman who wants me but is too afraid of where I'm from to do anything about it, I might finally find a way to hate her. And I don't want to. Not really. Not yet.

\

ALL KINDS OF refugees—that's what Ashtown is made of. Those fleeing religious persecution came with a little money and a lot of faith, and generally settled on the edge where the sand was more white than gray so they could pretend it was the promised land. A hundred years after that, those who fled from poverty and drought followed rumors of water and work, building the city. Maybe they believed that once the last shining skyscraper was finished and there were still plenty of vacancies, they'd be let in. I doubt they would have built the wall so high and sure if they'd known which side of it they'd be on. The builders' descendants became factory workers, less proud but just as efficient, until the factory was no more. Now, the factory workers' children work for Eldridge's industrial hatch, transferring materials from one world they'll never see to another.

A couple centuries after the building boom faded, those seeking refuge from war found Ashtown. They went to the city, wanting a place with walls and defenses. They insisted they'd been promised aid.

But the progressive Wiley City only keeps the promises it makes to itself. It is loving and nurturing and socialized . . . but only within its own borders.

So those hiding from war were left outside the walls, and war followed. Nik Nik's father was one of the most brutal fighters, and the infighting continued for a generation until Nik Senior stopped it, in the way a lion stops infighting among gazelle. When the dust settled, the new emperor was on top, challengers dead or exiled. He opened his mouth, blood still dripping from his jaw, and declared peace.

\

WHEN I LAND on 319, I see Dell has stopped playing with me. She left me no more than a quarter of a mile from the port. It doesn't matter, because this is 319 so I have an errand to run. I adjust the pack on my shoulder and walk into Ashtown.

If I figured anything out in these last six years, it is this: human beings are unknowable. You can never know a single person fully, not even yourself. Even if you think you know yourself in your safe glass castle, you don't know yourself in the dirt. Even if you hustle and make it in the rough, you have no idea if you would thrive or die in the light of real riches, if your cleverness would outlive your desperation.

This is a lesson I learned here, on 319, because there is one person in the world I thought was consistent, and I was wrong.

She's standing in the doorway of her concrete rectangle. She reaches for the pack without any pleasantries, because she's a garbage git through and through.

"Given me more this time," she says, then looks up. "Lots more."

She's not sad, but she knows what it means.

"Might not be able to make it back, wanted to make sure you were covered."

She brushes her black hair, waist long here instead of her usual severe bob, over her shoulder.

"Dust's high. Better come in."

Her name here is Aria, and I'm the one who got to tell her it means music. She pours me a glass of water that tastes half-iron.

"I can't stay. I've got—"

"You're an angel, yeah?"

"What?"

She sets the mug down. There's a scar across her lips that pulls at her mouth when she speaks, so she usually sits quiet. When she does speak, she keeps her mouth small to minimize the effect. But I still notice, because I know what that mouth is supposed to look like. The wide gap of it when it smiles perfectly.

"I'm not some rabid Ruralite. But you come, you bring food. I tried to follow you once and you just disappeared."

"You followed me?"

"Tried. If you're leaving, can't you tell me?"

"I'm not an angel. Nowhere near."

She's waiting. Of course she's waiting. No one in Ash does anything for free and I've been bringing her food and clothes since I found her, but I've never asked for more than this ass-tasting water. I have never touched this version of Dell, would never. Not because she wouldn't let me, but because she might. It would reek of gratitude. And maybe she'd be insecure, think she was less than me. I don't want to make Dell feel like that, don't want to make her feel the way she makes me feel.

"You just remind me of someone."

"She dead?"

"No. Face like a night sky, though."

She nods, understanding. We've got half a dozen phrases out here for the same thing: something beautiful and perfect that you can't ever reach. Except I've traveled through the stars hundreds of times, and I've still never gotten close to touching Dell's cheek.

"Face ain't like that," she says. She doesn't touch the scar on her mouth, but she might as well. "Not anymore."

She begins counting out the rations I've brought before I've finished my water. After a while she looks at me, not at me but at my shoes.

"If you're going for good, just go."

I go. Out her door I get a view of Wiley City, the only way I used to see it. She's picked a house right on the edge of Ashtown, so nothing impedes her view. She must sense all her other selves inside the city, living secure eighty stories up. She must know she's been cheated.

\

THE NEXT MORNING, Dell is quiet as she readies me for my long stay on 175. Just before getting the serum, she hands me a plastic sheet. I turn it on and see the space fill with information about Nelline.

I look up from the text to her. "You came through."

She goes cold in the face of my gratitude.

"You knew I would," she says, but not like she's proud of being consistent. More like she's ashamed she couldn't stop herself from help-ing me.

I scroll through the text and swallow hard. I was right to avoid this. It's harder than I thought it would be, and the buzzing in my head doesn't stop until I've shut down the screen. I hand it back to Dell like one hands an empty cup of bad medicine back to the doctor. I needed it, but I hated it.

She doesn't respond to my reaction until I'm heading into the hatch.

"Are you scared now?" she asks.

"Have you been talking to Jean? It's just a pull, like any other."

"It's a new place. That hasn't happened in a while."

"They're all the same place," I say, and begin climbing the ladder.

"But this one just killed you. Might have a taste for it now."

I look back at her from the top of the hatch.

"Why, Dell, you sound exactly like an Ashtowner."

She takes it as an insult, which I take as an insult. We can't ever really talk. I want to take her hands and tell her that, yes, she is better than me but that is because *she* is better than *me*. Not because Wileyites are better than Ashtowners, but because she is driven without being manipulative, she is ambitious but only until it edges over into cruelty.

Until we have that common understanding, we can never really speak, and that's something I'm just coming to terms with. Not pursuing Dell and being rejected, which I've always accepted as an inevitability, but never getting her to see me enough to even speak to me.

"Miss me," I say, from the top of the ladder.

She doesn't look up or respond. She just slides her headphones in. I climb into the dark.

In a few seconds, when the door is sealed and the vibrations hit just wrong enough for me to know it's a killing frequency, I will wish she had. I will wish her eyes, and not her downturned face, were the last thing I'd ever see.

PART TWO

A rotating black hole does not collapse to a dot. That's the old-fashioned thinking. It collapses to a ring, a ring of neutrons. And if you fall through the ring of neutrons vertically, you wind up in Wonderland. You wind up on the other side of forever.

—Michio Kaku

CHAPTER FIVE

When the bodies of the first traversers were recalled, there was shock at the thoroughness of the devastation. Twisted in and out, glistening with fresh blood and something else.

The scientists said, *We did not test it enough. We should have expected a backlash.*

And the spiritual said, *We did not petition enough. We should have expected a sacrifice.*

I'M NOT SURPRISED to die in the darkness between. Die exactly how I lived: belonging nowhere.

I know something is wrong the instant tuning begins, which means it's too late to do anything about it. Did Dell feel the resistance as she began the transfer? Did it come across like static, or a scream? It wouldn't stop her. Her job is to send me through, so she will. But this time, it will kill me.

The playful lick that usually just raises the hairs on my arms shifts dark, turns into a burn as it transforms from passive pressure to primordial rage. I've never really believed in Nyame. I carried her name, but only the way even atheist runners will wear Nicholas medallions before a tricky job. I wrapped myself in the pragmatism of Wiley City, a place so full of science and progress there is no room for superstition.

But now Nyame is as real as a backhand. I don't just feel her breath, I see her. She's staring down at a collection of universes like an old woman with a puzzle. She holds me up like a missing piece, but when there's already one where I belong she gets confused, frustrated, and tears me in half. It's a hallucination, I know, but I swear I hear her voice as my first bone breaks. But it does break, and it's my collar, so I don't think much after that.

Just before the blackout, one thought comes clearly: Nelline's not dead. Earth 175 me is alive and well. Eldridge was wrong, just like they were wrong once before.

\

THE HAPPIEST DAYS of my life were the first in Wiley City six years ago. It was my first taste of guilt-free joy. I'd made my way to the address on my cuff's digital ID, the apartment that was mine now. I found the house still packed up, Caramenta's things just waiting for me to put them where I would want them. And the box of journals detailing her life, sitting open on the rug like an instruction manual? It was fate smiling, I was sure.

But then the worry started. What they don't tell you about getting everything you ever wanted is the cold-sweat panic when you think about losing it. For someone who'd never had anything to lose, it's like drowning, all the time.

I set about the problem like I set about all problems. I made lists. I read Caramenta's journals and made a list of her traits, her phrases. She was faithful and pure and more than a pinch judgmental. But I didn't just want to be her, I wanted to be a better her, so I began reading the autobiographies of people who were born in Wiley City, and I made a list of their phrases too. They never called Wiley City *The Wiles,* so I wouldn't either. And they always referred to Ashtown by its proper name or simply Ash, never *Ashytown* or *Big Ash* like I used to.

I guess what I mean to say is this: I've been so consumed with keeping my job, with maintaining my stolen life, I'd forgotten the most basic fact I learned as a child. I was so concerned about getting fired, I'd forgotten that anyone can die, at any time.

You'd think someone who'd seen her own corpse would be smarter than that.

MY RIBS CRUSH in, then expand out with the suddenness of the new world. I made it through. I may still die, but my broken body won't be rejected and sent back like the others. Not quite a victory, but something.

I land on packed earth that used to be a river, and recognize it instantly. I'm in the wastelands. When I try to sit up, everything hurts. When I lie back, blood fills my mouth. I reach into the pocket of my vest and pull out the Misery Syringe. This is when I'm supposed to use it. It will block out the pain, give me time to contact Dell for a recall. The recall will kill me, but at least they'll know what happened. But I can't. I can't die here, in the dirt. Not like the last Caramenta, and all the others before her. Not like my mother.

I understand why the others followed protocol. I see why a scientist would choose the quick snap of certain death from recall over enduring this for one more second. But this hurts just a little worse than when I was twelve and mouthed off enough for Nik Senior to have four of his guys stomp me for it.

I'll have two minutes of pain-free movement once I use the syringe, but I'll need more than that to reach the road. I'll have to move, and regret moving, then move again, and only when I'm about to go down will I use the syringe. The damage is in the top half of my body: ribs, shoulders, jaw, and the one arm curled awkwardly backward like my

elbow's forgotten its job. The pain is only bearable in the space between breaths. Each time my lungs expand the feeling of ribs grinding
wrong makes me wish my jaw wasn't broken so I could scream.

I used to think the traverser's death was punishment for trespassing
into a world where you didn't belong. Now I'm sure it's a test. To see
if you deserve to stay as much as they do.

I breathe shallow, taking in too little air, to limit the movement in
my chest. Passing out is more likely now, but it's likely either way and
at least this way I won't hurt all the way to unconsciousness. The first
step is too hard, even moving my weight softly is violence, and I imagine, or I hear, misplaced bones tapping each other for luck.

If I make it out of the riverbed before using the syringe, I can buy
myself an extra thirty seconds to run for help. Versions of me have died
all over, but not this one. Never this one. If this is how I was supposed
to go, it could have happened when I was fourteen, or eight, or sixteen, or any of the other times it happened to other mes. I tell myself
it's just another shallow grave to crawl out of.

I cross out of the riverbed and onto the hard, gray land of Ashtown.
I'm losing my vision. It's time. I use the syringe, and move a second
before it takes effect. Bones already broken splinter, gashes already
bleeding gush, but I do find a road.

Just before I pass out, I get to the shoulder. This world is as medi-
cally advanced as mine. They should have pods. They should be able to
save me . . . if whoever finds me cares enough to try. If they're better
people than I was, when I found myself.

I set my cuff to an away message, so Dell will think I just wanted to
do this trip radio-silent. Better for her to think I'm being difficult than
dying, because the protocol for the latter would kill me. Just in case, I
rip off my collar and shove it into my vest. She won't be able to initiate
a proximity pull unless I turn it on again.

My two minutes is up, and in the snap of agony everything goes
dark for good this time. I'm whispering to Nyame that she can't have
it back. I stole this life, but that doesn't mean she can have it back.

I MUST BE dead, because life is pain and this is goddamn euphoria. The dark surrounding me is total, but for light-painted colors that I know aren't really there, like the aurora borealis left behind when you rub your eyes too hard. I don't know if I'm awake or asleep, still in the hatch or on my way to hell. All I know is I am not alone.

My body is broken to the point of delirium, and this is what my mind offers as a hallucination. I hear his steps before I see him, but I already know. I know the scent of his long hair, the sweat finely coating his neck and chest. I've avoided looking at him, even seeing his name in data, since I left Earth 22. I always thought I would panic when he came for me, but the sight of him calms me, because it means things are finally going as expected. I always knew he'd be standing over me when I died. Down deep, in the place behind my sternum where I keep all my shame, I am glad it's him. I want to be with Dell, but I wouldn't want her to see me like this. I want to seem strong and impenetrable to her. But him, he can be beside me when my heart stops beating, because he's always treated me as small and weak and precious anyway. For all the times Nik Nik has almost killed me, his presence now feels inevitable.

In the dream he asks why his name is on my back, and I don't know how to work my mouth into an answer.

Because I spent my money removing the other tattoos first.

Because I liked being reminded that once upon a time I belonged to someone, even if he was the worst person I have ever known.

Is my name still on your chest?

That's what I want to say. But the world is going watery, the black of the room closing in, and his face recedes into the blur like a light I've either been running from or chasing my whole life. The darkness takes me, but I tell him I hate him before I go. It's not much, as far as last words go, but it's one of the few things I can stand by.

BACK ON EARTH 22, I got the tattoo just after my nineteenth birth-day. I'd been hooked up with Nik for over a year, and he'd gotten me a present. That's why I did it. I don't even remember the gift anymore, but it made me feel happy and loved and I couldn't stand it. So I got the tattoo for him, thinking we'd be even.

His name, each letter as big as my hand, spread from shoulder blade to shoulder blade. I wish I could pretend he made me do it. That he'd held me down and branded me, like the stories say. I want to remember the pain of the needle, but when I think about that day I just remember the warmth of belonging and the thick in his voice when he said he was proud of me.

Nik Nik always said he was proud of me. He didn't say *I love you*. He'd say, *I'm proud of you*. Or, *I'll keep you*. Or, *You're safe*. But it was all the same.

It didn't work. We were never even. The next time I saw him with his shirt off my name was across his chest, and that warm feeling I was trying to hide from just came back again.

It was like day and night, the warmth of his approval just as out of proportion as the cold abuse of his disapproval. But it was warm for a while after the tattoo. Then one day I walked toward him with my arms open and he punched me in the gut so hard I pissed blood for a week. I don't even remember what I'd done wrong. It wasn't long after that he took me out to the river, to drown me for what he didn't know would be the last time.

\

WHEN I FINALLY wake from the dream about Nik Nik I'm sober enough to know I'm drugged, which makes the fuzzy disconnection terrifying. I am in a bed with something soft at my back propping me up. There's a cloth over my eyes. The cool material is thick enough to keep me from seeing anything, but my nose is telling me two things. The first is where I am. The air of Ashtown is hot and thick with dirt. I know I'm not on the edges, in the Rurals or the wastes; I'm near its heart, where the ground is gray and the air bites back with sulfur like breath from a not-dead-long-enough volcano. I haven't slept in a smell like this since I left my world. The Rurals smell like dirt, too, but it's honest. Salted maybe, but not this acidic.

The second thing I can smell is the boiled-down sap of wasteland bushes. Medicine. I'm being cared for. Sure, I can hear the mechanical whir of a pod over me, but that doesn't require more effort than closing a clasp and hitting a button. But someone has rubbed oil into my skin, placed the strong-smelling sap beneath my nose to calm me. This is *care,* but I'm not in the Rurals where it's obligatory. The House? Someone might have mistaken me for Nelline, but a quick movement of my mouth signals the telling pull of the veil. When I'm visiting a place where I was recently alive, Dell always gives me the face of a deep wastelander. Spotted with sun damage, cracks across the lips, filmy eyes—the kind of face quickly looked away from, even out here. Not the kind of person who would warrant medical care, and not the kind of face you'd trouble yourself to bring in. But Exlee's always been a softie. Maybe I just got lucky and caught them on a good day.

I hear a beep from the pod. Whatever drug has kept me disoriented and hallucinating, it's just administered another dose.

"Please . . ." I say, even though it's too late. Already I can feel the dull throbs lessening. I try to hold on to the pain, and the awareness it allows.

Someone in the room shifts closer, but I can't see and soon won't be able to think.

"You're awake. Can you tell me your name? Do you remember your name now?"

Now means he's asked before, but I don't remember it. The voice is quiet, and seems to come from underwater, but I know it. I just can't think clearly enough to place it. Pax? He was at the House.

Do I remember my name?

I do. I don't. I remember her name, but I can't remember my own.

Caramenta, Caramenta, Caramenta.

But that's not me. But it is. Or I am no one.

He shifts the material over my eyes, and at first I know it is a cold compress. But then I don't and it's a shroud and I'm high with a burial shroud over my face, waiting for the handfuls of dirt that will cover me. After all this time running, I have finally turned into my mother.

I start to cry. Loud, sobbing cries. Cries like I didn't cry when she died or when I thought I was going to. I see her on her dirt floor, her mouth a wide, dead smile and her eyes open to the flies. Am I smiling? I don't want to be smiling. I try to reach up to cover my face, but my arms are in the pod and it won't release me.

"No more. I can't . . . no more."

I want to say I'm not like her, I don't want it, but the words knot up at my mouth.

THE NEXT TIME I wake I am actually alert for the first time since leaving Earth Zero. Whoever has been watching me must have understood my plea, because the stronger opiate seems to be out of my system, though I'm still held in place by the pods. Pods, plural. It's not just the one plastic dome like the last time I was podded. When I first got pulled to Wiley, I hadn't been injected with the serum and I'd just suffered a world-class beating, so my touchdown at Eldridge was more of a crash landing. Dell sent me to an open clinic. I kept waiting for them to ask questions or demand payment, but I was Caramenta now. They put me into a scanner first, then a healing pod. Internal damage, external bruising, and a seriously sprained ankle, all fixed in fifteen minutes. In Ash the ankle alone would have cost a laborer his spot in rotation, would have choked his pay and kept food out of his mouth. But I was a resident of Wiley City, and residents, even former wastelanders who were not yet citizens, did not starve. I swore then that I would never be anything else again.

A warm rag is being dragged along my hands and shoulders, cleaning the parts of skin the pods will allow them to reach.

"I'm awake," I say, but my mouth is heavy. "Thank you."

The rag is pulled away, and I hear it splash into a basin.

"You're paralyzed, but don't be afraid. It's just a facet of the healing, not from your accident. Your collarbones and ribs are the last to knit. It's keeping you still."

There it is. The voice I heard before, only now it's clear enough that I recognize it. Not that I could ever forget it for long.

"You overheated from the healing earlier, but I'm sure it won't hurt to take this off while we talk," he says, and the compress comes off of my eyes.

I blink up at Nik Nik. Only the paralyzing agents keep me from flinching away, from rebreaking every bone in my body to get away from him.

The pods beep a warning at my dangerously spiking heart rate, and his eyebrows knit.

"Is the fever back?" he says, half to himself.

Then he places one monstrous hand gently against the side of my face to test my temperature, and I get to see what the emperor of the Wastelands looks like covered in my vomit.

\

YOU'RE PARALYZED BUT *don't be afraid*.

Don't be afraid.

It seems impossible that he said those words to me. Don't be afraid? It's like a lion telling a gazelle not to run, when everyone knows that's how he likes his prey best.

I kept my eyes closed and waited for him to retaliate for the mess I'd made of him, and myself, and the pod, but he just turned my head.

I don't want you to choke, he said.

Then keep your hands from around my neck, I thought.

Lying there, unable to move in the den of my greatest enemy, I listen to the wash, rinse, repeat of him cleaning and think about the plastic sheet Dell let me read before I left. Dell didn't have extensive biographical data on the Earth 175 me, but she had six entries uploaded from a pod used to heal Nelline that was kept at the palace. My injuries may be proof that Nelline is still alive, but those entries were proof she'd had cause to fake her own death. The first few were standard, bruising and a little internal bleeding from a beating. When I read those lines, I could remember the feeling of the punch that had caused them. But then the entries shifted to horrors I would never know, because I left. A miscarriage caused by trauma to the abdomen. An arm twisted to breaking. Twice, a broken jaw.

The pod fixing my ribs is probably the same one that fixed hers. The thought makes me almost as sick as the feeling of Nik Nik wiping my mouth. Am I being treated by the same man, in the same place? The veil should hold charge for three days, but what will happen if I'm still here when it dies and Nik Nik sees the face of the woman he's gotten so used to breaking?

I look around the room to avoid looking at him, afraid he'll be able to see to the real me if he looks too long into my eyes. I know this room. I'm home—*my* home, not Caramenta's home that I call my own the way a hermit crab wears a stolen shell. I've dreamt of it since leaving, so at first it's not strange to be here, in this bed. But then I remember this is Nik Nik's room first and foremost, and I'm a stranger who doesn't belong.

It's the room I shared with him, but different. From what I can see, it's less opulent than I remember. The wall of windows is unchanged, but the long red-and-gold drapes are gone. The bed I'm on is half the size of the one I remember, and the sheets are white instead of black-and-red silks. Gone are the oversized tapestries that only a lifelong Ash dweller would think passed for class. The walls are bare but for a few photo projections. He was always against portraits before. *Take the thing you love and frame it,* he'd say, *show your enemies right where to aim.*

I can't imagine a Nik Nik sentimental enough for pictures. I can't imagine a Nik Nik who doesn't show his wealth in heavy fabrics, sheets so smooth they're uncomfortable. I don't know if this subtlety makes him more or less dangerous.

After he finishes cleaning, he takes a seat beside the bed. He's holding a cup of something orange and steaming.

"Are you okay? Do you think you can drink this?"

I lick my lips and manage a nod, my head and neck the only mobile parts of my body. He holds the cup to my mouth.

"Can you talk?"

I can. I know how. I just have to remember how to speak without being afraid.

"Yes."

His smile at that is blinding. "Good, great. I was really beginning to worry."

There is something wrong with his smile, and it takes me a second to figure it out: it's all white. He doesn't have an onyx incisor. The absence of that dark flash inside his mouth is almost as disorienting as the absence of cruelty in his voice. My Nik Nik never smiled with genuine joy, and it pulls his face into a shape that I'm sure Nelline thought was charming. But if she was anything like me, she'd never be able to see his smile without thinking of its opposite, never be able to fully enjoy his good moods because of the inevitability of his bad.

This is like watching Nik Nik in costume. His hair is parted down the center, still long but not rowed on the side. He's wearing an embellished long-sleeve tunic that reminds me of the fancier ones my stepfather only wears when presiding over births and funerals. Until this moment I've never seen Nik Nik in anything but tank tops and leather when in his castle. It's hard to remember that, even when he looks like this, he's a villain. I go through the injuries Nelline suffered—the broken jaw, the internal bleeding, the miscarriage. That all happened here, in this place, and no amount of looking like a Ruralite is going to change that. Sure, he didn't kill her, but maybe she just used a particularly bad beating to fake her death and cover her escape. That's what happened with me. Earth 22 Nik was violent enough that I'm sure everyone assumed he'd gone blood crazy in my punishment, or that he'd left me too injured to defend myself and a water-mad deepwaster picked me off.

"Who are you?" he asks, and the softness of his voice can't stop me from thinking of this as an interrogation.

"No one. I'm no one."

"Why does 'no one' have my name on her back?"

"It's nothing. It was a joke."

"A joke?"

Shit. He's so easily offended, and I've forgotten the dance I used to do to avoid it. My jaw hurts from talking and there's a sharp buzzing growing louder in my ears.

"A dare. It's nothing," I say. "Do you hear buzzing?"

"No. Does your head hurt?"

"A little . . ."

"Open your eyes."

"They are open," I say, but they're not. I must have passed out again, or been close to it.

He holds more of what tastes like lukewarm lemonade against my mouth and I drink it, then he replaces the cold compress on my forehead.

"Get some sleep. You're not out of the woods yet."

"Don't kill me," I say, though I don't mean to.

"I won't," he says on a laugh, like this is a joke we're sharing.

"I—"

"Hate me. I know. Rest now."

IT WAS A list that brought me to Nik Nik, and a list that took me away from him. I've written thousands of lists since Pax first taught me to read in the kitchen of the House during his off hours. Even when my mother was kicked out, the House was open to me. I'm sure Pax already knew I wouldn't be cut out for the work, and he tried to make me qualified for something else, something lower-paying but easier to grasp. In my journal I've got a list written in Eldridge code of everything I know about Dell. It's two and a half pages long. Not much, really, for six years.

When my mother spun her last and Exlee told me I'd never make it as a worker, I made a list of options. There were only two.

Suicide.

Nik Nik.

I hid in the rooftops near his hangouts, and took note of the kinds of girls he never noticed and the kinds of girls he always noticed. He didn't like sweet girls; he didn't like girls who were quiet. But he didn't sleep with the street-loud type, the kind you want in your corner in a fight. He'd recruit them as misters, or keep them as friends, but that was all. I became what he wanted, something in between. I put an *x* in my name and pretended I'd been there before. And it worked.

The hardest part was trying not to like it. I had to remind myself that his newly dead father had branded my mom like a cow and taught me what a broken bone felt like before I'd even learned to read. Remind myself it was Nik Nik's runners who brought my mom her last dose. When I was in danger of forgetting, I made a new list, names of people who walked into his office but were found open-eyed and blood-drained in the wasteland.

My last night on Earth 22, *my* Earth, Nik Nik was drowning me because one of his runners had found my journal and told him about my lists. He wanted to know who was asking. He thought the governments of the walled cities had broken their implied agreement of mutual noninterference—we weren't allowed to vote in their elections or freely visit their towns, so they didn't ask taxes from, or offer policing to, us.

When I told him the truth, that I was doing it to remind myself who he really was, to keep myself from loving him, he'd looked . . . touched. Like he didn't think it would be hard for anyone not to love him. It had more to do with me being broken than him being worthy, but he still kissed me before he left me in the mud. He still went home expecting me to follow. And if I hadn't found my own dead body in the sand that day, I would have.

CHAPTER SIX

When I wake up again the sun has risen and Nik Nik is sitting in a chair at the foot of my—our, I mean, *his*—bed. He may have slept somewhere else, but he's settled in like he's been waiting a while even though the light tells me it's not yet full day.

He sees my eyes open and smiles. "Good news, as of this morning you can be reasonably assured you're going to survive."

I ignore what seems to be genuine happiness in his voice and look at the book in his hand.

"Why are you pretending to read my journal?"

He adjusts his glasses—fucking glasses?—and tilts his head. "Sorry? I didn't mean to invade your privacy. I was trying to find out who you are."

"Stop."

"Stop?"

"Stop acting like you can read."

That catches his attention. He's shocked, but not angry. Or maybe he is angry and this Nik Nik knows how to hide his rage to strike later.

He slides a nail into the book to choose a page. The nail is long like always, but not filed sharp to a stiletto's point or dipped black. He opens the book, and *reads*.

" 'Reasons I have lived: I don't know, but there are eight.'"

I try to sit up, but the pods beep at me. I slide a hand out to open the latch. I must be nearly finished cooking, because it only fights me a little and it's turned off the paralysis. I get to my feet and reach for the journal. Everything aches.

"You can't read that! That's in *code*. And you can't read!"

He holds me back as easily as he ever has, and I should stop. The journal isn't even important, just another collection of lists I began as a way to practice Eldridge code. It holds no secrets grander than my own fears. But he's taken so much—from me, from Nelline, from girls with my face on so many worlds—and I don't want him to have this too. I shove at his hands and reach for the journal again. He drops it and grabs me, his hand as big as both my wrists. I flinch and close my eyes. I don't know if I'm waiting for his teeth or the back of his free hand, but nothing happens. After a few breaths, I open my eyes. He's looking down at me.

"What did you think I was going to do?"

"What you always do."

"I'm not going to hurt you."

That faux-innocent voice clashes with the image of Nelline's twice-broken jaw. If I hadn't read the file, I would believe that what stands before me is a man with unbloodied hands. Sure, I've heard of killers like this. The calm, well-groomed ones with mommy issues who always do weird shit like skin their victims to wear their faces. But I'd always thought it was a Wiley City problem. I mean, Ashtown kills, sure. But we *kill*. We growl and we fight and we avenge and we retaliate. We don't do this polite coddling before we strike. We don't lick the tears. I'm not saying it's any better morally—a body's a body—I'm just saying I don't understand it.

I have hated Nik Nik for many things, but lying was never one of his sins. His enemies always know they are his enemies, and his friends always know they are safe. He doesn't smile and knife you in the back. This Nik Nik's behavior opens a new side to him, makes him not the man I know, or anything like him.

"Yes you will. Because you hurt everything you've ever touched."

I expect more of that chagrined smile, the one slowly making me believe I'm crazy. Or maybe for his mask to finally crack and reveal the rage of the man I know him to be.

Instead, he looks desperate. He picks my journal up off the floor.

"That isn't true. What you wrote in here, it's wrong. You don't know me."

Humans are unknowable, right? It should be easy to agree, to say I don't know him, fly under his radar until I'm healed enough to traverse. But the letters on my back burn, and I can't. I can't forget that he broke Nelline the same way he tried to break me. *Humans* are unknowable, but Nik Nik is an animal.

"Listen well, Yerjanik: I've *always* known you, and there is no evil you could not commit."

He shakes his head, less like he's denying the content of my words than denying having heard it at all.

"You should get back in the pod. You survived the fever, but your breaks need more time."

He leaves without waiting for my response, like he can't afford to hear what I might say next. I don't think he even realizes he's still clutching my journal to his chest. He certainly doesn't realize when I reach the door behind him, and keep the handle turned to stop him from locking it. He doesn't try. I prop the door so that it looks closed but doesn't latch, just in case, and then I change out of the pod gown and into my own clothes, left neatly folded on the chair by the bed. My pack is still missing, but it just contained food, backup tech, and emergency medical. The only real loss is the journal, and I'll get over it. I take the collar from my vest and check for a signal, but the fortress walls are too thick. I need to get outside to be free.

I open the door.

I know I'm not healed enough to get through the trip home without rebreaking a few bones, but there are pods on Earth Zero, too, and people less injured and with less to hide than me have died inside the palace. I'm unsteady, so I keep a hand on the wall as I make my way toward the east side of the house. The front door is perpetually guarded, but the side doors were always just locked and patrolled. All I need to do is time it right.

By the time I get to the side exit, I'm more than a little dizzy and weak enough to use the wall for more than just steadying. Still, I manage to stop and notice the shadows. They're too dark, and when a runner steps out from each side, I'm only surprised I didn't expect it.

One of the runners is a boy. He's no more than twelve, but he's already got his first mark: an eye tattooed behind his ear. The superstitious, and there is no group more superstitious than runners, used to believe the mark would improve aim while driving. I haven't seen a runner with it in ages. But then, Nik Nik never let runners under fourteen take a mark, so this is all new ground.

His partner, probably his mentor though he doesn't look much older himself, steps forward.

"No visitors on the log tonight. You trespassing?"

I can't process the question. I can only whisper, disbelieving, "Michael?"

Using the name is a mistake, but here my stepbrother stands, marked in every visible place.

His hands tighten to fists at the name. "Mr. Cross," he says.

Because what else would you name a runner you poached from the Rurals?

I think back to our last dinner, his red-stained hands as he tried to be something he wasn't. Or, at least, something I thought he wasn't.

"She's from the Rurals," says a voice behind me, and Nik Nik steps between us.

He's put his hand on my arm to help guide me back down the hall, but Michael calls after us.

"Bringing your aid work home?" he says, with more sneer in his voice than a runner should dare.

The hand around my arm goes tight, and Nik Nik rises to his full height as his spine straightens. He looks over his shoulder slowly, slowly. His eyes narrow, like a carnivorous bird spotting movement in the dirt.

Michael takes a step back, but it's too late.

"Your name. You said it was Cross?"

It's part threat, part statement, and not at all a question, but the runner answers anyway.

"Yes, sir," Michael says. The "sir" is as proper as he can make it, but he's trembling. It's fear, but also uncertainty. He doesn't know what the man before him is capable of. But I do. I tear my arm out of his grasp. Better to trust the wall.

The movement turns Nik Nik's head away from Michael, breaking the spell of his rage.

"Have a good night, Mr. Cross," he says, and resumes leading me down the hall. He does not reach for my arm again.

Walking through the palace with him is a strange déjà vu, something I've done a hundred times, but I've never done, and that I will never do again. When we get to the room I make no pretense before heading to the pod. The short walk has forced me to see how loosely my seams are held together. Every breath now is a dull ache, and there's no guarantee that I would have ever survived to the other side. I need another night in the pod. Tomorrow, I can contact Dell. I go into the bathroom to change back into the pod gown, keeping my clothes clutched to my chest.

Nik Nik is in the bedside chair reading my journal. *Again.* I don't write everything about my life like Caramenta did. I haven't written enough for him to still be reading. Either he reads slowly or this isn't the first time. He's still focusing on the first part. He's reading—over and over again—about himself. He takes his time before looking over at me. Once he does, once his eyes flick from the pages to me, I want to run. I have the heart of a coyote but he has the eyes of a mountain lion, a creature who doesn't need tricks because his teeth are real.

But the monster I saw in the hallway was different from the one I've known. This is a creature who knows what he is, maybe even regrets it. A monster who's seen a mirror. That must be what the journal is for him, another mirror to see himself.

"What would you have done to that boy?"

"You should know better than to call a runner a boy," he says. He lifts the journal. "You used to."

"That runner is barely eighteen. He's a boy. You're twice his age and size."

I don't know why it feels like I can do this, correct him. It's never felt possible before. I was never one of the women who believed she could change her abusive partner. I was just one who believed she could survive it. I bet Nelline thought so too. And she did survive, she must have, or I wouldn't be shaking as my pieces refuse to knit back into place.

"I want to believe I would never have hurt him," he says, answering my first question.

"But you don't like it when your men get mouthy?"

He looks up, his head tilted. "You're quick to treason."

I walk over to the pods, lifting them up. He comes to my side to help ease me into the bed.

"That's not what it means," I say, the machines beginning their high-pitched whir.

Nik Nik is reading my vitals on the glass of the main pod.

"Hmmm?"

" 'Treason.' You used it wrong. Whoever taught you to read mixed up a few things."

"You called them my men. It's treason to wish a ruler dead or over-thrown, which is what you do when you assume I rule."

In the hot room the air around me goes suddenly cold, and the pod feels unbelievably like a restraint.

"No . . ."

I should have realized. His hair isn't braided. I messed up. I've acted like a coward avoiding information about the emperor, and now I'm in a trap far worse than Nik Nik's.

"He's not dead here. The Blood Emperor's still alive? Your father is still alive?"

I pull one arm out of the pod and begin hitting the buttons to shut it down so I can open it. At least, I hope I'm hitting buttons. I might just be hitting it.

"You have to let me go. I need to go now."

I take deep breaths, try to clear my mind the way my office's psychiatrist taught me, but nothing will help the flashbacks from my childhood. A place where heads were displayed in windows to send messages, but not the tongues, because those were nailed to the doors of the surviving family members. A place where runners got their name using homemade monstrosities to mulch people down in the streets. It was a game. They kept score in tally marks on their doors. Another reason there are so few of me left alive: I was not a fast child.

I don't realize I'm still attacking the machine until Nik Nik grabs my hand.

"It's all right."

"It's not all right. Your father—"

"Died. When I was six."

The news calms me more than breathing exercises ever could. He notices, and releases me.

"How old was I when he died in your delusion?"

"My what?"

"In your journal, you think you know me. You've made an elaborate account of things that never happened."

"Right, I'm just a sun-crazed wastelander. I've spent too long drinking bad water. Once I'm healed up, turn me loose. We'll forget this ever happened."

"Why is my name on your back? How did you learn the code you use?"

"I made it up," I say, ignoring the first question.

"You're not a very good liar."

"Who taught you the code?" I ask back.

"The same person who taught me to read. My brother. Which is how I know there are no gaps in my education."

". . . Your *older* brother?"

"You've heard of him? He's absent in your journal."

"I have. He was a prodigy. Crazy smart, right?"

Smart and curious and as weak as a baby bird. Which is why Nik Senior killed him when he was fourteen.

"He's dead though," I say.

"Treason again," he says.

\

BACK ON MY home Earth, and I'm guessing every Earth where Nik Nik rules, the story is always the same. Everyone stopped speaking of the boy after he was killed; he was taken out of the records as if he'd never existed. Only I know, because his younger brother loved me and mourned him, that his real name was Adranik, *firstborn*. He was smart. Too smart. He understood numbers and stars but not how to please his father. He'd gotten sick when he was young, and never fully recovered. But even worse than being weak of body, he was weak of heart. He cried when his father took him hunting. He cried when the runners went on parade. When the boy was seven, Nik Nik was born. His mother named him Yerjanik, which means *happy*. An empty prayer. She must have known that wasn't in the cards for either of Nik Senior's boys.

By the time Nik Nik was five, he was already the biggest child in the wasteland. He hunted with Nik Senior's men in the deep wastes, where humans barely live and grazing animals get fat off plants and water too toxic for most of us. But the second-born son of the emperor didn't hunt the slower, lumbering prey. He speared predators with the glee of his father's worst soldiers. I was never sure if Nik Nik was born cruel, or just obedient.

The story from the emperor's men was that Adra's persistent illness flared up, killing him kindly in his sleep. And that was what you said happened if any of Nik Senior's men were in the room. But the real story, the one the workers who raised me heard from clients and passed around, was that the boy was taken into the black swamps. His throat was slit and his body shoved under.

They say the dead in the bogs don't decay. That they're perfectly preserved in a grave of black moss. I've always wondered, if anyone dared brave the runners and predators that far out, if they would find him still—a small boy with a huge brain and a perfectly serene face.

I spent most of my relationship with Nik Nik wondering if he knew what everyone else did. Or if his brother's murder was kept from him even after his father's death.

It was a long time before I finally felt secure enough to mention the boy who'd taught Nik Nik to write his name but died before he could teach him much else. When I did, he didn't answer directly. He told me a story. He said his grandfather's people came from a place across the ocean. A small country, but resourceful. Once, a larger country came in and massacred nearly everyone. But that, that wasn't the worst part. The worst part was that afterward, swords and sickles still drenched in innocent blood, they turned and said they'd done nothing. If the massacre was mentioned, they denied it, and no one was brave enough to argue. Nik Senior said *that* was true power. Not to kill a man, but to kill a man in front of his family and force them to agree you did not.

I asked him if his father was right, if that was true power.

No, he said. It was just blood magic.

\

NIK NIK HAS programmed the pods, and I intend to get into them as soon as he leaves, but he doesn't. He sits in the bedside chair, still in his tunic and glasses, looking every bit the holy man instead of the hunter he has always been. I should rush him out. I can feel the warning pulse of my veil losing charge, but I'm not as concerned as I should be. Half of me is wondering if having this version of him see me and not hurt me will heal all those broken pieces inside that therapy has blunted but not reassembled. The other half is wondering how many more pieces there will be if I'm wrong about him.

"Going to read me a story?" I ask.

"I was hoping you would tell me one."

"You don't want a garbage git's tale. All ours end in being eaten by a mudcroc."

"Important tales, those," he says. "You're not from the deep wastes?"

Dammit. I'm acting as if the veil is already gone. "Not originally. What story did you want?"

"How old was I when my father died in your delusion?"

"World," I say. "Just . . . pretend I come from a different world than you do, a world where things are mostly the same, but slightly different."

"How old was I?"

I stall, because he's asking like the answer could save his life, and I don't understand why.

"What makes you think it was different than here?"

"Here he died when I was six, but you were afraid of my father like you'd seen his rule firsthand. You're easily more than six years younger than me."

Can I still get fired for violating every traverser policy if no one ever finds out?

"I don't know. I was fourteen. Someone slit his throat while he was sitting at his desk."

I remember that day like it was the best birthday I'd ever had. I was so happy he was dead, runners showed up in my neighborhood to check my alibi. It didn't help that someone saw a small girl running from his office. I didn't kill him, but a girl that young alone with a man like him? I'd sharpen the blade and hand it to her myself.

"How old are you now?" he asks.

"Twenty-six. You do the math."

"And I took his place?"

"Yes, because Adra was already dead. He died when you were—"

Seven.

The dots start to connect. In the other worlds, Adra died when Nik Nik was six. Here, it was the father who died at that same time. But I'd bet a man and a teenage boy went out into the desert in all of them.

"Why do you want to know?"

"Why are you stalling?"

"Because you might kill me for telling the truth."

"I don't kill."

There's a shakiness in the proclamation that makes it easy to believe. It's different, and so much more true, than *I could never kill.*

"You were six," I say.

"The same age my father died here. . . . How did my brother die in your world?"

"I think you already know. Which means you already know your brother killed your father in this one. That's the question you want to ask, isn't it? In my world, in *most* worlds, your father killed your brother when you were six. In this one . . . Adra must have gotten the upper hand."

He stands, but doesn't approach me.

"Treason, every word."

"You said you wouldn't imprison me."

"No, I didn't."

"It was implied."

"Your injuries when you were found, did someone beat you for wearing my name? Was it my brother?"

There's real heat behind the question. I don't know where the protective rage comes from, I just know it should scare me and it doesn't.

"It was a . . . miscalculated landing."

This seems to amuse him. "You do this a lot?"

"It's kind of my special gift."

"World hopping?"

I swallow. "Dying."

Unsurprisingly, this gives rise to a dozen new questions. Mostly, I answer. I tell him more than I intend to about myself and where I've traveled. I realize too late that I have never gotten to talk to someone like this. Talk about world walking with someone who doesn't think it's a sin like my family or just a job like Jean and Dell. I like talking with him, and hate that I do.

I don't realize how many years I've been alone until I warm under a gift as simple as someone's undivided attention. I could say Wiley City has made me weak, but it's always been this way. Even my Nik Nik knew exactly how, when he wanted, to make me feel special. Just as he knew exactly how to make me feel like dirt. And I reveled in that tainted affection, like a plant settles for drinking dew because it knows it's never going to get real rain.

"You still haven't told me why my name is tattooed on your back."

"Not your name."

"Right. Another me."

"Now you're getting it."

"And what was I to you?"

He doesn't think I'm someone I'm not, so this is the longest stretch of conversation I've had without lying in a long, long time.

"A warm place to land."

"That's all?"

"Spoken like someone who's never been without a warm place. You should value them more."

"You're still talking like it's me you know. It isn't," he says. "I would never . . . hurt someone like that."

But he says it like it's something he wants to believe, not something he knows is true.

"Can I ask you a question?" When he nods, I continue. "Have you ever broken someone's jaw?"

He recoils.

"No," he says without a moment's hesitation.

The pulse of the veil is a steady countdown now. I could let it fizzle out on its own, pretend this wasn't a decision. If I just let the veil fall off, I am still committed to deceiving him. If I take it off, I am giving the man who looks like the monster that gave me every scar a gift. I turn the idea over and wonder how long I've been letting my most wounded self make all of my decisions.

I reach up and press the edges of the mask to release it.

It doesn't take long to see I've made a mistake. When he sees my real face, his eyes light with recognition.

Nik Nik lunges for me, and I scream.

\

"I TOLD YOU to go. You weren't supposed to come back. He's going to find you."

I blink up at him, surprised at the lecture.

"Did you really come back to him? He's going to kill you. He *tried* to kill you." He looks confused, but also tired. "I can't find you like that again."

We lock eyes, me not understanding him, and him not understanding why I don't understand him.

His eyebrows knit.

"Nelline?" he says, finally, actually looking at me. "What happened to your face?"

"You haven't been listening. I'm not Nelline." I push away from him, toward the tall mirror in the corner. "And what's wrong with my face?"

At my first glance I nearly scream again. I've had striations before, the tiger stripes of bruising that accompany traversing, but never like this. Even darker than my dark skin, they begin beneath my eyes and carry down as far as I can see. I lift my shirt, and see the marks across my torso. I lift the legs of my pants and find them there too. They might lighten with time, they've always disappeared before, but these survived the pod. Are they permanent? I press the marks that frame my cheekbones, but there is no pain. They usually act like bruises, but these feel like scars.

He touches my arm, and my whole body tenses. I turn away from the mirror.

"It was your brother, right? Adranik hurt Nelline."

"She was . . . his." He's still studying me. "You're really not the same?"

I shake my head. "Adranik was never the one to hurt me."

"In the times when he's not there . . . it's me?"

I don't know if he means when his brother's not in the picture, we are together, or, when his brother's not in the picture he is the one to hurt me. Either way, the answer's the same. I nod, and feel bad for being the one to tell him.

I can't find you like that again. There was real anguish when he said it. I picture Nyame punishing Nik Nik this way, forcing him to see and clean up exactly the kind of damage he inflicts on every other world.

"You can't stay here. He's gotten worse thinking she's dead. He'll want blood for the trick."

"I already tried leaving once today. It wasn't a roaring success."

"Daybreak will be safer. There's a runner I trust who's on watch in the morning, but he moves out to border patrol by the afternoon." He crosses his arms behind his back. "I can escort you out at sunrise."

I nod, and he walks to the door. Standing in the threshold, he hesitates.

"When you go don't leave a trace."

"I never do."

I'm so good at not making an impression it's a wonder I even leave footprints. Not once in my whole life have I been missed. I've collected marks from others all over, but I've never made one on someone else. As I close the door behind Nik Nik, I wonder how long it will be before I am less to him than a ghost.

\

THERE ARE SLIGHT advantages to being so often treated as prey. For instance, you tend to watch others more than others watch you. You tend, also, to only ever be minimally disoriented by a sudden loss of safety. But the most important benefit to being so often hunted is that you always know when it's happening.

So when the men come into the room somewhere after midnight, I am sitting in a chair facing them. I'd heard the footsteps gathering about half an hour after the pod had beeped to tell me I was as healed as I was going to be, and I thought briefly of escaping. But the boots had gathered at each end of the hall, and I'd rather be dragged out than give them the satisfaction by stepping into a trap. Eventually my patience outlasted theirs, and four runners entered my room.

"Can I help you?" I ask, like they're visitors to my sitting room, not soldiers who've cornered me.

Michael and the child runner are there, but they must be outranked by the one who speaks. Both look surprised to find me, sans veil, in the room, but neither says anything.

"Emperor heard his brother had company. Wants to meet you."

"Sounds like fun," I say, standing. I can be remarkably compliant when I don't have a choice.

They don't lead me down the way I expect. My Nik Nik kept his office on the right side of the palace. His father's had been on the left, but Nik Nik respected his memory too much to take it over. He left it as a sitting room, and he would meet those who had been friends with his father there. Adra must not care much for sentiment, which makes sense, if he's as smart as the stories say.

Taking a deep breath won't actually help, but as we near the office I do it anyway. The double doors I'm led to have only ever held Nik Senior in my memory, but I try to keep calm. It can't be as bad as that. No one could ever be as bad as Nik Senior.

I'm wrong.

I've been to worlds where plants kill, where people don't wear color, where the sun sets too soon. I've seen the impossible, but nothing so impossible as this. When the runners open the doors, I see him: Adam Bosch, father of interdimensional traversing and director of the Eldridge Institute, standing behind the desk, just in front of the chair where Nik Senior bled to death.

I see a man who has always been brilliant and kind to me, but with teeth covered in onyx and rows in his hair. I want to call him sir. I want to apologize for coming into his office.

The code. Of course, the code. If I'd questioned how Nik Nik and I both knew it, I might have expected this. But I didn't, so I panic and step backward. I lick at the sweat collecting on my upper lip and feel more like my mother lying in the dirt than I ever have. I know I'm facing death, because all of the shock and confusion and anger I expected to see on Nik Nik's face when my veil came off, I am seeing now on his brother's. Adam, Adranik, whoever he is, he killed me on this Earth. Or tried to. I should have known. Nik Nik isn't the only one who would have killed like his father.

The emperor steps back. He's afraid because his first thought isn't *resurrection* or *twin,* it's *ghost.* But then comes rage, the curling upper lip I remember from Nik Senior. It's impossible. Impossible. I know Adam . . . but then, you can't ever know another person. Which is why you should never admire anyone.

It's too late for me to learn that lesson.

"Why didn't you tell me it was her?" he says to Michael.

"She didn't look like that before," says the boy runner. He's defensive of my stepbrother, but there's too much apology in his protest. He wasn't cut out for this.

I won't get to see how they're punished for failing to recognize me, because Adam orders the other two to drag me to the dungeon. The hands grabbing my arms have fingers the size of my widest bones and no aversion to digging in as they drag me back.

CHAPTER SEVEN

In the dungeon, I add up the hours I've been gone and wonder if Dell has started to miss me. If she ever will. It's too early for her to be really worried. I've missed check-ins before, so she won't think anything's wrong tomorrow either. She'll go to Jean, probably, who will remind her I have history in the area. He'll tell her I have just let my curiosity get the better of me like I did that one time on Earth 68, and that other time on Earth 214, and that other time . . . maybe if I'd ever been reliable, they'd have the cavalry out.

Or maybe not.

Everything I knew about Eldridge is skewed now that I know the son of the Blood Emperor is running it. I've always believed Nik Senior killed his eldest, but apparently his narcissism was too great for that. He had wanted his second child to inherit, but he must have only sent Adam away to learn. On Earth Zero, anyway. Nik Senior probably tried to banish his son here, too, but this Adranik killed him for it.

The fact that Adam Bosch is my ex-lover's older brother is almost harder to process than him being a warlord. I roll the idea around as if tumbling the knowledge will wear the edges off. It doesn't work. It still seems impossible. I think about them, comparing their appearances in my mind, but there is nothing in my boss's face to remind me of the man I lived with for years. Even Nik Senior seems absent from Bosch. But then, when I think of the empress . . . yes, there he is. Adam has his mother's face.

All this thinking is just a distraction from the trap I'm caught in. The dirt is too hard to dig into on the hill the emperor chose for his palace, but the aboveground dungeons still *feel* subterranean. The walls are concrete, the door metal. The ceiling is made of puffy squares that keep sound from traveling to the floor above, a concession to Nik Senior's delicate wife. When I was a kid, I thought the empress was beautiful—and terrible. I hated her for standing next to a monster, for sleeping next to him and never clamping a pillow over his face. When I was a teenager, I thought I understood. She didn't like it, but she was secure the only way a pretty girl with no stomach for a hard life could be in Ash. But then, when I got older still, my understanding turned again, darker. Once I was with Nik Nik I began to wonder if the empress didn't mind the bloodshed at all, because for all the hell he bought the rest of us, Nik Senior could never do anything but love her. It is possible to love a monster, even if you spend every day reminding yourself that they are a monster.

I'm staring up at that ceiling when I hear the steps. How, how is it possible his footsteps sound the same in a wasteland dungeon as they do echoing off the high halls of Eldridge?

When I stand up, the voice comes from behind me. Quiet, but too forceful to be called a whisper.

"Don't stand. If you're not sitting when he comes in, he'll make you."

I turn around, but it's just me and the wall. I hold my hand up. The wall looks like solidly stacked cinder blocks, but enough of the mortar has been pushed away that I can feel air coming from the other side. I put my palm at mouth height and feel the warm breath of the intruder. Not a ghost, then.

I'm full of questions, but I hate to waste good advice, so I sit.

"Took you longer than I thought," I say when Adranik comes in.

"How did you know I'd come? I could have let you rot."

"You didn't order me dead. Means you want information. You don't strike me as the type who's patient when he wants something."

He walks up to the cell doors slowly, not caution but nonchalance. He doesn't open them. Wouldn't matter if he did. I could fight him in my world, where he has thin, delicate hands and a face that never quite meets another person's. But this Adam, callous and even-eyed, this one could kill me.

I think back to Adam Bosch's wide pant legs and white, white shirts. I should have known he was a wastelander. Only we know the true value of white fabric, because nothing stays white in the land of sandstorms and mudtides. And the slacks, the thin material flaring out instead of tucked into boots, an invitation to bloodmites and scorpions in Ashtown. Even I, for all my assimilation, still wear pants close and tight. He's not eccentric; he's just showing off. Does he feel exposed? Is it an adrenaline rush to dress the way he does? Or has he forgotten those old fears, a true Wiley City resident now?

I remember his smooth hands as he offered me fruit, knowing what produce would mean to me. *We're all rooting for you.* He might have been, because we are exactly the same and only he knew it. And I had worshiped him.

This one dresses like Ash: long hair braided twice on the side, thick pants tucked into metal-tipped boots, fingernails like stilettos, and a mouth full of shine. Adam Bosch is clean-shaven. Adranik wears a low beard against the desert wind.

"I told your brother everything."

"My brother doesn't ask the right kinds of questions," he says, flashing onyx teeth at me. Same voice, same easy authority as the man who signs my paychecks. The man who signed the letter of employment Caramenta gushed over like a sacred text.

He's right about his brother asking the wrong questions. Nik Nik wanted to know if sunsets are the same color on all worlds, and if there are places that still have frogs. He'd never even thought to ask how such a power could be exploited, how it was done.

"I'm not a threat to you. I just want to leave. I promise you'll never see me again."

He leans against the bars, hands and head hanging inside my cell. So at least he believes me about the first part.

"What game are you playing, Nelline?"

"I'm not whoever you think I am."

He looks at me, all of me, from the bottom up. "You think I don't know you? I *made* you. Why did you get my brother's name on your back? To make me jealous?"

I look at his hands without making it seem like I'm looking at his hands. Three scars around his index and middle finger. The emperor is married. The emperor is married and he's looking at me like he owns me.

She was my brother's. That's what Nik Nik had said. I should have focused on that. Should have asked, *Your brother's what?*

"We're not, I mean . . . I'm not your . . . You think I'm your wife?"

He laughs, loud and deep and cruel. "I'd never marry a garbage git. Much less a worker."

The voice in the wall gives a low rumble that's pure wasteland. I used to growl like that, before I came to the city and realized they never growled, or hissed, or spit to ward off curses.

Much less a worker. The emperor sounds like Nik Senior, full of derision for the House that keeps Ashtown running. Nik Nik wasn't like that. Peter, his best friend growing up, took the *x* and had his ear for sex providers ever since.

"My wife is elegant and pure. She's an angel," he says.

"Poor thing. She blind?"

"Mouth like that and you expect me to believe you aren't Nix?"

I bristle on Nelline's behalf at his use of her old name. If she did trick in Ash, she doesn't anymore, and his use of her working name means he still considers her open for business despite her wishes.

"I'm not."

"Then who are you?" His dark eyes narrow until he looks near manic. "Are you with them? The people in black suits who keep trying to kill me?"

"A rival gang squaring up on you?" I cluck my tongue. "The emperor in my world never had that problem. Neither did your old man."

"Your world," he says. "So you and my brother are telling the same ridiculous story. Say I buy that you are a duplicate from another world. How does it work? Can you show me?"

"Magic. And no."

He steps back, sliding his hands out of the bars.

"Thought you would have learned your lesson about telling me no."

He's not disappointed; he's not even curious. There's glee at my refusal, so I shouldn't be surprised by what comes next.

"The runners parade at dawn. You have until then to change your mind."

"You still . . ."

Memories overwhelm me. The modified vehicles, spikes and fire, the laughing. God, the laughing. I was small enough to hide, but rarely quick enough to get to a hiding spot. If you didn't cry, they didn't chase as hard, they got bored. But I was a child. Children always cry.

Can I activate my collar before they crush me? Will it even have finished warming up before they've ground me into nothing?

"You want to know what I know?"

He'd been walking to the door, but now he turns back, mistaking my rage for cooperation.

"I know that you are just like your father. Worse, even. You didn't grow up during the wars; you have no excuse for cruelty. You just like it. Your father was right. You are weak. A weak and useless ruler. Do you want to know where I come from? I come from a place where your brother is emperor and the wasteland rejoices. Everyone loves him. I don't have his name on my back to make you jealous, because not one person even remembers you. I have his name on my back because he is the best thing to happen to Ashtown. And you, you are the worst. The inadequate son, turning his father's legacy to shame."

It's a little lie sharpened to a knife, and it slices true. He closes his eyes, holds himself back from reacting. When he opens them again he's calm, focused. He looks more like Adam Bosch than I would have thought possible.

"You tricked me before, got me to kill you before the runners could have their way. It won't work again. This time, you'll go like the trash you are."

\

I'VE THOUGHT A lot about how I could die. Most gits do. There are ways that are acceptable, and ways that are not. Of course, sometimes we fantasize about not dying at all . . . but it's best to be practical.

My mother knew I would die in a palace.

One night, toward the end, she said, *You'll never keep your place, always reaching up.*

She was too out of it to remember the story of the man who flew too high and crashed to the ground, but she'd told me it enough times before that I'm sure, if she were capable, she would have reminded me again.

It was when she was sick for the last time, and everyone on the block knew it was the last time. Half because they thought this withdrawal would kill her, and half because they were sure if she made it through this time, she would never use again. I was in the latter half. But we were both wrong.

She was lying on towels, having sweated through her bedroll and blankets the day before, the last time she told me to keep my place. She said the first things to come out of her were my hands—fingers straight, not curled—because I was born reaching.

And that's how you'll die, she said. *High up in a tower where you have no business.*

I leaned in then, and said it. The last words she was coherent enough to hear from me: *Rather die in a tower than the dirt floor of a shack.*

I still believe it. I wish I didn't. I wish I could say that she didn't deserve to die like that. I wish I could call her death a tragedy or even unexpected. But you get the death you accept. Lying on that dirt floor, spinning one last time on a free dose from Nik, her favorite nightgown full of holes she never seemed to see, that was exactly how my mother was meant to go.

And if Adranik had put his hands around my neck and choked me to oblivion, it'd feel about right for me. Dying in a palace because I brushed too close to too powerful a man? It's been written in my stars on more than one Earth.

But death by runners? As an adult? No. The parades were the specter of my childhood. In the arc of my life, the time for them to kill me ended when I outlived Senior. It's a child's death, and I won't be made a little girl in the end. I'd kill myself before I'd face the parade.

\

I'M MAKING A list of options with too few entries when I hear the scratching travel up the wall and across the ceiling. It's the sound of a sandcat—a fanged rodent whose name makes no sense, except that they do eat other rodents, as a cat would, if there were any left small enough to fit the title. The scratching is a trick. It must fool the guards into thinking the sounds in the walls are made by the creature, but I remember the litter that invaded our house when I was a girl and this sound is off. The ceiling creaks too much for the weight of a single animal and the scratching is too precise to be a pack. I follow the noise to the corner of my cell, and watch as one of the ceiling tiles is pulled away.

The person who's come to my rescue is exactly who I expect: me.

I take a moment and stare fully at her. With Caramenta, half of the cheek was destroyed, the eyes discolored. I didn't so much *feel* it was me as I deduced it. But this is me and I know it in my chest. I am standing here in the cell but I am also staring out from the darkness of the space in the ceiling.

First, I go a little dizzy. Then, my heart beats quickly, a panic without reason. Finally, I vomit. In the space above she does the same. This time when I straighten, I keep my eyes closed. She doesn't, and starts vomiting again.

"You have to stop looking at me directly," I say. "Your brain thinks you're hallucinating. It's trying to make you throw up whatever toxic thing you drank."

"Got it," she says between retches.

When I open my eyes, her face is turned away and she's reaching down, holding out an arm as tattooed as mine used to be. I use the cell bars to lift myself up.

"I don't know what will happen if we touch," I say once I'm in the space beside her. "This has never happened before."

"Jesus, is that what I sound like?" she says in a voice as low and rough as an asphalt road. "Do you gargle with bleach or something?"

"Me? My voice isn't as bad as yours. You sound like coffee percolating."

We quiet as we realize that we must, in fact, both sound like this. Which is a letdown. Having been raised around people with voices as inviting and seductive as a birdsong sung low, I'd always hoped a little of it had worn off on me.

We replace the roof tile, then I shimmy in the crawl space behind her. She leads me to a gap between walls and we go vertical. She doesn't look back to ask me if I know how to climb the cinder block. I wonder if she has the same memories I do, of being exiled outside when Mom had overnight clients, of climbing up the walls to sleep on the roof, high above things that bite and sting, above ground that would suck you in at the first drop of moisture.

I think again about Earth 255 me. She couldn't do this, and because she couldn't climb she would never have to.

We climb until we can pull ourselves up onto the floor of a round, domed room. A portion of the wall is missing, and we slide through easily.

I look around. "The observatory . . ."

"The what?"

"The observatory. It was their mother's."

And in my world it was cleaned every day. The only portrait in the house was in this room. It was his mother, life-size on the wall just before the clear roof began. Here, it's all clutter and cobwebs.

"It's just a room they never use. It's safe enough," she says.

I look at her, but only from the neck down. I recognize her gloves, fingerless reptile hide. Mixxie gave them to me—us—after my mother died. All of the providers gave me something in the days after I buried her, even though she hadn't been attached to the House for almost a year at the end. They visited me one at a time, never more than a few hours apart, a suicide watch if I ever saw one. But it was Exlee who gave me the gift that saved my life: an invitation to stay at the House for a while, whether I took up the work or not. There they taught me how to seduce a man no one else had been able to keep, how to trap a predator by looking like prey.

I allow myself to look at her through a half squint. It's still disorienting, but there's no racing heart, no nausea, so I open my eyes fully.

Once I'm staring at her I can't stop. It's not at all like seeing myself. This dirt-caked girl isn't me. But it is exactly like going back in time, seeing a portrait of myself from when I was young. She looks—

"You look like my mother," she says. "But for those weird marks."

"I was just thinking the same thing about you."

"Figures."

She perches on a dust-covered desk, one leg hanging off and the other pulled close to her chest, her arms around her knee. And I know, because she's me, that she's trying to look casual as she reaches for the knife on her calf.

"We don't know what will happen if you do that either."

Her stretching fingers relax.

"I've been listening in the walls," she says. "You think you're the real me."

"A different you. My world just learned how to traverse before yours."

"Why?"

"Why what?"

"Why did you figure it out first? No, forget that. That's just luck. Why hasn't everyone else figured out how to traverse? Or have they?"

"No . . . they haven't."

"No one has? You've never seen another of these travelers—"

"Traversers."

"Whatever. None from other worlds have come?"

"No."

"Why not?"

I open my mouth to give the company line, that we might have been visited but they just haven't been detected, but then freeze. What if there are just too few Adam Bosches who aren't bloodthirsty emperors? How many Nik Seniors let their eldest sons live? How many Adraniks killed their fathers and took their places?

I could tell her this, but I'm not sure why she wants to know.

"I don't know. I never asked."

She leans back, a little smug.

I sit on a pile of what used to be curtains. "I don't question things. I'm just happy to have a position."

"A real position? You citizen?"

"Almost. Resident. Four years left."

She whistles low. "You told Nik you need to get outside to leave. But how will you get back if we don't have that technology here?"

She's staring at her hands when she asks, going for casual. I'm almost offended. Do I look that soft? I haven't been out of Ashtown *that* long.

"They'll pick me up the same place they dropped me off," I say. "The riverbed on the edge of town, the deep-waste side."

She nods. "Shift change at dawn. We'll leave then." She pulls out two thermoses, drinks from one, and holds the other out to me. "You'll need hydration for the walk. Not sure how the sun is where you're from, but here tomorrow's a bright day."

Only when she says it do I remember Dell warning me it was coming. A bright day, meaning don't go outside and bring in anything you don't want burnt or discolored. We haven't had one of those in a while. Or maybe we have and I missed it. In the city, they pull a dark screen over the sky to keep it out. We call the days overcast, and I've forgotten the shadow means fire on the other side.

I drink up, trying to remember the last time I had to face the white light.

"Thank you."

She waves off my thanks just like I would. "I'll head out soon. I've got more listening to do. Need something I can sell if I want to keep laying low."

"You spy?"

"I listen."

"Nelline . . . Why did Adra try to kill you?"

From the look on her face, the question catches her like a right hook. But she must have wondered, at least while it was happening.

When she answers me, it is, of course, a list.

"Because he wanted me and didn't want to. Because he wanted to prove he could live without me. Because he couldn't control me. Because . . ." She shrugs. "But I've been dosing myself with his paralytic, little bits, so it wore off quick. Took blood expanders on days when I saw him. Even if Nik hadn't found me, I wouldn't have even come close to dying for real."

Her voice shakes with the lie she's probably been telling herself. Lying there, bleeding out in the time before seeing Nik Nik's face, she probably felt just like I did on the desert sand after landing here. I wonder if she thought of Mom, too, when the darkness was closing in.

Odd, that 175 Nik Nik had saved us both.

I'd assume her relationship with Adra was like mine and Nik's. But no, I was never really prepared for him to kill me. I must have trusted him, at least that much. Trusted him to hurt me without killing me, to bruise me without breaking any of my most important bones. Is that still trust? Or just resignation?

Maybe Nik Nik was better than Adra so I was right to trust he'd never kill me, but more likely Nelline is just smarter than I was. That's why she's alive after facing Adra, and I was caught off guard by Adam: we saw the same face, and only she knew better than to trust it.

I shake out my pile of curtains and sit in a molding armchair.

Nelline was right. I *am* soft. Because I lied to her about how I'll leave, so I assumed she'd sneak out and spend her day waiting in the river for a transport that would never come. But I've been living easy for six years. Longer, if you count my years at Nik Nik's side as soft, which anyone in Ash would.

As sleep comes too easily, I realize what I missed, the most basic Ashtown truth I've let myself forget: a wastelander with two thermoses carries water and poison.

She comes over just as my limbs go fuzzy.

"Real sorry about this. His man says he'll pay teeth to get you back."

She gives me the reason even though I didn't ask. I like that. It means she respects me.

I know this death, and it's not a total one. It's a toxin made from plants found along the green sludge that passes for water in the deep wastes. Providers keep a bottle in their nightstands. Some even carefully cover themselves with it, an insurance policy against unruly clients. If a worker says no kissing, and you kissed anyway, you might go numb from the mouth down and learn a lesson. If a worker says their cock is off-limits, and you grab it anyway, you might find yourself unable to use that arm for a day or more.

Identifying the drug fills me with nostalgia. Being dosed with it— the easy blanket of a paralytic rather than the mind-churning panic of an opiate—feels like being close to home. I wish the paralysis hadn't started with my mouth. Wish I could tell her that I'm not mad, because I would have done just the same if I remembered enough about home to know who I really was.

CHAPTER EIGHT

How does Adranik become the bloodiest emperor? This is the question I mull over when I'm awake again but still paralyzed. He was the softer child, the one who couldn't even hunt without crying. How did he preserve the runners' parade when his carnivore brother didn't? How did he break his mistress's jaw when his own father built whole rooms for the comfort of his wife? Maybe that's the point. Everyone already knew Nik Nik was good for blood. When he took over he had nothing to prove. It was the opposite—people were tense, afraid he'd be worse than his dad. When he canceled the parades everyone breathed a sigh of relief, but still eyed him warily.

Adranik must have had everything to prove. Maybe he couldn't cancel the parades because everyone expected him to. Maybe it was self-preservation, the way the smallest animals are the first to growl, the first to bite.

Or maybe he only hated hunting because he was afraid of the game, and seeing someone else spill blood sat with him just fine.

I've been taken out of the castle. With half an inhale I can tell I'm not even in central Ashtown anymore. The acid tang is out of the air, and I don't realize how used to it I've already grown until it's gone. This room smells like a hospital, heavy-duty cleaner not quite hiding

the soft dirt smell. I open my eyes just a slit. The all-white room surprises me. I'm still in Ash, but the Rurals, I'm guessing.

I make out a shape loading linens into a large supply closet. He's
wearing the tunics I'm used to seeing when I visit my family, the ones
Nik Nik seems to enjoy here. This one started white, but is now the
dingy gray of a tea stain. I test my limbs—a little laggy, but good
enough.

I sit up and he turns around. Our eyes lock. Daniel. But he's not my
stepfather, not here. There's surprise in his eyes, but no affection. I
spring, shoving him into the supply closet he was loading, and force
the double doors closed against him. I wrap a sheet around the handles
to keep them closed. He's pushing against it, yelling, and already the
sheets are loosening. It won't hold long.

The smell of dirt and the presence of Daniel tells me where I am:
the vacant rooms in my stepfather's new church. I put my collar back
on and tap the center to begin the warm-up, then I run. I emerge in a
hall just off the main auditorium and sprint for the double doors at the
entrance. I've almost reached them when a shape steps into my path.

"You?"

Even though I recognize him, it takes me a second to remember his
name. Mr. Cheeks is still pretty, and still smiling, but now his face sick-
ens me. He's a runner in a place where they still live up to their name.
He looks just like the man who took my money a few weeks ago, except for the new tattoo at the center of his throat: a star within a star.

It strikes me, and I can't keep from saying, "Someone loves you?"

He tilts his head. "You read runner tattoos too? I knew Nelline
could, but I'd expect a girl well preserved as you comes from the city."

His mention of Nelline, Nelline as someone other than me, calms
me down. She had said "his man" told her Nik Nik wanted me. And
Nik Nik had said the runner he trusted went out to border patrol in
the afternoons. If I'd asked myself who worked border patrol in the
afternoons back home, I would have known to expect him.

"I do," I say. "I just didn't always."

He nods, casting a shadow over his love mark. When it goes bad, because he's young and it always does, he'll fill in the star with black and draw a circle around it. An ink-dark hole will mark his heartbreak.

"Let me go."

"Can't. Sorry, but we need you."

It wasn't what I expected to hear. *Sorry, he wants you,* maybe. Or, *Sorry, just doing my job.*

"Who's we?"

"She's coming."

I hear them now, the light and delicate footsteps. I should have guessed who they belong to, given my location, but when she enters the room I am unprepared.

Esther. My Esther. Her clothes are understated as always, but only the cuts are modest while the material is heavy, expensive. Nothing like she can afford back home. There's something off with her face. Once I identify what it is, I go a little rabid.

I start walking toward her. Mr. Cheeks moves between us. I push past him.

"Who broke your nose, Essie?" I get close enough to see that her front incisor is fake. "Who knocked out your tooth?"

Someone has been punching my delicate little sister in the face. Someone's about to die.

She smiles. It's sad and bruised. If she means to disarm me it has the opposite effect.

"My husband."

The words spin me. They're full of shame, shame she shouldn't own, and I connect the words with Cheeks's tattoo quickly.

He's standing too close to avoid the first hit, but he catches my wrist easily on the second and shoves me back. He's had a lifetime of fighting, and I'm out of practice.

"She's barely eighteen!" I scream in his face, the words half spit.

"Not me," he says. "I'd never."

"Then who?"

"Someone you can't attack, but thank you for thinking to try," Esther says, coming between us.

She's as gracious in this world as she is on mine. If there are souls that are pure, that are insulated from things that are done to them and remain the same whether they are gutter born or tower bound, Esther is one. The knowable.

My wife is elegant and pure. She's an angel.

It clicks.

"The emperor?"

She nods. "We hoped you could help us get him out of power. Nik said you . . . know things."

Adra was wrong. My sister is polite, but polite and angelic are two different things. Everyone makes that mistake. They think hair like snow means angel, and eyes like the sky mean saint. But my sister would ostracize someone to their death if they threatened her church. She could teach me lessons in ruthlessness. It's what I first liked about her. If she was what people saw when they looked at her, she'd have no more use than a porcelain doll.

She sits on the church's stage. In my mind the image overlaps with her sitting on my cot during my visit. She's younger than I was when I took up with Nik Nik, and I was still too young. Mr. Cheeks sits beside her, arm over her shoulders.

Sloppy runner.

I break for the exit, putting my palm over my necklace to make sure it's warmed up. Not quite, but close enough. Mr. Cheeks scrambles behind me, but he's too late. I'm almost to the doors and they're opening before me like the gates of heaven . . . except it isn't God, it's Nik Nik.

I slow to a stop and hear Mr. Cheeks doing the same behind me. I expect him to grab me, but he doesn't. He's looking past me.

"Why were you chasing her?"

"She can help us," Mr. Cheeks says.

"That's not your decision. You were to barter with Nelline for her freedom, not a new capture," Nik Nik says, looking down at me. "Is there somewhere I can take you?"

I move toward him cautiously, feeling like those birds that take food from the teeth of mudcrocs. He's holding open the door, and through it I can see the butane sky. The sun's not even up all the way, but it's a bright day, so it's nearly noon-light. My collar vibrates its readiness.

"Wait!"

Somewhere, deep inside, I must be looking for something on 175, something I haven't found yet. Because when my sister screams for me, I turn back.

"Look at you," she says. "Your skin has no spots, your teeth are whole. There's no film in your eyes. Your world has been so, so kind to you. Don't you feel anything, any . . . obligation to help us taste just a little of that peace?"

Nope. And it's on my lips to tell her so. To tell her that I got to the city on my own two feet, with no stranger from another world to help me, and I don't owe anyone anything.

Except, that's not true, is it?

There's the workers who raised me, who took me in after my mom's death and taught me how to seduce the most powerful man in the wastes. Did I ever reach back to them? Did I ever thank them? Have I ever thanked Jean? Or prayed in thanks for Caramenta, by whose blood I've risen to heights I did not even know the words to wish for? I look over her shoulder at Nik Nik, the sometimes Blood Emperor who nursed me back from death.

Sometimes, focusing on survival is necessary. Sometimes, it is just an excuse for selfishness.

Still, I shake my head. "Dethroning an emperor? This is none of my business."

"Please?" she says.

And the longer I stare at her, the harder it is to walk away. Partly because she's still Esther. Sure, the nose is twisted, but those eyes, those are my Esther's eyes. But mostly I'm struck because the parts of her that aren't like my Esther, the traces of shadow where a powerful man has been breaking his hand against her bones, those are me. Or used to be me. Or are me somewhere, on some world, right now. I don't know who I would be if I could turn my back on that. Someone else, probably.

I reach up, putting my collar back to sleep.

"You're a brat," I say.

She smiles, because even if this Esther doesn't know me, she knows what it sounds like when someone gives in.

"What, exactly, do you think I can do for you?"

\\

MR. CHEEKS GOES to free Daniel from the supply cabinet, and the rest of us wait in his office.

"You shouldn't stay," Nik Nik says. "It's not safe."

"Have to."

"You haven't seen what he does to you here."

"I can guess."

We're standing too close in a corner. His voice is low, but Esther is only pretending not to hear the conversation.

He looks at me, which makes it feel as if he's moved closer even though he hasn't. "Then why stay?"

"Because she asked me."

"And she means something to you? Like I did?"

"She's my sister."

Esther's illusion of disinterest shatters, and she looks over quickly. "Truly?"

She doesn't look disgusted, only interested. I wonder if she used to wonder what it would be like to have a sister. The way I used to, until I found out about her.

"And you know her?" Nik Nik asks Esther.

"She's my husband's mistress. And his spy."

"That's Nelline. Not me. I would never sleep with the emperor," I say. Nik Nik looks at me pointedly. "I mean, not *this* emperor, obviously."

Mr. Cheeks and Daniel are back. Esther feels so familiar I can't help but search Daniel's face for something recognizable, some spark I can cling to. But he's a void.

"She really isn't Nelline," Esther says.

Daniel shakes his head. "How can you be sure?"

"The way she speaks. Carries herself. I know the woman."

Daniel looks at me, then away. "Careful you aren't letting your hope lead you into gullibility."

Esther lifts her chin, looking older, much older, than mine but just as strong. "Careful you don't let your pessimism drown your faith."

Daniel's face goes red. He's petty, this version of Daniel. Weaker, without Mel to prop him up. He's nothing like the tower of warmth and goodwill I know.

Daniel looks to Nik Nik. "What do you think?"

"I believe her," he says.

Back home, Esther is Daniel's most trusted adviser. He would never take the word of some man over hers.

"I can prove it to you," I say, not realizing the words are true until after they're coming out of my mouth. "Your wife, did she die here? When Michael and Esther were two?"

"Adra's always known that, and I'm sure his spy does too."

"But does he know there was another woman? About a year later while you were preaching. She invited you in and you went. And afterward, you had a choice. You could follow through with the light you saw in her, marry her . . . or you could never look back, and dwell in your guilt."

He's gone ashen. Good.

"I live in a world where you married her, and it made your followers trust your words of redemption. You took in her daughter and raised her as your own. Where I come from, you smile all the time and you look five years younger than you do here, all because you weren't a coward."

He takes a while to respond, and when he does his voice is quiet.

"She died," he says.

"I know."

He blinks first. "Our parishioners tell stories. I never believed them.

A person from another world dropping down in the desert, then disappearing. In the stories it was a man. Are there more of you?"

"We rotate. This is my first time here. The man who used to come retired. The girl who came before me was . . . let go."

"You make it sound like a job," Nik Nik says.

"It is. My job is the only reason I'm here."

They all seem deflated by that. I'm not sure what they thought I was, but they find *employed* a letdown.

Esther overcomes her disappointment first. "Miracles can be found in the most inglorious places."

This is not a miracle, but she's got that preachy look on her face, so I know it's useless to correct her.

"You've seen worlds where Nik Nik is emperor? You'll testify to it?" she says.

"Testify to who? I can't be on record. My work gets most of your official documents, and I've broken enough rules already."

"Nothing official, just a group of people who aren't happy with the way things are, but don't have the imagination to see the alternative. They're coming here, and you can tell them Nik is better than his brother. Tell them they should support him."

It all starts to make sense. Why Nik Nik would hide me, why he would ask me to confirm the truth: that his brother committed regicide. It would make his rule illegitimate. This is a coup. And my naïve little sister is running the campaign of the usurper. Esther with her too little sense and too much faith, even in a man like Nik Nik.

"How do you even know he's better than his brother? He might just be more polite," I say, an accusation I never thought I'd lay at Nik Nik's feet.

Nik Nik hears the challenge in my voice, and responds the way he would on any Earth. He squares up.

"I'm better than the man you knew, and he's better than my brother."

"You don't know that. Even I don't know that. I haven't seen your numbers."

"Numbers?"

"Numbers. Your population, how many sick you have, how many are working, how many suffer, how many don't have to die but do."

"You can compare these numbers to other worlds? To prove concretely that we are worse off?"

It takes me a moment to realize what he's asking me to do: analyze. He's asking me to do the work of an analyst. The same thing I've been failing at on Jean's quizzes for weeks.

I look down at my cuff. I've taken ghost copies of data from all the worlds I collect so I could compare them . . . except I've never pulled from here before. I'd have to go to their port. And it's a bright day.

"I have the information from most other worlds, but not this one. I'd need to go to a port, but that's outside of downtown Ash."

Mr. Cheeks is looking at me like I've lost it. "There's no port in the desert."

"Not that kind of port." I hold up my hands like it will help me explain it, then I shake my head. "It's not a place where boats from other places come in, it's a place where data from other places comes in."

"Maybe tomorrow?" Daniel says.

"I can't stay another day," I say.

"Even if she could, the people are risking enough gathering here tonight. We can't ask them to do it again. It's only a matter of time before Adra links her escape to me, if he hasn't already," Nik Nik says.

"Does he believe she's from another world?" asks Daniel.

"No, this is worse. He thinks we have his spy," Nik Nik says. "I'll go to this . . . port. I'll get the information and be back by nightfall."

"No, I'll go. Even if you could find the port, you don't know how to access it," I say.

"Then I'll assist you," he says.

"No offense, but at least if you were cruel you'd be useful. You're not even that here. I'll take your runner instead. We'll dash out and be back in no time. I'm guessing he has a vehicle?"

Though the prospect of sitting in a runner's ride twists my stomach.

Mr. Cheeks sucks in air through his teeth, but Nik Nik calms him with a raised hand. He turns back to me.

"Even if I would order him from your sister's side, I doubt he'd listen. He'll remain here until Adra isn't a threat to her."

I study the pretty runner anew. It's an interesting match—my stained-glass sister the star on the throat of a killer with the face of a doll.

"Fine."

"We'll still need to find a way to convince the others that she's genuine," Esther says. "She looks just like her. They'll think she's just pretending."

"I can handle that," I say. "We'll just need to make a slight detour after the pull."

\

WE LEAVE AS soon as we can round up the gear, but it's not soon enough. Really, it's been too late since sunrise. Even under the reflective tarp, my cheeks and forehead begin to burn.

"Not far."

He yells it like there's a risk I won't hear him, but the world is so still it's like the sun has an invisible hand pressed down on us and not even air can rise. A bright day is as soundless as the hatch. I can hear our boots on sand and our rough breath. The tarp blocks everything from my vision except my feet and the ground slightly ahead, and the goggles turn even that into shades of red from blood to blush where true sunlight creeps in along the edges. If I threw all this off, I would see the truest, brightest white of my whole life . . . for a few brief seconds before everything went black for me forever.

This is what it's like to love Dell.

She's unattainably bright. It makes me want to touch her even if it takes my fingertips, to see her even if I'll see nothing after. And if I ever dared cross that line, if I ever got close enough to stand in the full light of that star, she'd request a transfer, or order one for me, and everything would be dark thereafter.

I replaced Caramenta without anyone noticing. Nelline could replace me just the same. But if ever Dell wasn't herself, I would know. She'd be dimmer, and I would know right off.

"Turn right in four steps, then go eight. I'll drive."

The vehicle is right where Nik Nik says it is. Even reaching out to open the door burns my fingers. I climb in, taking off the tarp and goggles only after everything is closed up again. My fingertips are still hot pink. I press them to my face. They radiate heat.

"You peeked," I say to Nik Nik, who has taken off his goggles and is showcasing the new pinks of his eyes where the whites should be. The goggles can only protect against secondary light, not direct, so he must have looked out from behind the tarp and caught the edge of the sun.

"A little. I couldn't remember where it was parked."

"Are you sure you'll be able to drive through this?"

This being thick mesh covering the windshield. I can make out shapes in the desert, but only if I strain.

"Of course," he says, which is exactly what he said earlier when I asked if he knew where the vehicle was parked. *Of course* apparently being shorthand for *I'll figure it out.*

"Fine, let's go."

The vehicle is part tank and outfitted for days like this. It crawls along with all the speed and grace of a squared-off stone. I could probably have run to the port faster . . . you know, if I'd ever done the weekly trainings that would enable me to run more than ten seconds without wheezing.

The port isn't visible, but its position is logged into my cuff. It's loud, surrounded by all that rattling metal, so I tap Nik Nik's arm when we get close, and point when he needs to turn. He shouldn't risk the run with already-burnt eyes, but he stands at my back as I work the port. The download is slow, and for a second I'm worried my credentials have been revoked because of my absence, but eventually the data speeds up like it always does. I move around as it downloads, releasing the heat from rising from the baked sand that's getting caught under my tarp.

"We have a problem," he says. "We're at high noon. We can't risk driving until it passes."

Because even anticombustion additives have their limits.

"We can wait it out in the car, but without the engine to run the fans . . ."

We could dehydrate before the heat shifts away, and pass out waiting.

I check the map Dell downloaded into my cuff again. "There's an emergency shelter just ahead. We can hide there."

I lead, keeping the tarp low and staring at the ground. Luckily the shelters are so camouflaged I couldn't get us there by sight anyway, and the verbal directions from the cuff don't require seeing forward.

A few times I almost stumble into cracks in the desert, a sign that mining continued here longer than on Earth Zero or Earth 22, but eventually I get to the square I need. I get on my knees, the ground reads my cuff's signal, and a square of earth lifts up and reveals a ladder.

I climb down and hit the button to seal it as soon as Nik is clear.

Temperature control and oxygen are working, so I peel off my gear as we wait for the sun to pass over us. At least, I wait. Nik Nik is wide-eyed, scanning every inch of the space. Eventually he goes to the emergency manuals and begins flipping through them, Eldridge code no obstacle to him. And now I know why. Because his big brother taught us both.

The sight of him reading competently is still strange, and it's a wonder my brain doesn't make me puke, because this could just as easily be a hallucination.

"It's just boring procedural stuff."

"Not to me. I want to understand the magic that brought you here."

I take the manual from him. "It's not magic. There's no such thing as magic. You sound like you've been spending too much time in the Rurals."

"And if I have?"

I look at him, his tunic, his helpful smile. "Fuck me. You're one of the faithful? That's why you had to take care of me when I landed. You *had* to."

Nik Nik the believer. I've seen everything.

"I didn't *have* to do anything. And I didn't take care of you because of religious obligation."

"Then why?"

"Because you are a miracle."

"Not a miracle." I shake the manual. "Science."

"What do you call science when it answers a prayer?" He takes the manual back, then moves away from me, finally, and I can breathe again. "That's what I was doing when we found you. I was in the desert, desperate, praying for an answer to the problem of my brother."

"It really bothered you," I say. "Finding Nelline like that."

It must have been the final straw that made his brother's cruelty impossible to deny. Nik Nik is obviously upset, clutching the manual like a man used to finding solace in texts. Because, here at least, he is.

"In your world . . . do they ever tell stories of the time we fought?"

Fighting is one word for it. Child abuse is another.

"Your father forced you and Adra to fight. He should have won. He was older, and Senior was testing his cruelty not his ability, but you found something to use as a weapon and . . ."

I shrug rather than finish. It doesn't matter if Adra surrendered before or after his little brother knifed him, the stories could never agree, it only matters that he did. Senior had already planned to get rid of Adra, most likely, but the fight primed Nik Nik for the loss.

Nik Nik is quiet. "It was a shard of metal. Sharp. Valuable. By the time I was old enough to realize my father left it there on purpose, he was long dead." He stares down at the cover of the Eldridge manual like it holds an entirely different set of answers. "When I held it, I felt the thrill. The same thrill I felt when I hunted. I almost turned on Adra, but I stopped. I knew. I was young but I knew that if I gave in, turned what I'd been trained to do to animals to a person, to my own brother . . . there would be no coming back from it. I dropped the shard, forfeited, and have tried never to hurt a living thing since."

That's definitely not how things went on my world. Or Earth Zero. Nik Nik had only stepped up his hunting game after the fight, and he had no qualms about using men as prey.

Nik Nik is still staring at his hands, so what he says next isn't a total surprise.

"But I still remember the thrill. After seeing what he'd done to that girl. Hearing what he's been doing . . . I began to think there was only one way out. That's why I was in the desert. I was praying for a way to stop the suffering that didn't end with me killing my brother. Then Mr. Cheeks found you on patrol. An angel fallen from the sky, with my name on her back so I would know the gift was meant for me."

"A fallen angel is a demon."

"A being who can enact great change, either way."

There is nothing left to say. He goes back to reading nonsense. I sit on the cot. He's gracious enough to pretend not to notice that I'm staring at him.

CHAPTER NINE

Time is flat. We process it linearly, but everything is happening at once, always. Right now I am kissing Nik Nik. I am leaving him. I am killing him, because surely I've done that before or will somewhere in the infinite. I am home with Dell. We are happy. We are not. We used to be happy and now she resents my lower status and I resent her resentment and we stay together because we've given up too much to do anything else.

I've always believed, like all rational people, that my selves are separate. That they—we—exist independently. But sometimes when life is too still, when I lie in bed in the quiet, I can feel it all happening. Not just my selves collapsing, but time collapsing, because past and future are other selves just as surely as those on different worlds. My mother is dying right now, and I feel it. But she also recovered, woke up, got clean, and I feel that too. I feel that somewhere I am not alone. And I feel that sometime, soon or not long ago, I will accomplish something great.

It's the latter I feel most strongly. The certainty that I am on the cusp of being worth something. But maybe that's just my justification for reaching, for disobeying my mother's last warning. Maybe she felt the flattened universe too, all things at once, there near the end. Maybe she saw how I would die, have died, will die again, and tried to tell me.

I feel those, too, when I'm not careful. I feel 372 deaths in my chest, hanging over my head like a heavenly host of guillotines. I should have known Nelline wasn't among them, because there was no tightness behind my ribs, no new death making room for itself among the others.

Right now, I'm trying to ignore the hum telling me number 373 is coming, for real this time, and soon.

"There's a voice," Nik Nik says. "In the desk."

"What?" I walk over. In the top drawer is an old-school receiver, whispering my name. I pull out the large earpiece Eldridge hasn't used in years.

". . . Cara? Cara, answer me."

"Yes! Dell?"

There's a silence where I can hear her breathing out, or holding something in.

"You're late."

"Miss me?"

"Don't joke. You missed check-in. Your cuff is still on your obnoxious away message. Do you have any idea the—"

"She's not dead."

"What?"

She asks the question, but her voice is laced with horror, so she must understand.

"My dop. She's alive. I was found in time, but I spent nearly three days in that pod."

"Over three, nearly four," Nik Nik says. "You didn't wake up until the second."

That explains her anger.

"Who was that? Do you have someone in the emergency hatch with you?"

"Of course not. That's against the rules."

"You need to come back. Now."

"I can't. It's a bright day. If I go aboveground I'll get burnt. I'll be home after sunset."

"Right at sunset?"

I look at Nik Nik. He shakes his head.

"After," I say. "A little after."

"People are already upset. The sooner you come back, the better it will be for you."

"I know," I say. "But I can't get back just yet."

"As soon as you can, right?" she says.

"Tell Jean I'm okay."

I hang up before she can object and place the receiver back in the desk. Nik Nik has finally put away the books and is staring at me.

"What?"

"That was Dell?"

"What do you know about Dell?"

"Flowers she likes, clothes she wears, and doesn't. Her favorite foods."

"I'm not sure I've forgiven you for reading my journal," I say, sitting back on the cot.

He sits beside me. "You were dying. I wanted to know who you were first. You don't want to die unknown, do you?"

"I am unknowable. Everyone is."

"Not to God."

"You really have been drinking the lemonade, haven't you?"

He ignores that. "Dell, she missed you."

"She's worried about her asset. She's too classist to really care about someone like me."

"How do you know?"

"Because I know her."

"But isn't she unknowable too?"

That, I ignore. "Is it past high noon yet?"

"Almost," he says. "Did I throw you away? Is that why you don't believe you could matter to her?"

Despite myself, I smile. "No, Nik. You always held on tight enough to bruise."

And what does it mean? That the only time I've had value, the only time I've been treated as precious, was not in the arms of my mother or my upstanding Wiley City boyfriend, but in the claws of a dictator.

\

WHEN WE GO back outside, the car is just as hot as before, but no hotter, which means we're on the plateau before the downside of the wave. Nik starts to drive back to the church, but I direct him to the riverbed instead.

"We'll have to take another break if we go out that far," he says. "But I know a place."

At first, I don't see her. She's a hidden mound among the ridges at the edge of the bank, gray-brown tarp protecting her from the sun and prying eyes. But when she hears our vehicle, she stands. She thinks this choking motor is opportunity knocking.

"Might need your help if she runs."

"Who is it?" he asks.

"Nelline."

I open the door and pull her inside. She doesn't fight enough, but then, she doesn't know it's me. Once I close the door and she pulls off her tarp—that's when the kicking starts.

I shove her up and over the seat, where she lands in the cargo space at the back of the vehicle.

"You really are exactly the same," Nik Nik says.

"No shit," Nelline says in that god-awful voice.

"Didn't you already know that?" I ask, for once more diplomatic than someone.

"At first, yes. But I talked myself out of it. It's so impossible. And lately I only saw her when her face . . . when she didn't look much like herself."

I look back at her, but she's not meeting our eyes. She doesn't like hearing about her injuries, her weakness, and I don't blame her. She's uneasy around Nik Nik, like he's a stranger.

"Weren't you two around each other socially?"

If she's anything like me—and I'll admit, she is—she would have sought out the emperor right when things got desperate after her mother's death. Surely they'd been around each other enough in the past nine years to become close?

Nelline is shaking her head. "Adra's orders. If I ever fraternized with little brother or any of his other rivals, I was out of a job."

I can feel her desperation to keep living as if it is my own. I understand it, and wish I didn't. I wonder if Adra knew Nik Nik was the one who took care of her after his bouts of rage.

"That's how he's always seen me, isn't it? Just another rival," Nik Nik says—to himself, I'm guessing, because we can't possibly know. "You were romantically involved for years, but he never even mentioned you to me."

"Romantically involved." She snorts and looks to the right. "Nonsense words. Adra's wife is an image. Seen by everyone. Watched. Asked for favors and done favors in return. We could never be *romantically involved* if I was to remain inconspicuous."

I wonder if that's what she's been telling herself; it wasn't that she wasn't good enough or that Adra was superficial, just that her job was incompatible with being his in public. I pity her. I may hate that Nik Nik loved me, but I know he did and everyone on Earth 22 knew it too.

She moves to escape at the same second I would, but I see her tense for it the moment before, which is just enough time to grab her tarp and shove it by my feet with my own. She's halfway to the door at the back of the vehicle before she realizes.

"You could jump out, but not sure how inconspicuous you'll be when you're a giant flaming blister," I say.

And she might still do it—I'm sure suicide has never been far from her mind, just as it's never been far from mine—but I hope she doesn't. It's unnerving to have someone who looks so much like me living, but it's also comforting. The universe erases me, but it also remakes me again and again, so there must be something worthwhile in this image.

In the end, she eases away from the door.

Her head is low when she asks, "What do you want me to do?"

The question gets at me, because it doesn't sound like the first time she's asked it. I have never had to kill a person, and I'm not sure that's true of Nelline.

"Nothing. You don't have to do anything. We just need you to prove I'm not you. You can go as soon as we're done."

She doesn't look relieved. She doesn't believe me.

When the car starts to jolt, I see where we'll wait for it to cool down. I feel warm, warmer than a bright day, and I want to thank Nik Nik except he doesn't know he's given me a gift.

We're still a block from the House when the temperature gauge starts shaking in the deep red, but I don't mind. I suit up and get out like a Wiley kid on the first day of school.

I'm still steps away when it hits me how different this House is from the one on my world. The door, twice my height and an extravagance in a place where the fight against the world outside is constant, is peeling. It's a light ash that looks like a wash made from local soil, and when I get close I realize it is. Back home—and even on Earth Zero, I've checked—the door is off-white, sheened in a wash of chemicals that makes it shine gold where light hits. Repairs haven't been done yet here that were done six years ago on my Earth.

I wonder if Nik Nik gives them extra money when he's in power, or if Adra is just sucking them dry. The rule that Houses are tax-exempt has been around since the same rule about churches. I wonder if he stopped honoring one, or both. It's not a smart move. Everyone knows workers do more to keep the peace than runners and bring more civilization than the holy in the Rurals ever could.

Nik Nik knocks on the door with his free hand. In my excitement I've left him to drag Nelline along alone. But I abandon him again the second the door opens, and I see a sliver of Exlee's face.

I push inside and strip off my tarp and goggles, because I'm thinking the sooner I get unencumbered, the sooner I get a hug. But all I get for my urgency is a slap to the face.

Exlee hasn't slapped me since I was a child, but even with that distance I know this hand feels different. There is no love here, no correction, only rage. I don't return it. Nik Nik has taken off his tarp now, sending whispers through the small portion of patrons who are actually paying attention. But Nelline is still under, content to let me take punishments meant for her.

"Filthy spy," Exlee says. "Going to report to your man so runners can drag more of my staff at dawn?"

"Who?" I ask. "Who did the runners take?"

"Mixxie, though I'm sure you already know."

I turn back and yank off Nelline's tarp. Another gasp, this time from Exlee. I've always wondered what it would take to shock the proprietor of the House. Now I know.

Nelline keeps her eyes down, and it takes me a moment to realize she's looking at her hands, not the ground.

"You betrayed Mixxie and you still wear her gloves? What is wrong with you?"

I ask the question and mean it. How could she? The love I had here was always unconditional. I don't know what it would have taken to break it.

"I didn't have a choice," she says.

"I bet you did. I bet it was a choice between betraying them or poverty. And that is still a choice."

She looks up at me, sharp. "You would have done the same."

"No."

But there's just enough doubt in my voice that she smiles.

She flexes her hands. "I bet you threw these away years ago. Or hid them deep so no one would know where you came from."

"Explain," Exlee says, an admission of confusion that is the closest to a concession of weakness I've ever heard from them. Their head is still high, though, so it's more an impatient demand for an explanation.

"I'm not Nelline," I say as the curtain to the main room opens and Pax enters the lobby.

Pax focuses on me like an underfed dog. His hand is in the air before I can say I'm not Nelline; luckily Exlee is there first, towering over Pax in shoes as tall as my forearm is long.

"That's not Lorix's girl," Exlee says, then turns Pax toward Nelline. "That is."

"What? How?"

Exlee shrugs. The confusion only dims Pax's rage for a second, and in the next there is fire in his eyes again.

"Should've known," Pax says, moving toward Nelline. He spits at the ground between them. "Your teeth are rotting, Nellie Girl."

Cara Girl. Pax has called me that a hundred times since I was small, and hearing him say it now drives home that he cared for her just like he cared for me. It makes me hate her all over again.

Pax leads her away to the House's holding area, but she looks back at me over her shoulder. Her eyes are full of rage and injustice. She still doesn't think she's done anything wrong. She probably thinks even betrayal is fair play in the game of survival. Looking at her is like looking at a worse version of myself, but not far off enough for me to feel superior. I could have been her, still could be.

Exlee turns back to me, then looks past me to Nik. "I've heard you've been making moves, Second Son."

Nik Nik manages not to flinch at the name. "What you heard before were rumors. I've only recently decided."

"You should have been on my doorstep the moment you did."

He should have, and my Nik Nik would have. I wonder if this Nik's time in the Rurals has blinded him to the value of Exlee and the House. A war can't be started, fought, or won without them.

"It was an oversight, but I'm here now."

Exlee gives a rare smile, a sure sign the offense is forgiven. "So you are. My office is this way."

Exlee begins to walk to the back of the House, then looks at me. I realize I'm waiting for permission before following, like the girl I used to be. Somehow, Exlee understands and nods.

That's not Lorix's girl.

But I am, and I always will be.

IN EXLEE'S OFFICE, Nik Nik suffers through an interrogation about what kind of ruler he would be and why the providers should show up at his meeting. It may not have been planned, but it's good we came. News spreads from the House faster than a yell, and before the meeting even starts everyone will be talking about Nelline's doppelgänger, and wondering who she is. They might just believe Esther when she tells them.

I, still half listening, wander around the office, touching the same shelves I touched as a child but that I haven't seen since I was a teenager.

We didn't live on-site often. I don't know if Exlee had a rule about Mom staying here while she was bingeing, or if Mom was too ashamed to let her friends see her like that, but generally she stayed in the House when she was doing well, and moved to the concrete units when she wasn't. And when she wasn't, when she tried to see clients on her own without the protection of the other workers behind her, things got bad. In worlds where clients forgot their place and killed her—or me, or both—it was always away from here. I've died all over the desert, but never in the House. The House has always been a sanctuary for me.

Exlee's office was a constant for me. Even when we lived on the edges, I was allowed to pass time here during the day while I waited for my mom to be free. I imagine it's like having a grandparent's house, if there were any of those around. The generation before my mother's didn't fare well; anyone over a certain age was forced to fight and patrol during the wars. Those who survived the violence had a short life-span thanks to food, water, and whole areas of air we didn't yet know had become toxic. That is the quagmire that made Nik Senior. That is the mix of fear and blood and death that made having a warlord for an emperor attractive. There hasn't been another civil war since him, but there hasn't been much of anything else either.

I watch the stages through the window. I don't know the man on the left stage, or the enby dancing center, but the woman on the right is familiar. Her name used to be Helene X, but we teased her about it so much I'm sure by now she's changed it. We all knew she'd been born in the Wiles, but there was no need to advertise it with a name like that. I never understood how a Wiley girl got to Ash. It couldn't be simple poverty—they have *systems* for that—and whenever I asked her about it she seemed more scared than desperate. When my mother died, Helene gave me a useless little pin, dark and wrinkled like a sea creature. Only after I came to Wiley City did I see my first real carnation and learn people there called them the flower of mothers. The black carnation was appropriate, and I wish I still had it.

Staring at Helene X like this without paying is stealing, so I move back to the wall of bookshelves. On a small silk cloth is a glass orb. I pick it up and hold it loosely in my palms so the light hitting it reflects stars onto my hands. I am holding the universe. I am Nyame.

"Nelline used to do that too," Exlee says. "She'd hold it just like that when she was a girl."

So did I, of course. We are cut from the very same cloth, but I have to believe I would never betray them. I have to believe there are limits to my ambition . . . but then I think about Starla. I called her friend, and sent her away with a basket full of apples and not one drop of remorse.

I put the orb back. I haven't actually been given permission to touch it here.

"Sorry," I say.

Exlee places a hand, painted gold up to the wrists, over the glass orb, caging it in black nails each as long as a pinky.

"You're better kept than she is."

"I live in the Wiles."

"Oh? The runners didn't mention a day-tripper."

"I . . . came round the back."

Exlee raises an eyebrow that means another question is coming, but Nik Nik intervenes.

"We need to be going. I hope to see you all tonight," he says.

Exlee ignores him and turns back to me. "Do you think he's worthy of being emperor? Or are we buying trouble for nothing?"

I look down at my cuff. "I don't know yet. But I'll know by to-night. If you come, I'll tell you the truth."

The sound Exlee makes isn't commitment, but it isn't dismissal, so I take that as a good sign.

When we get to the front of the House, Nelline has her hands tied behind her back and a fresh stinging slap on her cheek. She's looking at me like it's all my fault. She earned that mark in the shape of someone's—I'm guessing Pax, since he and Mixxie were so close— palm, but I feel it on my own skin. We cover her with a tarp before we go out into the light, but I'm afraid it will slide off and she won't be able to cover herself, so I spend the walk back to the car hovering close to her.

When we get back into the vehicle I look her over for new burns. There are a few hot-pink patches, unavoidable on a day like this, but I feel guilty anyway. It doesn't feel like she's a version of me at all. It feels like she's a sister, or a daughter, or a mother. Someone I was supposed to take care of and failed.

\

I THOUGHT THE House would fill me up, but it's just left me raw. My heart hurts, and for the first time I'm actually feeling the loss of 22, my first Earth. I did keep Mixxie's gloves, and Helene X's pin. I preserved every gift and lesson the workers ever gave me. But I didn't have them with me when I came over. I might have had the gloves, but everything I was wearing became an offering to Caramenta's corpse. I won't find them in any keepsake boxes in my apartment on Earth Zero, because Caramenta's mother never died, and so there were no grief offerings to receive.

Coming to this world has derailed me. How long would I have been content to move forward, never thinking about the past? Forever, probably, as long as there was one more goal in front of me, one more pull, one more test, one more promotion.

"You look upset," Nik Nik says in a quiet pause before the last leg of our trip.

"I'm fine. Tired."

Even if I wanted to talk to him—and I do, I do—I would never give Nelline the satisfaction of hearing me say *I don't know who I am anymore, I don't know who I have been.*

When we get back to the church, I commandeer Daniel's office. I force myself not to look over my shoulder when Mr. Cheeks takes Nelline away. Loud noises come from deep within the building— shelterless wastelanders hiding from the heat of the day, just as my stepfather promised at the dedication.

I hit the projection function on my cuff and generate a list based on worlds whose census list Nik Nik as emperor. I stare at the two hundred or so numbers. I wait for the nervousness, the defeating apprehension that has come during every practice test. It never arrives. I do the initial comparison in half the time I would be given on the test. I double-check my data, but I didn't make a mistake.

The results are good news for the revolution. Ashtown in Earth 175 has a higher death rate and shorter life expectancy than 90 percent of the worlds where Nik Nik rules, and those where it is close are so highly numbered there might be environmental factors contributing to the mortality rate. I'm relieved, but not surprised. I'd already decided that if it weren't that way, if Adra was all bark and no bite and people were just as well off, I'd duck out into the desert and leave Nik Nik high and dry. But Adra is killing people who get to live almost everywhere else.

Once I review the primary figures, I go after little things. Ashtown here exports fewer goods to the Wiles. They seem to make less of everything, and they import more. They are operating at a staggering deficit, fabric and produce bought in bulk by the emperor from Wiley.

But why? He couldn't hope to sell it back to his people for profit, since most don't make enough in actual currency to buy their weekly expenses. Nearly half of the House's clients pay in barter—favors, grown food, weatherproofing materials, any kind of metal.

I call out, hoping for Esther, but Nik Nik comes in.

"Yes?"

"Those eight or so buildings a mile from here? Is that still an interior farm?"

Nik Nik shakes his head. "You mean Hangars Row? That's the runners' machine shop, and Adra's base in the Rurals."

"Why does the emperor have a base in the Rurals?"

"I don't know. I've never seen it. But he has a base in the deep wastes too."

"What does he charge for the food he buys from Wiley?"

"Three days' wages will get you a week's ration for those who can swing it. Otherwise, he'll take metal. He takes metal for almost anything."

"And no one grows their own?"

"Not openly. He banned individual farming two years ago. He says it's dangerous. But some of the poorer families never stopped. They grow aboveground, and they're just as healthy as the rest of us."

I turn back to my screen. "He should be buying synthetic soil from Wiley City. Not whole produce."

But the emperor wants his people dependent on him for food. Why? So he can hoard their scraps of iron?

Nik Nik leaves me in peace. I bring back the master list of worlds. I'm missing something, but I can't see it. I scroll through screen after screen, barely scanning the ruler histories, bothered by the problem of Adra's stockpiled metal.

\

"MISS ME, KITTEN?" Nelline says, biting at the rough skin on her lip. Her hands are chained to a cot. Even from here I can see the straps cutting into her wrists. I picture Mixxie's face, trying to hate this version of myself, but I can't. I just feel sad, like I've failed somehow.

I step forward. "I think it's a trick of the brain," I say. "The way I can't make myself hate you even though you're a bloodrat."

She hisses at the insult but stops short of denying it. She sold people out to runners. There is no worse thing a person can be in Ashtown.

"It doesn't go both ways, if that's what you're thinking," she says. "What do you want?"

"Help." She snorts, but I continue anyway. "I'm missing something. I can't see it, but you know this world better than I do. And you know everything about Adra."

She sits a little taller under the compliment, but keeps her face disinterested.

"And I should help you why?"

"Because you'll want to be in Nik Nik's favor when he comes out on top."

She shrugs. "The idea of being in the pocket of an emperor lost its appeal when the current one tried to kill me."

I take a risk. I sit beside her.

"Do you know why I have his name on my back?"

"You told Adra—"

"That was a lie. No one gets the emperor's name tattooed because he's good at his job. Part of his job is letting Ashtowners hate and blame him for our lives. No, I got it because I did the exact same thing you did. I failed at being a sex provider, so I weaseled my way into being the emperor's kept woman. I thought being with him was the worst thing that could happen to me . . . but now I've met Adra."

"He didn't beat you for getting the tattoo? For letting everyone know?" The surprise in her question makes her sound young, and the hope in it makes me feel old.

"No. Nik Nik on my world was violent too. He was quick with a backhand. He'd throw something when he was mad, choke me when I said the wrong thing. But he was more like a child than a tyrant."

She sneers at me. "You loved him," she says, like I can't be trusted.

"I didn't," I say, and this time I'm sure it's true. "This Nik Nik seems to be better in every way than mine. But I don't really know him, so that could be a lie. I'm telling you that even if he's no better than the man I know, it's still a better pocket to be in than Adra's."

She's staring down at the concrete floor. The lights overhead make a dull shine between her feet. She takes her time, but eventually she looks up.

"What do you think you're missing?"

"I don't understand the way Adra does business. In most worlds there's an interior farm in Hangars Row, so they don't have to buy produce from Wiley City. Some of the other buildings are used for textiles or pottery that get sold back. It's like this Ashtown doesn't make anything themselves."

"You're right. You are missing something. Adra is paranoid. He's sworn for years that men in black suits are trying to kill him, but no one else has ever seen them."

"Is he using?" I ask, though he'd be the first emperor that I know of with the taste.

"Obviously. Though whatever he's taking is so pure he never has any of the side effects. It's definitely not what he distributes to the masses."

"What does this have to do with Hangars Row?"

"Because his paranoia inspired him. Hangars Row is a weapons stockpile. Adra reinvented the gun."

I CANNOT, AT first, process what she's saying. Guns haven't existed in my lifetime. But I remember when I was a girl, people saying that if runners had to use guns instead of vehicles, they would do far worse than killing one or two people each.

There has never been weapons manufacturing in Ashtown, but it was Nik Senior who destroyed all available weapons brought from across the desert and the ocean beyond. He made the law that metal could be used only in domestic or industrial settings—partially a warlord's attempt to ease the fears of his new people, and partially to disarm any would-be usurpers. Runners had to make weapons out of vehicles, and knives had to be useful for kitchen work or tanning even if you'd only intended them for murder. Even the emperor would learn

to kill with chemical-filled rings and teeth when denied the easy avail-
ability of an obvious weapon. An art he passed on to both his sons.

Wiley City's stunners are what some think of as guns now, but the
city's been without guns even longer than we have, so they aren't really.
They are plastic and shoot a pulse that temporarily paralyzes but won't
kill. Nik Senior's edict didn't stop killing, but now people have to be in
contact with their victims, have to feel their deaths.

In the wake of Nelline's revelation I try to imagine what my childhood would have been like if Nik Senior's men were armed. How I
would feel if the deaths were quieter, quicker, but more common. I
wonder if you feel it less, with guns. If so many people are killed with
so little effort, is it easier to pretend they aren't lives? That everything
is fine? It's different, I imagine, from seeing flattened forms like blood
ghosts on the sand or hearing the screams in the streets during the parade. No, killing should take longer than a heartbeat. Murder should be
unignorable, always.

CHAPTER TEN

The church isn't nearly as packed as it was at the dedication, but there's enough nervous energy that it might as well be. Esther's invited representatives from different groups, rather than whole populations, so what stands before me is a handful of the most powerful people in the wastes. Most I don't recognize, but some hold power on every Earth I've ever been to.

Standing tallest, of course, is Exlee, who's sporting a lush beard that appeared so suddenly it supports the theory that their body hair is as synthetic as their breasts. Beside them is Tatik. She used to be a runner for Senior back in the day, but now she's the mistress of the deep wastes. She watches over those no one else cares about, and brings reports to the emperor when they have something they need or something to give. At least, that's what she did on 22. I don't know if Adra uses her here, where he's paranoid enough to have a base even in the vastness beyond the river. Under Nik Nik's reign Tatik is still called mister, even though she gave up the post, and she outranks everyone but him. This version is thinner than she should be, but she holds her head just as high.

Viet's presence is a surprise, though I guess it shouldn't be. As a deathkeeper, he's supposed to be neutral in all things political, his calling transcending anything as petty as politics. But he does preside over life and death, so I suppose this concerns him too.

Daniel, Esther, and Nik Nik round out the powerful people I recognize. A few of the strangers are runners, and I can read from their marks that they're important. Esther is holy, but she's not trusting or naïve, so they must have shown their loyalty to her some way. Or maybe they're just loyal to Mr. Cheeks. He spots me and starts walking over.

"You're late," he says.

"A bit." Nik Nik wanted me here early, but I'd spent too long trying to disprove my fears . . . only to confirm them. "What are they fighting about?"

Mr. Cheeks shrugs. "You, I suppose. Or Adra. You're both pretty sizable pains in the ass."

Nik Nik is addressing the group, standing tall and calm. He's changed clothes since we got back. His tunic is black, high-collared, with gold embroidery. It's a little flash on the humble garment that marries him to the Nik Nik I used to know. He handles himself well, and I spend a little time watching him listen and respond to the concerns of people who are not yet his. I wait for rage, the indignation he always showed when people dared question him, but this Nik Nik is different from mine. He's only just about to taste the power that would give him that kind of arrogance.

That is, if I don't ruin his chances. If I don't tell the whole truth.

"I would like you to trust me . . ." he says, answering some comment I didn't hear. "But I don't require it. I only require that you use common sense to know we can't go on like this."

"If you'd lived through the last civil wars, you'd know it can always get worse," says Tatik, who was Senior's right hand when he was nothing more than the son of a warlord.

She's not wrong.

Eventually Esther sees me, and my time as spectator is over. "Here, here she is."

The others turn to me, and their faces tell me everything. The ones who think I'm a stranger just distrust me. The ones who think I'm Nelline and know her, hate me. Judging by her pursed mouth and tightly crossed arms, Tatik is in the latter camp. But Viet only squints, trying to picture me as a baby so he can recall my name.

Tatik spits at my feet as I approach. "If you'd told me this was your source, I wouldn't have wasted the gas to get here."

She starts to walk off but then Exlee snaps open a massive black fan and the sound stops her dead.

"Hang around, General. The Second Son has a trick up his sleeve."

This stalls Tatik long enough for Mr. Cheeks to come back with Nelline. He drags her out and pushes her next to me. Her hands are tied. They can't think she's a threat right now, which means the restraints are just to shame her. It's not working. Her chin is high and she's smiling. It's a cruel one, and I'm glad I rarely smile if that's what I look like doing it. We share a look, she gives me a slight nod, and I know that if I don't mention Adra's advantage, neither will she.

"We've all heard about the visitors," Esther says. "Tatik, your domain has the most sightings of them all. That's what she is. She's Nelline from another world."

"Or the bitch has a twin," Tatik says.

"No." This, finally, from Viet. "Lorix delivered only one."

He should know. A child hasn't been born in Ash without his hands on it since his mother died.

"Then it's a coincidence! You can't expect me to believe . . ." She hesitates, her eyes landing first on Nelline and then darting to me. Eventually she shakes her head. "You can't expect me to believe this."

Tatik is the linchpin. If I can get her to believe me, the runners will follow. It can't be that hard. She was so connected with Nik Nik, I must have enough of her secrets to leverage.

"Does he still call you Jadda, when no one else can hear?"

She looks at Nik Nik, half-amused and half-irritated. "He calls me Jadda where everyone can hear, the stupid boy. Always has."

Shit. My Nik Nik hid his affection like a blight. All of the emperor's secrets I held on 22 are poor currency in a place where Nik Nik doesn't deal in shadows. There's only one thing . . . I take a second, hoping I don't look too nervous while I do the math. Nik Senior died when Nik Nik was seven here. The empress hadn't been dead long. Was that enough time?

"Your child, she was a girl, he made you"—I stop short of saying *kill her,* given what I now know happened to Adra—"send her to the city."

There is a moment of silence, where the whole room watches us. At first, Tatik's face doesn't change. Then it softens.

"No," she says. "My daughter was stillborn."

I was wrong. Nik Senior didn't live long enough here to father the child that only Nik Nik suspected was born in my Ashtown. I hear Esther's disappointed sigh behind me, but before I can deflate too much Tatik continues.

"But if he'd lived longer, I would have had another," she says. "And the plan was always to send her to the city."

"Her? How did you know it'd be a girl?"

"Girls are all my family makes." Now, she smiles. "Where you're from, we had a daughter survive? Did it work? Her integration into the city?"

I know what I'm not going to tell her. I'm not going to tell her the theory of the birth was only corroborated by Tatik's depression and withdrawal from the world. I'm not going to tell her that her child and any evidence of it disappeared so thoroughly, we talked about it as another floating corpse in the bog. She was so old by that point even that girl had been a miracle. Everyone knew she'd never have another.

I say, "She never came back to Ashtown," because as far as I know that's true and it's the only thing any Ash parent wants to hear.

I thought I was protecting her, but her face goes hard enough for me to know I've somehow told her the whole truth.

"I'm not saying I believe you, but I'm listening," Tatik says.

Esther speaks excitedly, taking advantage of the momentum. "The strangers don't just come here. She's been to many worlds, and learned from them."

"Always a spy, then?" Exlee asks, eyebrow raised in a perfect waxed arch.

"Not always," I say, because Esther's going pink from the interruptions and I'm probably the only one who knows she's got a temper like a solar flare. "In some worlds I'm a provider. Some worlds a grower in the Rurals. In most that I know about, I'm dead."

I hadn't thought about it being the same—my traversing and Nelline's spying—and I don't like to think the reason we've both made it this far is that neither of us is bothered by stealing the facts of other people's lives to secure our own. I activate the projector on my cuff.

"These are the mortality rates where Nik Nik rules." I show them a graph that has an average of the worlds I've analyzed. I overlay it with another. "And this is here. You're dying sooner and more often than you need to. Your quality of life is worse. On Earth Zero you grow your own food. You sell excess back to Wiley. Here, you only spend."

I continue, highlighting other basic criteria that might matter to them. I'm not sure if they believe I am who I say I am, or if they are even following the numbers being projected in light against the wall, but they stay quiet.

Finally, I get to the more personal section.

"These are just a handful of people who are alive, right now, in ninety percent of the worlds where Nik Nik rules, but who are gone here."

I hit a button on my cuff and turn the wall into a sea of faces. Mixxie is slightly larger, near the center. It's cheap, manipulative propaganda, but it's true.

Esther lets them marinate for a bit. She looks no less serene and ethereal than before, but I recognize her ruthlessness.

"You must see—"

"But there is a risk," I say, turning off the wall of the dead. A new graph appears; it's a steady line with a sharp spike settling eventually at a lower, stable point.

Nik Nik studies the graph with narrowed eyes, but Esther grabs my arm.

"What is that? What are you doing?"

When I answer, I speak to Nik. "It's the average casualty rate for worlds where you take power from your brother. It's the cost. Tatik is right. It always gets worse before it gets better."

"How?" he says. "He doesn't have enough loyal runners to enact this kind of damage."

"No. He has guns."

The news hits the others like water on wasps.

"He wouldn't dare," Tatik says. "That was his father's edict."

"He would and has," Nelline says, looking casually amused at their fear.

Viet shakes his head. "I honor life. That's all I do. I cannot be party to anything that would cause such loss."

"The change in power makes things better, there is no doubting that," I say. "How he's running things is wrong."

They're not listening. Exlee is waving their black fan, watching as Nik Nik tries to salvage the meeting. I'm guessing they knew about the guns, or at least suspected. Nothing happens in the wastelands without the House being aware. Eventually, Exlee gives a throat-clearing *mmhmm*. It isn't loud, but it silences the others.

They address Nik Nik and Esther. "Can you think of any way to mitigate this damage? A transfer of power without the casualties of war?"

Esther looks confused, then lowers her head. Of course she can't, because she's a believer. Believers would never consider assassination, and that's the answer Exlee's looking for.

Nik Nik is looking at his hand like that long-ago shard of metal is there again, like he's being asked the same question he was that day. Eventually he shakes his head.

"No," he says. "I can't."

I close my eyes. Nik Nik knows the right answer, but he can't do it. And that's why they're all going to die, bloodily and completely. Adra's known how to murder his way to power since he was a sickly teen. Cruelty is a science he learned early and well, just like all the others. It hits me then that Adra is smarter than his brother. Colder, worse, but smarter. Which means he must have seen this coup coming.

Exlee is finished, so the arguing resumes. It's loud, but beneath the din I still hear it. I hear it in my spine, the way a praying mantis hears a bat's shriek, the way any prey can always hear its predator: the roar of a dozen motors, far away, but getting closer.

It's a parade of runners, and it's too late to escape.

\

"THE DOORS! GET away from the doors!"

Nik Nik cries out his warning while I'm still speechless. But of course, he's lived with the parade every day, and I haven't heard them in over a decade.

"We don't *run* in the Rurals," says one of the runners, but no one responds.

"Are you still sheltering my people here?" Tatik asks.

Daniel nods. "They were waiting out the bright day."

It's all she needs to hear. Rather than waiting to see if an exit emerges, she disappears to the back of the church. She'll get the deep-wasters out, or die trying.

An engine revs in place, then squeals out, and a moment later the double doors splinter inward. The vehicle that skids into the church has four wheels as high as my hips. He doesn't stop accelerating until he's halfway into the room. I jump onto the stage, but he's not aiming for me yet. He slides sideways and Daniel disappears under his massive wheels.

Esther screams and lunges toward him, but Mr. Cheeks is already pulling her back, away from the newly broken-open entrance. He must know a rear exit or a bribable runner. I should follow, but I can't move. It's the first runner death I've seen since Nik Senior's funeral, but the smell of gasoline and blood takes me instantly back. I want to go to my knees. I want to scream.

Three more runners ride into the church, these on the two-wheelers whose speed ensures they match the body counts of the larger models despite being half their size. I see the wide, deep treads of their wheels, like teeth on a creature from the deep wastes, and I can feel those marks across my spine. How many times? How many times have I died with my back to a runner? One less, I decide. Not this time.

The men dismount and begin splashing gasoline on the walls. They each have a second canister on their bikes, and I know it is acid. They'll leave it in their wake, so that anyone who tries to run through the front door will be hobbled before they can reach it. They must already be at the rear of the building and expect those seeking shelter to come this way.

Exlee hasn't moved. They just sit perched on the edge of the stage like they're about to sing, casually flicking that large, feathered fan like a bored god. When I walk past, they raise an eyebrow, then turn to watch my progress.

Finally, Exlee stands. "Who could use a little favor with the House?"

Quickly, one of the two motorcycles pulls up and Exlee sits on the back, finger-waving goodbye as the runner rides them both to safety. I hadn't thought they would have as much pull in this world with Adra trying to choke the workers out, but apparently even with an ash-washed door there is nothing so valuable in the desert as a safe, warm place where someone will touch you exactly how you want.

I'm not looking for anything safe or warm. I'm looking for Adra. I want him to have to kill me with his own hands.

I walk forward until I am face-to-face with the line of runners keeping us inside. They are blocking the door, waiting for their cue. We started the meeting when the sun was already half-set, but night never comes slower than on a bright day, and past the broken doors the sky is still the bright blue of chemicals burning.

From outside comes a hot-wind hiss that feathers the hair from my face. It's as good as a slap, the universe asking why I'm walking toward my killers. It's Nyame leaning in, tilting her head, trying to understand why I'm choosing to leave life this way. I expect any one of them to rev forward and claim my life as their point, but they don't. Which means someone with authority is watching.

"You out there Adra? You hiding from me?"

I hear the rustle of his long coat before I see him, but eventually Adra enters the square of horizon I can see over the runners' shoulders.

He tsks his tongue against his teeth. "Nelline, Nelline, Nelline."

"Wrong. Your girl's back there."

He doesn't believe me. There's merriment in his eyes, amusement at my little game, until he looks past me. I'm not sure how she got out of her cuffs—I'm guessing she could have done it anytime—but I feel her at my back even before his eyes go wide. I look over my shoulder, and she blows a mocking kiss at him as she steps forward. I look back at Adra, hoping that Nelline will do the smart thing, the survivor thing, and use my distraction as a way to escape.

Adra looks back at me, afraid this time. Finally.

He's dressed in the full regalia of a wasteland emperor: rings on every finger that shine only half as well as they cut, huge black boots recklessly tipped in silver, black hide pants, and a wide-sleeved coat of gold and black that drags a few feet behind him. I've seen Nik Nik in that coat, but for ceremonies only. He always said it made it seem like he wasn't prepared to fight. But Adra has six runners between him and me, so I doubt he's expecting to have to throw a punch.

"Who are you?" he says, stepping forward in a jingle of metal.

In addition to the rows designating his line of succession, he's wrapped the ends of his braids in silver, another tradition Nik Nik hated. I wanted him to dip his braids. I can still hear his response: *Telegraph my location? Walk around like a fucking wind chime?*

"Your brother told you who I was. I'm a visitor."

"The stories aren't real. People can't just come . . ."

"From other worlds?" I say. "Don't act surprised, Adra. I know you. You figured out the mysteries of the multiverse when you were still a teenager."

"When I was a teenager, I was ruling Ashtown," he says, pride mostly, but a little regret.

Someone comes up behind me. Someone else facing death while the smart people take their chances hiding or finding a hidden exit.

They know they're wasting their time. They know a runner never enters a building unless the others have surrounded it. But they want out before the building is razed, and I can't blame them for that. Runners sometimes miss, but fire never does.

"Tatik is in there. You can't do this," Nik Nik says. "She's an elder."

"A traitor has no age."

Nik Nik flinches. Killing Tatik isn't technically the same as killing their own mother, but it's not different in any way that matters.

"She wasn't participating in anything. This was my doing alone."

Adra's glare is potent as he looks at his brother. "Oh? My missing runner had nothing to do with this? My missing *wife*? The Ruralites whose house you use?" He shakes his head. "Don't worry. You will pay, but so will they all."

Nik Nik swallows. "You'll leave us here? To die in the fire?"

Adra tilts his head. "Oh, you'd like that. Leave you here to disappear into one of your hidden passages? Or to die and burn only to have your followers lie about it, turn you into a myth to use against me? No, I'll kill you myself."

He nods to the runner at his left, and the man punches Nik Nik in the stomach. The blow makes a sound that's both wet and hard and Nik Nik doubles over, only to have the same runner knee him in the face. This should make me happy, seeing the man who towered over me brought low, seeing his mouth go red for every time he fed me my own blood. But it doesn't. It doesn't make me feel better, and I'm not sure if it's because I know this is not my Nik Nik or if this kind of revenge never really heals.

"Thought you said you'd do it yourself," Nik Nik says, spitting. "Are your eyes watering for me, brother?"

All our eyes are watering. We're still in the mouth of the building, and the mixture of gasoline and smoke is overwhelming. But the comment has the effect Nik Nik wants, and Adra, who's been covering his nose and mouth with the sleeve of his robe, nods toward the door.

"Come on," he says.

As we walk, Nik Nik reaches over and touches my necklace. I get the hint. Outside means escape, and he must have remembered that before he manipulated Adra into it. He's telling me to teleport. I should have thought of it first. I look over my shoulder. Esther and Mr. Cheeks hopefully knew another way out. I don't see Nelline, but I feel watched, so she's not far. The only person I'll really be leaving to die is Nik Nik, and it's not like he's never done the same to me.

I press my collar to warm it up.

Out from the overhang of the burning church we're greeted by the long stretch of empty desert. Somewhere, in the darkness outside visual range, are the river and Ashtown and the concrete slums that brought me up. All I need to do is leave, and I won't lose a piece of myself here. But if I leave everyone in this mess, am I still myself? Or am I Nelline? She could tell herself she didn't do anything wrong, just passed on information, just survived. Will I be sitting in my apartment, telling myself all I did was go home? All I did was survive and there's nothing more important than that?

Adra grabs Nik Nik by the hair, biting at his throat and tearing open a gash far clumsier than the thin slices Nik Nik and his father used for murder. He's bringing up his hand, loaded with the poison rings he inherited, when I reach out and put a hand on his wrist.

"Do you want to see it?"

Adra goes stiff. "See what?"

"You know what. The dark between stars. When you were a boy you wondered what it would be like to walk inside it. I can show you. It won't take long."

His mouth twitches, revealing a black incisor turned brown from its new-blood sheen.

"Let me guess, all I have to do is spare him?"

"No. You have to make him an example. You're too insecure to let him live. But let it wait until you come back. He means something to me on another Earth, and I don't want to watch him die."

"You think I care about your other worlds?"

"You do. I know you do. I know you used to use rocks as models of the planets and stars, used to look up at night and know that all that darkness couldn't just be absence. If you want to see what lingers there, this is your last chance. I can slip away with or without you, and my kind won't be coming back around here for a long time."

I'm counting on at least some of what Adam Bosch said about his childhood being true. Only now am I realizing that his stories of sitting surrounded by rocks he called planets were not the stories of a boy pretending to be an astronaut. It was a boy pretending to be a god.

Adra licks his lips. He is an impenetrable emperor, wearing his embroidered jacket like an ermine robe and his gilded braids like a crown. But what flickers in his eyes when he looks at me is the wonder of a child. The boyish curiosity that has survived all his cruelties, because it existed before he murdered his father, before he heard the wet screams of his people under spinning tires.

"Show me."

\

"DELL?"

I haven't done the math of how many hours have passed since I last spoke to her, but I'm expecting someone from the night shift when she answers.

"You had better be calling for a pull."

"I am. My collar is broken, so it's not clasping. I need a proximity retrieval."

"How wide?"

I look at Adra. "Four-feet radius?"

"There's too much lingering interference."

"I told you it was a bright day."

"Best I can do is a three."

"That'll work."

"Two minutes."

She goes quiet, and I picture her leaning forward as she perfects my frequency. I'm so newly stitched together, and I've stayed here so long, the journey back will be a rough one. Not, however, as rough as it will be for Adra.

I walk up to Nik Nik. His hand is pressed against the wound in his throat, but he's more shocked than scared. He must not have thought it would come to this, between him and his big brother. He must still love him. I take some sealing bandages from my vest and hand them over.

Adra is talking to one of his men, so I lean forward and whisper, "When you take power, promise me you'll melt them down. Resist the temptation to keep them."

He nods, though he still must not expect to survive this. "May your life be long and easy."

It's a common blessing out here, but I've never dissected it before. Why are we, who are so unhappy, fixated on long lives? What is the point? An easy life isn't a blessing. Easy doesn't mean happy. Alive doesn't mean anything at all. Sometimes the path to an easy life makes you miserable. The only person I've ever heard value happiness is the former empress. She named her second son *happy*, hoping it would be true. She knew the cost of an easy life, and the uselessness of a long one. She had both. She wished neither for her child, only that he at some point be happy. Was he? Was anyone?

I step close to Nik Nik and inhale deeply. The scent of him, of the skin at the junction of his shoulder and neck, is instantly familiar. I never want to stop smelling it. I never want to smell it again. I take my fill, because it will be the last time.

When I step back, he's staring at my mouth. He looks disappointed as I put more distance between us.

"Goodbye, Yerjanik." Saying it eases an old ache in my chest, like I'd always meant to do this, to look him in the eye and tell him I was leaving.

"Goodbye . . ." He stops; his eyebrows furrow, then relax. "Caralee."

I haven't heard him say my name in so long that it uncoils me a little, and I'm not mad he read my journal anymore. The Nik Nik I knew before had a hold on me. Maybe I've never noticed until coming here, but my fear and ambition are both rooted in my time with him.

I left, but never really stopped carrying him at my back. Knowing this Nik Nik has freed me. I always thought I'd have to kill him to feel free, but hearing him say my name kindly is the balm that I thought only seeing his blood would be. Maybe it just takes this, glimpsing him as a different person who is whole and undamaged and who would never have hurt me. My Nik Nik was not a supernatural monster, not an inescapable god. He was just a flawed person who could and should have been better. Just a pitiable boy who cut his brother once, and became so lost he could never find his way back. Seeing this version is like seeing a wish I never thought to make for him come true. It would never have been possible for me to forgive myself for staying with him so long, but it seems possible now.

It's close to the two-minute mark, so I move back to Adra. "You'll need to stand close to me. Within three feet."

He could have told his men to kill Nik Nik the moment we've gone, but I'm hoping he wants to do it himself. How else will he ever again taste the kind of power he felt when he killed his father?

Adra steps up to me and plants his hands on my hips just to do it, but I barely feel his touch beneath the familiar tingle of Dell calling me home. Adra gasps, feeling the electricity too. Maybe stronger, maybe it already hurts a little.

I see the flash of movement from the corner of my eye, just before we're about to disappear. She's bided her time, but her goal has never changed. She wants out of Ash, and she'll take my life to do it. Nelline charges us, pushing her way into the three-foot perimeter.

"No!"

But it's too late. We disappear.

\

I AM THE first to enter the space between worlds, because I was at the center of the pull. It feels familiar like a recurring dream is familiar— something that is not real, but you've been there before just the same. The handbooks explain that anything unbelievable you see is a hallucination, images pulled from the subconscious to explain the sensations and absolute void of dead space. But the searching, prodding whisper feels real. I tense, remembering how quickly that muzzle turned to teeth last time. But there is no anger, no retribution. Nyame passes me easily.

It's Adra's turn, so I face him. I know it will be ugly, but it is my ugliness, so I watch. In the very back of my mind I was afraid he was just as strong and determined as I was. I was afraid he would somehow live and push through, broken but alive.

I needn't have worried.

I can almost see the dark shadow of Nyame's hand as she wraps it around the front of him like a child picking up a doll. There is no indecision, no trying to make him fit like there was with me. In a flick of motion, she lifts him, presses her thumb to his sternum, and breaks him in half. She squeezes the new shape of him together, and I am grateful this dark space is silent, because I never want to know what it sounds like for shoulder blades to fuse to knees, ribs to thighs. After he is bent he is pulled, stretched apart from the center out until bone and joints give and sinew and muscles are extended like red and black taffy somehow catching shine in this place with so little light.

The wet, lumpy horror that once was Adranik, brother of Yerjanik, son of emperor and empress, is flicked back into the void. He will reappear in the place we were standing immediately, no time passing between our exit and his reentry, and the people who know him will try to understand how such utter and wanton destruction could happen in the blink of an eye, how an entire body could be undone between one breath and the next. If the runners live up to their reputation of self-preservation, they'll abandon their loyalties and choose the brother who now has the upper hand. I have accomplished what Nik Nik could not envision: a peaceful transfer of power, bought with the blood of only one.

Nelline drifts beside me like a waiting ghost. Her eyes are wide and shining, but her mouth is set in a line. She knows. She saw Adra's death and she understands. She's reached too far this time, and it's the end.

Adra's death came first, because Adam Bosch is firmly rooted in Earth Zero, so there was no decision for Nyame, or the forces we give her name, to make. But once the pressure at my back lessened and she accepted me on my way to Earth Zero, it was over for Nelline. We can't both make it, and she's made her choice.

Time moves differently here, or it doesn't move at all. So maybe Adra's death was instantaneous, and my mind slowed it down to process. Maybe Nelline is already dead, too, but I still wish I could move, take her hands, smooth her hair down and tell her everything will be okay, the way I hope someone will do for me when my time comes. But I am caught in the tide of traversing, and I can't break out to move toward her.

I don't want to see her torn apart like Adra, but I bought this death too. I opened the door to every escape she'd ever wanted, *we'd* ever wanted, and I can't be surprised that she tried to walk through it just like I did.

I expect Nyame's disembodied hand, a shadowy force that our scientists have told me again and again is just pressure, a swath of dark energy meeting particles that do not belong. Instead, I see myself come up behind her, just like I wanted to. No, not like me. Younger, untouched, a version of myself that probably has the voice of a nightbird.

Caramenta.

I try to say her name, but I can only make the shape of it. She wraps her arms around Nelline. Nelline feels it. I don't know if she sees that the pressure is coming from one of us, but she doesn't look so scared anymore. Caramenta whispers in Nelline's ear, though I know sound doesn't travel here, and begins to squeeze. She hugs her tighter and tighter, until Nelline's mouth and eyes open wide and stay that way. Finally, there's a quick snap, and Caramenta's arms sink further into Nelline's body than ribs would allow. It's still a murder, but she carries her toward me like a child, delivering her to my feet with the delicate care of a sister.

Caramenta fades into the dark. I alone survive . . . again. Nyame lifts me toward my destination, aided by whatever sound Dell plays to please her. She fingers at the newly healed seams along my ribs until a few sing apart. It hurts, but it's not fatal and I never stop moving forward. I'm not dying, not yet.

The break of Earth Zero accepts me, and suddenly the feeling of being nowhere gives way to the feeling of being home. The darkness just feels like walls blocking out light, not the deep black of a place where direct light doesn't exist.

I'm in the hatch. I made it. And there, at my feet, eyes wide and body collapsed in, is Nelline. I thought she'd be sent back like Adra. But maybe my being in the space between rather than on Earth Zero lets her stay. Or maybe Nyame respects determination.

I crouch. The pain in my side and chest flares, but not enough to keep me from touching Nelline.

"You made it," I say. "You did it."

I know it's too late, but if she can hear me I want her to know she's not in Ash anymore. Whatever she was running from, she succeeded. She's in Wiley City, which is all we've ever wanted. She's free.

I can't crouch anymore so I roll carefully onto my back. Amid the pain of the rough trip, I feel the ball in my chest like a rock being shimmied in. A new loss, a little more weight to carry along. I welcome Nelline's death, and the everlasting memory of her.

I don't know how long I lie there before the hatch opens, an angry creak that lets in too much light. My fingers are entwined with Nelline's, but I don't know when that happened.

Dell crouches before me.

"Stop crying," she says. "I'm here."

But I didn't realize I was crying.

"I'm injured," I say. I don't know how I'm going to get up from the floor with these ribs, much less climb out of the hatch.

"But not dead," she says.

I want to ask her why that's a good thing. I want to tell her that I'm not even sure I can die anymore, that I think my destiny is this: to watch every version of myself bleed on different ground until I am all that's left. But medical is here, and I have just enough sense to keep quiet.

PART THREE

If you must know anything, know that the hardest task is to live only once.

—Ocean Vuong

CHAPTER ELEVEN

When the recruitment campaign began, we learned Eldridge needed a very select group of people—those who lived with enough risk to have died over and over and over again . . . but had somehow survived here.

And the scientists said, *Interstellar travel has always belonged to the few. Of course the people we seek are a paradox.*

And the spiritual said, *Heaven has always belonged to the few. Of course the people we seek are a miracle.*

ELDRIDGE'S PHYSICIAN HAS been clucking over my scans since they came in. Except for a few hairline fractures that reopened during my jump back home, the injuries I sustained getting to Earth 175 are just dark shadows of new healing on the projection. But the doctor can tell how bad it was, because he keeps looking from the scan to me and back like he's being tricked.

"How did you survive?" he says, at last.

Because I don't know how to die.

That would be a good answer, said with just enough cheek to let him know I don't care. But when I close my eyes, I see Nelline's broken corpse and I want to scream, *I didn't, I didn't. I died. I'm dead. Again.*

Instead, I say, "Someone found me and thought I was worth something."

I tell him how long I spent in the pod. I tell him about the fever. He clucks some more and presses his cuff.

"Your body is probably more acclimated to the pressures of traversing than any other human being," he says. "Your extensive experience is likely what saved you from the dop backlash."

Jean told me the same thing when he visited the infirmary, once my twenty-four hours of observation were up. Only, he worded it as *Nyame knows you well. She was lenient.* They are both saying I survived jumping to a world with a living dop because of how many times I survived jumping before. As if not dying is a skill I've honed, not just blind luck.

"You're the only duality survivor we've ever seen. They'll want to get a detailed account from you."

Dell comes in as the physician is taping my ribs. Half of a watcher's training is in medical, so I know she understands the extent of the damage on the scans, but if she's concerned or impressed she doesn't show it.

"Why aren't you podding her for these fractures?" she asks.

"Because she fractured along pod-healed injuries. She already had the healing fever once over there. She might not come out of a second bout without lasting damage."

She spends a bit longer staring at my face. "And these traversing bruises?"

The doctor shakes his head. "Never seen so many marks. They survived her podding on the other world, so they're likely . . ."

"Permanent," Dell says.

Her study of my face turns to actually looking at me in an instant, and I don't know how I can tell the difference. "Who took care of you?"

I shrug. It hurts. "No one. I mean, he wasn't a doctor or anything, but he kept me hydrated and tried to keep me cool."

Her face goes plastic, unreadable. "I'm sure he did," she says.

Her attention makes me feel exposed, and as soon as the electrical tape begins to pulse I reach for the Eldridge Institute shirt Jean brought me. Trying to lift my arms makes my whole body scream. I take a sharp breath and leave the shirt in my lap.

Now they're both looking at me.

"I can give her something for the pain, if someone can commit to seeing her home," the physician says. He stopped addressing me directly the moment my watcher entered the room. I'd hate him for it, except hate takes focus and I'm in too much pain.

"I'll see her home. She has no family in the city."

"Traversers never do," he says, not quite far enough under his breath.

The injection works quickly, and when I stand my head feels full of air and my mouth full of cotton. I turn to Dell. "I live off the fortieth floor."

"I remember," she says.

It's on my tongue to tell her she's never been to my place, but she's already holding open the door.

\\

SOMEWHERE ALONG THE way, Dell has learned where I live. She walks slightly ahead of me, but never looks back to ask where we're headed. Or if we're moving too fast. Or how I'm doing. But who's bitter? Not I.

I realize too late that being alone with Dell while I'm this wrecked is probably a bad idea. All of the little annoyances I usually swallow seem intolerable now that my ribs are hissing and I can't remember my last good sleep. Only when my apartment door slides open does she come up short. She studies the walls, head tilted in a way that somehow cascades her perfect haircut without ruining its shape.

"It's . . . different than before."

I haven't decorated as much as I should have for six years, but now that I've spent real time back in Ashtown I realize I've collected images that remind me of home: rough fixtures made of imperfect metal, paintings in shades of gray with just enough shape and splatter to feel industrial.

"Here," she says, pointing to a distressed piece of wood I've hung above my couch. "You had a picture of flowers here, didn't you?"

No, but Caramenta did. It was the only thing hung among the half-emptied boxes. It's in my closet still, because even though it's hideous I assume it meant something to her.

"When did you come here?"

She looks over her shoulder. Her face is no more expressive than usual, but I swear I see a glare in her dark eyes.

"Why are you pissed at me? Is this about being late? You saw the scans. I was half-dead when I got there."

"You stayed after you were well."

"It was a bright day!"

The yell costs me an echoing screech along my sides, but it would be worth it if it got to her. I want her to step up, come at me, yell back that she's not stupid and she knows damn well when the sun set on 175. But she just looks slightly annoyed before turning away.

"Where is the bedroom?"

I hobble after her. "That would be the thing you can't find. Does even knowing where my bed is break protocol?"

She's glaring at me again.

"It's down the hall, Dell. Obviously. I don't have a spare."

Her face empties, leaving no trace of anger; the indifferent night sky I've come to dread.

"We should get you into bed. You're irrational."

"I'm not irrational. I'm in pain."

Her eyes soften. She takes my arm, about fifteen minutes and thirty floors too late.

"Come on."

I don't need her help to walk, but I let her lead me. I hadn't made my bed when I left, so it's easy to crawl into the crumpled mess while she answers her beeping cuff.

"Not going to tuck me in?"

She looks up. "You've been placed on leave. I would have recommended it anyway, with your ribs, but I don't know if this has to do with your health or your delay."

"How long?"

"Two weeks."

Tension constricts my chest. "Paid?"

She nods, and I relax into the pillows.

I stare up at the ceiling, bright white and high enough to make me feel like I'm floating. I feel a slight panic at the prospect of losing my job, but it's distant, muddled by more than painkillers. I grew up fearing death, every day. Tasting that terror again mutes my reaction to unemployment.

"I killed someone," I say without meaning to.

"What did you say?"

"Nothing."

"What do you mean you killed someone?"

"Nothing. It's an Ashtown expression."

It's not, though I'm sure enough people there have said it.

She studies me for a second longer than is comfortable, then looks away.

"That girl following you into a jump . . . I'm sure it wasn't your fault."

That girl. Like Nelline is some other garbage git. Like she wasn't me.

"What will happen to her body?"

"A week for tests, then the incinerator most likely. I doubt anyone wants to bother with a burial," she says.

"I'd like to. Bury her, I mean."

Dell is staring at me again, and I think she'll tell me no. But eventually she nods.

"I'll arrange it." She adjusts her coat. "You have my number if you need me."

"Not going to stay and watch me sleep? What if there's an emergency?"

"Then you should call emergency services."

I close my eyes. "Go if you want. Can't stop me from dreaming about you, though."

"Don't be cruel."

I don't understand her response, but I'm tired of teasing Dell, of trying to irritate her just to make her feel something at all. I fall asleep before I hear her leave, but I'm sure she does.

\

ADRA VISITS ME in the night. I see him bend and break. I know I couldn't have seen his face, not once he was snapped backward, but I've invented it—eyes wide as stars, a blood curtain hanging from his mouth—turned toward me in accusation. Somehow, too, I've added sound into the void. I replay the memory and make myself sick with it, until I know the particular hurt of dry-heaving with fractured ribs.

Do you want to see it?

Those weren't the last words he heard, but they might as well have been, because he was dead as soon as I made the invitation.

Two days fighting nightmares in my apartment prompts me to make an appointment with Sasha, the same psychologist who helped stop the panic attacks I'd thought were normal because so many people who grew up with runners had them. In Ashtown, our therapists work out of the House. If Sasha were from Ashtown, her office would be filled with incense and we'd both be lying down when I spoke to her. She would cover me in oil made by pressing one of our few flowering plants. She would stroke my hair and rub my back and I would believe her when she told me my mind was wonderful, and that I would survive this and so much else.

I miss having a place where someone would touch you, just hold you if that was what you needed, or hold you down if you needed that more. But no one in Wiley touches—not me, not each other—and Sasha especially doesn't.

Sasha's office doesn't smell like smoke, or sex, or anything but clean, and we sit feet apart as she tells me I'm exhibiting a totally normal grief response. She doesn't believe I knew Nelline well enough to account for my grief. She thinks it's myself I'm mourning.

You understand you're alive, don't you? she says, more than once. *You are alive, Caramenta. You are still whole.*

She calls me a dead girl's name, and pronounces her alive. But even if she'd gotten my name right I wouldn't really believe her. I used to be at least 382. Now I am 7. How can I possibly be whole?

Maybe if you touch me, I want to tell her, *maybe if you were stroking my hair like a sister, I would believe I was alive.*

But they don't do things like that here, and it's embarrassing to realize after so many years in the city I still need it.

I'm just getting home from one of our sessions when my cuff beeps a call from Esther. I'm grateful it's a voice call, rather than the standard video. My family doesn't know about my injuries, or my new marks, and I'd like to keep it that way until I can see them in person.

"Hey you," I say, but once she starts talking, I realize my tone is too light.

"I'm heading for the wall, can we meet? I don't have much time, but I need to talk to you."

I don't like the panic in Esther's voice, but I like the quiet even less. It means she's hiding her trip from those around her, which can only be her family.

I'm already opening up a new screen from my cuff to order her a quick pass as I answer.

"Of course. Always."

And when I say that word, something that began to slide into place in Sasha's office clicks home. I have to be alive, because there is someone who needs me.

\

WITH HER FAIR, uninked skin and her biblical, *x*-free name, my sister could probably slip through Wiley City without a pass. But that's not

Esther. Esther does things by the book, not just *the* Book, but any book.

She spends the first five minutes of our visit touching my face and scolding me for not telling her I was hurt. She says she would have brought me root paste for the pain in my ribs, so I say smelly mud is precisely why I didn't tell her. I can tell by the way she looks at them that she doesn't understand the marks are permanent, and I don't try very hard to convince her. Hearing her voice heals something inside of me, even if she is just nagging. To hear her speak without fear or shame, different from the last version of her I heard, is its own gift. I stare at her, looking for hints of damage or signs of abuse. But there is nothing. This is an Esther I haven't yet failed.

Soon enough, she shifts from examining me to examining the city. We're in a garden section near Wiley's entrance so she doesn't have to waste too much time going back home. We're forty stories in the air, but plants grow from the ground like they never will in her backyard. She's not impressed. To her the plants must seem useless. Trees and bushes and flowers—pretty things, inedible.

"Gardens like this are for aesthetics and air quality. They do have vegetable gardens and orchards here too."

"It's very nice," she says, *nice* somehow becoming its opposite. "No flies?"

"No, but there are bees. I've seen them."

"Honey?"

". . . No, just bees."

She nods. Selling honey to the city is one of the main sources of income for people in the Rurals. They can't really harvest enough to compete with the cheaper, shipped-in supply, but some residents in the Wiles have a sweet tooth almost as big as their need for philanthropy. Overpaying for honey from the poor makes them giddy.

"Does Mom know you're here? Does Dan?"

She shakes her head. "I'm supposed to be helping the women of inner Ash."

"They let you go alone thinking that?"

"Michael's downstairs. But he doesn't know why I'm here either."

I sit on a bench. "Neither do I."

"I need help."

"I figured."

She sits beside me, arranging her pale-blue skirt against her thigh so she doesn't take up extra space. Her people are good at making themselves small.

"I've been noticing things missing during inventory," she says.

"Like parishioners helping themselves to more food than they're allowed?"

She waves her hand. "I would never care about that. It's the powder. Michael's powder."

I have just enough time to process that she means explosives when she adds, "It's been happening since the dedication and it's gotten worse."

I've just sat down, but I stand up again, pacing. I stop when the Wileyites start to stare at me. The others in the garden had been stealing glances at us; Esther's long sleeves and apron draw attention in exactly the same way as a visiting monk's orange robes. She's so Wiley-looking but for her skin that sees the real, unfiltered sun, they want to hover close to the safe, familiar-yet-just-exotic-enough novelty of her. They are smiling in a way they'd never smile at someone from downtown or the deep wastes. It's still patronizing, the look you give a puppy, not an equal, but it's less fatal than the distrust the rest of us get.

"Did you tell Dan?" I ask.

"I did. He just smiled and said there must have been an error recording it before, or that Michael had been practicing and forgotten to log what he used. He told me to let it go."

"But you didn't."

Because of course she didn't. Esther is as self-reliant as a mountain. She wouldn't come to me unless she'd exhausted all the ways she could solve this on her own.

"No, I didn't." She looks down, a little guilty, maybe, but not sorry.

"I help some of the people in downtown Ash. I don't preach like Mom and Dad, just help, and they like me for it. I asked one I trust if he'd heard anything about anyone trying to sell it. He said no, but his man's a runner, and after I asked he kept an eye out for me. One night he overheard something about our building. He gave it to me directly, but I don't know what it means and neither did he. It's runner tongue."

She doesn't ask me if I know the tongue, which I like because it means she won't ask me how I know. It feels utterly without judgment, and I can see how the population of downtown would be seduced by her easy manner.

"Play it," I say.

Esther has a handheld, not the pricier cuff, but it's loud enough for me to easily hear the clipped, barking message. I listen to it twice, not because I don't understand at first but because I want to buy time. I look out over the trees. I picture her here, safe and away from runners and sandstorms and Nik. But she wouldn't be Esther without her flock, and I know she'd never come, even if I were allowed to sponsor someone full-time.

After a long silence in which Esther doesn't play the message a third time because she knows I'm stalling, I say, "You know Nik Nik?"

Her faith keeps her from expressing anger verbally, but she's got eyes that harden with hate and it's a shift that makes her warm, frothed-ocean irises seem like they were actually blue-veined marble the whole time.

"I'm familiar."

"He donated to your church's building. A lot. That's not how things usually work. Usually new builders pay him."

She's sheltered, not stupid, so she nods.

"You think the missing explosives are his tribute?"

"Maybe. Even if it is, you don't have anything to worry about. Runners have stolen powder from Ruralites a dozen times. But even experts hurt themselves with that stuff. Wait for a bang and find whichever runner has some newly missing fingers, then accuse them of theft as if the emperor is innocent."

"What exactly did the message say?"

"They're coming back to collect Nik Nik's due. It's usually a phrase used for tribute or tax money. It's code, but they must be talking about the powder."

"When?" she asks, and I wish she hadn't.

"Why does it matter?"

"Because I can—"

"Stop them?"

She closes her mouth, deflated, but only a little. "It sounds unreasonable when you say it."

"You can't fight the emperor," I say, but, because the decision isn't mine to make, I add, "You have ten days before they come, according to the message."

She looks down at her feet, smooths her hands along her apron. "Do you think my father knows?"

I want to say no. I've long thought of Dan as one of the only honest people in Ashtown, and it's difficult to lose that image. But he conspired with Nik Nik on 175, so anything's possible.

"Maybe. It might be that he made an arrangement in exchange for funding his building, or it might just be that he can deduce who would want the powder and knows enough not to get involved. Either way, he doesn't have much choice. He keeps quiet and your congregation is left in peace. You fight back and . . . Nik Nik will still get what he wants."

"That makes it worse," she says. "Being bought, not forced."

The words of someone who's never been forced.

"Trust me. Ignore it. When next week comes, close your door and pretend to sleep. Don't try to fight the thieves."

When she goes, I hope she'll listen. I hope she has one-tenth of the sense of self-preservation that I do. If she doesn't, if she acts on all the righteous anger in her eyes, she'll end up with a tiny cut and a quiet death and I'll have to go to other worlds to see her.

\

THE DAY OF my debriefing at Eldridge, I'm woken by the proximity alert on my doorcam. I shuffle forward and make it to the door just in time to see someone retreating, ducked down so I can see only a shape I first assume is a black-clad shoulder. Too tired to be cautious, but just awake enough to be curious, I open the door and find a note—an actual paper note, not a plastic vidscreen—folded and tucked into my door. It's the kind of thing Esther might do, if she was in the city, but when I touch the paper I know it's not her.

I have an affinity for paper that is as little understood in Wiley City as it was in Ashtown. When I make my lists, I like to write them physically, not type them into a coded file on my cuff. This is precisely what got me into trouble with Nik Nik back on my home Earth. The paper that's been placed on my door is softer and smoother than Ashtown paper, because in Ashtown paper is made from blending root plants and dirt, and here the paper is made from other paper. Ashtown paper is brown to tan, depending on the quality. Wiley City paper is the gray of other people's ink. Someone from Wiley has left me a note.

For a moment, I entertain the fantasy that it's from Dell, but then the careless scrawl sets me straight. Dell practices calligraphy like other people practice meditation, and I imagine her handwriting carries the structured fluidity of anyone who is also fluent in a kanji-based language. Whoever wrote this is unused to writing physically. A tech head, for sure.

I know what happened on 175.

Beneath the declaration is a meeting place and time. I read the words again, trying not to react, forcing myself to fold the note back along its seam when I want to crumble it into nothing. I close the door and rewind my doorcam, but whoever left the note stayed tucked below its range. All I can see is the same dark bump on the edge of the feed where they didn't hunch down quite low enough. It might be a shoulder, but it might also be the curve of a back, the top of a head, or the edge of a hood. All I know for sure is they were wearing black.

My cuff beeps an appointment reminder. It's time to get ready.

JEAN IS WAITING for me just inside Eldridge's doors. His eyebrows go up as he studies my face.

"They didn't fade."

I touch my cheeks. I've mostly forgotten about the stripes that begin at my cheekbones and continue all the way down my body, just slightly darker and more purple than my own skin. He's wrong, they did fade a little from that first day. Just not much.

"They're permanent," I say. "Do you think it's the price for surviving?"

He shakes his head quickly, severely. "You don't pay with scars so you can survive. Scars are the badge of honor to prove you survived. This is your Purple Heart."

I could tell him Wiley City has never actually given a Purple Heart, and I'm not sure anywhere else has in decades—not since war became so technological and killing became letting the wrong people starve—but I like his explanation too much to disagree.

"Are you ready for this?" he asks, leading me to the elevator.

"I have a choice?"

"Of course," he says. "You could choose quitting. Failure."

"Then I guess I'm ready."

It's the right answer, and he smiles as he sends our elevator up. We're going all the way to the one hundredth floor, the highest artery in the city for now. They've already approved the next round of construction—soon there will be a 120th floor—but this one will still be high up enough to barely be shaded. I've never been on this floor. Adam Bosch's office is here, and all the important meeting rooms, so I wouldn't have clearance inside the building without Jean's fob. I guess I could go to the hundredth floor outside the building, make use of the exterior elevators to get to their public-access parks, but there are fewer of those on the hundredth floor than any other, so why bother?

"You're tense," Jean says as we climb. "Are you concerned about the exam?"

"No, I'm sure I'll pass."

The gut-churning nervousness that once came when I thought of the analyst test is gone. I've taken three practice tests during my leave and scored nearly perfect on every one.

"Then what is it?"

"Do you know if there was an Eldridge courier sent to my house?" I ask.

"There was," Jean says, then, before I can get excited over the clue, continues, "I sent you study materials. Did you get them?"

"I got them. I meant today. Was anything sent to me this morning?"

Jean frowns down at his portable screen. "Nothing from me or Dell, and no one else but HR has your address. Why?"

"I got a weird note. I can't tell if it's a threat or not."

"What did it say?"

The elevator doors glide open on a whisper, and suddenly there are too many eyes and ears around us.

"I'll tell you after."

"I meet with Mr. Bosch after. Monday?"

I nod, suddenly nervous as we walk to the meeting that I've been told many times is not actually an interrogation, no matter how much it feels like one.

The debriefing room is dominated by a large half-moon desk that can seat up to ten people. Today, it holds only six: two investigators in the center, my advocates on each side of them, a Human Resources representative on the end to ensure the questioning is fair and act as a mediator between the company's representatives and mine if things get tense, and then there, on the far end, is my therapist.

Sasha isn't like Dell or Jean, who have blood from somewhere else. Her people have been in Wiley City since its founding, and in a city just like it before that. Only someone whose family hasn't had to deal with uncontrolled UV rays for a dozen generations would have skin or eyes as white as hers. She's as much Wiley City as I am Ashtown, but she's never looked at me like I was anything but a person. When we first met years ago, she told me I'd grown more confident. Of course she was comparing me to Caramenta—a sweet, sheltered girl a few weeks out of her mother's house—but I liked the compliment and I liked her for giving it to me. She wanted me to succeed, to have a piece of something that used to be just hers.

Sasha's supposed to make sure I don't get too agitated by the questioning, and I trust that's what she'll do. The company pretends it's a protection for me, but it's not. If I have a breakdown during their debriefing, they'd have to take care of me, citizen or no. Wiley City might pride itself on how well it takes care of its people, but when it comes to damage to employees directly from employers, their policy has always been *You break it, you bought it.* Within the city limits, anyway. Back when Wiley companies operated in Ash, they'd fire children clumsy enough to lose a limb at their factories, fine families for the cleanup if an overworked loved one committed suicide there. But when dealing with their own people they are models of compassionate responsibility.

My advocates are my watcher and my mentor, Dell and Jean. Jean takes his seat and begins sliding through the files on the briefing screens that have been provided. He's trying to hide his nervousness, but he's sweating just enough for his dark skin to pick up shine from the lights overhead. I don't know how many children Jean has—not because it's a secret, but because I've lost track—and between his children and grandchildren it's as if he doesn't know how to turn off caring for anyone more than twenty years younger than him.

Dell is too professional to ever look bored, but she does look indifferent. Her hands are folded, and I'm sure she already has the information for the meeting memorized.

I am seated at a table alone. There is a microphone floating above me and a pitcher of water on the desk. To my left on the far side of the wall is something I'm sure doesn't happen for other hearings: a gallery of people—scientists, I'm guessing, because instead of the simple reading screens they've brought processors and they're tapping away at them even though nothing has happened yet. They aren't part of the committee; they're just an audience waiting for the show.

"Okay," says the ranking investigator, "let's begin."

At first, the questions are broadly curious. They say they want to know what it felt like when I first landed, but they don't. They don't want details about the taste of blood or the unique, shifting agony of being unmade and dropped in a new world like a skinned cat. They want to know how many bones I broke, how many days I was out, how high my fever got. Nice, clinical numbers that are easy to process. I tell them I don't remember much.

"And the DD-905?" asks the lead investigator.

"The what?"

Dell leans forward. "The Misery Syringe."

The lead investigator tilts his head at that, but continues. "Protocol dictates that in the event of dop backlash you call for a pull after using the dose."

This is the first lie I'll have to tell. Heart rate scanners and other anti-lie tech are supposed to be illegal for employers to use against employees. Maybe Adam Bosch would care, but I doubt Adranik does. Just in case, I hedge my answer so it's *technically* true.

"I'd left an away message on my cuff. When I was passing out, I couldn't call for a pull."

With some carefully moved pauses, I've told the whole truth. I can't tell them I broke protocol and used the painkiller to get help rather than accepting the death sentence of having Dell pull me back. Pigeons aren't supposed to value their lives more than the mission.

"I don't know what happened to the syringe," I say, also true. "I must have dropped it when I passed out, or when I was moved."

The second investigator turns to the lead. "Ashtown has a severe drug problem. Someone probably just thought it was their lucky day."

The room shares a lighthearted laugh. Except Jean, because he wouldn't laugh at a joke that hurts me, and Dell, because she never laughs.

It's not my fight. It's not. Even though my time spent on Earth 175 makes it feel like I am fresh from the ash. I bite my tongue when I want to call them out. Like Ashtown has the resources to even have an intra-

venous drug problem? When Wiley City has such a lockdown on plastic and glass? No. Ashtown junkies smoke rock shards as black as their
emperor's hair in pipes they make themselves from clay they dig out of
the ground. My mother would trek for miles because she *swore* red clay
left a better taste than gray. And even an Ashtown user is too smart to
take drugs from a dead body. They know what tainted looks like, and
they can smell a trap better than any sandcat.

Dell taps her pen on the table, once, hard, which snaps me to attention. I've been glaring down, fingers gripping the desk. If the investigators had bothered to look at me, they'd know I was angry. And then
they'd remember I was a traverser, and traversers don't come from the
same places as the rest of them.

I sit up straight. I start to smile, then remember Nelline and what a
smile actually looks like on my face. I settle for not grimacing in a way
I hope looks neutral.

Next they want to know what it felt like to see my dop. The scientists sit up for this part. They must have petitioned for a chance to interview me and been denied. I wonder if Dell or Sasha made that call.
I tell them the manuals were right about the vomiting. They ask me
how long it took the brain to adjust. I don't know if my mind ever
adjusted—I still don't know what to do with Nelline—but I tell them
it took about twenty minutes for the nausea to wear off.

"And what was phase two? What replaced the nausea?"

This from the quieter investigator.

"After the nausea it didn't feel like looking at myself. It felt like
looking at a relative, a sister or a cousin. And I felt . . . inexplicably
protective of her. I know it was just my mind extending its own self-
preservation to a being it saw as also me. But it felt like . . ."

"Affection," Dell says.

I nod. The tapping on the screens to my left grows frantic.

"Did this protective instinct drive you to bring her here?" the chief
investigator asks.

"No! I mean, no. I knew what would happen."

"But you called for a proximity pull. Why?"

"My collar was broken," I say.

"Was it?" the lead investigator asks, and in the silence that follows I realize my mistake.

I messed up. I called for a proximity pull, then showed up wearing a perfectly functioning collar. Do they think I was trying to smuggle Nelline in and forgot about the dop backlash? Or do they think killing Nelline is exactly what I was trying to do? It doesn't matter. They know I lied; they just won't know why.

I know what happened on 175.

Well, apparently everyone else does too.

CHAPTER TWELVE

R ight, this mysteriously broken collar that seems to have disappeared from our inventory," says the second investigator.

"It what?"

I touch my neck, half expecting the collar to be in the last place I remember it. I look at Jean, but he seems as confused as I am.

Dell leans forward, looking straight at me even though she's giving testimony to the investigator.

"I inspected the collar when she arrived," she says. I'm sure she sees my panic before she looks away. "It was crushed. I had already suspected as much when the frequency was too weak to find her. The cleaners must have seen it and assumed it was a piece of damaged tech to be recycled."

She's lying, but I can't figure out why.

"This is where I have difficulty. The collars are made to sustain any trauma, to keep our people from being trapped. Even a pressure strong enough to break bones shouldn't have damaged it to that extent," he says. "You say it was crushed?"

He leans back, shaking his head. I drag a finger on the side of my glass.

"Have you ever heard of the Ashtown runners? Not the errand boys, the old runners. They still ride on Earth 175. And their cars aren't like Wiley City cars. They aren't lightweight, or solar. They are made of the heaviest metals and ornamented in stone. They are meant to run into people and buildings and each other. And they get twice as heavy on a bright day, when they add more metal panels coated in a cheap reflector. They don't just break bones. They liquefy bodies."

I hadn't meant to go that far. I'd just meant to offer up an alternate explanation so he'd stop looking at me and Dell like we were hiding something. I'd never meant for her to get wrapped up in this.

It takes a second, but he turns to the galley. "Would that compromise the structure of the collar?"

The scientists murmur, and then one stands. He looks nervously at me, then back at the investigator. "If the day was hot enough that the collar's structure was already taxed . . . possibly. If such a vehicle does exist."

"They exist."

The voice comes from behind me and everyone stands. I stand and turn, even though looking at Adam Bosch is like stabbing myself in the chest. He smiles and nods at me, kind like always, and the guilt could crush me to dust. I want to tell him I'm sorry, but he won't even know what I'm sorry for.

"Mr. Bosch, we weren't expecting you," says the chief investigator.

"I didn't mean to interrupt. I thought you'd be done by now."

His name is Adam, but *Adra, Adra, Adra* bounces inside my head. I don't know how long I can stand there, but luckily Jean saves me.

"I won't be much longer," he says. "I'm sure we're nearly done."

"Of course. I'll leave you to it," Adam says.

The room feels darker when he leaves, but I can breathe again.

\

THE NIGHTMARE THAT wakes me the next day is another quiet one, more sad than horrifying but a nightmare nonetheless. Nelline, who was somehow also Caramenta, and somehow also my mother, was lying beside me in bed, telling me over and over again that she's not here. That she is gone. That everyone is gone. Except me. I am alone in an infinity of universes. I actually miss the quick and easy horror of the Adra nightmares, where his mangled corpse tries to point a finger at me, but he has no fingers, only bloody stumps.

I'm half-dressed when someone buzzes at my door. Nelline's body won't be released to me until I'm at the city border, and I'm not expecting anyone else. When I check the feed, Dell's on the other side.

My first thought is that she came because she wrote the note. That the note was about me lying about the collar and she's come to collect. But I still can't square the choppy handwriting with her elegance. Besides, what could someone like Dell possibly want to extort from someone like me? I gave her my most valuable possession when I handed over the earring.

I open the door. "What are you doing here?"

She walks in without waiting for an invitation. "Today is the burial, isn't it? I'm going with you."

"You want to come with me into Ash?" I look her up and down. "You're wearing all black."

"It's a funeral."

"It is, but—"

A second buzz interrupts me. This time the screen fills up with Esther's face. She's staring wide-eyed into the camera and standing way too close to the door. I let her in.

"What are you doing here? Who sponsored you?"

She nods toward Dell. "Ms. Ikari. She told me you had a friend die, and we thought I should help you with the burial."

"I don't need help." I look back at Dell. "From either of you."

Esther steps forward. "Do you remember the prayers for the dead? The peace ritual?"

Of course I don't. When someone dies in Ashtown, we just hire someone from the Rurals to say the words. Or a sahira from inside the city, for those who lean a little more toward the pagan. I wonder if

Esther has ever been hired to bury the dead. I wonder if Caramenta ever did.

"Besides," Dell says, "the van is rented out in my name. Unless you planned on transporting her in the trunk of a company car?"

These are both excellent points. "Fine. We'll all go."

"You're going into Ashtown wearing all black?" asks Esther, whose long dress is in the customary gray of Ashtown funerals, though today's apron is brown.

Dell narrows her eyes. "All right. I give up. What does it mean if I wear all black?"

I shrug. "It means you're a professional, and you're not dressed like a runner."

Dell looks down at her dress. "I'm dressed like a prostitute?"

Prostitute is another word I learned only after I came to the city. *Worker, provider, comforter, house cat,* on and on—we have as many words for them as islanders have for water and northerners have for snow, but *prostitute* isn't one of them.

"Don't be ridiculous, Dell. A mere worker would never dare wear all black," I say. "All black is for the elite."

Dell looks down, then raises her chin twice as high as before. "I would be elite."

\

BORDER PATROL STOPS us the moment we cross into Ashtown proper from the ambiguous stretch of desert that separates it from Wiley City. This time, I pull far off the road and into the dirt, so they'll know I mean to deal. I get out before he can make it to my window. He stumbles a bit, but then so do I. I'd forgotten this was his route. I look back at Esther in the center seat of the van, and wish it had been any other runner.

"Mr. Cheeks," I say.

There's no star on his neck, but otherwise he is indistinguishable from the version I left on Earth 175. Seeing Mr. Cheeks, plus my earlier talk with Dell, slides something into place for me: The note was left by someone wearing black. Runners always wear black.

It's farfetched—how would a runner know something you would need Eldridge access to know?—but the idea takes hold like catching the scent of an old enemy. Doesn't having the note hanging over my head make me feel hunted? And who has always specialized in hunting me?

"Miss me that badly, had to come back again?" he says. "The price is still three hundred."

I hold up the cash. "I need a guide." I nod to his vehicle, a massive truck with tires the size of my car. "Can you take us into the deep wastes?"

He walks over and looks through the windows in the back of the van. I haven't looked in the cargo hold since they loaded it, but I know he must see the unmoving chrysalis of Nelline, wrapped in a white, plasticized sheet that clips closed on the side.

"For a body dump you'll need twice that to buy silence, and I don't need you to come along. You can trust I'll do the job."

Esther steps out from the side of the van. Maybe she thinks he'll take a local more seriously than a Wileyite, or maybe she thinks her being a holy woman will help him understand our purpose. Either way, I hadn't wanted him ever seeing her at all, but now that's ruined. As she stands tall with the early-morning sun catching her hair and an ethereal shine to her serene expression, I'm sure he'd propose to her here and now . . . if her eyes weren't so hard. If she weren't looking at him like he was less than dirt.

I should have warned her not to let on that she knows they've been stealing from the church, but I doubt she could hide her distaste anyway.

"It's not a body dump. It's a proper burial," she says, short, clipped. "Is that a problem?"

This is more than distaste; this is a challenge. Esther wants to look a runner in the eyes for stealing from her.

Mr. Cheeks looks from her to me to the van, baffled by her irritation but more interested than offended. "No problem, but I've only got room for four."

"We're only three," I say.

I take his picture with my cuff, standard safety procedure for Wiley-ites who take a ride from Ashtowners. It's such a tourist move, but I've got Dell with me in clothes that scream *kidnappable*. He lets me record his image without comment, which means he either isn't planning on double-crossing us or he has no fear of Wiley City's retribution. He presses his wrist to the vehicle door and the old locks open. Even with the parades off, runners are married to their vehicles. I'm not surprised he's embedded a chip instead of just using a removable cuff or carrying a fob. He makes a call on his car's radio, then motions us inside.

"You all make yourselves comfortable," he says. "I'll get her."

"How do you know it's a her?" Esther asks.

Mr. Cheeks just nods toward us like it's obvious.

I sit in the passenger seat to keep Esther from being beside him, but she just sits behind the driver's seat so she can glare into his rearview mirror. The cab is separated from the back storage by a shell, so the only time I have to see the body is when he transfers her out of the van. He doesn't throw the bundle over his shoulder. He carries Nelline like a bride, and I'm grateful.

\

"YOU WANT *WHAT*?"

We've made it to the edge of the deep wastes, and I've just told Mr. Cheeks my plan.

"It's not much farther."

"It's not the distance that worries me; it's the obstacles. No one's supposed to even go near the bogs."

"Is that strictly true?" Dell says. "I'd always heard that was where you took all the Wiley citizens who come seeking assisted suicide."

I turn back to her. "How do you know about Akeldama?"

She shrugs. "I imagine most in Wiley do. It's good advertising, since it's a service we can't get there."

"Those are different. Special," Mr. Cheeks says, though the correct word is *cursed*. Either way, I'm glad we're in agreement that Nelline won't be sleeping with the nameless.

He's not happy, but so far he's doing a fantastic job of watching his language around Esther, an effort I appreciate only half as much as I resent it. He's even muted his callbox so we can't hear the types of calls runners typically exchange.

Dell is tired of our arguing. She sits forward. "How much? How much more to take us to the *un-special* ponds?"

"Bogs," the runner and I both say at once.

"Whatever. Twice what she gave you?"

Mr. Cheeks is biting his lip and doing the math. He was already making out for half a day's work. A runner on border patrol can go a week without a shakedown, and even if he'd reported the six hundred honestly, no one would ever expect him to pull double. Right now there isn't a mudcroc in all the wastes big enough to deter him from that kind of payday. Still, he looks in his mirror, at Esther.

"I know you runners are becoming a greedy lot, but surely that is enough money for you," Esther says.

I'm sure when they were deciding to skim from the Rurals, the runners considered Dan retaliating, or even Michael. But it's Esther's temper they should have thought of first.

"Mouthy princess," he says, which means he recognizes her. Still, he folds and starts the engine again.

Despite the absence of a marker, he turns left and begins cutting through the desert at a diagonal from the river. He played scared with the bogs, but he's been there before. If his actions on 175 are any indication, he's the type of runner who obeys only the rules he respects, and will turn his back on an emperor who stops acting with honor. He's the type of runner I didn't think existed, one I certainly never saw as a child.

We encounter no animals, predator or prey, which makes sense given how heavy and loud the runner's truck is. Even the laziest grazing animal would have felt us coming far enough off to move, and the predators here are too well fed to be concerned with taking down what must look like a very difficult meal.

We reach the bogs in the midafternoon, and I'm just beginning to think that everything is going too well when Esther speaks up.

"I'll need to open the wrapping on the body to prepare her."

I exchange a panicked look with Dell. I'd known we'd have to take Nelline out of the burial shroud if I wanted the bog to preserve her, but I hadn't realized Esther would be with me when I did. I don't know how to explain Nelline's identity, even if there was time. But Esther knows what I do for a living, knows there are other worlds with other versions of ourselves. I'll just have to trust her to process it and understand without being too traumatized by the sight of something that looks an awful lot like her sister's dead body.

Mr. Cheeks carries the shroud-wrapped form to the edge of the bog, where the dark sand is cooler than it should be, covered in a green-black sheen unlike anything else in the area.

When he moves to undo the clasp for Esther, I stop him.

"I'll do it," I say.

He shrugs and moves back to his truck, far enough away that he won't be able to see her as Esther performs the ritual. I undo each clasp slowly, leaving the latch by her face for last. Finally, I open the shroud.

Whoever held the body must have been paid something, because she's been prepared. The blood that trickled down her face in the hatch is gone. Her sunken chest is now propped up. Her open eyes, closed.

I am better prepared for horror than this, this sleeping girl, this untouched face. When I feel the hand on my shoulder, I think it is Esther, but when I place my fingers over it, I know it's Dell. Too cool, too large, to belong to my sister.

"You need to let Esther work now, so we can send her off while it is still light."

Burial by the sun is a custom that remains the same on both sides of the wall. I stand, making way for Esther. I assume Dell will move away then, but she puts an arm around my waist.

"Is this all right?" she asks.

I nod.

"Did you pay the deathkeepers to make her up like this?"

"Morticians," she says. "They're called morticians in the city."

I knew that. It's another word from my list. Viet would be called a mortician in the city. But also a midwife. Keeper sits easier than either. Odd, after all this time it's getting harder, not easier, to pretend.

"You didn't answer my question."

She shrugs against me. "You didn't need to see her like that again."

Esther is kneeling beside Nelline. I wait for her scream, her questions, but she only goes rigid for a second. Then she takes Nelline's shoulders and lifts her, pulling at the simple gown to see down her back. After a moment I realize she's checking the tattoo. Whatever she sees must satisfy her, because she shakes her head and lays the body back down.

"It's not me," I say.

"I know. She has tattoos, but they're different from yours," Esther says.

Dell doesn't say anything, but her gaze shifts to my back like she can see the mark that's there through my clothes.

Esther is touching Nelline's face. "Is she from another world?"

"Yes. The journey back . . . it killed her."

"Does that happen often?"

I swallow. "It's happened before."

She looks at me for a long moment before nodding, and I feel like I've answered an entirely different question.

"I'll need her name. Her real name," she says.

"Nelline," I say.

Esther turns from us. She is gentle as she pulls the limbs out of the shroud and tucks the material beneath the body. She cuts a finger's worth of Nelline's hair and puts it into a jar, then grabs a handful of the dark sand and pours it over the strands.

She takes out a small vial of oil and pours it on the ground to make a paste, then uses the paste to make a cross on Nelline's forehead.

She's ready to begin.

Esther sits with her legs crossed. She closes her eyes and bends forward, her face by Nelline's. She will sit like this, taking deep but measured breaths, until she has finished whispering the first prayer into Nelline's ear. We are not allowed to hear. No one living is allowed to know it, only the practitioner and the dead. The superstitious believe that if you can make out the words, your time is soon coming. Most people look away so they don't risk even interpreting the shape of the words.

Oddly, though I'm not the one meditating, a calm comes over me, a spell woven by the warm heat and my sister's barely audible prayer. The minutes of inactivity should pass like an eternity, but when she finally straightens and opens her eyes, it's too soon.

"*So let it be done,*" she says, and the first part of the funeral has finished.

Next, Esther lights a cigar and sets it aside. Using her fingers, she draws a symbol in the sand that looks like a big cross, with little crosses filling in the four sections around it. Lastly, she draws an awkward number seven over it all.

She sees me watching. "To open the gate," she says.

I should reply *I know* or *Of course,* but I'm tired of lying so I just nod.

She closes her eyes, letting the smoke from the cigar waft around her and Nelline. I don't know how long she waits, or what she is waiting for, but suddenly she opens her eyes. The door must be open, because she repeats the ritual, only this time drawing a different symbol on her left side. This one looks like an outlined cross filled in with stars, with coffins on either side.

Esther takes from her pack another bottle that smells identifiably alcoholic and pours it over each symbol, making a puddle. Then she reaches for the cigar, which has by now burnt down enough that she can add a little ash to each side too.

She closes her eyes to wait for the second symbol's work. I don't know how she senses it, but she opens her eyes at the exact moment the cigar stops burning.

Esther stands, and the second part is finished.

Now it is the final part. The only portion of the funeral I've ever been able to see from my usual position in the back of the crowd. This is the long prayer. We have to witness and repeat it to send Nelline on her way. It doesn't seem like there are enough of us to help her make the journey, so I'm glad when Mr. Cheeks steps closer to join in.

Like all things with the death ritual, the prayer is broken into three parts.

Esther stands and faces the sky, because the first part is not being spoken to us or Nelline, but some great beyond.

"Holy host above, I call as your servant, sanctify our actions this day. Receive this child into your arms that she might pass in safety from this crisis. Forgive our living and our dead, those present and those absent, our young and our old. Whomever you keep alive, keep him alive in you, and whomever you cause to die, cause him to die with hope. Wash her with dirt and ash and oil and mercy. Give her a home better than her home and a family better than her family. Admit her to the city, where living beings have no pains, but receive only pleasure. Where the rain always comes, and the sun is kind. Where swans, peacocks, and parrots sing.

"Make her grave spacious and fill it with light."

We repeat the last line three times. Dell and I move forward to the body. Next we will send Nelline away, so this is our last chance to give her a message. I kneel down first. I hadn't intended to give a secret for the dead to carry, but when I get close the whisper comes out of me.

"I'm so sorry, Nelline. Tell Caramenta I'm sorry about her too. And tell her I wish it was me. Every time it happens, I wish it was me."

I move and Dell leans forward. I'm surprised she has a message for Nelline, or some other dead, but she stays beside the body longer than I do. When she's done, we each grab a strap on the bag and carry her body to the bog. We slide her off of the bag and for a moment she floats on top of the viscous liquid. But then, slowly, Nelline begins to sink.

Esther turns her back to us, and says the second part of the prayer to the dead.

"*Nelline, I am commending you into the arms of the earth, the preserver of all mercy. I am returning you to everlasting peace, and to the denser reality of the creator of all. Don't be scared. Don't regret. Whatever time you had, it was enough. Whatever you accomplished, it was enough. We will remember your good deeds for the rest of our lives. We will forget your wrongdoings forever. Thank you, thank you, thank you, for spending your time in the dirt with us.*"

We wait for the bog to consume her. It is quicker than waiting for the body to be shoveled in like an earth burial, but it is much, much quieter. I can't keep the words from the send-off from repeating in my head. *Don't be scared.* Was she scared? Of course she was. She had no training in traversing. She didn't understand what was happening, why she had to die for following me. She must have been terrified. But was she scared *anymore*? Did she feel anything? Did she have enough consciousness to find her way back to peace? Or was that terror in the dark the last thing she would ever know, for all eternity?

Esther doesn't turn back to us until the body is submerged. The final part of the prayer is for our benefit. Nelline is gone.

"*The phenomenon of death is just the separation of the astral body from the physical body. It is the five elements of the body returning to their source. In the divine plan, every union must end with separation. Whether it was now, twenty years ago, or twenty years in the future, you were always going to lose her. We are pilgrims at an inn. When we leave is immaterial, because we are only meant to leave.*"

There is comfort in the inevitability. It makes my part in her story unremarkable. I didn't change her fate; I don't have that power. My presence just changed her timing. We were always going to separate. We must always separate. Time is a flat thing and we are always separating. When we are together we are already gone.

"*I take refuge in the dirt. I take refuge in the ash. I take refuge in the oil.*"

We chant the affirmations three times.

"*I go to the dirt for refuge. I go to the ash for refuge. I go to the oil for refuge.*"

When we finish, Esther says "*So let it be done*" for the last time, and then it is.

\

MR. CHEEKS HELPS Esther build a small fire as we wait for the sun to go down. Only once it is no longer visible in the sky can we leave without a guilty conscience. Leaving in the light means you don't really care if the dead find their way. Only the truly arrogant arrange morning funerals, putting that much faith in the devotion of their loved ones and that little stock in the strength of the Ashtown sun.

Dell's cheeks and ears are turning the telling pink of an outsider, and she goes to wait in the runner's vehicle before it can graduate to a full burn. When only half the sun is still visible Esther finishes at the fire and brings me the mourning candle. It looks like oil, but it's just wax that hasn't cooled yet. Inside will be the lock of hair that Esther took, and dark sand from the place beside Nelline's grave.

"I don't need that," I say when she offers it. "We weren't that close."

She looks at me square, a sign I've entered into an argument I won't win. "You are as close to her as anyone ever can be. You are her," she says, and shoves the still-warm jar into my hands.

"It . . . doesn't work like that. Being the same isn't the same as being close," I say, but I clutch the jar anyway.

Esther gives a satisfied smile. "Light it when you want to talk to her. Or when you want to remember. It will run out when you don't need her anymore."

That part I know is a lie. I couldn't afford a full burial when my mother died, but Exlee paid for my mother's candle. It ran out too quickly. I still needed her. I still do.

After I take the mourning candle I think, and fear, that she'll go back to giving dirty looks to the runner, who is now crouched by the bog watching the horizon for signs that the night predators are waking. Instead, she stays with me.

"Do you know what I have to do to prepare for this? To make myself worthy of ushering the dead?"

It's a trap. The answer is no, but it should be yes, so I stay quiet.

"I have to be anointed in oil and wholly cleansed. I go to a cave known only to me, my father, and the one who will take over my duties if I ever leave or die. There is a hidden spring there. I drink from the spring, and bathe in its waters to become pure. Afterward, my apprentice works holy oil through my hair."

"Sounds . . . slippery."

"You can say it sounds strange. Even when I was the apprentice I thought so."

"You apprenticed?"

She looks at me. "I used to prepare Caramenta."

Caramenta. Not *you*.

CHAPTER THIRTEEN

H ow long have you known?" I ask. I realize now that she wasn't checking the body to see if it was me; she was checking to see if it was her real sister.

"From the very beginning."

My mind stutters. I think back to every interaction we've ever had, and all along she knew I wasn't her sister. A phone call stands out. When I was getting ready for the dedication, it was Esther who called to tell me Joriah might come.

. . . *you remember. Tall, red hair? He moved out here for a little while when we were young, but then left for the deep wastes as a missionary.*

She wasn't making small talk. She was feeding me information.

"Was it the tattoos?"

When I realized my mother was still alive here, that Caramenta had a family, I rushed off to see them. I still had tattoos on my forearms then. I thought I kept them covered, but if Esther was used to bathing Caramenta naked, she would have known something was off.

"No."

"The way I talked?"

"You certainly sound more like her now than you did at first. But no. I knew you weren't her because you brought me a gift."

I remember that. I was always the youngest around my mother's friends and colleagues. I didn't know what a twelve-year-old girl would like, much less a twelve-year-old girl from the Rurals. But I wanted to bring her something, because I had a little sister and first impressions matter even if she didn't know it was a first impression. I settled on some strawberry lip gloss, which my mother quietly "lost," and some dried flowers pressed into a necklace, which Esther was allowed to keep.

"She would have known not to bring you lip gloss," I say.

"She wouldn't have cared enough to try. Caramenta hated me."

"What?"

Esther wasn't half as spoiled as she could have been for being the Rural leader's heir. She was kind when she didn't even have to be. Who could hate her?

"Cara had a thing about men, and boys. She liked Michael, she loved Father, but she had no use for me. As I got older, it was like I was worse than in the way. It was like she saw me as some kind of obstacle. A problem. She made things . . . hard for me. I don't know what I would have done if that offer hadn't come in from the city. She didn't want to take it, but Dad thought the money would help out here. She said she'd do it for no more than a year. In my head, I thought, *Oh good, I'll be thirteen before she moves back. Plenty old enough to run away.*"

"Jesus, Essie." I swallow my reaction, a horror-concern cocktail that's years too late. "Thirteen is too young to run away. So is eighteen, by the way, for a girl from the Rurals."

She smiles at me—nice, wide, and bright—like she doesn't know I'm not her sister.

"But I didn't have to leave. Because things changed when you came back. You didn't scheme with Mom anymore, and you smiled at me. I'd been praying for Cara to become different. I hadn't known exactly what I was asking for . . . but I wasn't sorry. Even after I was old enough to realize you being here meant she must have died working, I wasn't. I prayed for you, and you came. To regret that would be to reject a miracle."

That's twice now someone called me a miracle. And again it comes from the mouth of someone whose sibling I killed.

"How did it happen? Did Eldridge really think they could replace her without anyone noticing? Was it to avoid paying out the death benefits?"

I shake my head.

"You know why she was recruited?" I ask.

"Because she died on a lot of worlds and you can't travel to a place where you're still alive." She says it like she's twelve again, reciting the facts of traversing exactly as they were first explained to her.

"Right. And if you try to go to a place where you're still alive, it kills you. Usually. Almost always, with the very rare exception. She tried to come to my world, and died because I was there. I found her body. Eldridge doesn't . . . actually know I'm not Caramenta."

Her eyes go wide and her mouth goes small as she processes that I am not the company's contingency plan, just a first-class grifter.

"No one knows? Dell?"

"Just you," I say. "I didn't have a good life. My mother is the same person as here, but she never made it to the Rurals. She died when I was sixteen, and I didn't have a lot of options. When I saw Caramenta's body, when I heard Dell saying she was bringing her back . . . I didn't even care where I was going. But I got lucky. I got you. And your family. And an apartment in the city."

She takes a breath and looks back over the horizon at the nearly downed sun. She's giving more thought to her response than I gave to looting a body and taking its name, and she's younger now than I was then.

Finally, she makes a decision and looks back at me.

"I understand that the multiverse means there are many of you, and some live and some die. But I think, I *believe,* there is a reason for those who live. Death can be senseless, but life never is. There's a reason you're here and she's not."

"People get lucky every day."

"Is it easier for you to believe in chance than the will of the universe?"

"Yes? Obviously?"

She shakes her head at me. These days she only looks truly young when I'm irritating her. I reach up to wrap an arm around her neck, kissing her head the way she hates because it makes her feel small. I need her to be small. I need her to be small and stationary and easy to protect forever.

"You're a pain," she says. "But I'm still not sorry I wished for you."

When we finish talking I notice the sun has mostly set. I hadn't heard Dell leave the car, but she's walking quickly back from the bog now, like she's running from something. I go to the bog's edge to investigate. The surface is a darkness so still and total it may as well be the hatch. I will Nelline to sink down into the perfect black until she comes out the other side, going home the way she came.

Mr. Cheeks starts his car, and the headlights shine on something in the liquid. I can't reach it, and it's sinking slowly, so I lean down until I can make it out. At first, I think it must be a rock, the kind from the mountain that contains enough metal to wink if the light hits it right. But then I recognize its shape: an Eldridge collar, fully intact, sinking to a place no one will ever find it.

I look over my shoulder, but Dell is already in the vehicle, staring at her hands.

\

ESTHER STAYS THE night with me, and we hardly sleep for all our talking. She asks me questions she couldn't ask Caramenta, or any other Ruralite, even though I try to answer as if I am one of them. She even asks about my last job. I don't hold back, so by the time I'm finished my little sister knows everything about me. Nearly. I don't mention the note, because I don't want her to worry, but I give her everything else.

I thought she'd get caught up in the murder, but not my teenage sister, who'd squealed like a teapot when she'd heard about me dating Nik Nik in my old world.

"Wait, so he had the hots for you on this other world too?"

"No . . . maybe . . . it doesn't matter. It just means Nik Nik's type is consistent across the universes. I probably remind him subconsciously of his mother or something twisted like that."

"Does he remind you subconsciously of your father?"

"Wait, what?"

"'Cause you had the hots for him twice now too."

Her eyes are wide as she looks up at me. She's sitting cross-legged on my bed with her hair braided for sleep.

"I did not."

"Some things are inevitable."

"Nothing is inevitable," I say. Nik Nik is the tide I've been kicking against for the better part of a decade, and I have to keep kicking because I'll drown in him as surely as a tar pit.

"Besides, I don't want him."

"Who do you want?"

I hesitate. Only the most hardcore Ruralites have issues with the way the rest of Ashtown looks at gender and sexuality as a casual gradient. But Esther is a leader's daughter.

I say it quick, because I don't want to pretend to be something I'm not with her.

"Dell."

She goes stiff, then tilts her head more in disbelief than disgust.

"You're really nothing like her, are you?"

"Dell?"

"Cara." She starts picking at the edge of the comforter. "I saw her once helping a congregant, a sweet girl, Sarah, who had an obvious crush on her. I told her I thought they looked nice together and she got mad. It didn't make sense, because no one cares, maybe some of the ancients but no one *really*. But she was so angry . . . she started being really cruel to Sarah after that. Which I guess means I was wrong."

"No," I say, "it means you were right."

I'm starting to understand Caramenta now, a girl who started out just like me, but had been given the kind of stability and care I only dreamt about. She'd want to be perfect to make sure she could never get thrown away again, even if that meant hating anything in herself that strayed the slightest bit.

"And Caramenta *really* didn't like Dell. I think she even filed a complaint against her once during training."

"Seriously? No wonder she hates me."

Esther's lips quirk. "You still think she hates you? That she attended a funeral in the Ash and dropped that kind of money to get you to the bogs because she hates you?"

"Money means nothing to her. It was probably less than she spends on a good dress."

But the argument is weak and my little sister—who looks all of fourteen in the T-shirt and pajamas I just bought her—is right. Dell is being kind.

When Esther hugs me goodbye in the morning, carrying a bag full of the lotions and cosmetics I'd been saving for my next visit, I ask her to come back. The next raid of her explosives stockpile is less than a week off, and I want her to spend that night with me, if just to keep her from standing in front of the pantry doors armed with only a rolling pin. She shakes her head, but promises not to do anything stupid. Before she leaves, she calls me by my real name.

I watch to make sure she meets Michael on the other side of the wall, and the whole time I'm thinking that now, if I died here, Esther could bury me properly. Before, it would have been under the wrong name. I never would have made it through to where I belonged. It's a morbid comfort, but still a comfort, to know that even on the wrong Earth someone carries your name.

\

"WHERE DID YOU get this?" Jean asks.

Since Jean went to meet Adam right after my debriefing, I've had to wait until my first day back to bring him the note. I've been watching him read it carefully. At first, the shock on his face was total. But then it gave way to anger. I made the right choice. He didn't send it.

"Someone left it on my door."

"Did you see them on your cam?"

I shake my head. "They were careful. I'm guessing they went with paper because digital messages can be traced."

"Or they just know how you like paper."

"I doubt they're trying to get on my good side. It sounds like a threat."

"You think so?" he says, in a way that tells me he doesn't. "Are you going to go?"

"I have to."

"You don't. Leave the note with me. I'll get it sorted."

"I didn't tell you so you could fix it," I say, then trail off because I don't know why I did tell him.

I shove the note back in my pocket, and Jean takes the hint that I'm done talking about it. For the rest of our meeting we go over results from my practice test with the updated information, and I'm unsurprised by the light in his eyes.

"This is really good stuff, Cara. Excellent work. I was only concerned about the memorization, but your reports have gotten cleaner too. You've really used your time off to your advantage."

He's so proud that it hurts me not to smile back. When I try, his face drops.

"What's wrong?" he asks.

"Nothing, it's just . . . don't you think I'm going to miss it? I'm giving up world walking for a desk."

He leans back in his chair like I'm a virus he doesn't want to catch. "A desk on the sixtieth floor. With opportunities to climb up."

"How many stories up am I when I traverse?"

He shakes his head, but a slow smile spreads across his face. "It's been a long time. I'd almost forgotten . . . there's nothing else like it, and I won't pretend there is."

"So, maybe I don't go for analyst. Maybe I go for a Maintenance position, something that will still get me sent—"

"No." He says it more harshly than he's ever said anything to me. "Maintenance is phased out too. This equipment is self-repairing. If you don't go for the analyst job the only place for you to go is home."

His snapping surprises me, and I want to remind him that I'm not actually one of his grandchildren. Instead, I nod.

"Okay, okay. I'll do the test. Analyst is better than nothing. I was just . . . I don't know, dreaming."

His smile is back. "I just don't want to see any of us fail."

I don't know if he means traversers or black people or people from outside in general, but I accept the explanation.

He looks down at his hands, and I know what he's going to say before he says it.

"Cara, about the note."

"I'm not leaving it with you."

"Please . . . don't go to this meeting."

"I'll be fine. *I know what happened on 175.* It's not even a proper threat. They're probably just trying to blackmail me. I'll show them my bank account and then we'll both walk away weeping."

He shakes his head, but doesn't say anything else.

Only after I'm out and on my way to my first pull do I realize I missed something: Jean never asked what happened on 175.

\

I DON'T REALIZE I've developed a fear of traversing until it's too late.

I hadn't been afraid as I made my way to the elevator to meet Dell. Sure, I'd hesitated to get in until a co-worker behind me—Maintenance, I'm guessing, given the black jumpsuit—cleared his throat and growled *It's open* at me. But that hadn't been fear, that had been my profound desire to go home. That had been the certainty that I didn't belong— not in this office, not in this city, not even in this world. What does it mean to miss the taste of ash on your lips? What does it mean to crave something toxic?

No, only after I'm dressed and veiled and Dell slides the Misery Syringe into my pocket does terror come for me. Seeing the syringe, a reminder of what can and has gone wrong, puts the taste of iron back in my mouth. When I climb the ladder to the hatch, my hands are shaking.

I've just landed inside when I start to panic. It's dark, true dark, and even though there hasn't been enough time, I'm sure I've already left. I'm hurtling toward a place I don't belong, but I'm not going to make it. She'll never let me. Nyame will bite through me, then rip along the perforations her teeth create. And I'll deserve it, because I used her to kill. Seeing Adra's death in the dark was as much a prophecy for me as it was for Nelline. It just took longer for the universe to catch me. Such a stupid mouse, to run back into the trap.

I feel her claws around my torso. I pound at the hatch door, but it's too late. It was always too late. Words from Nelline's funeral come back at me. This was always going to happen. I, maybe more than anyone else, have only existed to die.

Suddenly there is light, a starburst that feels like the end of the world even after I recognize Eldridge's traversing room.

Dell has lifted me half out of the hatch and into her lap on the platform above, her hand on the back of my neck. Even in this she's not sweet, not gushing. She is squeezing my neck with a firm and clinical distance.

"Breathe, Cara," she says. "Breathe now."

And I do. At first it's just short, panicked gasps, but slowly I take in more air and hold it longer. My panic is gone but I'm still wrapped up in her.

"I used to be stronger than you," I say, the space under my arms already sore from her sure, hard yank.

"You've spent too long avoiding physical training. You're light as a bird."

"I'm okay now," I say.

She takes her hand from the back of my neck. "Would you like me to call Sasha? Or . . . do you have someone else in the city I should contact?"

"I've never had anyone else."

"You used to. What was his name? The one with the"—she waves a hand around her head—"the hair."

She's just trying to get me talking, but it works. Impossibly, I laugh.

"Marius? From four years ago? After his mother threatened to have a breakdown, the novelty of a kept Ashtown creature wore off."

"He called you that?"

"No . . . she told him we can't love. That people from Ashtown can't. That we don't even really feel, we just survive."

"I think you've proven that's not true."

She manages to make crawling look elegant as she moves to the ladder and descends to the office floor. But I'm staring at her, too struck to move.

"What?" she asks.

"You're right. I . . . it's not true."

I was never sure. For years, I've been unsure I was capable of anything but ambition. I think back to the days lost crying for Nelline. Feeling guilty for Adra. Feeling hope for Nik Nik. Sometimes you have to bleed to know you're human. I am afraid, panicked, and ashamed, but I am also grateful. I hadn't thought all this misery would bring its own gift.

"I'd like to sit in the hatch."

Her first expression, before she masks it with her constant disapproval, is worry.

"I don't think that's wise."

"Please. I just want to sit until I can stand it. Promise me you won't try to send me anywhere. Just let me stay there."

She sits. "Do whatever you want. I doubt we'll get a pull in today anyway."

She's typing into a pad, no doubt pushing back deadlines because of me. I drop back into the hatch.

It's easier this time, to slide into the dark. The perfect black isn't such a surprise, an impossible thing my mind has lightened in my memories in the weeks we've been apart. And it is a *we*. I see that now. What felt like suffocating on my first attempt feels like entwining the second time. I'm not so far gone that I think the pitch-dark space is sentient, but we are partners. I wish I knew what material made this sphere possible, but even asking will get me fired, labeled, and perma-banned from Wiley. Or worse. I can't picture Adam Bosch ruling with Adra's iron fist, but Eldridge's secrets have never leaked, even across worlds, and that doesn't happen purely through kindness inspiring loyalty.

I sit in the dark until my heartbeat goes so quiet it's not there at all.

I press my cuff. "I'm ready. Send me."

Dell's reply, when it finally comes over the cuff, is cool. "Absolutely not."

I climb halfway out of the hatch, glaring down at Dell seated at her desk. She's still not looking up.

"Dell. Program the pull."

She sighs, but eventually addresses me. She stands first, of course. Dell is taller than me, like all Wiley City residents are typically taller than Ashtown's people—a result of never having to guess where break-fast is coming from as a kid, or not growing up where only those small enough to hide from runners or be passed over for armed service had any chance of survival. I like addressing her from above. The way she has to tilt her head up makes her look open, vulnerable. I wonder if I look like that to her. Or if I looked like that to Nik Nik, the emperor being an exception to the rule of Ashtown's shortness, any of the times he tried to strangle me.

Dell leans with her fingertips spread out on the desk. "I am not going to approve this. What if you panic in transit? There's nothing I can do about it then. If you panic when you land and I have to bring you back it's a waste of a pull."

"So? I'm owed a wasted pull. Don't forget I did do the job on 175."

"You pulled one port on 175. You were supposed to pull four."

I wave my hand at the technicality. "Oh please. The backup ports carry so little intel that's not overlapping, it's really like I pulled from three and a half."

She tilts her head. "How do you know that?"

Oops.

I give her a look I hope passes for charming. "I'll tell you if you let me do this pull?"

She rolls her eyes.

"Oh, come on, Dell. It's my first day back and I don't want to waste it. What are you afraid of? Losing me?"

This hits home. She can keep denying me the pull, but then it will look like she cares.

"Fine," she says, sitting. "Is your veil still secured?"

I nod, feeling the tightness across my cheeks.

"Close the hatch."

She must have shut down the tuner, because I spend enough time in the dark for it to warm back up. For a second, I'm sure she went home, leaving me here as a lesson for pushing back. But just when I'm about to give up I hear the whisper that Dell calls a signal and Jean and I call a petition. It surrounds me and embeds in my skin. And just like that I'm traversing.

At the edges of the total darkness are packs of swirling light, bending out of shape, gravity turning beams into rings. It's been years since I've really paid attention to the act of traversing, the feeling of weightlessness, of being nowhere and also the center of everything. I feel the presence I will probably always call Nyame now, and that Dell will always tell me is just a mix of pressure and hallucination. Nyame is not angry with me. Her touch is gentle, a welcome back, as if I've always belonged here and my absence has been noted.

It opens up something in me, maybe not as deep as what I felt sharing time with my sister, but close. It feels like being seen, and how long have I been missing that? Suddenly I want my job again, not because I'm terrified of carving out a living in Ash, but because my job is to walk among the stars. How can I have viewed it as a paycheck for so long when I would pay to do this? I see now that it is a gift, not a life-line.

One day soon traversers will be obsolete, and I was so focused on the next position I hadn't considered what that means. But even if I get an analyst job with a pay raise and citizenship and two bedrooms on a higher floor, I will have lost something I can never get back.

CHAPTER FOURTEEN

The meeting place is on 80, so before I go I dress in the kind of clothes I learned to value by watching Dell. I'd checked before, and the coordinates on the note lead me to a public garden owned by Adam Bosch, which adds evidence to the "employee" column on my list of suspects. A runner would probably want to meet somewhere low and populated. Another piece of evidence in that column is the wording: *I know what happened on 175* instead of the more proper, *I know what happened on* Earth *175*. It's a shorthand we'd use, but anyone outside the company would feel the need to specify that they were talking about an Earth and not a street address or elevator line.

Bosch has kept this public garden since he purchased the block-sized mansion next door. It's a known place to spot him, either on his balcony or when he takes his own turn in the massive greenspace. I used to believe the garden sightings were just a man oblivious to his own celebrity taking a walk and getting caught. But now that I've seen how much shine Adra donned, I'm sure he drinks in attention like cracked ground drinks rain.

The garden is full of frivolous flowers and fruit-bearing trees, half edible and half purely aesthetic. It looks like he did what any of us would do—picked out the brightest flowers with the biggest petals he could find, the kind of plant that would be singed to brown ash by the time noon hit back home.

I grab an apple and sit at a bench where I can pretend to watch a fountain while watching the park entry. I'm looking, I realize, for Starla. Who else knows where I live and stands to gain from bringing me down? She was in charge of 175 for eight years; maybe she established some way of getting info and put two and two together. She was deported, but the walls aren't perfect, especially if you have friends on the inside. And she must have had friends, right? Even if I never saw them. I couldn't have been all she had.

But I don't see the waist-long shine of her dark-brown hair, and the bright silks she favored would stand out in this crowd. More than half of the visitors are in tight pants and the kind of boots that could keep you dry during a mudtide. Wiley City's upper class is appropriating the desert-dweller look in droves. No one's gone for the onyx teeth, rumors of loss of taste and a shortened life-span are probably enough to isolate that trend, but I see a few metal-tipped nails. Funny, there's no gold dust on the fingers. They don't want to be Exlee, only the emperor. Anyone from Ashtown would have made the opposite choice, because not only is Exlee's power greater, it's cleaner. Somehow using someone's need to keep them in line is less awful than using their fear.

I eat my apple slowly, but soon enough I find myself sliding teeth along the core, trying to milk the shavings of the fruit. A new one, lush and green instead of the red I've been devouring, appears over my head, held dangling by its stem.

Once I take it, Adra—Adam—walks around the bench to sit beside me. My heart pounds, but I try to keep my voice steady.

"I've heard stories about taking fruit from a man named Adam," I say.

"Pretty sure that one was the other way around."

"I guess I wouldn't know."

It's been a long time since our first conversation, when I hinted I wasn't really from the Rurals. He gave me fruit then, too, but I hadn't hesitated to eat it. I have no reason not to trust him, but panic washes from my head down just the same. My heart and skin are reacting like he's Adra, like I'm in danger. I picture that little piece of Nelline's ghost in my chest, roughing up my ribs because I'm talking to the enemy.

He looks sideways quickly, twice. Most of us wear cuffs or carry fobs, but Bosch has one of the few ocular ports. They say it allows all of your messages and news and research to come up instantly on the side of your vision. Messages are cleared by looking left, and notifications are shut down by closing your eyes for five seconds. They also say the first wave was an utter failure, that you have to use eyedrops every four hours or you'll want to rip the whole thing out . . . but probably not to his face.

"What are you doing here?" I ask, like it's not his garden.

"Meeting you, of course."

"You . . . you left the note?"

"Well, not me personally. But yes, I had it left."

His face is lined in that soft and perpetual smile that makes him look like a puppy even though he's the smartest man in the city. So different from Adra, but not different enough for this to feel like anything but talking to a ghost. It's too much. I look away from him and for the first time notice we are the only ones in the garden.

"Where is everyone?"

"In other parts of the park. The paths leading to this area were redirected due to maintenance," he says.

"Maintenance?"

"Maintenance . . ." He waves his hand, as if to remove the meaning of the word, so much an emperor there is no excuse for me not having seen it before. "It's almost always code for something else, you know."

I nod like I understand, even though I don't. I'm out of my depth. I hold up the apple. "I prefer the red."

"I had to guess. You didn't leave enough skin for the cameras to pick it up. I figured I'd bring you a new one before you attempted to swallow the core."

"I like to finish what I start," I say.

"Do you?"

From anyone else it would be some kind of sexual innuendo and I'd be disappointed in Adam but not surprised. But his tone is charmless and menacing, and it penetrates the dreamlike encounter. I remember all at once who he is, who I am, and that I'm not behaving like someone who doesn't know he's the son of Nik Senior.

I move slightly away from him. "Why did you summon me here?"

"Summon?" he says.

Fuck. Summon is what emperors do. I should have said *invite.* I'm blending him with Adra again.

He's staring at the bench, at the new space I've put between us. "Don't be afraid of me."

Easier said, and all that.

"Why am I here?"

"I wanted to make sure you weren't her," he says. "Two of you came back."

"But you said, 'I know what happened on 175.' What did you mean?"

He doesn't speak, but I can wait him out. I begin on my second apple. The first taste is always too much. He must be decades out of Ashtown to think anyone from there would prefer the green. Sourness isn't a novelty back home; it's in all the fruit we grow, the price we pay for our little bit of sweet. This apple just tastes like Ashtown's best efforts. But it's still free food, and I'm still me, so I keep eating.

"Do you know I'm the only one who sits here? This bench is always unused."

This is not an answer to my question, but I play along.

"Really? But it's the only one in the shade."

"For that to have value you'd have to know the sun can be dangerous. No one here does."

". . . But you do?"

He takes time answering. I see him swallow twice before he finally nods. His confirmation puts me on edge. I am no one, nothing, why tell me this? Nelline's ghost is screaming in my chest and the sour in my mouth is nesting like a rock in my stomach.

"I suspect you learned my name on Earth 175, but I'll ask you not to say it."

"I'm not going to blackmail you."

He smiles. "But you thought about it."

"Only for, *maybe,* a second."

He laughs loud and clear. "God, you remind me of home. I look forward to working with you more closely."

"This is about a promotion?"

It can't be, not really. He would have just come to my office, or had me come up to his. He didn't need to leave a cryptic note, or empty out a public garden, if this is just about a job.

He tilts his head. There is a famous picture from over a decade ago—it originally ran on the front of a news projection but now a version of it is blown up in the lobby of Eldridge—of a twentysomething Adam Bosch at the moment they figured out the frequency to send an animal to another world. The picture was taken right before the sequence was discovered, and it captured the genius at work just before his breakthrough. He is giving me the same look now that he gave the problem of worlds.

"This area of 175 is going through a leadership transition, and it wasn't before you got there." He turns, stretching his arm along the back of the bench but not touching me.

"Does that matter?"

"It does." His smile, at last, has wavered. "I summoned you here because you killed me."

\

ALL THE WORDS I could say crowd at the front of my mouth until only the smallest can squeeze through.

"No. Yes. What? You . . . yes."

His next laugh is loud enough to echo off his house. He laughs like Nik Nik, utterly unconcerned about disturbing others. I'd envisioned many reactions to him finding out I killed Adra, but glee was not on my list.

"Jean's always said you weren't the killing kind, but he doesn't know Ashtown stock like I do. Your bonus will be on your next check, but I was hoping you'd be interested in more work like that."

"I'm not Ash stock," I say, but then the rest catches up with me. "Bonus?"

"Yes, the bonus."

"My bonus . . . for killing you."

Things are connecting too slowly, and I keep looking at him, waiting for the world to coalesce into something that makes sense.

"It's more than generous. We would have gotten to him eventually, but 175 was always so paranoid. You've saved me a lot of hassle."

Why hasn't everyone else figured out how to traverse? Or have they?

No . . . they haven't.

Why not?

Nelline would have gotten it right off, but it's taken me this long. What better way to stop an invention from being made again than by killing every version of the man who invented it? Even if that man is yourself?

The sour taste in my mouth now is all bile and no apple. I let the fruit slide from my hand and roll into the grass.

"Do you feel it? When they die, do you feel it in your chest?"

His mouth opens, then closes. "Of course not," he says, but he has to look away first.

"How many of you are left?"

"About two dozen."

Three times what I have.

He's uncomfortable with my responses, obviously not in line with what he remembers from "Ashtown stock." I've played this meeting badly, but he's played it worse.

"You don't need to decide right away," he says. "Think it over."

I stand up too quickly. It looks like I'm running away . . . because I am.

"I've got a meeting with Jean." This is true. Jean just doesn't know it yet.

"Wait," he says, and I have to.

He stands and I try to look impatient, not disgusted or terrified.

"Take care. I pay close attention to those who carry my secrets."

It's not a threat, but it is. I should never have come here. There's no record of this meeting except the paper. I could disappear right now. I was safer when he thought I was just opportunistic and conscienceless. If he knows I'm horrified I become a liability, because people with morals do illogical things. I need to be Ashtown in his eyes.

When I open my mouth, it feels like Nelline is speaking.

"You get me that bonus, and I'll be quiet as the river."

He smiles wider now, because geniuses like it when things make sense, I guess.

"I'll personally make sure it's on your next check."

"Appreciate it," I say, all teeth, making a polite threat of my own.

When the gate to his garden opens I exhale and head down to 70, where Jean lives. It's an area mostly populated by new-money-rich immigrants. The houses are still expensive and it has just as many parks as 80, but people from higher floors travel here like it's a novelty. I don't bother going to Jean's house, because I know he'll be at his wife's restaurant. She advertises it as authentic Ivorian cuisine, but Jean has confided in me that she doesn't make it right for the public. I believe him, because the leftovers he brings me from their house have twice the smell and spice as what she serves for pay.

When I walk in I clock four of Jean's grandchildren serving customers while two of his children shout in the kitchen. Jean is occupying his usual booth in the back, though he often wanders around and talks to patrons about his homeland or his old job, depending on whether or not they recognize him. They usually recognize him.

He's sitting now, and as I slide into the booth across from him I wish

I'd spent the walk planning what to say. As it is, only one word comes out: *Murderer.*

I want to say it angrily, but it comes out like a plea. Like I break my own heart by saying it when I wanted to break his.

He folds his hands.

"I told you not to go to that meeting."

I open my mouth again, but he holds up a finger and looks over my shoulder.

"Sita," he says, and moments later a granddaughter, or great-granddaughter now that I think of it, appears at his arm. Her hair is buzzed short and it's a redder brown than the other children's, but she has Jean's round cheekbones and his wide, bright smile.

She pulls out a paper pad and a marker. She can't be more than five, and the pad is covered in stickers.

"Two juices please. Ginger and tomi," he says.

She pretends to write our order by drawing stars and what looks like a fat tree with skinny arms, all while nodding seriously. Jean kisses her on the head and lets her go.

I'm silent until she comes back with the drinks, spilling a third of each before setting them down and walking away.

"Did you call her over because you thought it would soften me?"

"I called her over because I was thirsty," he says, and then has the audacity to smile. "And because I knew it would soften you."

I keep my face dead. He doesn't need to know that the child has utterly spoiled my rage, leaving only hurt.

"I'm right, aren't I? You know what Adam is doing? You knew he was the one I was meeting?"

Jean takes his time, sipping deep from his ginger juice, though I leave my tamarind untouched. I'd never had it before him, and I don't want the taste to remind me that it is the least of things he's done for me.

"I knew he's been wanting to recruit you to wetwork since you were hired. When I saw the note . . . I assumed it was him," he says.

"And you've just been letting him get away with this the whole time?"

He takes another sip, then looks at me. "Do you remember where I came from? What I was?"

Somehow I am the one who feels ashamed. I can't look at him when I answer. "I know what some of your other selves were."

"Say it."

"A child soldier. That's why you were a traverser candidate. You . . . you died a lot."

He twists his glass along the table. "By the time Eldridge found me I was already old enough to think I knew how my life would go. Too many children and too little money, living in a desert not unlike your Ashtown. Mr. Bosch brought me here, showed me the world, and yes I was valuable because I was rare, but I was also valuable because I was willing to make others even rarer."

"You killed the other Adams for him?"

"Hardly. Mostly his father did, or he killed himself as a teenager. So few made it out to Wiley City, he was never his own greatest challenger. There were others. Competition."

"Competition? He just killed any scientist who could do what he did? And you let him?"

He opens his hands. "There were not so many."

"If there's one, there's three hundred and eighty. If there's five there's . . . a fuckload. Jesus, Jean."

I set my hand down on the table hard enough that it lights up with menu selections. I slide them away because I want to do the same with him, with this information, with everything I'd ever wished was true about him.

"I've killed more for worse men, with far less reason. But this was all years ago. After I'd shown my loyalty, he decided I had more value as a traverser and face. By the time the scope of what we would need to do became clear, there was a department devoted to the . . . unpleasantness of maintaining a technological monopoly."

"There's a whole department? How . . ." But then it hits me: "Maintenance."

It's almost always code for something else, you know?

Adam told me himself, but he wasn't the first. Adra had raved about people in black trying to kill him, men who had disappeared before anyone else could see them.

"That's why you lost it when I said I wanted to join Maintenance. They're a kill squad."

"*Were*, Cara. You're years late to this. Occasionally some young upstart will make Mr. Bosch nervous, but for the most part Maintenance sits back and collects a check. I wasn't lying about them being obsolete. The only job I've heard of this year was another Maintenance worker who couldn't keep quiet. Which is why I didn't tell you. You have nothing to do with this. Your hands are as clean as my baby granddaughter's. You shouldn't die for these sins. And dying is all you will do if you try to expose Adam Bosch. I will tell him you're declining his offer. Take the analyst test. Spend the next four years doing an honest job and sending money back home and then when you get your citizenship you can go work somewhere else. It's too late for all of this."

"Just pretend Eldridge hasn't killed thousands of people?"

"Tens of thousands, and yes. Extend Eldridge the same courtesy you extended your other government. I don't know much about the history here, but I would guess the blood runners in your past saw as much judgment as the juntas in mine. Once they're in power, no one cares how they got there."

It doesn't matter how you got it. If you have it, it's yours.

Nothing says Ashtown like accepting mass murder without protest. Because that's what you do to survive. That's all Jean's asking me to do, to shut up and survive. I should be grateful he talked me down. I should have been able to talk myself down without coming here at all. I should have known to let the powerful man kill whomever he wants, just like I always have.

"When you came to Wiley City, didn't you want it to be better?"

"Warlord, emperor, CEO . . ." Jean shrugs. "No difference. You can't save the people he killed. You can only damn yourself. Unless you think some trial, some murder sentence, will please the dead?"

No, the dead won't thank me for trying to get Adam Bosch arrested. And if Adam Bosch mostly killed himself and people on other planets, the families of the victims wouldn't even know if he did go to trial.

I rub my face. "You're right."

"I know this is hard to accept, but you will see it is best. If you are still upset when you get promoted, just use some of your new salary to save lives back in your hometown. It all washes out."

He pushes my cup toward me, like he's offered everything from coffee to healing tonics hundreds of times in the last six years. If I accept it, it will mean nothing has changed. That I'm falling back into routine and looking past the bodies it took to pay my checks.

I drink every drop.

I won't act against Adam Bosch. Jean is right. This isn't the first time I've been kept by a man ruining other people's lives to hold on to power. What Jean doesn't know is that even when I intend to do nothing, I have to know the exact shape of the thing I am allowing to happen. Now, high up in Wiley City, I'll do the same thing Nik Nik drowned me for doing in Ashtown. I'll sit at my desk, and begin a list of names.

\

MY LIST GROWS and spreads in the days after my meeting. It started out small, a handful of scientists who expressed regret about Bosch's breakthrough because they'd been *so close*. Three names, all Wileyites, with a mortality rate that rivals mine. Those three represented just over a thousand murders, but rivals have continued dying off ever since.

My list now has fifty names, all dead across the majority of worlds, but none dead here. Killing on Earth Zero must be too real for Bosch, because while he dispatches his merry band of murderers to every other world, here he just buys the institutions of his rivals and runs them into the ground. He's aggressive in Wiley, but utterly ruthless in shutting down competition in every other walled city with even a half-functioning tech center. He doesn't even recruit the scientists, just leaves them to find work in another field. They must learn their lesson, because none have remained in interuniversal travel.

That kind of razing is a tactic I recognize from his father. It was Nik Nik who folded in upstarts, who turned any would-be rival gangs into sanctioned runners wearing his colors. Nik Senior would kill them all or leave them and their families without defense or supplies in the deep wastes. It is the descendants of his enemies who still haunt the edges of the wasteland, mouths blistered and minds rotted from two generations of toxic water and polluted plants.

I won't tell enforcement, but knowing how many dead I'm ignoring is like knowing how to spell the name of the demon who bought your soul. When I was with Nik Nik, I wrote the names of people he'd hurt in a book while wearing his gifts. That's all I'm doing now, looking Adam's crimes in the face while getting lightheaded over the size of the kill bonus he gave me.

It doesn't take long for Jean to call me, early enough in the morning for me to know he's not just checking in.

"You know I can see what my username is pulling up, right?"

"I'm not doing anything about it," I say, because that's what he's actually called to ask. "I just need to know."

He isn't really angry—irritated, maybe, but mostly concerned—so when he gives in with a sigh, it's more pre-planned theatrics than an actual shift in his mood.

"Get it out of your system, Cara," he says. "But keep it to yourself. Give Adam Bosch no reason to take his due."

"You make it sound like he's going to garnish my wages or something."

He clucks his tongue at my ignorance. "The only due powerful men recognize is a life—in service or in sacrifice."

Something about what he says slides into the back of my neck like a talon, and even after he hangs up I can't shake this new uneasiness. Only when I'm getting ready for work does it hit me: *The only due powerful men recognize is a life* . . . and the runners said they were coming to the Rurals to collect the emperor's due. I check the date on my cuff, but it's too late. If they stuck to their plan, they went last night. I'd forgotten, among all of the corporate espionage and murder and selling my soul, I'd forgotten that runners were coming for my sister's stash last night and she didn't want them to take it. I think about the star on the runner's throat on 175. Maybe the funeral wasn't the first time he'd seen her. Maybe he'd come for exactly what he had on another world. Or maybe Nik Nik decided to get power in the Rurals on this Earth the same way Adra claimed it there.

I press my cuff so I can call her, but before I can dial, it rings. When I see my family's number, I expect it to be someone saying Esther's name and calling me home through sobs, so when I hear her clear, even voice I calm instantly. I'm prepared for whatever comes next, because it is not the worst.

"You're okay?" I say. "I thought the runners were coming for you."

"Not me," she says. "They took him. Michael's gone."

In the background I can hear my mother, frantic and wailing while my stepfather tries to soothe her.

"Gone how?"

"There were runners here this morning. Mom thinks they kidnapped him."

Mom thinks means Esther doesn't. Which means he's run away with them, probably.

"I'm on my way."

I call Dell to let her know I won't be in. What would Bosch do if I didn't call in? Does the information I hold make me unfireable? He does have an entire murderous department standing around with too little to do, so probably best not to risk it.

It's midmorning when I make it home, but I'm already sweating in my Wiley City clothes. Esther offers me use of her closet, but I'd rather dehydrate than wear the light dresses of a Ruralite. My stepfather hugs me tight and I feel his wet face against my shoulder. I realize then that this man is too open for subterfuge, regardless of what he was capable of on 175.

"You were never letting the runners take powder from you, were you?" I ask.

Confusion clears his grief a little, but he shakes his head. "The missing powder? I think it was just Michael taking extra without logging it. He was practicing, probably."

Not practicing, stockpiling, because he knew he was leaving soon. The runners were only ever coming for him. He was the emperor's due all along.

"How long has he been gone?"

Daniel shakes his head. "I don't know. It was sometime in the night. Some of his clothes are missing, but most are still here."

Of course they are, because a Ruralite turning runner isn't exactly going to bring his collection of tunics. I bet he took only the white tank tops the boys here use as undershirts.

I turn to Esther. "Did you hear him go?"

I doubt there was a struggle, but Esther's room faces Michael's.

"No, I . . ." Esther looks down. "I stayed up in the storeroom all night."

Because she thought they were coming for her powder, and because I've never been able to make her listen to me. I tell myself her stubbornness was for the best. She would have tried to stop Michael, and this way she missed the runners entirely.

"I might know where"—I slide my gaze over to my mother—"they would have taken him. I'll see if he's there."

"It's too risky," Daniel says.

His concern allows me to separate the 175 version from this one. This is my stepfather, and he loves me. Or, he loves who he thinks I am and that's the best I've got.

"I'm a resident. They'll think twice before trying to hurt me. Plus, I have money, hopefully enough to buy him back."

Or to tempt them into casting him out. Runners are a loyal bunch, but if I can get to him before he takes his first mark they won't feel obligated to keep him.

"I'll go with you," Daniel says.

My mother squeals.

"If the head of the Rurals is seen at a runners' den, word will travel," Esther says. "I'll go. I do outreach in the heart of Ash all the time. It won't be unusual for me to be seen there."

There is no sound of distress from my mother at putting Esther in danger.

Daniel takes my sister's face in his hands. "Send both my girls out into that vile town? My most precious things?"

I doubt he even remembers that I was born in "that vile town" anymore, his mind rewriting Caramenta's history so it is no different from his Rural-born children.

"It will be fine," I say. "I'll keep her safe."

Daniel looks a little sad, but he smiles. "And who will keep you safe?"

I don't have an answer for that, but Esther does.

"You don't know, Father? God herself holds Cara in the palm of her hand."

I glare at my sister for what I think is a tease, but her face is open and sincere.

CHAPTER FIFTEEN

Three hundred and eighty-two worlds and I bet every Hangars Row smells just like this: sweat, dirt, gasoline, and smoke. It smells a little like the side rooms at the House, but mixed with a zoo. The smell hits me like a wall that is half revulsion and half memory, but I can tell it hits Esther harder, a hell of a smell for a girl raised around open earth and interior farms.

The space used to be a warehouse, back when corporations drilled and polluted our land, working even our children till their hands bled. They were based in cities like Wiley, but like all the city-based companies, they didn't adhere to any of the same labor laws once they weren't dealing with citizens. That's why the emperor had to send a message.

It only took a little murder and a lot of vandalism for those places to learn that whoever had given them access to the land had lied; Ashtown was not theirs to claim or pillage. The Blood Emperor himself disabled the last drill. Our water's been cleaner and our ground more steady ever since, or so the story goes. Even Eldridge's industrial hatch—the machine that brings in resources from other worlds—is careful to treat its Ashtown workers fairly, with runners checking in every so often to make sure.

The first runner to see us slides out from under her vehicle. The monstrosity she's working on is technically a bike, but the two tires are wider than any two ordinary car tires combined. She hisses a little at me, but nods at Esther.

"Thought you stuck to the alleys. No souls to save here and we don't need your food."

Esther's smile is different from Daniel's. It's calm and benevolent, but it leans close enough to a smirk that she never looks naïve.

"I would never bring aid here," she says. "I'm sure you all eat better than any in my congregation."

"Damn right we do."

"Mr. Scales, that's enough."

The runner turns away at the command, which means the one who gave it outranks her.

"Don't tell me you've caught another body?" Mr. Cheeks says when he sees us.

Mr. Scales ducks her head when Mr. Cheeks passes, bringing her chin so low they almost look the same height even though she's easily half a foot taller. He taps her on the shoulder, telling her she's not in trouble, and suddenly she's the tallest in the room again.

"No, I'm looking for someone. He's a new recruit. He would have arrived last night," Esther says. "I don't want to cause trouble, but I do need to speak with him."

Mr. Cheeks either doesn't realize *I don't want to cause trouble* is a threat or doesn't care, because he's already shaking his head. "Once a runner, a runner for life. Not even the princess of the Rurals can convert a runner."

"I'm just here to say goodbye. It's . . . he's my brother. Please."

Up until now I've been silent, not just because my sister has things under control, but because I wasn't sure how much she wanted to show. She's trusting this runner with the truth that Michael, the de facto prince of the Rurals, has defected.

"You're more polite when you need something," he says.

"Last time we met, I thought you were stealing from me."

He laughs a little at that, maybe surprised her distaste hadn't just stemmed from his occupation, or maybe just surprised she felt she had a right to be mad about theft.

"We've not skimmed from the Rurals in over a decade," he says.

"I know that now," she says. "I'm sorry I was short with you, but you have to let me see him."

I step forward. "He probably hasn't even taken marks yet. You don't owe him sanctuary," I say. "Name your price."

Mr. Cheeks stiffens. "Keep your money," he says before turning on his heel and disappearing.

We've been waiting for five minutes when I get the feeling Mr. Cheeks isn't coming back.

"This is my fault," I say.

"No," Esther says. "It is most decidedly mine."

"That other world? The place where I got stuck? Michael was a runner there. I should have warned you it was possible. When I heard the message, I should have known they weren't just coming for powder they didn't even know how to use."

She smiles for me, a kinder and less all-knowing version than she shows the world. "I have always known it was possible."

"If they bring him out here, do you have a plan?"

She pats her bag. "Of course."

Finally, the door opens. Michael enters with Mr. Cheeks following close behind. No, not Michael. He's gotten marks, one on each arm, which means he can never be Michael again.

"Esther, we're too late."

Her eyes are wet, but she's still smiling. "It's been too late since we were ten."

The two runners stand opposite us. Michael doesn't reach for his twin, and to her credit she doesn't reach for him. She holds her head high. From the outside, they could be strangers, representatives from bordering territories negotiating a contract.

"Mr. Cross, I presume," I say.

He flinches, and in his uncertainty I finally see a hint of the boy I've known for years.

"How did you know that?"

"Big sister knows a lot of things, like what a shit runner you'll be. You know they only want you because of the pyrotechnics. Runners haven't had explosives in years and you're too oblivious to know they're using you."

I don't pretend I won't hate him for this. This will tear apart Esther and my parents. Not to mention what it will do to Daniel's reputation. They'll say he was such a bad father his own son chose the life of grit and blood and oil.

He's going to yell at me, maybe for the first time in his life, but Esther moves.

"It's okay," she says, touching his arm. Her palm has landed on his mark. "Will you tell me what they mean?"

He looks over his shoulder to check with Mr. Cheeks.

"The one on the left is loyalty." I say. "It's always the first. The one on the right . . ." I squint, trying to remember a language I was last fluent in when I was Nik Nik's. "It means he has a partner in the field, I think."

"No," he says. When had his voice gotten so deep? When had he grown up?

He looks back at Esther. "It means half to a whole. Some runners get it to commemorate their partner, but I didn't."

Esther understands the tattoo is for her the same moment I do, and now it's easy to see the water in her eyes, though she seems determined not to cry.

"You'll need to stop using words like *commemorate*. I want you to fit in," Esther says. She manages to sound like she means it. She opens her satchel and pulls out a woven bag. "Food. I know they tend toward meats and bread and you're used to produce. It's just a little to help you while your body adjusts. I made you gloves. You should have gloves."

Inwardly I cringe, expecting the pastel gardening gloves Ruralites are known for, but the gloves Michael takes out of the pack are black and thick. They can't be leather, Ruralites don't do animal work, but she must have taken the material from their bright-day tarps. I can see a hint of silver dust adorning the knuckles.

"They'll protect your hands if you get near anything too hot."

She knows, I realize. She must have known he would go, and what he would do for them once he left. I wonder if she'd known this was an option the moment explosives went missing and she just chose to believe it was all the runners' doing.

"I thought you had a plan," I say.

"I do. I plan to love my brother, whatever life he chooses." He gasps at that, and she goes weak. She takes his hands. "The tunic has a high collar and long sleeves for a reason. Anything at all can be covered over."

He jerks away, but he keeps her package pulled tight against his chest. I make out the hard edges of something that is definitely not fruit or clothes. Because he never publicly preached I don't know which holy book Michael favored, but I'm guessing the book she's hidden in his things already has his name inside.

Michael doesn't hug her. He nods goodbye, then turns his back and stomps away. His steps are an awkward mimicry of the runners' march, but I'm sure he'll master it soon enough.

That leaves us with Mr. Cheeks, who looks no less bewildered than when we dared him to drive to the bogs.

"He came to us," he says. "We didn't poach."

She nods. "I know. I don't blame you. My father might, but I won't."

After that they just stare at each other. I look from one to the other, but neither is looking at me. I clear my throat. Esther blinks. I liked it better when she couldn't conceal her hatred of the runner. This new mutual respect is dangerous.

"Thanks, for letting us see him," I say, and usher Esther out. Once we're in the car, I say, "I thought you'd be more upset."

"I couldn't possibly be more upset," she says, and I know beneath the affected calm, she's telling the truth.

"Surprised, then," I say. "You're definitely not that."

"Do you know why Michael took on the ritual of explosives when he was a boy? I asked him once. He said he liked not knowing what was going to happen. He didn't hope for it to go well or for it to go poorly. He didn't care either way. He liked that uncertainty. That kind of curiosity is ill fit for people who are supposed to want only the best in all things for everyone, all the time."

"What about your rituals? If only one person is allowed to hold the knowledge at a time, how will you cope without Michael?"

"We've been without a bombardier before. After my grandfather died, my father wasn't allowed to practice it, because he was an only child. The congregation did without for twenty years before Michael declared that he would read the texts and began practicing. We'll bring back the simple fire bowl. It will be enough."

"You won't practice, will you?"

When she looks at me, she's lost the fight against tears. There are fresh tracks on her face.

"I'm an only child now. It would be forbidden."

I think about Michael, drawn to a runner's kind of danger even at ten. And about Cheeks and Esther, the way they froze as if seeing some greater part of each other. Maybe I'm not the only one who feels the tugs of my other lives. Maybe they hover over us, steering us, constantly. I told Esther before that nothing was inevitable, but that was before I felt so helpless to change absolutely anything at all.

\

DELL CATCHES ME sleeping at my desk the next morning. I'd stayed too late at my family's house, first to comfort Mom, then to help Esther and my stepfather arrange a prayer to send Michael safely into his new life. The whole thing felt like a funeral, and if you judged by my mother's wailing, you'd think it was. By the time I drove back to Wiley City, it was already late.

"I was just resting my eyes," I say, wiping at my mouth.

She sets a cup of coffee in front of me. Usually Jean brings me coffee, but he's kept his distance since our discussion at the restaurant and Dell must have noticed. I look from her to the cup. Dell lives and works on the eightieth floor, but this is the second time she's been down here, like my desk is somehow on the way.

"I take it things did not go well with your family emergency?"

I shouldn't hesitate to tell her, but with everything I've learned about Adam I can't help but think she's down here so often now because she's spying on me. In the end, I remember Nelline's funeral, only possible because of her, and the sight of my undamaged collar drifting down into oblivion.

"Michael joined the runners. We tried to talk him back, but it was too late."

"Wasn't that dangerous?"

"Not really. I dressed like you, so they mistook me for a real Wiley City resident, thought I had value." I throw a smile on it to make it a joke, even though it isn't.

"You shouldn't. Multigenerational citizens dress more like you do," she says. "The way I dress is too traditional. It marks me as a child of immigrants."

"You dress like an Ashtowner's dream of Wiley. It's the first thing I noticed about you."

Her brow furrows, uncertain as she so rarely is. "Why do you pay so much attention to the way I dress?"

"Why are you at my desk when you live and work on eighty?"

Her eyes widen and I realize she's just remembered why she was at my desk, which is not actually what I wanted to know.

"You missed the announcement yesterday. Adam Bosch called a special assembly for this afternoon."

My stomach drops, not just at the mention of the murderer I used to admire. "You think they've reached remote capabilities?"

I've been preparing for this, I even have a career path for the day I can no longer traverse, but my heart will break just the same to never walk the worlds again.

"I can't think of what else it could be," she says. "I'm sorry, Cara-menta."

I almost believe her.

\\

SOMEONE POKES MY side while I'm loading up on free food before the assembly. I turn with a scowl that instantly melts.

"Dresden, Dresden, Dresden, look what the sandcat ralphed up."

"I do so miss your idioms," he says, reaching over me to load up his plate on the company dime. His eyes settle on my face. "I'd heard sur-viving a dop left its mark on you. Those permanent?"

I touch my face. I'd forgotten, again, that I'm branded.

"They're permanent."

His smile never dips into pity, and I'm grateful.

"I like it. Goes with your whole hard-ass brand. Probably have re-bellious teens tattooing their faces before the year's out."

"Thanks. You back on rotation?"

"In a way. They brought me in when you were out, and I fill in since they're letting you get away with a low rotation. I'm just on call now, like the rest of us who aren't you."

He doesn't say it with any kind of malice, but then, he doesn't need this job so much as it amuses him. Dresden is the rare traverser who was worth something before taking the job. He's pure Wiley City, from his ice-light eyes to his nearly white hair. He'd burn up like paper where I come from. He's even paler than the others, because he was confined to his room until mid-adolescence. He suffered from a genetic immune disorder when he was a child. He shouldn't have survived, but on this Earth he did and on one hundred others he didn't.

"I'm sorry about Turner."

Dresden's partner was let go last year when my dop on 245 died. It was the last world he had keys to that I didn't. They fired him, and increased my rotation.

Dresden waves away my apology. "Better him than anyone else. I can keep him here."

"For what it's worth, it looks like we're all going to be in the same boat pretty soon anyway," I say, motioning toward the stage.

He nods. "You see the front row? It's not the board this time. All reporters." He grabs a handful of grapes. "Might as well eat the bastards out of house and home on our way out."

Pretty soon I see two other traversers present for the assembly. They've never greeted me with the friendliness of Dresden, but my existence doesn't threaten his way of life like it does theirs. Still, whatever bitterness they harbored must seem irrelevant now, because they sit with us as the assembly begins. Others in the audience take piteous glances at the four of us, but we keep our heads high, a quartet playing proudly as the ship sinks.

In the corner I spot a pack of black jumpsuits that used to mean nothing to me. I look in their eyes for some mark of the things they've done, but workers in Maintenance just look like people, younger than you'd expect and laughing too loud at one another's jokes. Someone else might be surprised that so many are Wiley City stock—assuming, against all evidence, that cold-blooded murder is a desert trait—but I know better. I'm only surprised at how many of them are still employed. I've taken more comfort than I deserve from the idea that they're mostly inactive, but there are nearly twenty in attendance. Even if I didn't know what they really did, I'd hate them. They're too excited, making jokes on the morning the only other world walkers in the company will be getting unemployment notices.

The lights dim, and a hush falls over us. A woman I don't recognize talks about Eldridge's legacy, something that doesn't usually happen. This recitation must be for the reporters' benefit, because she's only telling stories we've heard a dozen times. Eventually she introduces Adam Bosch, and the applause is so much louder than usual I look for the speaker playing the track.

Once Adam takes the stage I assume the announcement will come quickly, but he's in a storytelling mood. I used to relish this part, the human side of the genius letting us in and, in his awkward way, begging us to understand him. Now I just see a tyrant establishing a legacy. He wants his journey recorded, not in the universal desire to be remembered, but because he pictures every word he says going on a plaque somewhere. He doesn't want us to feel closer to him; he wants us to worship him.

I feel Nelline's long hiss building in my chest. It's probably just my own dislike, but it feels like a warning.

I know, I think at her. *Fuck him. I know.*

I bite into what I can already tell will be the first of many danishes.

Eventually he starts revving up for the kill. He's made his voice louder but clearer and more careful, like this is the clip he wants news outlets to replay.

"And so I struggled with how to share this amazing experience. I believed there must be a way to open it up to others. Now, I am proud to say that I have found that way."

"Here it comes . . ." Dresden says.

"I am thrilled to announce the first ever commercial traversing trip, made possible by our new inoculation against the backlash of duplicates."

"What the shit?" I say, the words half pastry.

The reporters are shouting questions, too many at once to differentiate. Adam holds up his hands.

"This is by no means the beginning of a commercial wave. This inoculation is made from limited resources, and incredibly tedious to distill. For our initial trip we will only have five doses available. We'll begin auctioning those seats for a traversing trip to leave early next year. I want to stress that we have no intention of taking more passengers than we consider absolutely safe."

The rarity will increase the trip's value for buyers, I know better than anyone.

My mouth is dry. The cheering continues even as he starts taking questions.

Dresden starts clapping. "Looks like we get to live another day," he says.

\

"YOU KNOW DAMN well there is no inoculation. You have *felt* Nyame. You can't inoculate against her."

Jean sits down behind his desk. I didn't have an appointment, so after the meeting I just went to the elevator and started bleating into my cuff like a goat. Eventually he sent the elevator down. Unlike Dell—and, really, anyone under forty-five—Jean doesn't have his security clearance integrated with his cuff. He carries a manual fob, which means he had to get up and come to the elevator to keep me from making a scene.

He tosses his fob on his desk before sitting with a loud sigh. He looks distressed, and I want to believe the press conference turned his stomach just the same as mine, and the prospect of the commercial traversing trip is weighing on him.

"I'll admit, it is . . . sudden," he says. "But I'm not in the loop on R&D, and neither are you. Maybe he developed something."

"Something of this scope? How? You're the one who told me business was becoming *less* lucrative. And then he magically finds a way to milk five of the super-rich for capital? That's fifteen hundred people dying."

"No, it's five. Only five on each Earth. No one will experience more than five deaths. And that's only if he plans to kill the dops. As much as you hate him, don't forget he is a genius. He may very well have found a way around the backlash. Maybe it was because you survived. Maybe there was something in your blood that helped them figure it out."

I'd already thought of that. That's why I'd spent time since the press conference scouring Eldridge's network for proof that the work had been done. But no one had accessed my blood sample since the day I came back. No one but the doctor had accessed my medical file at all—

except Dell, probably looking for an excuse to put me on yet another period of limited rotation.

"If he'd found a way around it, a scientist would have done my pull today."

"We don't know that."

I lean forward, putting my arms across his desk and maintaining eye contact so he doesn't look down. Is this what I look like when I make excuses for my own comfort? Weak and ashamed? It must be.

"We'll see," I say, then stand and walk out.

His office door is the kind that slides open into the wall, so I can't slam it, but I wish I could. I settle for walking heavily back to the elevator. My boots are heavy desert stock, and the sound is as satisfying as punching a wall. The slapping sound reminds me I've been dressing more and more like Ashtown since I got back from 175. It hasn't been a deliberate change, but I don't care enough to fight against it.

I still love Jean like an uncle, but I can feel the rift forming between us. I sit down at my desk and shake the fob I stole from his office out of my sleeve. I didn't want to steal it, but he couldn't have maintained his denial and still given it to me.

I tried to do this the easy way, tried to prove the legitimacy of the discovery by following the trail of research on Eldridge's servers. But even with Jean's credentials I couldn't find anything. No funds allocated to it, no scientists moved to the project. I found one reference attributing the discovery to a specific department, but all their files are locally stored. Meaning I would have to be on a terminal in their department on the seventy-eighth floor to access it.

I wait until the last person has left my area for the day, then go to the elevator and use the fob to unlock upward access. I get off on 76 and take two flights of stairs up, in case an elevator going to that floor would attract attention, but I'm still waiting for someone to stop me. When I walk out of the stairwell and onto the floor, it's dark. Not dark like my floor is dark, meaning everyone's gone home and there's only ambient lights from computers and appliances, but perfect dark.

I'd expected this floor was still research and development, just working on a different project. I was going to access their computers to either see the research for the inoculation, or prove there isn't any because the inoculation doesn't exist. But Adam hasn't even bothered to set up a dummy department. There are no desks, no computers. Just empty space where a miracle was supposedly manufactured. I make my way through the floor by touch. There aren't even the required holograms pointing out the exits. Nothing.

Jean will say this isn't proof. Bosch might have the floor mislogged to protect the breakthrough. He might be concealing the names of the scientists to keep them from offers by poachers. But Bosch has eliminated any competitor who could make use of his staff. There are no poachers, and there is no inoculation. He just plans to kill the winning bidders' dops. I knew it in the auditorium, I knew it when I tried to look up the department, and I knew it when I lifted the fob from Jean. I was just looking for an excuse to turn away.

Convinced, I find my way by feel back to the door to the stairwell, but when I turn the handle nothing happens. I jiggle the handle, throwing my shoulder against the door, but it doesn't budge. So . . . logging the floor was a trap. Which I would have known if I'd stopped for a second to ask myself if the smartest man in the city would *really* let it be so easy to discredit him.

I'm wondering if I can bust open a lock in the dark, when I hear it: the high-pitched whirring of a building electrical charge. Of course. The auto-locking door is the trap's cage, but the electrical net will be the glue.

Security nets are usually built into the floor and designed to electrocute trespassers, incapacitating them until private security or public enforcement can be summoned. Something tells me Adam Bosch doesn't have this particular alarm set to inform city enforcement. If I go down, I'll disappear forever. Dell would ask where I went, but Jean wouldn't. He'd know.

I spider-climb into a corner, playing a real-life version of *the floor is runners' acid* from my childhood. I've been climbing since I could walk, so I'm able to put yards between the ground and me. At first, I see the

glow of shock go through the floor and think I'm safe. But then it begins to climb too.

The thorough asshole has put the conductive mesh up the walls.
My left side is propped on the wall with the elevator panel, and it remains dark. But the light is moving steadily toward my right. I try to
outclimb it, but it follows. I move my hand at the last second, but then
I slip and instinctively try to catch myself again on the wall that is the
bright blue of a lightning strike.

The electricity screams through me and I shake so bad my eyes blur.
The floor charge has gone out, so when I slam against it the most I get
is bruises. Bruises I can't even feel, since I'm numb on my whole right
side. I should be unconscious, but my Ashtown boots have mitigated
some of the damage. Some, not all.

I'm half-blind and I can't walk. My ears must be working fine
enough, because I hear steps coming. They are careful, different from
a runner's only in that they are lighter. Security has come to see what
the net has caught. No, not security. I can hear the wrinkling of a plastic jumpsuit. A Maintenance worker's coming for me.

I try to drag myself back toward the door, but I only have one
working arm and leg and even those are twitching. I barely have the
strength to slide my hand against the locked door, much less break it
down, and the footsteps are getting closer.

I'm seventy-eight floors up, reaching where I don't belong, and yet
somehow I'm still sure I'm not going to die.

Not yet, I say to the dead in my chest. *I'm not coming yet.*

And I'm right. The moment I have the thought, the door at my
fingertips opens and I'm hauled up. I know it's not one of Adam's
people, because I know just what she smells like and she had to pull me
up the same way last week.

Dell hooks my dead arm around her neck and closes the door to the
seventy-eighth floor tight behind us. The guard will have to unlock it
to follow, if he sees any reason to check the stairwell at all. Since I
should be unconscious on the floor, he might convince himself the net

malfunctioned. Dell isn't taking that chance though. She drags me up the stairs and out of the building's exit on the eightieth floor.

When we get to her apartment, the shaking in my left side has stopped, though I'm still numb on the right.

Dell all but drops me on her couch when we enter, then begins messing with her cuff. I'm guessing she's checking Eldridge's security memos to see if they've reported a break-in. Or maybe she's telling Bosch I'm the intruder, and that she has me. It's impossible to tell; her face always goes blank when she's concentrating.

"Last person who found me incapacitated made me juice. Just saying."

My words are slurred, my tongue fat and pressed against the sides of my teeth.

"Stop fighting unconsciousness. We'll talk in the morning," she says, bringing a throw from another chair and draping it over me. As she tucks me in, she leans down to whisper, "And I was the last person to find you incapacitated, don't forget."

She's right. I don't remember how I got out of the hatch after landing from 175, but I do remember her finding me and telling me to stop crying. I want to smile at her scorekeeping, but my mouth only half cooperates.

"See you."

She must nod, but my eyes are already closed. I wonder if I'll wake up to her, or a group from Maintenance. I still manage to go to sleep, so I must not care. Or maybe I trust Dell . . . just a little.

CHAPTER SIXTEEN

The smell of food wakes me long after the beeping of my cuff should have. At first, I don't move. I'm thinking about yesterday, about everything I've learned. Does knowing Adam is planning another kill campaign change things, when I've already agreed to ignore the ones in the past? I have never considered my own moral character. I've never known exactly what my limits were. I still don't, but I know that this is too much. Glossing over murders that have already happened so I can keep collecting a paycheck? I can take that. But standing by while the next round happens, and the next round, all so I can retire a citizen? I might as well jump in the bog beside Nelline, because that will take me to a place just as dark and suffocating.

I have to do something. It's probably the worst mistake I'll ever make, but I've got to.

I'm a little shaky, but I manage to chase the smell of food until I stumble into Dell's kitchen. The space is roughly the size of my whole apartment, minus the bedroom. She has a formal dining room, I'm sure, but there's a table here too. Everything in sight is either clear or silver, and all the lines are sharp and clean. Dell is bringing two plates to the table when I enter.

I take a seat at her table, rubbing at my neck, which is kinked from being pressed against the arm of the couch.

"This high up you must have at least one guest room. Afraid I'll dirty the sheets?"

She levels a glare at me across the table. "The bedrooms are all on the second and third floors. You were in no condition."

The sound of her setting a plate—loudly—in front of me calls me an ungrateful asshole more pointedly than words ever could.

"Sorry . . . I just wasn't sure what I would be waking up to."

She nods, acknowledging my apology and letting it go. At first, I think she's being extremely cool under the circumstances. But once I'm finished eating she slides something across the table. It's a jade teardrop earring in a plastic bag.

I look back up at her. She's wearing the pair.

"Fuck."

"Indeed." She leans forward. "It and its mate are one of a kind. But I now have three. I saw the otherworld menagerie on your wall, all in Eldridge specimen bags . . . with one empty space. Care to elaborate?"

I finger the edge of the bag. "This is what you want to ask me? You find me half electrocuted on a restricted floor, and this is what you want to know?"

"I've wanted to ask you for a while, but you were so upset when you first returned I thought it best to wait. I'm done waiting."

I can justify hiding my reasons for breaking into that floor, because she might report me to Bosch. I can't justify lying to her about this anymore. I never could, really.

"It was part of my collection. When you lost yours, and I had an extra, I gave you mine."

"And what is that collection? Half of it just looks like dirt, or water. And did I see a sample of Lot's Wife in there? What are you thinking?"

"It's perfectly contained. It all is. I just save things that don't exist in my world. Or"—I look down at the earring—"things I can't touch here, but was allowed to touch somewhere else."

It takes a second, but her entire face contorts when she understands. I expect disgust, but there's only confusion. Like this is an impossibility.

I'm afraid of what she'll say next, so I jump ahead.

"You approached me. I tried to slow things down, but in the end spending a night with you was a gift and I took it. We drank and we talked and you treated me like an equal because, in worlds where you don't know where I came from, you actually let yourself be attracted to me. I was going to leave before things went too far, but you were charming and open and lonely and you *wanted* me. I know it wasn't real. But you wanted me before I said a word. I'll say I'm sorry it happened if you want me to, but I won't mean it."

I take the bag and shove it in my pocket, angry for no reason. I'm more sure now than ever that this memento is the closest I'll ever come to holding her.

Dell's made a temple of her hands and pressed her face into it. Her eyes are closed as she slowly shakes her head.

"Stupid girl."

At first, I'm sure I've misheard the whisper, but she says it again, and then once more. When she finally opens her eyes, they are wet and raging.

"Do you not have a single memory from before your first jump?"

"Not . . . really."

"I kissed you! After our training, before I knew you'd be assigned to me. You invited me to your apartment and I kissed you and you kissed me back and the next morning I had a long message in my cuff saying I was the devil sent to tempt you. You called me a sinner and said if I ever so much as looked at you for too long again you would file a harassment suit."

My mouth is dry. "No, that's not . . . no."

"*Yes.* After we were matched for our first jump, you said you would request a transfer when you returned. But you never did. It was worse than that. You flirted, pushing at me, teasing me with what you knew I wanted, when I already knew you would destroy me for acting on it."

"I wasn't . . . That's not what I was doing."

But it was exactly what I was doing, from where she sits. In her universe. The multiverse isn't just parallel universes accessible through science. They are in each of us, a kaleidoscope made of varying perceptions. Dell and I were in different universes this whole time, and I should have known. I thought she was ignoring her attraction to me, but I was torturing her with it.

Isn't Dell unknowable too?

A warning from Nik Nik, but even that had already come too late. I broke Dell's heart before I even knew I had it, and I've been breaking it and breaking it again ever since, thinking I was the victim the whole time.

"I thought you were just classist. That's why you pretended you weren't attracted to me when there were times . . . times I could tell. I thought you were telling me I was beneath you every time you pulled away. I didn't know what she'd done."

"She?"

"Me, I mean I didn't remember that I'd—"

"You said 'she.'"

"I know what I said!"

I stand up. Dell stays sitting. I see it now, every ounce of hurt I'd missed before, that I'd caused. Or Caramenta had. What must she have thought? Me flirting with her after threatening her like that. All that subtle anger I'd harbored against her, thinking she thought she was better than me, did she feel it? Did she think it was Caramenta's Ruralite hate? I owe her so much. I owe her the truth.

"Imagine, just pretend, that I came back from that first pull six years ago . . . different. Pretend that I was a girl who'd never set foot in the Rurals, and wasn't properly trained to work for Eldridge, and when I was called to this Earth yours was the first face I saw and I wanted you. And I didn't know anything about what happened before, because that was Caramenta and not me, but I knew you were holding yourself back. I assumed the worst."

Because I always assume the worst of Wileyites. Because I have a chip on my shoulder as big as a mountain and twice as sharp. Because at the end of the day, *I* was the one who couldn't look past class, not Dell.

Dell shakes her head, stops, then shakes it again. "That's not possible. Bosch himself programmed first pulls. It's just . . . not possible."

It is, and if I leave her alone with it long enough she'll put it all together. Leaving her alone is the least I can do, but it's also all I can do. I take the bag out of my pocket and slide it across the table to her.

I replay the moment I gave it to her, the way her eyes lit up—had it been hope?—and then darkened. And I read that shift all wrong, punishing her when I should have been comforting her.

"What am I supposed to do with three earrings?" she says, picking up the bag.

"Whatever you want," I say. "I really didn't know. I'm a con and a liar and a garbage git and anything else you ever thought of me, but I really didn't know what had happened between us. You've got to believe that."

She doesn't stop me with more questions as I go, though I'm sure she has them. She's probably weighing whether or not they are worth asking, now that it's too late to change anything. We've wasted six years looking at each other and thinking we knew what we were seeing. Now it can't be anything but too late.

Walking home hurts, and takes longer than it ever has. I spend the rest of my weekend woozily recovering from my run-in with high voltages and the truth about Caramenta and Dell. It doesn't help that every news projection is rehashing the details of Eldridge's announcement, which feels so long ago but was only yesterday. In a later press conference Adam Bosch confirmed plans to repeat the journey every two years.

Because you can't have a mass murder *every* year. That would be too much.

He's had to be a little bitter; being subsidized by the government means he has to be overseen by them. It must feel just like having a father again. He wants enough money to be independent. The industrial hatch makes money, but not enough for the truly ambitious. And

I know he is, because I am, because all of us who were told we were nothing will never stop trying to be everything.

\

WHEN I'M SUMMONED to the hatch for my first pull on Monday, a man is waiting for me.

"Oh sorry," I say. "Must have double-booked."

"Wait. Caramenta, right? I'm really excited to meet with you. I've never seen a traverser who's done a three-hundred-pull year."

His smile is almost blue-bright, standing out against his gold-toned skin. Gold, not an ordinary brown or beige. Providers at the House sometimes use dust to get the same effect, but they start out with skin ranging from tan to dark brown to a black so rich customers line up to rub against it, so it makes them all look like earthbound gods. On his Wiley-descendant skin, the gold tones make him look like a pearl. There is a line of white at the base of his dark reddish-brown hair where the roots are beginning to grow in. He's a Wileyite trying to pass as something else, and I can't quite figure out why. Doesn't he know we still die for not being what he is?

"Three hundred and two," I say when I'm done sizing him up.

He takes my response as a good sign and holds out his hand. His palms are undyed, and they seem flat and pale and almost blue compared to the rest of him. I take his hand, my skin suddenly looking darker than it has since coming here. I've gotten paler without Ashtown's real and untamed sun, but I'll never catch up to those whose blood has been in the city for as long as mine has been in the desert.

"My name is Carrington, and I'll be your watcher for today's pull."

I yank my hand out of his. "They fired Dell?"

He laughs. "Ikari's position is more secure than any watcher in the sector, thanks to you."

"Oh . . . good. Where is she?"

"She's just taking some time off from this part of the job," he says. "Don't worry. I promise I won't get you killed."

I don't want him to think I don't trust him, so I hide my displeasure.

"Sorry, I don't like change. I've never pulled with anyone but Dell before."

"Never? Weird," he says, and begins my prep.

It is weird, I guess. In six years Dell's never taken a vacation while I worked, or called off long enough that we couldn't just reschedule pulls for another day. But then again, neither have I. We've never said aloud that we didn't want to work with anyone else, but we've both done our part to make sure we never had to.

Until now.

The ache in my chest isn't just for a missing romantic prospect. It's also just missing Dell. I've seen her face nearly every day since I hatched in this land of strangers, and I wish I'd realized she was my best friend, not just the girl I couldn't have.

She's removed herself from seeing me, which makes her wishes clear. I won't reach out to her, won't burden her with having to respond to some grand romantic gesture. But if she ever chooses to talk to me, I'll promise to do whatever she wants. I'll never flirt again if she'll stay in my life. I'll always want her, but I won't make that her problem.

\

WHEN I FINALLY see Jean again, I'm ready for a fight. Working with Carrington has spoiled my mood like milk on a bright day. The watcher and I have nothing to talk about, but that doesn't stop him from talking.

I sit down, sliding Jean his fob across the desk.

He looks more irritated than surprised.

"You know, if I'd reported this stolen instead of just malfunctioning they would have GPS tracked it to your house and you would have been deported before sunup."

"I'm sorry, but I had to know. Are you going to cut me out of your life too?"

He looks at me from just under his eyebrows, holds on to that disapproving scowl for about three more seconds, then softens.

"I heard Dell requested desk duty. She said she was behind on her files. How are things going with Carrington?"

"Do you know how many horses he has? Twelve. Do you know their names? I do. They're named after the signs of the zodiac. Did I ask for any of this information? I did not."

He laughs. "Dell will be back. It's been six years with a mouth like yours, who wouldn't need a break?"

"Keep talking, old man, and I'll tell Carrington where you spend your off hours. He's a *big* fan."

"Carrington is a world-walker groupie," Jean says. "Careful he doesn't try to sleep with you to taste the stars."

I gag audibly.

Sitting across from him shouldn't still feel like sitting with family, but it does. I notice he's looking down at his fob, so I wait. He draws a quick circle around it with his finger, then taps it like he's made a decision.

"What did you find?"

This is a good sign. If he was going to ignore what was happening regardless, why would he even ask?

"I was right. There's nothing there. No R&D department, just a security net to trap anyone who comes looking."

"Did you get hurt?"

His concern is genuine, which makes it that much harder to be at odds.

"I managed to get out before the shock deployed," I say, a lie that protects Dell and thankfully takes some of the fatherly fear from his eyes.

"That was a close call. They'll only get closer from here," he says.

"You're not going to try and talk me out of acting against Bosch?"

"Would you listen if I did?"

"Maybe, if you could give me a good enough reason." I lean forward. "What are your reasons, Jean? What do you tell yourself to make this okay?"

He's studying the top of his desk like he can see a pattern in the plastic. I've seen this look before, when we were discussing my odds at getting analyst. He's deciding how much sugar he needs to coat the truth he's about to give me.

"Have you seen the list of leading bidders? The youngest is two decades older than the life expectancy where I come from. Every year walled cities get richer and more developed, and every year rural provinces get poorer and sicker. The other side of the scale tips down because of their rise, and they do nothing to balance it. I'm supposed to care about these five, when they have ignored entire plagues just outside these walls? I will give their deaths the same courtesy they've given the deaths of my people and yours. I'm going to kindly look away."

I don't have the right to say he's wrong. I was born at the tail end of Ashtown's wars, and I was a child through the time of the blood parades. But Jean was born and grew to adulthood in war and starvation and pestilence. He watched his eldest child born surrounded by the same violence and death he'd grown up with—violence and death driven by a lack of resources, while cities like Wiley grew higher and higher on the horizon.

"I can't use that as a reason to ignore this. It's your reason, but it can't be mine."

"I know," he says. "You realize that even if Bosch does not kill you for meddling, you will lose your job and your place here?"

I shrug. "We've always known me getting citizenship was a long shot. Me making it to thirty has always been one too."

"What is your plan?"

"I've been gathering information, the names of people he's ordered killed. I'll have a comprehensive list in a few days. When I tell the authorities what I think he's planning, I'll add the evidence I've collected so they can see he's done it before. This place is still mostly government funded, so his board will comply with enforcement even if he doesn't want to."

"And if he learns it is you who began the investigation?"

"Will you tell him?"

It's a question I should have asked before running my mouth, but I can't stop feeling safe with Jean.

He shakes his head. "I won't."

I believe him. Not as a kindly grandfather who wants to protect the young, but as a once-and-always soldier who would never put one of his own in danger.

"But if a complaint is made anonymously, the accused is allowed to read it. You may give yourself away."

"I'll deal with the consequences, whatever they may be."

Jean leans forward and puts his hand over mine. His hand is darker and larger, but still more like mine than Carrington's could ever be.

"Their indifference has killed you on hundreds of worlds, and here you are, sticking your neck out to let them do it one more time. I want you to know, after this goes bad and you're facing whatever end you've engineered for yourself, that I do admire you."

"Thank you. I mean it. Don't think I'm not still grateful for everything you've done for me. This doesn't change that."

"Will you still take the analyst test?"

"Jean, I'm *definitely* going to get fired for whistleblowing next week."

"Good thing the test is first thing Monday." He puts his hand over his heart and makes his eyes wide. "For me?"

I roll my eyes. "Yes, fine. I'll take the test."

That weekend, I finish assembling the packet detailing what I've found out about Eldridge's competitors dying unusually on other worlds. I add a letter explaining what I think he plans to do with the highest bidders to facilitate his lucrative commercial trips, including what happened when I visited the department that made the breakthrough.

On Sunday, I airdrop the information to Wiley City's Tech Crimes digital box.

On Monday I take the exam, dressed like an analyst in my business best.

When the time is up, the screen dings a perfect score. The victory is a little bit of ash on my tongue, but a victory nonetheless. I look around at the Wileyites surrounding me, their expressions ranging from open dismay to disappointment. I want them to know I did it. That I, an Ashtown child so worthless they've let her die hundreds and hundreds and hundreds of times, have scored perfect on a test made for them.

I message Jean about my score, then I walk back to my desk and wait to lose it all.

\

IT'S ILLEGAL FOR Wiley City to investigate a citizen without their knowledge, so I'm sure enforcement will be here soon to inform Adam Bosch of the case. If they come to interview traversers, I won't hide who I am. Once Adam reads the complaint, he'll know it's me. I was mostly anonymous in the letter, but I made sure to mention that I was a high-volume traverser. It may condemn me, but it protects Dresden and the rest of the part-timers from being caught in the crossfire. Once I get the boot they'll all get an increased rotation. Plus, I never have to hear Carrington talk ever again, so that's another bright side.

But Maintenance makes their move first. I see them coming from a long ways off, leaving their offices on the far end of my floor. There are three, walking in a *V* formation in those awful black jumpsuits. They dress how a child imagines a bad guy would dress, and I still hadn't known they were killers.

"Who do you think is on the chopping block?" Dresden asks, suddenly at my shoulder.

Me. They're headed right for me. But he doesn't know what they really do, so I shake my head. "What do you mean?"

"First Wiley City dispatches enforcement here, and then—"

"What? When?"

"While you were taking your test. You didn't miss anything. They went straight to the top floor and came right back down and left. But now Maintenance is on the move, so they must be clearing out someone's stuff, right? Changing the locks?"

"You're thinking of Building Maintenance. They're Off-World Maintenance," I say. "That's not what these guys do."

They're only eight feet away now, so I stand and turn around. I want to face them. They won't do anything to me in front of Dresden, he's a citizen, so they must just be escorting me off the property.

Standing doesn't make it easier to pretend I'm anything but prey, and my breath goes shallow as they approach. Why does it feel just like a runners parade, even after all these years? But they pass me without slowing down. The woman at the front offers a glare, but the man on the left greets me with a wide smile. They must know. They know I've killed one of the Adams. The one with the smile winks like I'm one of them, like we're in on the same fun secret.

They march past me to the elevator. I watch the display, expecting them to go straight to 100, where Adam's office is. But they stop at 80. The rock that's been growing in my chest plummets into my stomach. I run to the elevator without thinking, remembering only when I'm there that I can't make it take me where I want to go.

I pound at my cuff, trying to call Jean, but there's no answer.

Finally, I dial Dell.

"You don't have to talk to me, I just need you to send the elevator down so I can go to the eightieth floor. It's an emergency."

She closes the connection without saying a word.

I begin to pace, frustrated and helpless, but then I hear the ding of the elevator opening behind me. I get in and see it's programmed to return to 80. Whatever else is between us, Dell came through.

I rush out as soon as the elevator arrives, hitting my shoulders on the sides of the doors. I run toward Jean, but I've been late to see him so many times no one even looks out of their offices. Or maybe up here they already know what I've just discovered, and they're burying their heads because they saw Maintenance come this way.

I run into Jean's office, but the only ones here are the three I followed in. They freeze in a tableau—one righting a knocked-over chair, another sliding glass from a shattered award into the trash can, and the third spraying what smells like bleach over what looks like blood on the back of Jean's chair. I shake my head, letting denial hold me in place for just a second before I turn and run in the opposite direction.

No one came down the company elevator, which means whoever took Jean must have exited the building on this floor. I run outside wondering if they went down the escalator, or used an exterior elevator, but then it hits me: we're on the eightieth floor. I run in the direction of Adam Bosch's garden. Once inside, I look for the paths with holograms that say CLOSED FOR MAINTENANCE. The path leads me to a clearing so close to the back edge of the garden I can see the desert beyond.

At first, all I can see are leaves and a wall of black jumpsuits with their backs turned to me. I try to push past them, and in the struggle of them pulling me back and me raging forward, I land on my knees in the clearing, face-to-face with Jean. Adam is standing over us, his constant smile in place. There's blood on the cuff of his customary wide-collared white shirt. It's Jean's blood. I couldn't see it at first, but there are wet rivers crawling from his mouth and temple.

"You're beating a man old enough to be your grandfather. What is wrong with you?"

I look around at the others, but their expressions are either gleeful or empty. Adam could be at a speaking engagement for all the change his face shows. Only his eyes are a little off—not unfamiliar, just different.

"Traitors have no age," he says, his voice too light for his statement.

And then I understand why his eyes look familiar. They're his father's eyes, and that was his father's line. Usually he said it about children executed for carrying messages of rebellion, but I learned from Adra on 175 that it applies on the other end of the age spectrum too. I'm only now realizing Adam didn't so much inherit his father's traits as he was possessed by them.

I push myself to my feet, even though I hate standing over Jean. I never wanted to be taller than him.

"Jean isn't a traitor. He's loyal to Eldridge. He's grateful for everything you've done for him. He knows what kind of life his family would have had without you. He tells me all the time."

This seems to please Adam, but it doesn't stop him from rearing back and kicking Jean in the spine, sending him forward onto his hands. I can't contain my scream, so someone steps up from behind and does it for me. The gloved hand covering my mouth smells like crude oil. It tastes like it, too, when I bite their fingers.

"I can tell this upsets you," Adam says. "But he sent a very incriminating package to enforcement. I don't know what I'll have to do to shake them. It's . . . inconvenient."

"It was me." I can't get the words out fast enough. "Everything you think he did, it was me."

"We already know it was a traverser with access to information your clearance doesn't provide, and his fob was used to access a restricted floor last week."

"That was me! I used his login when I found the information. I stole his fob."

"This fob?" he says, pulling it out of his pocket. "This fob that was sitting on his desk when we came in to question him?"

"Yes, I just . . . I gave it back after."

Adam clucks his tongue. It sounds like I'm lying. I kneel down and pull Jean back up from the ground so we're both on our knees.

"It's all right, Cara," Jean says. He's calm, but his jaw isn't connecting right.

"It's not all right," I say, then look up at Adam. "Let me take him to a pod."

Adam tilts his head. "But we're not half finished yet."

"Do it to me. Whatever punishment you have planned, I'll take it."

"No," Jean says, too clear for someone in as much pain as he must be in.

"You're being irrational," I say to Jean, then to Adam: "Don't do this."

"He's already told us that no one else has his login, and that he's never lost track of his fob," Adam says. "You're too late to lie for him."

I reach out to Jean, because I want to touch him somewhere, but I can't tell where he's injured. He holds my wrist, and I hold his in return. His hand could be the hand of my grandfather, could be Pax's hand, could be anyone I'd call family. In this land of strangers, he is the only thing that has ever looked or felt like home. He doesn't need me like that, he brought his land and people with him in a dozen other family members, but I have always needed him.

"Tell them it was me. You have to tell them," I say. "You have, I don't even know, sixty-four grandkids who need you."

He smiles, small and painful. "Do you know how many lives I've taken?"

"I don't care."

"Of course you don't, but I've started to, as I've gotten older." He looks back to Adam and clears his throat. "And that is why I went to the authorities. I wanted to go out doing one good thing. . . ."

He squeezes my wrist so hard my bones ache. He's so strong, even after all these years.

"Let me."

I refuse and keep refusing. I scream his innocence and my guilt until two Maintenance workers each take an arm and drag me away. It doesn't stop my screaming. They let me go wild until we get near the entrance of the garden, then one threatens to drug me. He isn't mean about it. He tells me he understands. He says the first colleague is always hard, but it's time to pull myself together or he'll do it for me.

They escort me all the way home. Once I close the door in their faces, I call Jean on his cuff. He doesn't answer. My next call is to enforcement. I tell them a man's being hurt in the back of Bosch Garden. The automated voice on the other end records coordinates and issues me a file number in case I want to follow up, then disconnects. It's the only time in my life I've ever missed the runners, because I'd give anything for the call bot to be a violent human looking for an excuse to let their blood boil over.

I call Jean back, and when he still doesn't answer I try again every fifteen minutes. Thirty-two calls and eight hours later, someone picks up. But it's not Jean. It's his wife, Sopia. She gets out two words, but then she can't speak. I hear rustling.

"Cara?" The voice is clear and strong, the emotion in it subdued.

"Aya?" I say, and it must be. Jean's level-headed oldest daughter, who went into business school when the rest of his children chose art or cooking or agriculture. But he loves her just as much despite her differences from the rest of the family. He loves them all. He loves me.

"Yes, it's me," she says. "We've just gotten Dad's cuff working again and . . . there was an attack. They say he was checking on the industrial hatch just outside the city. Runners found him. He must have tried to fight . . ."

"Is he okay? Aya, is he going to be okay?"

There's a moment of silence, and I wonder if she's had to answer this question yet.

"He's dead, Cara. They killed him."

PART FOUR

Dear brother from another
time, today some stars gave in
to the black around them
& i knew it was you.

—Danez Smith

CHAPTER SEVENTEEN

When asked what this discovery could teach us about what mattered, about death, and human nature, and how to make the world a gentler place, both parties were silent.

But we were right, the scientists said.

And so were we, the spiritual said.

WE USED TO believe the universe was stable. We saw its cycles, the reliable circles it traced, and called the pattern static, meaning unmoving. Then we learned its wildness—asteroids that leave their own clusters and impact with planets that've also abandoned their orbits, everything dancing off track to the music of chaos.

I believed I was stable. I thought my ability to go to work, to visit my family, to eat and sleep, meant that I was. I confused routine for reliability and reliability for safety. I had no idea the chaos I was capable of holding inside of me. Now the only thing "static" about me is the buzzing rush in my ears when I try to think, a hiss like the sound that comes through the speakers when Dell tries to contact Earths that are lost.

I am lost.

I spend my days in bed, leaving only to eat and go to the bathroom, staring up at a ceiling that calls me murderer.

The day after Jean's death, I'm guessing the second the news reaches the desert, Esther petitions for a day pass. I deny it. She petitions every morning for the next week, but I deny those too. I don't deserve her. I didn't deserve Jean. They both loved and encouraged me and I can't figure out why. Have I done anything for Esther? Had I ever done anything for Jean? Sure, little presents here and there. Bringing him lunch occasionally. But I'd never done anything to earn the way he always tried to lift me up. Just as I've never done anything equal to Esther's kindness, her acceptance of someone she knew all along to be a stranger.

I am a rot to the people I love, and the world keeps giving me gifts I don't deserve. This apartment, this life, the sound of Jean's laugh, the smell of Dell's hair—all memories of things I never deserved to experience in the first place. And how do I repay the world for my luck? By infecting everything with my darkness. By taking the light out of Dell's eyes and taking Jean away from his children.

Eldridge closes until the weekend in honor of Jean. I spend the days wandering around my apartment forgetting to eat. Sasha sends out a department-wide message encouraging anyone struggling with his loss to make an appointment with her or one of the other grief counselors. I delete it. She can't help me. This isn't a Wiley City kind of grief, grief at the unknown, a twist of fate taking a life. This is grief because a powerful man killed someone I love but will never see consequences and it's Ashtown all over.

For the first week of work after Jean's murder, I don't go in. I don't do anything. Finally, on the third day of my second week out of work, something moves me. I shower and dress and drive the hell out of Wiley City. When a runner I don't know pulls me over I throw the money at them without even turning off my car. I don't go toward my family's place. I drive into the heart of Ash and get out at the House.

Exlee must be surprised at my appearance, but nothing shows on that painted face.

"What do you need, child?"

This, precisely this. I need someone to call me a child.

"I don't know." My eyes are suddenly too wet, and I wipe at them. "But I have money."

"Of course you do."

Exlee motions me forward and takes my hand. I've seen Exlee lead others back, usually with an arm around their waist or draped over their shoulder. But I am led like a cousin, an intimacy that has nothing to do with sex and everything to do with safety.

I think I'm being taken to one of the other providers' rooms. But I'm led down the enby wing and eventually into Exlee's own work suite.

Exlee rarely sees clients. At first, I'm afraid. What if they've forgotten me? What if Exlee doesn't recognize me as a daughter, and tries to give me something I've never wanted here. But then they pull out the duvet I used to curl up on as a toddler. But I'm not a toddler anymore, so they push it against a long couch draped in warm, red velvet.

"Lay down. Tell me what breaks your heart."

I'm crying before I even make contact with the couch. Exlee lies beside me, and I curl around a body broader than mine but just as short without the advantage of shoes. I cry into the chest, arms, and hair of a person who feels more like home than this world's version of my mother ever could.

I'm not even sure if I'm talking, if I'm coherent, but I feel Exlee saying, *I know. We all know. We understand.* As they stroke my back and gently massage my neck, I realize it is touch I want, touch that is making me feel a little bit whole again, and it is touch from a person who is part castle, someone I cannot destroy and who will always be safe.

Maybe that was Nik Nik's appeal. Not that he was powerful enough to keep me safe, but that he was too powerful for my curse to touch him. I can destroy almost anyone. My mother, Jean, even myself over three hundred times. Death hangs over me like too-fine dust settles on the skin—weightless but impossible to remove, no matter how hard you try.

I sleep through the night for the first time since Jean's death. In the morning Exlee brings me breakfast. I say I'm not hungry.

"You will eat because I'm charging you for the food, and you're still too much Ashtown to waste that."

I eat a meal of stringy meat, the eggs of a ground-lying bird, and a tough grain loaf. There are better meals at the House, they have access to even Wiley City's ingredients, but Exlee has given me flavors I would not even find in the farming-centric Rurals. Food that tastes like blood, and gives me a little piece of downtown Ash's strength to take with me.

I am fed twice more before I go. I'm never given a proper bill, so I take what I remember from the menu back at my world's House, and triple it. As I leave Exlee reminds me to say Jean's name each morning and each night until the burial, because our dead are only weights on our backs when we won't let them walk beside us, when we try to pretend they are not ours or they are not dead.

When I get home, I am still sad. I am still distraught and full of guilt. But I have taken a step back from the edge of true despair, or something even more dangerous.

\

JEAN'S FUNERAL IS a Wiley City event. His family is there, down to the smallest member, eight rows of love with their arms entwined like a net to carry the heaviest burden. And that is what they will have to do now, because Jean's absence is exactly that.

The mayor speaks about Jean as a treasure, an explorer, one of the first to return from the dark unknown that claimed so many lives before him. It doesn't take long for her to digress into the political, saying Jean's murder is exactly the reason Wiley City needs to "intervene with added security measures" in the land outside the wall. In the past, additional border security has always been unpopular, because the same things it is supposed to fix were supposed to be fixed by the numerous vertical wall extensions they've already authorized. Border security never lowered crime rates the way they said it would, and eventually

Wiley accepted that they were murdering and stealing from each other. It wasn't worth it to spend on external security, not when so many still remember what Nik Senior paid them out for trespassing last time. But Jean's death has ignited a new hatred for runners, for Ashtown, for dirt itself, and this time people applaud.

Eventually she remembers this is not a rally but a funeral. She tells us that we've lost a rare kind of hero, the kind of knight who would fight a dragon. She says it must have taken such great bravery, to traverse when before they'd only recovered bodies. I'm sure, but not nearly as much bravery as it took to accept someone else's death, knowing no one would praise you for it.

I want you to know, after this goes bad and you're facing whatever end you've engineered for yourself, that I do admire you.

Would he still mean that if he knew this was what I'd bought?

I've forgotten myself and worn gray, a speck of ash in a sea of black. It's not the kind of funeral I'm used to. No one speaks to Jean, only about him. We are never invited to approach him with our secrets. I settle for whispering *I'm sorry, I'm so sorry* to myself and anyone who'll listen. I say it to his family after the service, but they think it's *I'm sorry you lost your father,* when I mean *I'm sorry I got him killed.*

Dell is here. I sense her looking at me, but I can't look back because I don't know how to seem like I don't need her, and it wouldn't be fair to use Jean's death like that. Sita is in front, the dark-brown girl with hair the color of clay and a face just like her grandfather's. I remember Jean holding her quickly, kissing her head as she squirmed to leave. I hope she remembers too. I hope she never forgets, because it will be all she has left now.

It's too much. I duck behind a tree to wait for the crowd to thin. Footsteps follow me, but they aren't the ones I want.

"Fuck off."

His amused chuckle grates like a knife being badly sharpened. "I like your rage. It means you're loyal."

I turn on Adam Bosch. It hasn't been that long since I was afraid of him, but now I feel nothing at all.

"To *him*. I was loyal to *him*. If you wanted to make anything but an enemy of me, you should have let him go."

He tilts his head, studying me like a puzzle.

"I don't expect you to approve of what happened to Jean, only to learn from it." Too casually, as if we're discussing the weather, he takes out a vial of eyedrops and drops liquid into his enhanced left eye. "I don't need to earn your loyalty. I just need to give you time to understand that you don't have a choice. You Ashtowners are very good at figuring out your options."

"*Us* Ashtowners, Adranik. You've more than earned the Blood Emperor title."

I want to insult him, but he doesn't get angry. Just peers closer.

"Do you know there are five worlds where we've been lovers?"

I know of one, but I won't tell him that.

"Five whole worlds where I'm brain-dead? Tragic."

"In two we're still together, in the other three . . . you've died."

"Suicide, I imagine."

"No, and I think you know that." He steps forward until he's practically against me. His closeness is threatening but not human enough to be sexual. It's like I'm being threatened by a rock, a robot, a weapon. "I just want you to understand that I've killed you in worlds where you meant something to me without a second thought. And you mean nothing to me here."

"I told you to kill me last week. And you should have."

"And waste such potential? After all the trouble I went through to get you?"

"Don't you get it? I don't care about potential. I am the one who betrayed you. You killed an innocent man."

He laughs, just a little, just enough to piss me off. "You think Jean outsmarted me? That I didn't know he was lying?"

I shake my head. "Then why—"

"If he had betrayed me, and I killed him, I killed the traitor. But if I killed you, whether you were the traitor or not, I would have lost him. He would have reacted irrationally. But if you were the traitor, and I killed him, you would learn the consequences your actions have on those around you. You still need Eldridge. Jean did not. I removed the element I could not control."

I run through his words twice before I truly understand them. He didn't even kill Jean because he hated him, or because he felt betrayed. He killed Jean because it made the most sense. Murdering Jean was just the answer to a riddle.

He's still studying me like he's trying to see beneath my skin and behind my eyes.

"You hate me, don't you?" he says.

"More than anything in this world."

This seems to surprise him. *If I'd killed you . . . he would have acted irrationally.* Adam Bosch doesn't understand hate.

"But you'll still report for work when your personal leave is up, just like everyone else. I could tell you all the ways I'll kill your family if you talk, how many pieces your sister can be severed into, but I don't think it matters, does it?" he says. "In every world, you are ruled by blind ambition, not familial love or loyalty. You're not going to throw your chance at Wiley City away over this."

Something's been bothering me, but I couldn't quite figure out what until he says this last part.

"What trouble?"

His smile drops. He tilts his head at me.

"You said you went through so much trouble to get me. But you didn't. It was just a recruitment letter."

When his eyes settle on me, I can't find a trace of Adam. All I see is Nik Senior.

"I think we both know that's not true, Caralee."

Hearing my real name from his mouth pitches me close to vomiting. Dell told me he programmed the pull himself, but I was so distracted by our fight I hadn't listened.

"You killed Caramenta? But why . . . why bother?"

"Before her first pull Caramenta came to me, her conscience bruised because of some heavy petting with Ikari. I knew then she'd be useless to me."

"Because she wouldn't kill for you?"

He lets out a bark of a laugh. "Kill? The little Ruralite would have gone to the authorities over insider trading her second day. Too self-righteous. But even then it would have taken two dozen people to access her worlds. Your worlds."

So he sent her body into my path, and hoped I would do what Ashtowners always do: take what wasn't mine. And I did because, in his words, I've always been blindly ambitious, or, in my mother's, I was born reaching. But I wasn't exactly what he wanted. In the garden he said Jean had told him I wasn't cut out for murder. Jean had kept him from recruiting me to Maintenance. What if he hadn't? Would there be as many traversers as there are Maintenance workers now, while I put all of the black jumpsuits out of work instead? Would I have taken the job when I was just a broken bit of a girl from Earth 22? Before I learned generosity from Jean, or compassion from Esther?

My memory of our first meeting, once my favorite, turns rotten. The way Adam came down to see me, and told Dell to be patient. It was because he knew I never went through training. He knew who I was the whole time.

Nelline was a killer and a spy, exactly what Bosch wanted. Did he plug her death into the system without full evidence, hoping she'd faked it and history would repeat itself if she found out about my body? He said he'd come to my meeting to see if I was her, but did he *hope* I was? Did he start planning to kill me as soon as he found out I'd been studying for the analyst test? Or did he just get bored with the version of me that wouldn't kill, when he was about to need so many more people dead?

"How does it feel?" I ask, finally. "To turn out just like your father?"

For a moment, the space between one heartbeat and the next, I am sure he will hit me. What he threatens instead is worse.

"Do you want me to fire you? Will Jean be properly avenged if you die working as a whore in the desert? Will that sate your righteous fury?"

I hesitate, not for long, but long enough for Adam's smile to turn real.

"Of course not. Because for all your words, you don't know how to go backward, Cara."

I'd wondered why he didn't kill me, too, and here it is. He couldn't control Jean, didn't have anything he needed anymore, but he can control me. He sees me like a toothless dog on a leash, not really a threat despite all my growling.

He takes a step away and puts his hand in his pocket. A half smile creeps onto his face. He looks like the Adam Bosch the papers show.

"I meant to tell you congratulations on your perfect score. I understand you landed in the first round of interviews. I'm sure you're concerned about getting another mentor with as much experience as Jean Sanogo, so I want you to know that I've had you assigned to me personally as protégée."

"Eat a whole dick, Bosch."

He chuckles, actually chuckles with Jean's body not yet fully buried. "You do so remind me of Ashtown."

"Don't kid yourself," I say. "You never left."

\

I TAKE OFF my mourning dress for the second time in a month, and put it in the top of my closet. My hand glides against the cold jar, and without thinking I take it down. I'd tried fruitlessly to get Esther to take Nelline's mourning candle back, but Esther had insisted like only the princess of the Rurals can.

I light the candle at my small kitchen table. You're supposed to know what you want to say, or at the very least who you need to speak to, when you light it. My mind is swirling with a hundred questions and twice as many dead, most of whom wear my face.

I remember a line from one of Esther's songs, and speak it.

"I do not know which way to go, but my eyes are turned toward you."

I watch the smoke for what feels like an hour, looking for an answer in the shapeless gray. The room fills with the smell of the bog at sunset, as if I'm sitting back there watching Nelline go, but there are somehow also hints of the neatly clipped grass from Jean's ceremony. The two deaths are entwined, not separate griefs but wells digging into the same dark reservoir inside of me that is growing wider by the day.

I revisit the realization I had at the House. I am a creature that destroys all who stray too close to her.

My fingers flex on the candle and I understand the words anew.

I am a creature that destroys . . . and Adam Bosch has strayed too close.

Will Jean be properly avenged if you die working as a whore in the desert?

Adam thinks I hesitated because I care enough about my job to make me malleable, but really I hesitated because as he spoke I got caught on the word *avenge* and have been ever since.

The sound that fills my head is something between a laugh and a chant, shapeless and expanding like the smoke in my kitchen. I look down at my hands, hands that aided a coup against Adranik, hands that killed him. Not only can I destroy Adam, I already have.

My mistake was thinking that his were Wiley City crimes and that those should be handled in the Wiley City way. I went to the authorities because I thought a citizen had committed a crime. I thought he would fire me, then wait for the notoriously long Wiley City judicial process to take its course. I didn't know that even here he was an emperor, but I do now. Adam may have forgotten what happens when you kill the wrong person in Ashtown, but he'll remember soon enough. Blood is the only answer for blood in the desert.

Thinking this way is dangerous. Murder has a cycle just like water. In the same way water becomes a cloud, then becomes water again, when blood calls for vengeance the blood from that vengeance calls too. If you plan to give death, it will always return to you. But I'm not worried. I've been close enough to death to see its shadow my whole life. It always misses me, but only just, like the person who leaves the room before you get there but whose scent is still in the air.

If this is how death finds me, at least it will be different. I have died a hundred ways, but never in defense of another. Not until now.

I make a list of what I need to accomplish, which is long. Then I make a list of people I can trust, which is short. By the time I finish planning, the candle is out, though the smoke still hangs heavy like a ghost.

\

I DRIVE INTO Ashtown so slowly that even the most distracted runner could have clocked me. But when the heavy boots walk up to my window, it's not who I want to see.

"Where's Mr. Cheeks? I need to talk to him."

The runner tilts her head. At first I think her tight expression is suspicion, but then I realize it's less serious and more complicated than that: jealousy. That's when I recognize her. The mechanic. The tall one. Mr. Scales.

After letting me sit with the sun in my eyes, she finally looks away.

"He's on the later patrol," she says. "It's still morning."

Technically it's noon, but I give her the cash without haggling and start the car.

"Don't you want your receipt?" she asks.

I shake my head. "Won't do me any good."

I drive back toward the Wiley City border and wait. The city has increased perimeter patrols since Jean's death. The conversation that should be about what Adam Bosch has done is instead about outer-city crime.

When I'm sure enough time has passed for it to no longer qualify as morning even for a group of night owls like the runners, I drive back toward Ashtown. This time I recognize the giant vehicle with a back like a winged beetle that pulls me over.

I get out before he does, and at his first sight of me he closes his eyes, looking for all the world like Esther when she prays for patience.

"What now? First you want me to trespass on the bogs, then you want to leave a runner a care package. What career-threatening event do you have planned for me today? You want to give the emperor a lap dance and need me for access?"

I decide to spare him the knowledge that I've already given his boss a lap dance, and it was as subpar as all my other sex work.

"I need to talk with you about a job, but I didn't have any contact info."

"A job?"

"Consider it a consult."

He looks back at his vehicle. "No time now. Tomorrow?"

"Okay. I don't get off until five, but I can get you a day pass."

"You want me to go into the city? Now?"

He has a point. Jean was a hero. It will take a long time for the city to stop raging at the people they think took him.

"Is there a place in Ashtown we could meet? I don't want your colleagues to think you're making side deals."

He thinks for a moment and shakes his head.

"I'll come to you," he says.

He reaches into his pocket and hands me a piece of metal that is as wide as two fingers but paper thin, though it doesn't bend when I press it. His name has been punched out at the top, and beneath that is his contact info.

"Next time, just message me."

"Seems less fun when you're expecting me."

"Oh, it's never fun. Don't worry about that," he says, and we walk back to our separate cars.

CHAPTER EIGHTEEN

When I'm summoned to the hatch I expect to see Carrington again, but it's Dell. Seeing her so unexpectedly, bent over a screen while light from the window turns strands of her dark hair to pure shine, is a fist in the throat. I manage to control my reaction enough to keep from running to her. I walk quietly, like I'm trying to catch a bird.

I get close enough that I can see the heading of the file she has up on her screen before she notices me. It's information about Earth 22.

"If you want to know about me, you could just ask."

I'm certain she didn't know I was standing there, but she still looks up casually as if she isn't surprised. On her face I see everything she wants to say to me. In the end she settles for the most familiar: indifference.

"I just wanted to see what went wrong, to prevent it from happening again."

"Little late for that. If it happens a third time, I may just have to accept that someone is trying to kill me."

It's the truth, but I've gotten good at telling Dell the truth in a way that's so obvious she can't hear it.

"Right . . ." She looks down at her reader, tapping on the desk with her index finger.

"Just ask."

"Ask what?"

"Whatever questions have your face all corkscrewed."

"My face is not . . ." She takes a breath. "Your name. It's not Caramenta, is it?"

I shake my head. "Caralee, though, so when you abbreviate it I can still pretend you're saying my name."

I didn't mean for it to sound flirtatious, but it does and we both look away.

"How did you know what to do?"

"You. You walked me through it. I saw myself as a corpse lying in the desert. I heard a tiny voice saying a name that wasn't mine. I put the earpiece in and you told me, 'Make sure your collar's secure.' So I took off her collar and put it on. And then you said, 'Make sure the pouches on your vest are closed so you don't lose anything on the jump.' So I took her vest. The only things of mine that came over were my boots and tattoos. The cuff had an ID with her address and emergency contact information on it. Her front door was keyed to my face. It was . . . easy."

"I should have known you weren't serumed. When you came back you were too bruised for such a short jump."

But she didn't say a word, because she didn't want Caramenta to think she'd been studying her body too closely. The rift between Dell and me is mostly my fault, sure, but I hate Caramenta for her role in it too.

"I wanted to tell you I'm sorry," she says. "Jean was a good man."

I don't think he would fit her definition of good, but he does fit mine, so I say, "The very best."

"He cared about you. I know it seemed like he cared about everyone sometimes, but the way he spoke about you to others . . . even I was jealous."

The tears come fast and hot, lacing the edge of my vision. I stare at the bright outside to dry my eyes, but the regulated daylight could never be hot enough.

"Thanks."

"There are rumors . . ."

"Rumors?"

"Rumors that he wasn't alone," she says.

She does not say he was with me, though that must be what she is thinking. Which means she understands his death is partially my fault, even if she's off on the details.

"What do you think?" I ask.

"I think he had no reason for being in Ashtown, so it would make sense that he was with someone else who had business there when the runners found them."

It's been a long time since I let myself give a good, hard, Ashtown hiss. I do it now.

"Runners don't kill their customers."

"Customers? You think extorting people is a financial transaction?"

"No, but they do. And you Wileyites *love* it. You tell your friends how you bribed your way into the desert, even though it's not a real bribe. Just like you come to the craft bazaars *knowing* we've overpriced everything, just so you can tell yourself you've haggled when we let you pay fair value. Every dead Wileyite is a hundred more who will never come, and never pay the toll for coming. Runners aren't stupid. The House would punish them for the damage a killing does to business."

She's staring at me, her face unreadable in the same way a star chart is unreadable when there are no lines to mark the constellations. It's not that you can't make out a shape, it's that you can make out so many shapes you'll never know which one is right. If I wanted to, I could read longing in her distance. But if I'm honest, it's probably just my own reflected back by her indifference.

"What?" I ask, because even lovely puzzles get tiring if they're un-solvable.

"You used *we* when talking about Ashtown."

"Does it bother you?"

It might. The Caramenta she was attracted to was perfectly tame—a Ruralite, a farm rose, not a garbage git. How would Dell react if I threw away every attempt at assimilation? How quickly would she and everyone else spit me out if I became that unpalatable?

But she surprises me. She smiles her real smile, wide and white and nearly perfect but for how much longer it stretches on the left side of her face. It's the same side of the face where the Ashtown version of her carries a scar.

"I've gotten used to you pretending you're from nowhere. It's a change to hear you declare yourself."

Declaration sounds too formal, but I have claimed my home more in this conversation than I have in six years. Maybe just existing as what I am is a statement.

Dell inserts a vial of serum into the injector. "It's time," she says.

After my prep, when I'm climbing into the hatch, Dell calls my name.

"What?" I ask.

She's looking down at her desk, but eventually she raises her eyes.

"Jean loved fiercely. It fits the story of his life to die protecting someone he loved. The only person who should feel guilty is the monster who beat him."

Her dark eyes have the shine of sincerity, and I want to tell her everything. Maybe I should never have let her hold my real name, because it seems I can't keep anything from her now. But I can't tell her what really happened to Jean, or what I plan to do about it. Not just because she might be connected to Adam, but because she might try to stop me.

"I'll keep that in mind," I say, and take the ladder down into the dark.

\

ESTHER BUZZES AT my door as aggressively as the technology will allow—which isn't very, but she caps it off with a scowl into the camera. When I open the door an inch she pushes it open three feet, and my calm, Ruralite sister stomps into my home like Nik Nik's meanest runner.

"Oh? You're not dead. Interesting. I was sure you were dead. I messaged you a hundred times. I even got a digi of Jean's funeral coverage so I could see you, but you weren't in it."

"I was in the back . . ."

"And then I hear that you have, not once but *twice* crossed the border but didn't see fit to let me know you were okay? I was halfway to picking ingredients for your candle!"

"I'm sorry I didn't think . . . wait, who told you I'd crossed the border? Are you still talking to Michael?"

The flame of her rage flickers, then surges. "It doesn't matter! I thought you were dead! I thought they'd killed you with Jean and nobody cared enough to inform us."

Did she think a new replacement was coming? This one just as off as I was?

"It's my fault."

"Yes, it is."

"No, not that."

Her glare narrows.

"I mean, yes that too. I should have called."

The heat of my sister's righteousness can rival a brush fire, but so can her empathy. That's why she puts out her rage with a sigh.

"You can't blame yourself for Jean," she says.

"Why not? He's dead because of me. This is why I didn't call you back. I knew you'd make me feel better and I don't deserve to."

She swallows what's probably another balm, another sweet comfort I don't want and haven't earned.

"Fine," she says. "Tell me. You can tell me everything."

And I do. I tell her things I couldn't tell Exlee because it would be too exhausting to explain, and things I can never tell Dell because she doesn't know me well enough to understand. I tell Esther, first and only, everything. I've already told her about what happened on Earth

175, so it's easy to tell her of Adam's bonus and how I found his other murders. When I tell her about turning the packet in to enforcement she says she's proud of me, but I can sense her hesitation because she still lives in Ashtown so she knows what a bad idea it was.

By the time I finish telling her about Jean and what Adam said at the funeral, she's pacing my tiny living room, her flowing clothes swooshing around her ankles like a mudtide.

"You can't let him get away with this."

"I know. I just need a little help."

She nods. "Anything. What do you want me to do?"

"Not . . . from you."

And up goes her eyebrow. "Then who?"

There's a suspicious pitch in her voice, and I have a feeling the leniency my grief bought me is about to run out.

"You're not the only one I invited here tonight." I'd hoped to tell her before the runner actually arrived, but my door monitor beeps with the proximity of my new guest.

Mr. Cheeks is lingering near the entrance. He's wearing a high-collared jacket and gloves, covering every inch of skin from chin to fingertips, but even without the tattoos his identity is obvious. It's not even his desert skin or silver teeth. It's the narrowed, wary set of his eyes. No one else in Wiley walks around looking like they're expecting to be jumped.

"*Him?*" Esther turns toward me. "I don't like him."

"Why not? He was never actually stealing from you."

"I know, it's just . . . his presence. Has he killed me on another Earth? That might explain it."

It somehow feels wrong to tell her what I know, like ruining a surprise.

"Not that I've seen. But this isn't the only world where you know each other."

Mr. Cheeks has picked a peach on his way to me, and right now his head is craned all the way up, staring at the steel and glass the same way

I did when I first came. At first I think his awe is pure, but after he lingers too long I see the two enforcers just at the edge of my feed. He's probably been wasting their time for hours, and he's determined to make it stretch.

I open the door. "Taking your sweet time?"

"Just having a bit of fun." He smiles wide. "You see the light out there? Sun's half set but it's still day bright."

"They want people to commute home in the light, so they don't switch to nighttime until about half past seven, regardless of the time of year."

"They just push back the sun?" He shakes his head. "That's city stock for you."

I start to nod in agreement, then realize he's including me.

When Mr. Cheeks steps into my apartment he becomes the second person to enter my home and instantly begin lecturing me.

"What are you thinking? She shouldn't be anywhere near runner business," he says, pointing his half-eaten peach at Esther.

"Why? Because I'm a Ruralite and we all know Ruralites are thick as rocks and full of judgment?"

"No, because you're an only child now. That makes you sole heir. Business with runners has consequences, and the emperor'll strip me if I cause unrest in the Rurals by letting its future wander into sinking sand."

He's not wrong, but my sister will claw before she backs down, so I step between them.

"This is just a conversation. Esther's here to visit me, but she won't be involved. She knows how to handle herself. She only looks soft."

"Soft?" He says it like the word is an impossibility. "Soft like a diamond, maybe."

He means to insult her, but he doesn't know my little sister has waited years for someone to see her and know she can cut.

When he sits on the couch, he tosses his gloves aside and begins eating the veggie snacks I've set out by the fistful. Esther sits beside him. I don't like the look of them so close together, but that's because when I look at her I see a twelve-year-old and when I look at him I see Nik Nik.

"Tell me your story, and I'll decide if we can do anything for you."

"This won't make sense unless you know I'm a traverser."

Mr. Cheeks chokes on his food. "Thought you guys all got the slip?"

"No, I'm still working. And there are a few others in the sector who are part-time."

I don't know why I need to correct him, except maybe I need to hear it myself. I'm still working. I still have a job. I don't have to do this.

"Last month I was trapped on another Earth and when I was there . . . I had to kill that version of Adam Bosch. It was self-defense, kind of, it doesn't matter."

"Who's Adam Bosch?" he asks, not so much as blinking at the murder.

Esther all but rolls her eyes as she turns. "The king of the interstellar empire? The inventor of traversing? He made the first portal when he was barely out of his teens in a neighbor's shed? Everyone knows Adam Bosch."

He nods. "Right, the white shirt."

"Any other questions?" I ask.

"Just one." He wipes his hands on my couch. "Is that where you saw me?"

Suddenly he's staring at me, eyes clear and mouth hard, and I realize he was playing stupid to disarm me. And it worked. It worked like it would work on any Wileyite . . . or an Ashtowner who's forgotten that the runners want the smartest along with the strongest.

"Why would you ask that?"

"Because of your face when you first saw me for the burial, and how you've trusted me like we've got history since, and how you just answered my question with a question."

All good points.

"Fine. Yes, you were there, and we were on the same side. But that doesn't matter here," I say. "When I got back Adam Bosch on this Earth gave me a bonus."

Mr. Cheeks furrows his brow. "How much?"

"A lot."

"Five thousand?"

I nod.

"Adam Bosch paid you for a wet job."

I nod again. "It turns out when Eldridge first started he had his men kill him and anyone else who could have figured out traversing on other Earths."

Mr. Cheeks just shrugs. "You called it an empire. That's how they're built."

"I know. That's why I thought I could keep working for them despite the past. But when he announced his new commercial trips, I figured out he planned to kill the highest bidders on other Earths to make it happen. I sent an anonymous tip to enforcement. But they thought it was sent from my mentor."

"What was his name?"

He asks casually, but I understand his cunning now, and I'm sure he already knows.

"Papa Jean," I say. "Jean Sanogo."

He leans forward, metallic nails disappearing as he clenches his fists.

"I've beaten my runners up and down trying to find the one who crossed your Jean. I should have known he was city-killed. We don't kill Wileyites unless they come to the blood field, begging for it and willing to pay the fee."

If Jean had gone that way, Viet would have had a record. Even if the keeper couldn't be bothered to watch the news, whichever mister is acting as executioner would have come forward.

Mr. Cheeks looks down at his knuckles, eyes moving like he's doing math, then he shakes his head. "If that's how this Adam does business, he'll do it like that all over. He's going to make five dead—five *rich* dead—and we'll get pinned on whatever world he kills them. They're already crawling into our edges over one man. They come knocking on our door every time a pretty-enough Wiley girl checks in too late. Five dead? They'll raze the town."

I hadn't thought about that. But nothing about Maintenance leads me to believe they are equipped for anything more sophisticated than violent murders. Even if all they do is traverse them back and count on the backlash to kill them, that's still five bodies that look mangled enough to have been run over. Who better to take the blame than runners?

"Enforcement won't do for you. He's got that machine bringing in oil and metal from god knows where. They'll treat him with the soft touch until they've got enough for building the next twenty floors," he says. "What's your plan?"

"My plan . . . is to kill Adam Bosch."

Mr. Cheeks allows me five whole seconds before laughing. "Nah."

"Oh, Cara . . ." says Esther.

"What?" I look at them. "Why can't I kill him?"

"Don't you pay attention to projections about him?" Esther says. "I only skim them because I knew he was your boss, and even I've heard the stories."

"What stories?"

"He keeps the secrets of traversing to himself. He doesn't trust anyone else with unlimited power to access worlds, so he won't allow it to be re-created. I'd thought he was being noble, but I guess he's just power hungry. He still does core diagnostics himself. Without him things would run fine for a while, I'm sure. But once something broke down, or went wrong, there would be no way to correct it. Maybe if one of his rivals could look . . ."

I shake my head. "He's put them mostly out of business. Forced them into other fields for years now. They'd probably be able to catch up, but it would take time." I look up at them. "Is it the worst thing? Maybe we've had our time in the stars, and if letting that kind of evil live is the price, we should let it go."

"It's not about your fucking job," Mr. Cheeks says. "That industrial rig stops bringing in metal and oil from other worlds, Wiley City's going to look for somewhere else to get it. They'll violate the treaty and come to take what Ashtown stopped giving decades ago. And the runners will parade again."

Hearing a runner make that proclamation sets my teeth shaking. Funny, for all the glory attributed to the blood runners, Mr. Cheeks seems to share my dread at the prospect.

How badly I wanted to kill Adam Bosch. I still do. If I hadn't reached out for help, I might have started a war without even knowing it. I can't kill him, but I need to stop him from sending out Maintenance.

"Could you . . . blow something up?"

"Depends on the something," Mr. Cheeks says, but he's already smiling.

Esther looks concerned.

"We traverse using a machine called the hatch. I know the materials are unstable, because most of Eldridge's training manuals are about how to keep it from exploding. Losing the traversing hatch just stops people from traversing. The industrial hatch is rough. It can't sustain anything that breathes or bleeds, so resources would continue to come in uninterrupted, but there would be no way for the assassins or bidders to get to another world."

"Bosch will rebuild," Esther says.

"I know, but it'll buy us time."

Mr. Cheeks is nodding. "Blowing up a thing that wants to blow up? That's a party. The hardest part would be convincing Himself to outsource us. We can't accept jobs. He can only loan us out. You'd have to have something he'd really want for him to agree, and he doesn't want for much."

What do you get the emperor who has everything? Last time I asked myself that question, I ended up with his name on my back.

"I'll figure something out. If I can find a tempting enough payment for him, will you get me the meeting?"

He looks suspicious. "Don't offer cash, you know. He won't like that."

"I know."

"I'll set the meet, but if you waste his time with my name attached to you, don't call on me again."

"I won't."

The meeting slowly dissolves after that. When Mr. Cheeks stands to leave, he smiles at me.

"So this other world? Was I the same?"

"Almost exactly. You were a runner, but you were loyal to Nik Nik, even though he wasn't the emperor. And . . . you had one more tattoo."

I can't quite keep my eyes from darting to his throat. He notices, and his eyebrows go up.

"Definitely not fun, but certainly never boring," he says.

Mr. Cheeks agrees to see Esther home, but before she goes she corners me.

"Wouldn't it be wise to include Dell in your plan?"

"No," I say, and as soon as the word is out I know I've said it too quickly. "You and Cheeks aren't from here. Neither are any of the other runners who will help. Enforcement has no jurisdiction over you. I'm the only one they can hold accountable, and I'd like it to stay that way."

She believes the excuse, which is true, if only part of the whole truth.

I watch them go, then sit down to list out what bits of gold might interest a dragon like the emperor.

\

I BURST INTO the prep room with more momentum than I intend, startling Dell into dropping the veil she's holding.

"Any chance I'm scheduled for a pull on 175 today?"

Narrowing her eyes, she picks up the delicate bit of plastic and wires. "You are not."

"Do you know when I will be?"

"You assume they'd send you back?"

I just look at her, because we both know the fact that I'm salary means they'll send me before booking a freelancer.

She sighs, setting the veil on the counter. "You'll be returning in three weeks."

"I need to go today."

"Cara, it's not just against policy for you to fraternize with those from other worlds, it's unhealthy and . . . and I think you've done quite enough of that."

If I were doing this for any other reason, her plea would have changed my mind.

"I'm not going to fraternize. I left something there, but I know where it is. I need to get it back. Please."

I haven't asked her for anything since the day Jean died. Even if she denies me now, I'll still owe her for that. Because of her I was able to see him one last time. I couldn't save him, but Dell gave me his good-bye.

"This place almost killed you."

"I know. But that was because Nelline was still there. She's . . . not there anymore."

Another bit of loss, another senseless death. And if Dell doesn't give in, it may all be for nothing. I've spent the two days since my meeting with Mr. Cheeks thinking of what would tempt an emperor, and I think I've finally got it.

"Fine." She looks back at her desk. "Will you require a veil?"

"It's too late for that."

"You'll have thirty minutes, and this time you will not lose your comm or turn it off. I need to be able to reach you directly."

"Fine."

"Swear it."

"I'll swear on my mother's grave if it'll get me to Earth 175."

"Your mother isn't dead."

She says it so quickly, I can't quite hide my reaction. I flinch. She notices, her face falling as she realizes that just because Caramenta's mother is still alive, it doesn't mean mine is.

"Cara, I didn't think. I'm sorry."

"It was a long time ago, long before I came here. Imagine my surprise to see her again," I say. I try to keep my tone light, but her eyes are heavy on me. "So, 175?"

"Give me ten minutes to reset."

"Thank you."

CHAPTER NINETEEN

When I land in the dirt banks of the dry river, the smell of hot sand and ash hits me like other people must be hit by the smell of their mother's cooking. After a second I lick my lips and the salt and acid taste of the air settled there isn't the shock it was last time.

I hit my earpiece. "I landed. There's no nuclear wasteland, no raging fires. I'm alive."

"Stay that way," Dell says back.

I walk along the road that will, eventually, lead to the emperor's palace. The sun is high and the wind is angry. Mr. Cheeks is the first person I see, hovering at the entrance of the palace. He takes a deep breath when he sees me. There's surprise and irritation on his face, but no malice.

"Knew you'd be back. Trouble always comes twice."

"You know you give me that same exasperated look in every world I see you?"

"Good. Means the other mes have a level head."

He turns around and motions for me to follow him.

"Are you really off patrol now? Such a sellout."

"That seems to be the general opinion," he says. "The emperor wanted me close by, and it's a hazardous post now with Adra's holdouts waiting in the wastes. I wanted something more stable."

Because he's in love, and he has someone who depends on him.

"Is Esther all right?"

"Almost," he says.

"Was she burned badly? In the fire?"

He shakes his head. "She burned, but not bad. Her trouble's not that. Adra tasked Mr. Cross with killing the wastelanders who were seeking refuge that night."

I close my eyes, not just at the former emperor's cruelty in sending a Ruralite runner to kill those he'd grown up learning how to protect, but because touching those from the deep wastes only ends one way.

"Tatik killed him?" I ask.

He nods.

"And Daniel didn't make it?" I say it like a question, but I already know. The vehicle that hit him that night was too heavy to do anything but obliterate. Even if he'd survived the running, the condition he'd have been in after would have made a bullet a better remedy than a pod.

His nod is short. "She'll be steady soon enough. She's been throwing herself into setting up the new government."

Nik Nik has taken the same office he had on my world, leaving the office of his brother and father alone. When we get to the door, I turn to Mr. Cheeks.

"Do me a favor? Don't tell Esther I was here. I won't be coming back and I can't stay long. There's no point."

He nods, then opens the door. "I'll be right outside."

Nik Nik is staring out the window, looking like a man I've seen a thousand times, rather than just a dozen. My Nik Nik used to stare like that too. Anytime he needed to think I could find him at a window. Granted, mine would have died before doing it in a tunic, but still.

"Shouldn't you be wearing your fancy coat?"

He turns quickly, and when he sees me his face passes through hope and joy before settling into the kind and welcoming expression of all Ruralites. He walks toward me slowly, hands clasped as always, like a man who is constantly keeping himself from doing something. Given his blood, it's probably for the best that this is the type of man he is.

"It didn't agree with me," he says. "I found it cumbersome."

"You always do."

"Do I?"

"I've never known a Nik Nik who wore the cloak for anything but ceremonies and very public appearances. You'll find the hair adornments won't agree with you either."

"No, I didn't think they would."

He's in front of me now, so close that if I don't look up I'll see only his neck.

"The braids look nice though."

He has three rows on the side of his head, the ends of which are braided loose down his neck. It's one more than the other Nik Niks I know, because he's not the second in his family to rule, but the third.

"Why are you here? My first thought was that you'd come to stay. But now that I see your face, I think you must need something."

"You've gotten good at this mind-reading thing."

"They say the emperor is omniscient. What is it? You must know I can deny you nothing."

I was going to dance around it, but there's no point and I don't have much time. I meet his eyes.

"I know you kept one. I need it."

He doesn't play dumb. He turns away and kneels by his desk. I can't see him, but I know there is a small, hidden safe beneath the emperor's chair. On 22, it held a fresh cache of poison. It could either be put into his rings, or, if the palace were ever overrun and the emperor saw defeat on the horizon, he could retreat to the office to rob his enemy of at least one victory.

I wonder if the contents here serve the same purpose.

When Nik Nik rises, the light catches on the object in his hand, held delicately between his palms like a wounded bird. A small gun. A pistol. Something I've only read about. He holds his hand out to me and I take it.

"I melted the rest down, just like you said. It was Mr. Cheeks who thought this one should be saved. It belonged to my brother."

Fitting, since it's going to destroy him . . . just not in the way a weapon usually destroys.

"I'll need to take this. Are there bullets?"

"Only six. We destroyed the means of production and I've . . . ordered that the knowledge be lost."

Meaning anyone who attempts to pass the information along would be killed, and there's a fat reward for whoever turns them in. There aren't many willing to turn bloodrat in Ashtown, but there are enough.

He gives me the bullets. I hold them in one hand and the gun in the other.

"I thought they'd be heavier."

I know metal. I know vehicle parts, and window blocks, and the thick clumps of it that get passed around as a rough currency. I'd expected something more like that. Not this fine work, this jewelry.

"It doesn't seem like it's enough to kill," I say.

"It kills. Adra had been . . . practicing. That one will put a hole through an entire man. There were others. The runners say they could blow off limbs."

A coward's machete.

I put the gun in my largest pocket, but put the bullets in my vest. Technology that runs on electricity fritzes out during jumps—the more complicated the tech, the less chance of it surviving. I don't know if this counts. It feels more mechanical than electrical, more like gears than circuits, but it doesn't need to work to accomplish my purpose. It just needs to look like it does.

"You'll be leaving now?" he asks, but it's not really a question. When I nod, he continues. "I can't help but think, with a request like this, you may be in trouble."

"More often than not, these days."

"You have no enemies here. Whatever ugliness has led you to need such a weapon . . . this can be your sanctuary from it."

It's a nice thought. Just step into the hatch and disappear forever.

Earth Zero isn't even my home. I'd just be leaving Caramenta's world for Nelline's. I could start over, never think about Maintenance or Adam Bosch again. Maybe this guilt belongs to Caramenta, too, and I can shed it when I shed her name.

"It's kind of you to offer. Kinder than I deserve. But I think this time I'll stick around and see what I can do."

"If you change your mind, we're here. I'm here."

"Don't wait on me."

He tilts his head, acknowledging the gentlest refusal I know how to give.

"Your Dell, did she miss you?"

I lower my head. "No, or if she did, she won't anymore. You were right. I was judging her and I was wrong."

"There is no undoing the damage?"

I shrug. "It's not really my call. Can I ask you one more favor?"

"Of course."

"Do you have an image of your brother as emperor? It can be digital or physical."

He freezes, but nods. I expect he'll go back to his desk, but instead, he reaches down into his collar. On his neck is a small fob. When he hits the button on the side, a hologram of his brother in full regalia projects out. As I watch, it cycles. His mother and father are in the fob too.

It only takes a second to plug his necklace into my cuff and copy the image.

"Can I take your picture?"

"Sure," I answer, a little crookedly because I'm saying yes before I understand the question. It's not easy for me to deny him anything either.

He doesn't ask me to smile, just points the fob at me and takes a quick snap. This is a sign that he's letting me go, storing my image with the rest of his dead.

I don't hug him goodbye. I just walk out. I'm only in the sun for a few seconds before I'm back in total darkness again.

When I climb out of the hatch, Dell is studying me.

"What is it?"

She blinks, shaking her head a little like she hadn't realized she was staring. She pulls her comm out of her ear.

"I just thought it would take longer," she says. "Did you find what you were looking for?"

"Not exactly," I say, because she might ask to see it.

She turns away from me. "You can go. I've fixed the schedule. You'll need to do a double tomorrow. It will bruise."

"With the marks I've got now, I doubt I'll notice."

She looks over her shoulder. "Even if it doesn't show, it will hurt."

"I know, but it will be worth it."

I mean that pulling the double will be worth it because now I have something to tempt the emperor. But I also mean everything else. It will be worth it, all this pain. It has to be.

\

AS WE WAIT for the emperor, Mr. Cheeks seems even more nervous than I am. He said he could get me a meeting with Nik Nik quickly, and he wasn't lying. It was only Thursday that I got the gun, now it's Sunday and I'm waiting in an empty warehouse for His Royal Pain-in-the-Assness. I haven't been granted an invite to the palace, which isn't surprising. If Mr. Cheeks had gone through any official channels, I wouldn't be meeting with the emperor at all, only his emissary.

Mr. Cheeks pushes back his already-slick dark hair.

"He must trust you, to agree to meet like this," I say.

"He trusts me now. Ask me if he still does when this is over," he says, and returns to his nervous preening.

Two runners open the double doors and Nik Nik steps through. He's come out in full shine—nails, boots, and rings. His long vest was made from a giant wasteland reptile, in case anyone forgets that he was a hunter first. It isn't as cumbersome as the royal coat; it doesn't drag and he can freely move his arms, but it inspires far more respect in those who've seen the creature it was made from.

Seeing him feels like being back on Earth 22, in all the worst ways. I was uncertain when I first met the Nik Nik on 175, because he didn't look like I expected him to, and so I wasn't sure how he would act. That was a blessing, because this one looks just like mine, which means I know exactly what he's capable of.

He comes with only two runners—not the six Adranik insisted on—and even those he dismisses when he sees me. He must trust Mr. Cheeks very much indeed. I've tried my best to look important but nonthreatening in my thick Wiley City shirt. I've brought a jacket of my own, white as bleached bone, the kind of thing that no one here would ever waste money on. But I don't live in a place where all bright things turn gray anymore, and I need to show it.

When he tilts his head, his long braids slide against each other, snakes cradling the side of his face.

"I told my boy that no matter what you were offering, I wasn't in the mood to lend out my runners. But now"—he looks me up and down, sucking at his lip—"I'm suddenly open to negotiation."

It's an intimidation tactic, nothing more. The emperor takes surprisingly few lovers, and when he does he prefers the professionals at the House to unvetted strangers.

"I'm afraid that's not on the menu, not even for Your Imperial Majesty."

I don't quite bow, but I give a deep enough nod to make him smile. Nik Nik is made up of as much ego as the rest of us are water, and giving him respect has always made him respond in kind.

"Shame," he says, motioning toward the marks on my cheeks, "I've never had a cat before. Should have figured the preacher's eldest would leave me blue."

I want to laugh at that. Nik Nik thinking I'm too pure to be poached, not understanding that I am nothing if not my mother's daughter.

"Show me what you have for me," he says.

I see Mr. Cheeks relax in my periphery. If Nik Nik hadn't liked his first impression of me he wouldn't have given me the chance to present. We're over our first hurdle.

I open the pack at my side and pull out my silk-wrapped bundle. When I pull away the wrapping, Mr. Cheeks audibly gasps. Nik Nik keeps his face from changing, but his eyes look hungry.

I hold the gun out to him quickly so he won't confuse this for an assassination. I don't need to tell him what it is or what it can do. Even decades out of circulation, their legend hangs heavy over us all. My grandfather killed himself with one. His grandfather used one to kill too many others to name.

"How do you have this?" He holds the pistol awkwardly at first, but then it finds a place in his palm like it was always meant to be there.

"Did your runner tell you what I do for a living?" I ask, because saying Mr. Cheeks's name would suggest a familiarity that might put the emperor on edge.

Nik Nik nods. "You're a world walker."

"I smuggled that in from over a hundred worlds away. Last of its kind. The means to reproduce it doesn't exist here, and they've just been destroyed in the other world."

I can tell by his renewed focus that the pistol's rarity is tempting him more than its shine. I know that look. He wants it, and he'll do anything to have it. I wonder if he's already trying to decide if he will keep it a secret or wear it on his hip to show the world.

He holds the gun up and points it straight at me.

"I'm listening," he says, finally lowering the weapon when I don't react.

We've passed the second hurdle.

I lay out the plan as Mr. Cheeks and I have rehearsed it. He warned me that once the meeting started he would have to pretend to be an uninvested observer, and he wouldn't be able to help if I forgot something. I recite everything just as he taught me: how many men we would need, for how long, and how much of a bonus we would front for the families of any men for whom the job went south.

Nik Nik listens quietly. He lets the gun hang loosely in one hand while he stares at the other, dragging the tip of his thumb over stiletto nails like he's testing for sharpness.

"And for allowing my men to take this job, I keep the gun."

"The gun you can keep as a thank-you for meeting with me. If you allow your runners to do my job, you'll get the bullets. There are only six, but time it right and you'll only ever need one."

Mr. Cheeks suddenly straightens, giving a nervous shuffle, but I can't see why. Nik Nik is smiling . . . too late I realize he's just showing all his teeth.

His coat hisses like the creature it once was as he moves even faster than I remember. Suddenly he's behind me, his arm a bar at my throat while his other hand presses against the back of my neck. He had been testing for sharpness after all, because with a curl of his hand four of his nails puncture the side of my throat.

"You think I need the rumor of bullets to secure my throne? You think me impotent? In need of a weapon?"

I lock eyes with Mr. Cheeks, who seems to vibrate as he's torn between duty and honor. I keep eye contact as I shake my head. I can handle this. I've been here a hundred times before. I focus to calm my beating heart. He's letting me have a little air, that's good. I can feel the hardness of his chest like a boulder at my back. This Nik Nik is mine, exactly the same. Which means I know how to make him stop.

I don't fight. I go soft against him, prey showing its belly. The weaker I become, the looser his hold, until I can finally squeak out something to distract him.

"Your . . . brother . . ."

He all but drops me.

"What did you say?"

"If you don't want the bullets, fine. I'd think you'd take the job to get back at the brother who abandoned you."

He doesn't look at me like I'm lying, just lost.

"My brother died when we were boys."

He believes what he's saying. Good. If he'd known what really happened, I would have lost my fail-safe.

I press my cuff, calling up an image of Adam Bosch. Nik Nik glares a little.

"Another too-soft Wileyite, so what?"

I slide to the picture of Adranik in regalia. Finally, Nik Nik reacts.

"It . . . can't be."

"This is the world where the gun came from. He's the emperor there, because Nik Senior died when he was fourteen."

Nik Nik doesn't hear me, so he misses my accusation of murder. I don't exist. He's walking over to the hologram of Adranik like he can touch him—to embrace or choke, I'm not sure.

He looks over his shoulder at me, half-feral. "I want to see the other one again. Put them side by side."

I do what he says with trembling fingers. I've never seen him like this, on any world. He's not quite saying his brother's name, but his mouth opens like he wants to. I give him time with the images, and do my best not to make a sound. Finally, he turns.

"And this is who you want to ruin. Your employer. My blood."

Brotherly loyalty is something I hadn't counted on, after all these years.

"He killed my mentor, and blamed it on your runners. You might not have known who he was, but he definitely knows who you are. He still knows his old name. He knew the runners were yours when he pinned it on them."

Truthfully, Adam Bosch has likely not thought once about his family since his father sent him away, but framing this as an insult might be the only way to make him forget mine.

Nik Nik looks back at the images, then away again.

"We have a deal. For the gun and bullets, you'll have whatever you need."

"Thank you—"

"This is no longer a loan of my men, but an authorized action. You are just access. The credit for the attack is mine to claim, not yours."

"I understand," I say, meaning I understand the order, but also I understand what it's like to have a hurt so bad you need your hands in something vengeful to lessen it.

"A week?" he asks.

"Less. It needs to be this Friday. They're hosting the analyst interviews and we'll need the influx of strangers to hide our presence on the elevators."

He nods one last time, then snaps his fingers. The two runners outside open double doors. He walks out stone-faced, accompanied by the whisper of his coat. Long after the trio has gone, Mr. Cheeks moves toward me. He lifts my chin to check the bones of my neck.

"Not broken," he says, letting me go. "You didn't tell me they were brothers."

"You would have been obligated to tell him, and I would have lost the advantage."

We're both staring at the door now.

"If you don't arrange the attack, he'll launch one himself. No turning back now."

"I'm getting that."

"I thought I'd seen all of his moods," Mr. Cheeks says. "But never this."

"Rage?" I ask.

"Hurt," he says.

When I finally make it back to my apartment I peel off my clothes. Blood has snaked from the puncture wounds on my neck down my white coat, making a mockery of my attempt to be from here. I'm not just a child of ash, I'm a child of blood, and it's a giant cosmic joke to think I could ever reach higher than that. A line across my throat is already starting to darken, and the bones of my neck hurt so bad the throbbing is traveling up into my skull. The worst part isn't the pain; it's the familiarity. It's how many times I've felt this before and how many times I've sworn I would never feel it again.

I sit on the floor, the years collapsing. Yeah, time is flat, but it's never been flatter than right now, and all the nights I've nursed a throat crushed by Nik condense until I am a girl on my knees in the emperor's bedroom. A girl who never found a body, never got out. Never free, but endlessly dreaming of freedom.

Never has it been easier to know who I really am, because Caramenta didn't feel violence until the day she died, and I've never been more than a step ahead of it.

I should go to a pod and get instafixed, or at least get an injection of euphoria that outlasts the pain of healing. Maybe in the morning. Tonight is for living like I'm still on Earth 22, for feeling every ounce of pain, and converting it into rage. Rage is dirty fuel, but it burns hotter than grief ever could.

\

"WHAT HAPPENED TO you?"

The naked concern in Dell's voice gets at me. "Nothing. It wasn't even really a fracture. It's just the bruise left."

She doesn't listen. She circles me, prodding along the discolored skin.

"I told you, I've already been podded."

"These cuts are newly healed. How did you . . . ?"

But then, standing behind me exactly as Nik Nik had and at roughly his height, she puts her hand against the spot and must see the way her fingers line up perfectly.

"Who."

Oddly, there's no question in the word.

"No one." I move away from her. "Where am I headed?"

"Nowhere. Doing a pull today might aggravate your injury. We'll resume tomorrow."

"I don't want to get behind."

"You're injured."

There is something in the way she says it that sets me on edge. She's saying it with the same tone she used after Jean's death. It's the same tone she's been using since she learned where I'm really from.

"I liked it better when you talked down to me. This constant pity is your worst look yet."

Her eyes harden, which is what I was going for. She can hate me all she wants, as long as she stops feeling sorry for me.

"I'm canceling the pull. That's final."

"It's a short jump."

"The decision is made."

"I'm fine."

"And I'm the watcher. Which means this conversation is over."

I grab my jacket. "It's never a conversation, Dell. It's just you giving orders."

"I'm doing my job. I suppose Carrington was gentler about it."

"I liked Carrington. *Loved* him. He had twelve horses and a sunny fucking disposition."

"Oh, he's a bore and you know it."

"A ray of sunshine compared to you, sweetheart." I move to the door, but it slides closed in my face. I turn to see Dell's hand on the desk's lockdown button.

"Send me on a pull or let me go," I say.

"Is there something going on? Something you need to tell me?"

And there it is, the truth sitting on the tip of my tongue, begging to run to her. I grit my teeth.

"Not a thing."

Dell stares me down. I stare right back, even though making contact with those dark pools is not unlike getting trapped in a bog.

Eventually, she forfeits and releases the lockdown.

"Don't expect me to clean up your mess next time," she says.

I don't know if she's talking about hiding my unbroken collar, or helping me escape security when I was electrocuted, or sending me to Earth 175 off the books, and the fact that there are so many options fills me with gratitude out of place in the argument.

"I'd never ask you to. Wouldn't want to soil your hands."

She takes it as sarcasm, but it's the truest thing I've ever said.

I spend the next morning in my customary post-fight-with-Dell bad mood, and running through pithy responses I wish I'd used is enough to distract me from my imminent corporate sabotage. On my way to breakfast, I hiss at everyone who smiles at me and glare at everyone who doesn't. Dell has taken me off rotation for an extra day, and when I try explaining this audacity to my sister she just says, "So . . . she's protecting you?"

I hang up on her. My day shifts from gray to black when I get an ominous text from Mr. Cheeks: *Expect a batch. Act surprised.*

A batch is what you call ten to fifteen runners, but if he means they'll be here in Wiley City it might as well be a brood, or a whole goddamn parade.

Before I can reply my cuff notifies me that someone has requested a day pass on my residency. I open it up, automatically expecting to approve Esther . . . but then come up short at the name.

Yerjanik Nazarian.

The emperor himself.

I quickly hit the redial on Esther, determined that, in at least this, she would be sympathetic.

"This can't be possible, right? He must be on the restricted travel list."

"Would you restrict the ruler of a neighboring principality? Particularly one known for . . . less-than-diplomatic responses to insult?"

I'm not sure where Esther is, but judging by her breathing I'd say she's weeding the interior garden.

"Cara, you did approve it, didn't you?"

". . . I'll call you back."

I confirm the pass.

CHAPTER TWENTY

When Nik Nik arrives, he has brought a posse, and if I hadn't received the text from Mr. Cheeks I would have fainted at the sight. I haven't seen this many idle runners gathered together in years. And there is nothing more terrifying than an idle runner.

I step aside, motioning them in quickly. It does no good; none of the runners will move until Nik Nik clears the threshold, and he takes his sweet damn time. He's wearing a black sweater that he must have purchased here. Full-coverage clothes in Ashtown are always thin, because they're for protecting against burn and sand rash, not the cold. But the sweater the emperor wears is a thick, soft material. If it weren't for his onyx-dipped teeth he could be a Wileyite—one of the bored, rich ones who adopt the Ashtown aesthetic for fun. His rows are tight, shiny, and new. If I didn't know any better I'd think he's dressing up for someone, and I can only keep my nausea at bay being sure it isn't me.

"What are you doing here?"

"Lemonade," Nik Nik says, ignoring my question and answering the one I should have asked.

"I don't have lemonade. It's not as popular here in the city."

"What do you have?"

"Coffee, soda . . . things it takes a machine to make."

"Water, then."

I bring Nik Nik his water. Because of the text from Mr. Cheeks, I'd gone out for extra drinks and food. I should have figured His Royal Pain in the Ass wouldn't want any of it.

"You guys can help yourselves, but you'll have to share. I don't have that many cups."

The runners shrug and half of them make their way to the kitchen while the others stand on either side of Nik Nik, who has taken a seat in my favorite chair. No one else sits.

"How did you get them all here? I only approved the pass for one."

I couldn't approve this number if I wanted to. I'm a resident, not a citizen, which means the most I can do is three in a week, with no more than two in a single day. Even fewer if it's for something longer than a day pass.

Nik Nik drinks his water without answering.

"We built your city full of holes. Ins and outs, where only we can find them," says one runner, using the slightly maniacal voice they use on outsiders.

Mr. Cheeks steps forward. I've been avoiding looking at him, remembering he'd said bad things would happen if the emperor suspected we were conspiring separately.

"If we get caught, they may decide to mark us as ineligible to return because we don't have proper papers," Mr. Cheeks says, respecting me enough to talk to me like I'm Ashtown instead of Wiley.

"And it wouldn't do for the emperor to be marked, so he comes in legitimately," I say.

Mr. Cheeks nods. The runners who raided my fridge—and, from the sounds of it, my pantry—have returned so the second half can take their turn. They're working in shifts, never leaving Nik Nik unprotected, with the exception of Mr. Cheeks, who forgoes refreshments to stay at his master's side. I'm not sure if it's loyalty or if he just doesn't trust the emperor with me.

"Why are you here? I thought we weren't moving until Friday?"

"We need to scope out this hatch."

" 'Scope out'?"

Mr. Cheeks shrugs, this time another runner answers.

"Scope out. Figure out how thick the hull will be. Record how long it takes to cut through. Plus, Mr. Cross wants dimensions."

My mouth goes dry. "You want me to get you into Eldridge? Fifteen of you? No way. There's no way. I'll only be able to get you in on Friday because all the interviewees have to go to that floor, so it will be set up for outsiders. I can't even make the elevators take us there today."

My discomfort is amusing, and laughter rolls through the batch like thunder. I am surrounded by my enemy, and it makes the back of my neck twitch.

"Adam Bosch has a replica in his mansion. A nonfunctioning prototype," says another runner I don't know.

They speak based on who has the relevant information, not who has the highest rank, and it leaves me ping-ponging between them.

"He's having a party tonight, so rear entrances have biometric access disabled for vendors. We slip in, get the info, and slip out."

"Okay," I say, "but do you really need sixteen people for this?"

They laugh again, higher this time. I don't want to make them laugh a third time.

Nik Nik answers this time. "Half to do the job, and half to distract security somewhere else." He drags a finger against the arm of my chair. "Runners play in the park to send a message, we slip in while the city scum scatter."

"But why are you *here*? Why did you come to me instead of just heading straight to Bosch's place?"

The emperor sits forward, so he can reach into his back pocket. He pulls out a cloth and tosses it at my face. I unfold it, rubbing the material through my fingers. It's black, but catches a metallic shine in the light. Without testing I know it's breathable, but will keep dust out of your lungs on a long ride. I'm holding a runner's bandanna.

I drop it and step back. The image I have of the bandanna is not Mr. Cheeks, is not any of the runners I don't hate. It's of the parade. The bandanna is a talisman that takes me back to a time when the cloth covered the mouths of the cackling drivers, laughing loud enough to be heard over engines and screaming.

Nik Nik takes my reaction as an insult, and maybe he should. In the next breath he's on his feet, sharpened nails digging into my biceps as he grabs me by the arms.

"You wish to use us as a tool and think yourself clean? Are you like them? So city, so Wiley that you can let someone else do your work and be satisfied? Are you afraid of Adam Bosch?"

I can't stop myself from hissing at that, and the emperor smiles and lets me go.

"The choice is yours," he says, and I almost believe him.

I bend down and pick up the bandanna. This is what Adam does. He dispatches operators to three hundred worlds, killing in his name, and thinks himself civilized because he doesn't go along. Maybe if I never go, I'll pretend afterward that this had nothing to do with me. That Jean was avenged by some stranger, instead of someone who loved him.

"I'll ride with you tonight. But I don't want to be part of the distraction. I need to get inside Adam's house."

Nik Nik's smile widens, a black shine that mocks me and knows me well. "Leave your scent where the enemy sleeps?"

"Something like that."

"Very well. The path we take will keep us out of view of surveillance, but if you're caught later . . ."

"I'll be on my own?"

He shrugs. "You're not a runner. But you can rest easy knowing that, with or without you, we'll make Bosch kneel."

"That's all I need."

I head to my room to get ready, pulling clothes out of the back of my closet that I haven't worn in years. They were the first things I bought when I landed, before I understood what I needed to pretend to be.

Just a few months ago when I was packing for my stepfather's church dedication I agonized over how to dress for Ashtown in a way that still showed I was a resident. Dressing between two worlds was difficult, and I weighed a dozen variables before I could decide on one outfit. Now, the clothes I need leap into my hands, because I remember who I am. Black, and lean, and ugly—I dress in my Ashtown best and I don't pretend it's anything but that. I am Caralee through and through. I'm a garbage git and even the air in the Rurals is too clean to agree with me.

They say hunting monsters will turn you into one. That isn't what's happening now. Sometimes to kill a dragon, you have to remember that you breathe fire too. This isn't a becoming; it's a revealing. I've been a monster all along.

That's why when I make it halfway down the hall, I turn back to my room for something else.

When I come out, Mr. Cheeks sees I'm wearing gloves.

"They won't scan prints. They won't even know we were there," he says.

"Just in case," I say.

"Have you thought about how to keep him from rebuilding? He might care enough about his legacy to train someone if he was going away, but I think we both know enforcement putting pressure on him is a long shot."

"I'm working on it."

Before we go he helps me fasten my bandanna, tying it tight over my nose and mouth so only my eyes are visible. He pulls up his own, marked with three needles to designate rank. With his face covered, he's all lovely eyes. Without the shine in his mouth and the line of his jaw, he has the eyes of a doll and the lashes of a vidscreen model.

"It suits you," he says. "If things go south . . . we're always looking for a few good misters, and not even Wiley's best can reach into Ash."

If he'd said that to me three months ago I would have spit in his pretty face, because I believed that anything that wasn't a Wiley City citizenship was failure. But I find myself nodding, accepting a vision of a future that might want me more than the city ever has. I could become the thing I'd always feared, and then I might never be afraid of anything again.

\

WHAT SURPRISES ME the most when I'm moving with the runners is that Nik Nik doesn't demand deference during the run. All of the pomp and circumstance he'll usually kill over—lowering your eyes when you speak to him, never questioning him—all of that goes away as we navigate the scaffolding of Wiley City. They use a construction elevator for thirty of the floors, but then we have to get off and take a dark stairwell from the sixtieth floor to the eightieth. If we weren't dressed like runners, and if we weren't about to commit a public disturbance, we could just take the public elevators up. Anything outside of the buildings is public commons, and access isn't restricted the way it is in buildings like Eldridge.

About halfway through our climb my gasping is louder than the stomping of fifteen pairs of boots, and I can hear Dell lecturing me about physical activity in the back of my mind. We part ways near Adam's land. The runner who will be leading the distraction grabs Nik Nik's shoulder without asking. I expect the emperor to turn around with a backhand that's heavy on the rings, but instead he returns the gesture, grabbing the man's shoulder in a display of affection and a wish of good luck.

I didn't understand how Mr. Cheeks could be so loyal to someone like Nik Nik, but the creature he obeys wears a face I've never seen. This Nik Nik—a man who is focused and sure, who issues confident commands and moves with the swiftness of the creatures he once hunted—*this* is the man Mr. Cheeks chooses to obey. Not the insecure, spoiled child who has choked me either once or a hundred times.

When we get to the edge of the garden that houses Adam Bosch's mansion, Nik Nik holds up a hand to stop us.

"Follow my path exactly. Cover to cover, two at once."

He points to Mr. Cheeks, then me. Mr. Cheeks nods and moves beside me. We move through the yard in starts and stops, until the mansion is close enough that we can break for the door in a final sprint. We don't break for it though, not yet. We're all crouched, silent and staring at nothing, but I'm the only one who seems antsy. Just when I'm about to ask what we're waiting for, I hear it. The screaming starts a moment before I see the smoke, then a chainsaw rages to life in the distance.

Nik Nik sprints from the brush and we all follow.

Adam may have turned off the biometric requirements for his party, but the door still locks automatically when it's closed. Unfortunately for Adam Bosch, the door is metal and we've always known more about metal than city kin.

It takes me a moment to place the woman who moves to the front of the pack, but that's because I've never seen Mr. Scales in glasses before. She rolls up a sleeve, revealing a gauntlet laced with magnets. She slides them along the exterior of the door, pressing her ear to it to hear the progress. Eventually, the door slides open. As she reattaches her magnets, Nik Nik touches her bare arm—not her shoulder like the others—and when she catches me noticing she looks away and so do I. She nods to him, then runs back to the perimeter while the rest of us duck inside.

Once we're inside, the group begins to move down the hall, but I linger behind.

The emperor notices before Mr. Cheeks does, and his awareness, as always, makes me uncomfortable.

"Scared?"

I shake my head. "No, I want to find his room."

I expect him to ask me why, but instead he just smiles wide with teeth like an oil slick. He pulls out a fob necklace exactly like the one he carries on 175. He pushes a button and projects a map of the mansion against the wall. "There, the far corner. If you aren't out in ten minutes, they'll notice you leaving."

The others begin to make their way to the prototype held in Adam's home lab, but Mr. Cheeks lingers behind.

He waits until we're alone to ask the question I'd expected from the emperor.

"Why?"

"I just want to see if there's some evidence of what he's done. I know enforcement is slow, but we might be able to give them something they can't ignore."

He shakes his head. "Man's a genius. He'll keep himself clean."

"I'm just going to check."

He's looking at me like I'm lying. And I am lying. But he lets me have it and goes to meet the others in the prototype room.

Adam Bosch's walls are lined with news projections featuring him. There are no images of his friends or adopted family. When I finally reach the double doors of his room, I realize I never needed Nik Nik to give me directions. Adam sleeps exactly where I would expect: in the rear of the house, with an entirely clear wall overlooking the desert in the direction of Ashtown. Does he miss it? I didn't, but my upbringing and his were as different as gold dust and dirt.

I go through his things quickly, but the search is as fruitless as Mr. Cheeks said it would be. The only thing of interest is a digital filing cabinet mounted on his wall. It's cut off from the network, safe from hacking, so I'm sure every file is encrypted. But there's nothing to stop me from reading the menu. I have to take off a glove to scroll through the headings on the screen, but I use my palm just in case it's a trap complete with fingerprinting. The screen is filled with options. Some file names I recognize as boring procedure, others read like math I don't understand at all, but then I get to the impossible.

My name, my real name, is a file on Bosch's personal server. Why? I open it, even though all the files inside will be password-protected. They are. I can't open them, but I recognize the type from the extension at the end of the names—they're from medical. Why is Adam Bosch getting copied on all of my medical workups? There are enough files to go back to before Jean died, before 175, almost to the start of my employment. Did he get copied on all the high-volume traversers, and now I'm just the only one left, or is he watching me specifically?

I leave the filing cabinet alone and put my glove back on before surveying the room again. Even here there are no images of anyone who might matter to him. His space is as bare of sentiment as the emperor's, and I wonder if it's for the same reason. I tell myself that just because he doesn't keep images of friends or family doesn't mean there isn't someone out there who loves him.

The Nik Nik I knew understood it was important to view your enemy as a whole person. Think of a traitor as a father and a husband too. He didn't mean grant mercy. He meant when you kill him, know him well enough to know who might seek revenge. If Adam had studied Jean better, he would have known I'd end up in his bedroom, puzzling out the problem of his existence.

This is how I would kill him. In the place where he sleeps. According to Adam Bosch's walls, there is no one who would seek revenge. Just like there will be no one to get revenge if—when—he has me killed.

Only Mr. Cheeks texting me that I'm running low on time reminds me that I can't do what I want. I can't wait here until he enters and turn him to bloody pulp the way he did Jean. Because that would start a war, and even though those hypothetical deaths feel distant and unimportant against the loss of my only friend, they wouldn't be.

If we can't get rid of Adam, he'll just rebuild the hatch. The next one will be bigger and more protected and in a few years' time Jean's death will be a blip on the otherwise uninterrupted pattern of Adam's greed. Only I'll be gone, and there might not be anyone else who cares. I can't let that happen.

When Mr. Cheeks sends me another, more irritated message, I'm in Adam Bosch's oversized bathroom. I rush out into the hall and hear a gasp. I turn slowly, but I already know. I always feel it when she looks at me.

Dell is standing at the other end of the hall. She's never looked more beautiful, and we've never looked more impossible. She's wearing an evening gown, a sea of black crystals interrupted only by the bright *V* of her skin from collar to belly button. Her eyes are wide with horror, and a glass of Champagne hangs from gloved hands.

We're both wearing gloves. We're both wearing black. There our common ground ends. Seeing her like this is like seeing a star from the mud. I can't say this is a misunderstanding, that this isn't who I am. I can't lie the way I've been lying to myself for years.

I can tell from the hurt just beneath the shock that she recognizes me behind the bandanna. I'm not surprised. We've spent so many years together now, she could recognize me in the dark just like I recognized her scarred and covered in ash.

Before I can speak, before I can step toward her, Mr. Cheeks comes from the other side. He grabs me by the arm and drags me away. I look over my shoulder, but with the runner's appearance her eyes have turned cold.

Nik Nik and the others are at the edge of the property. I take a second to empty my pockets and throw their contents and my gloves in a nearby incinerator.

Nik Nik raises an eyebrow. "They won't—"

"Scan for prints, I know. Just being thorough," I say. "Where's your mask?"

Nik Nik smiles. "I wanted him to see my face."

Wanted Adam to know that he knew they were brothers, more like. I want to scream, call him stupid. He's tipped our hand and jeopardized the whole thing, but there's an energy in his eyes I've never seen before. His hands are fists, clenching and unclenching.

"When the bomb goes off, he'll know it's the past calling."

I hadn't believed Mr. Cheeks before, when he said Nik Nik was hurt by the news of his brother, but I see it now, clear as a knife wound. He hates his brother. But he also wore his best shirt and had his hair freshly done before seeing him.

"I'll take her home through the shadowways, and meet you back at the palace," Mr. Cheeks says.

Nik Nik nods. "Watch yourself until you've passed downtown. They'll chase us over the border for this."

The two men grab each other's shoulders, and then the emperor departs. Head high, steps long but slow, not at all like a man trying to hide.

Mr. Cheeks leads me back down the scaffolding to the dark elevator. We pull down our masks, and he pulls up his collar once we're on my floor. We walk slow and close like a couple out for a stroll until we're in front of my door.

"Are you sure you don't want to stay the night?" I say.

He shakes his head. "Light will be no friend of mine. And I need to be with the rest."

"I understand," I say, but I don't.

With the exception of my too-brief stays at the House when I was a girl, I've never been a part of anything. I thought of Nelline as being tragically lonely, without so much as a lover who would claim her in the light. But now that I've lost Jean, I'm not much better off.

I'm looking up at him, finally coming to terms with the fact that he might be the one Esther chooses, and maybe he wouldn't be the worst pick in the world, when I see the slender fingers work around his throat, grab his bandanna, and yank.

\

MR. CHEEKS'S HEAD snaps back with the violence of a whip, and for a moment I think it's over that quickly. But then he ducks and turns, spinning away.

My mind stutters at the sight. "Dell?" I ask, but she ignores me, slamming a hand into Mr. Cheeks's throat that leaves him sputtering.

Dell is taller than either of us, but Mr. Cheeks is a runner. He should have retaliated by now. He keeps his hands at his sides.

I wrap my arms around Dell's shoulders. She shakes me off.

"Dell, stop!" I say, but she's already going for him again. "He can't fight back. You're a Wileyite. He can't lay a hand on you. It's not fair."

She snaps her head toward me so fast her hair spins like a propeller.

"*Fair?* I suppose it's fair for him to choke you, then? When you're so small? Is it fair for him to make you smuggle guns for him and break into mansions?"

"What? No, that's not what happened."

"I know you must . . . feel for him. But no one should treat you that way. Use you like that."

Mr. Cheeks is laughing loud now, and Dell's confusion at the sound gives me an opening.

I step forward and touch her hand. It's trembling. "He's not for me. He could never be for me."

"You think I'm dragging *her* into this? That's a laugh. She hired me and mine. We're working a job for *her*." He shakes his head and glares at me like it's all my fault. "Sucker-punched by a Wileyite. The shit you get me into."

Dell looks back at me. "You hired him? I thought . . ."

"I know what you thought. That I'm a tiny little Ashtowner, easily led astray." I turn to Mr. Cheeks. "I'm sorry. I owe you."

"Yeah, yeah. What's new?"

He rubs at his throat, and points at Dell, squinting. Then he abandons whatever threat he meant to deliver and shifts his gaze to me.

"Trouble. White-hot trouble, that's all you are."

"That mean you're rescinding the job offer?"

"Like I'd let you land anywhere else."

"I'll see you later, Mr. Cheeks."

He nods, then steps back, merging into the shadows.

Without a word I usher Dell into my apartment and try to figure out where to start. Her eyes are on my neck, and I realize I'm still wearing the bandanna. I pull it off and remove my boots, hoping I'll look more like the Cara she knows when we talk.

I sit in my chair, hands on the arms the same way Nik Nik sat. When I notice, I take my hands off and fold them into my lap.

"You eavesdropped on me on Earth 175."

Dell rolls her eyes as she sits down. She's removed her coat and I see that she was fully prepared to start a fight in her scrap of an evening gown.

"Yes, please make this about an invasion of privacy," she says. "Some watchers listen to their traversers' every trip. I've obviously allowed you too much leniency for too long. A gun? A real, working gun? Are you crazy?"

"It only has six bullets, and it can't be re-created here. Besides, I didn't have a choice. I needed it to pay Nik Nik. Otherwise he wouldn't let me use his runners. He still almost said no. I insulted him." I touch my neck. "He's . . . sensitive."

"The emperor of Ashtown choked you?" She looks away. "You sounded like friends on 175."

"On Earth 175 he's my friend. On every other world he's an enemy." I feel guilty about the half-truth. "On 22, he's my ex, but that just makes him even more my enemy."

She leans forward. "You don't need to do this. Whatever you want, I can get it for you. You don't need to hire wasteland runners to steal for you. I have money."

It's strange, her talking about her money like I should think of it as mine.

"I didn't hire them to steal from Adam Bosch. I hired them to destroy him. Tonight was just a test run."

"Why?"

I look down, calculating. She was at his house tonight. She could be more than his guest; she could be an accomplice. Jean knew what was really happening; maybe Dell does too.

"How did you find me that night?"

"What night?"

"You know what night. The night I was electrocuted."

"I was on fortieth. I saw you taking the elevator up instead of down and I thought you might be coming to see Jean. But you got off on seventy-six, so I followed you. I lost you in the stairwell, but then I heard the net go off and knew it was you."

"And you didn't wonder what I was doing up there?"

"I've become adept at overlooking things about you that don't add up."

"How generous," I say. "Why were you on fortieth? You live and work on eighty but lately you've been down on forty an awful lot."

"I have my reasons."

"And what were you doing at Bosch's place?"

"He was having a party. All of the elite got invited."

"Must be nice."

"Oh, be more bitter. I never get sick of it."

"Why were you heading toward his bedroom?"

Her eyes flare before they narrow—rage and insult, but not guilt. I've missed the mark.

"Why do you think that's any of your business?"

She doesn't make it easy to trust her. We've never communicated well, but between tonight and our fight yesterday a canyon has formed between us. We danced around each other for years because neither would tell the other the truth. If I keep quiet, she'll walk out, and we'll spend whatever time I have left navigating around each other like ships and icebergs. All because neither of us is brave enough to show our throat first.

"Adam Bosch didn't create an inoculation. He's just going to kill the dops of the winning bidders. I made a report to enforcement and he . . . he thought Jean did it."

I don't spell it out, and it takes no time for her to get it. She sits up straight.

"Adam killed Jean? And then he spread the rumor that it was your fault, that you were there?"

I hadn't known Bosch was responsible for the rumor, but I should have guessed.

"I was there. Jean made him let me go."

She runs both hands through her hair, though even after that dishevelment it resets to perfect.

"I'm so sorry. I should have . . . I'm so sorry." She takes a breath, then lets it go slowly. "I checked the record from your . . . Caramenta's first pull. It had a death entered without enough evidence, just like

175. I got suspicious. I was hoping to speak to Bosch alone about it. I wasn't headed to his bedroom. I was headed to his library. Why were you in his bedroom?"

"Looking for evidence. He has a file on me, but it looks like it's just filled with medi-scans?"

She nods. "I forward all of your scans. Quarterly bloodwork too."

"Did he request that from all of the high-volume traversers?"

"I wouldn't know. You're the only one I've ever had. But"—her eyebrows furrow, like she's accessing information stored deep down that she'd never thought she'd need again—"once I compared the serum compound I had to what Anthony gave Starla. They weren't the same."

"The serums are individualized?" I ask. "Or Starla's was special?"

"Or yours was, and he gets the medical scans to track its effects," she says, which feels like an obvious option now that she's said it out loud and everything.

Has Adam experimented with me? I wonder if Jean knew. The urge to call him up and ask is so strong I could cry from it.

"You should go," I say. "Nothing good will come of you being seen lingering around my apartment."

"Is there anything else I can do?" she asks.

I struggle with how much to tell her. I don't want her getting in trouble over this, but it's not fair to let her get taken by surprise.

"Don't come to work Friday."

"Friday? *This* Friday? That's only three days away." She tilts her head. "Cara, you can't kill Adam. If he dies, the hatches will stop working."

"I know. Trust me, no one lets me forget," I say. "I'm just going to disable traversing for a while. I'm working on something for the long term."

"The hatch?"

I stay quiet.

"No, I understand, don't tell me." She stands. "I thought after Jean died you spiraled and got involved in a dangerous relationship. I could see you were sneaking around, hiding something. I just thought it was your runner boyfriend trying to ruin you."

"And your solution was to beat up a man who beats up people for a living?"

"I wasn't thinking clearly."

"You? I didn't think you ever lost control."

"Only every single time something happens to you," she says, putting on her coat. "These last few weeks, I've felt you truly slipping away from me for the first time. I handled it poorly. I'm sorry."

I know what it sounds like, but that might just be what I want it to sound like. She's gone before I can form a response. Which is just as well, because I don't know what to say. At some point, maybe when she gets home or maybe when it's already too late, she'll realize she's right and I am slipping away. Adam will know that someone on the inside helped the runners, and he knows I hate him for what he did to Jean. I'm not going to get away with it this time. But I'll leave that nightmare for Friday. When she gets a call, or sees a news report with my name on it. Until then, let her think we're fine. Let her believe we can keep up this dance forever.

\

THE NEWS PROJECTIONS catch fire after the runners' display. They used flamethrowers, chainsaws, and motorized skates to terrorize the garden with one clear message: *We didn't kill Jean Sanogo.* I scan the coverage obsessively, making sure none of the images contain my eyes or utterly unique facial striping. I'm in the clear, but I may have a new problem. There's a capture going around of Adam Bosch just after the runners receded, which means it's Adam Bosch just after he saw his brother's face for the first time in decades. He looks wide-eyed and utterly shaken, but just beneath it all, where another person would have confusion or hurt, there is cunning.

My building access still works, a Maintenance gang doesn't come for me in the night, but I'm still convinced he's making moves.

I monitor things around the office to make sure he doesn't increase security in anticipation of Nik Nik's next act. But as far as I can tell he hires only a little more security for his house and garden. Maybe he thinks Nik Nik will strike only at him personally, not professionally, so he's not thinking about protecting his company. Or maybe he's made preparations I won't see until it's too late. But it is too late, too late to think of something else and too late to pull back. The pieces are already in motion, and we're about to find out if Adam or I played the better game.

CHAPTER TWENTY-ONE

The day before we strike, I find myself looking at everything like it's for the last time. When I pack, I expect a mountain of possessions, heavy as an anchor, to prove I did belong here. But it's just a backpack's worth of clothes and a box filled with my collection of items from other Earths. Soon my name will be off Eldridge's books, off rotation, and these sealed bags will be the only evidence that I once walked among stars, that I was valuable and the universe looked me in the eye.

Instead of dread or sorrow, it's gratitude that fills my last normal day. When I get breakfast at my usual place, I'm compelled to say thank you, and then say it again when the first goes unheard. *Thank you for always being open. Thank you for always being as rude to me as you were to every other citizen patron, even when I barely passed as a resident.*

I walk slowly through the street gardens, staring in wonder at the tall buildings like I haven't since my first week here. Under a flowering tree I thank the city for treating me better than any stranger deserves. For giving me a comfortable place to sort out who I really am. For letting me know what security felt like, even if just for a few years that feel briefer now that they are coming to an end. And I thank the city for letting me know Dell, not just because she's beautiful and I got to see her, but because I was able to know a person who carried strength and perseverance, but was utterly devoid of self-pity.

When I get to work, Dell doesn't quite seem to know how to interact with me. She avoids my eyes in a way she never has. I'm desperate to bring up what she said in my apartment, just to hear the parts of it again that make it sound like she loves me.

The closest I can manage is to look her in the eyes and ask, "Any plans for tomorrow?"

"No," she says. "I might take it off. Personal day."

I nod. When she doesn't pick up the thread of conversation, I climb into the hatch and let her send me away for the last time.

I stretch out to touch Nyame's muzzle eagerly, and the energy doesn't withdraw. I let her know she's going to be alone again. But then I see pictures of shamans in trances and dancers in drum circles and children sleeping and I know she's never been alone. She's never *needed* us. There have always been those who transcend, and traversing is just one way to walk between worlds. I don't think she'll miss me, that's too limited a way of thinking, but she makes me feel like she's noticed me, and I am grateful for that too.

When Dell pulls me back I sit for a moment in the total dark, saying goodbye to this space, the womb that brought me here, the grave that took Nelline. By the time I climb out of the hatch for the last time, I'm near tears.

"I got you something for your interview tomorrow."

Dell hands me a box. Inside is a suit, the kind I've always admired but never purchased because I was saving my money like an idiot to remove tattoos I might as well have kept.

"You asked me how I found you," she says. She's looking at me squarely, and I can hardly take it. "You asked me why I was always on the fortieth floor if I lived and worked on eighty."

I lick my lips. It's a nervous habit, but the attention it draws only makes me more nervous.

"Why were you?"

"For the same reason I have never taken a promotion or a vacation, Cara. I'm always on the fortieth floor because that is where you are. I will always want to be wherever you are."

I drop the box so I can pull her close, wrapping my arms around her waist so I'm surrounded in her scent. I stretch up to kiss her, because what the hell. I'm sure the tears I taste are half hers, but when I step away her eyes are clear. She holds my face and kisses me again. I close my eyes and let her make me feel small one last time.

"I love you," I say, out loud and formal like I never have before. Wiley words for my Wiley girl. "You know that, right? I've never said—"

"Come home with me tonight," she says, Ashtown all the way.

And I don't think there is a version of me on this or any other world that could say no to that. The walk to her place passes in a giddy haze where the buzzing reality of touching her—really and finally her—is only matched by my disbelief that this is happening at all.

In her apartment I learn that our height difference means I'm perfect for her on my knees, and that her being strong enough to toss me around brings all the thrill of Nik Nik with none of the cloying fear. Most important, I learn that you can love someone so much and so thoroughly it chases away even thoughts of death.

The bubble doesn't shatter until late in the night when we're lying in her bed and she says, "It's going to be okay, Cara. Everything's going to be all right."

They're her last words before she falls asleep, and once she goes soft with oblivion I get up and head toward her kitchen. I won't leave, I'll soak up every inch of her until I have to go, but I stand naked in her kitchen and use a knife to cut sizeable chunks from the hair on the side of my head. I find paper wrappings and bundle two chunks separately before writing a note for Esther on the outside.

For you, and Dell.

I creep back into bed, where Dell fell asleep thinking everything is going to work out. It won't. Not after tomorrow. But she hasn't figured that out yet, so I hold her until morning, and in her sleep she holds me back.

When I think of Wiley City, this will be what I miss. Not the magic pods, or freely growing food, but this, being close to a woman who inspired me and challenged me, and changed me for the better. Touching, finally, the night sky.

\

I WAIT FOR my interview in the lobby. Without looking, I see six black jumpsuits, Maintenance workers on a day they don't usually work, waiting with me. I'm dressed in Dell's suit, and it makes me feel confident. I guess it's easy to be confident when you're helpless, easy to be fearless when you have nothing left to lose. I'm bobbing along in a tide I've set in motion but can no longer control.

When the time comes, I buzz up. The voice that answers scans my face for identification and unlocks the elevators. When I step on, Maintenance steps on with me. The black jumpsuit nearest me elbows my side.

"Mr. Scales," I say. "For a mechanic, you spend a lot of time away from the row."

"Heard we're blowing up some rich guy's stuff. Wouldn't miss this party for all the silver in the world," she says.

She's younger than I first thought, younger than me, and it makes me hate Nik Nik all over again. It's refreshing, simple, and familiar to hate him. It reminds me that, months ago, before crashing on 175 changed my whole life, hatred for him was my only complex emotion.

The only way to get past the guards is in plain sight. I count on Wiley City classism to keep the employees from looking Maintenance in the eye long enough to realize how Ashtown this batch is. It's a risk, especially after being so wrong about Dell's classism, but they've been in the building for half an hour and no one has looked close enough to sound an alarm yet. When they review the footage, they'll see that I'm the one who let the vandals in. Adam is too smart to think that's a coincidence.

Michael is huddled toward the back of the elevator. He's probably hoping I don't recognize him, but I knew he'd be here and I need a favor.

"Mr. Cross?" I take out the package with my hair and note in it, and hand it to him. "Can you see that this makes it to the Rurals . . . if anything happens."

He takes the package, frowns at its lightness. Then he must understand, because his eyes dart up like he's scanning my scalp for the missing piece.

"You're not going to die."

"Actuuaaaallly . . ." says Mr. Scales, before someone else elbows her into silence.

I smile, or try to. "It's okay. I know."

When we get off the elevator, the jumpsuits turn right toward the hatch and I turn left. The waiting area is full. They only took the top 2 percent of applicants to the interview stage, but between all the testing groups there are easily over two dozen. It seems every research head has been forced to take part in the selection process. A woman with a portable screen is going from applicant to applicant, dividing us into groups depending on who our interviewer will be.

Someone grabs my shoulder. I recognize the creaking plastic of the jumpsuit before I turn around.

"You're on the wrong floor," the Maintenance worker says as I face him.

My heart bounds, but I nod in resignation, following without resistance as he leads me to the elevator. He's focused on me, which means he doesn't see the counterfeit Maintenance crew heading fast toward the hatch. I don't know what's about to happen to me, but the runners will do the job.

The elevator is programmed to go up, which makes the destination obvious. When we get off the elevator at Adam Bosch's office, I expect more Maintenance armed with anything from stunners to chains. But it's just Bosch's secretary, a woman so Wiley City she could be made of ice. She ushers me back, past the interior fountains and lush ottomans, into Adam Bosch's office.

He doesn't stand when I enter, and I don't want to sit. While I'm watching, he rubs at his eye.

"You look like shit," I say, trying not to sound nervous. "Trouble with your super-tech? This is why smart people wear cuffs."

He takes a bottle out of his pocket and tries to squirt a few drops into his eye, but it's empty.

"The next model will be self-lubricating. That will solve the problem." He scoots closer to his desk. "Please, sit."

I raise an eyebrow and take my seat. "Are you pretending this is a real interview? I figured this was either the part where you tell me you'd never hire me for analyst, or you hire me, but give me a stern warning that you'll kill me if your secrets ever get out."

He laces his fingers. "Maybe there's a third option. Maintenance pays better than analyst ever will. Plus, we've recently developed a need for more workers in that arena. It's harder than you can imagine to find people willing to do what I need."

The offer is an empty one. There's an edge to his words, not quite concealing his rage. He's angry at me. He knows.

"Is it? Your brother always made recruitment look easy," I say. "Is he why I'm here?"

He leans back, too relaxed. "I didn't peg you for a planner. That was my mistake. I thought when you wanted revenge, you'd come into my house and kill me. But to sell me out to my brother? That . . . that was an interesting move."

I curse Nik Nik for showing his face. I curse myself for expecting anything less from the peacock of an emperor.

"Was it?"

"Of course. When you have no power, it's best to align yourself with those who do. A pawn recruiting a king to fight on its behalf. But this isn't a game for pawns, Cara. That's why I went to him directly, king to king, and made a friend."

Fuck. What's a gun to the kind of power Adam can offer? My mouth is dry, but I try to hide it.

"You made a friend of the emperor? No easy feat."

"I made him an irresistible offer. I told him I would secure jobs and visas for some of his more promising staff to work in Maintenance for me, and I sent along a pile of cash to sweeten the deal."

I've been spiraling since he began talking, imagining what I would do if I'd been double-crossed by Nik Nik, but then one word sticks out.

"Sent . . . you didn't . . . you didn't *send* the offer, did you? You took it in person."

"I hardly have time to be running into the desert," he says, but his face is already twisting. Some part of his brain is aware he's made a mistake.

He could have had me. He could have beaten me easily. I laugh. I can't help it. I laugh and keep laughing.

"So you insulted the emperor by making an offer remotely, you insulted him further by giving him cash, and then you insulted him a third time by assuming he would part with his men if you paid enough. They aren't his slaves; they're his family."

Adam licks his lips. *Hubris.* That is the word that will be written on his grave. He's spent decades studying any space he's ever wanted to conquer, any person he's ever wanted to win over, but he didn't bother to check even the most basic things about Nik Nik. Because, despite his blood and his birth, he thinks of us as simple, stupid, greedy creatures.

And me, for my part, I was saved by my knowledge of him. I will bring Adam to his knees because I spent years yielding in his brother's house. Every bruise and broken bone, every moment of self-loathing and tainted desire, has led me to this: sitting across from the smartest man in the universe, and having the upper hand.

"Nik Nik was supposed to just blow up the hatch, but now I don't know what he'll do," I say.

He still looks calm. His hand is steady as he presses his ear.

"Communications for the building have been down for five minutes," I say. "Don't panic. Buildings like this are meant to contain an explosion. And the hatch is so unstable, you took extra precautions in that room. No one will get hurt."

"Nothing is going to happen. The emperor is a smart man. He knows how valuable it will be to have friends in the city. He needs someone like me. Besides"—he smiles wide—"I'm his big brother."

"You are. And you have no idea what he is capable of doing even to those he loves."

I check the countdown on my cuff. Fifteen seconds. I grip the arms of the chair and brace myself. He opens his mouth to speak again, some bravado to hide his fear, but it's time.

The shaking is subtle twenty stories away, but it's enough to set the sirens off and for Adam to understand.

I expect rage, but as the smoke slowly drifts up past his office window he only leans farther back into his chair. His face is pinched as he works at this problem, this puzzle it's too late to solve.

Moments later a second explosion goes off, louder than the first, though it's farther away. When I look out the window it's easy to see the second wave of smoke, as big as a city block.

"Looks like your house is gone. You really should not have sent cash."

"You did this, all of this, because of Jean?"

"And to stop you from killing the bidders."

That hits him.

"You care?" He laughs. "Why should you care? They're no one to you. They're nothing."

"They're people."

That only makes him laugh louder. "If only I'd realized how surprising you would be. This could have been fun. You know it's useless, don't you? I'll just rebuild. You haven't done anything but waste my time and signed your own death warrant."

I pull a pair of gloves out of my pocket and slip them on, then I walk over to him. I sit on the edge of his desk, sliding my hands along it. It's actual wood, and I don't think I've touched real wooden furniture since I've been in the city. Shame I can't take off the gloves.

"You weren't *so* wrong about me. You're a genius, after all."

I lean forward. He should stop me, but he doesn't, because he's intelligent and the downfall of all intelligent creatures is curiosity.

"You said when I wanted revenge I would come into your house and kill you. And that's exactly what I did."

I grab the empty vial of eyedrops he shoved away when our interview started.

"You've been putting Lot's Wife into your eye every four hours for the better part of two days. First, your iris will bleach, then I imagine your hair. But soon enough your entire body will be a white and frozen statue. Best guess is you have three years, but you'll be blind long before that. You can either begin training someone else in how to keep the hatches running . . . or let them break, and let your legacy die with you. No one remembers traversing, and no one remembers your name."

"I would have known."

But I can tell his eye burns more with every word I say.

"Decide who you want to be, Adam, with whatever time you have left."

"I'll kill you," he says. "I'll tear you apart."

"I very much expect you will."

He hits a button on his desk. It must be on the local network to buzz his assistants, not the larger communications that a runner named Mr. Splice jammed, because moments later four Maintenance workers enter, thick jumpsuits rustling like leather. For the first time I realize the jumpsuits are easy to rinse off; that's why they wear them.

"Grab her. We're going to the border."

My chest is singing as I am yanked out of the room. I tell my dead hush. I tell my dead I will see them soon. There was a time when the thought of ending up in the same desert I came from was the worst possible fate, but now I am comforted by it. Being beaten to death on the same sand that raised my sister, that made me enough of a fighter to get me here, it feels like coming home. If it's good enough for Jean, it's good enough for me.

Fingers dig into my arms, and only then do I realize I'm dragging my feet; my body reluctant though my mind is at peace. Then the office's double doors open, and I see Dell. At first, I think I've invented her, because I wanted her to be my last thought and because I want her to be there when my heart stops beating this time. Selfish, I know, to wish that violence in front of her.

But then I notice the enforcement officers standing on either side of her.

"Good, you've already detained her," Dell says. She nods to enforcement. I'm close enough to read their patches so I can see they're immigration. "That's the one, you can take her."

The enforcement officers grab me, gentler but just as sure as Adam's team.

"What is going on here?" Adam says, not quite in control again, but who would be?

"I filed the report with HR last night," Dell says. "She's been caught violating company policy. Smuggling, fraternizing off-world. Her visa was dissolved this morning. Immigration has orders for her immediate dismissal."

It's all moving so fast, but I understand, just barely, that Dell has saved my life. I look over my shoulder at Adam, expecting rage, but instead he's calm. He can't follow me. He won't risk himself or his men being caught in the wasteland after the message Nik Nik sent with his mansion. But he's already looking past me and through me, which means he believes me about the Lot's Wife, and I just became his least-important problem. Maybe he'll figure out a cure, maybe he won't. He's an evil man, but the world will lose something unique when he goes.

"I hope you choke on every lungful of ash, knowing you will never taste clean air again for the rest of your days . . ." His eyes shift from mine down to the scars on my face, and he tilts his head. "However long that may be."

"What does that mean?" I ask.

He smiles. I knew he wanted me to ask even before I did, but I couldn't help it.

"You have no idea what I've been putting in your veins. Even I don't know all of the long-term effects. How long did you intend to live, Caralee?"

Three hundred and seventy-odd deaths in, it's a stupid question to ask.

"I don't, Adranik. I never did."

I could tell him I didn't want this. That every time it's happened, he's made me kill him. But I let him keep his anger, even though I can't match it.

"Take her," he says, and they do.

Immigration allows me ten minutes to pack while supervised, but I only need five. I take a moment to drop my gloves and Adam's eye-drops into the incinerator. Bringing Lot's Wife into the world feels no different from bringing in a gun. I've taken precautions to contain the damage of both, but anything can happen.

I grab the things I packed yesterday and I'm ready. They confiscate my cuff, but I've already messaged Esther that I'll need a pickup at the city gates. It doesn't feel like much, six years of trying as hard as I could, but it's all gone now. When I walk escorted out of my apartment, Dresden is waiting for me. His smile is crooked, not sad but awkward, and I shrug at him so he knows it's no big deal, that I'm fine. He hands me a basket, and I know without lifting the cloth cover that it is full of apples.

I hear Starla in my head from what feels like a lifetime ago.

It'll be you soon enough.

She was right. She always was.

Enforcement leaves me in the desert. I stand in the sun eating an apple from my friend while waiting for my sister and feel very, very lucky.

\

THE ACIDIC AIR only burned for the first week. After a few days I can't even taste the salt on my lips. Early on, I spend most of my days feeling my own pulse, waiting for it to slow. Adam Bosch made it seem like the long-term effects of the serum would kill me, but after the second week I have to admit that I'm feeling better every day, not worse. It's possible the smartest man in the world was wrong or just bluffing. But maybe it isn't one of those quick corporate deaths, like the factory accidents from long hours and lax safety protocols, maybe it's one of the slow corporate deaths, like that dust that settled in our grandparents' lungs until there wasn't room enough for air.

I'm not dying quickly, but I can still starve. I'm not eligible to work at any of Eldridge's import sites or processing facilities, so I start out doing scavenging, but that only pays out big once every so often, with a lot of starving in between.

Esther pressures me to come back to the Rurals, but to join with the holy I'd have to confess my sins, including murder, and if I can't regret it I won't be allowed in. And I don't regret it. I could lie, I'm sure I wouldn't be the first liar in a tunic, but it's time to stop pretending I'm anything but a girl from downtown Ash.

Mr. Cheeks keeps dropping stronger and stronger hints about becoming a runner. But a runner is a runner for life, and if I've proven anything it's that I never go anywhere to stay.

My obsession with writing lists finally pays off, and pretty soon word gets around that I'm good with a pen and I know how to talk like a Wileyite. Suddenly I am a resource. At first, it's just a favor I do for parents who want to write to children who have been granted full-time enrollment in city schools. They want to talk to their children without their children being embarrassed by them. So I write their letters, translating what they want to say into something that sounds less like home. Then vendors from the bazaar come around, looking for help writing an ad to increase traffic from the city. They don't want the full Wiley City treatment. They want it to sound enough like Ashtown to be quaint and original, but not threatening or crass.

By the time the emperor's adviser brings me a job, I've accepted that this isn't side work anymore. This is what I do. I act as an intermediary between two worlds, a traverser like I've always been. A vendor I

write for offers me a desk in her shop to use as a base, as long as I keep
an eye on her goods while she's out, and I take it. I like having a place
to work. She likes having the increased traffic of curious locals wanting
to see a fallen world walker, the girl with the traverser's skin. I've had
the space a week when Michael comes in, marching perfect like he's
been doing it a decade. He's got three times the marks he had last time
I saw him, and most are achievements. He's thriving. The shop owner
and other customers are watching too closely, a decorated runner
enough to make them nervous. He drops an unopened package on my
desk.

"Told you," he says.

"You win," I say, and tuck the package away. "How's business?"

He shrugs. "Things went tense right after . . . Himself was in a
mood."

"I can imagine," I say, and then, because I can't quite resist, add: "It
can't be easy, to find out your brother left you behind."

He snarls a little at me, showing off the runner's tooth he always
wanted. He leans forward on the weathered desk I use to write.

"You taught me how to leave, Cara. I learned to chase the edge
from watching you."

It's not an accusation, I realize. He's thanking me.

"You were always going to find your place. Didn't matter what I
did."

"Maybe," he says, and takes those careful runner's steps away from
me. "They're making up, you know. The brothers. They've been talking. They're only fighting now, but . . . you know."

I do. I remember Michael and Esther fighting in the backyard, and
this is no different. Fighting means there is something worth fighting
over. It means you care. I enjoy the image of Adranik and Yerjanik
together again, for the first time without their father's cruelty or their
mother's apathy. It's an odd place to find love, but I hope they do.

I have a job in Ashtown, and no plans to move. For as long as I've
lived, my mind has been on the next thing, reaching for something

higher and better. I did not think I was capable of contentment. And I did not think it would be so lonely once I found it.

The biggest surprise is Nyame. I still see her. At night when I sleep, she shows me images of the worlds I used to know but am cut off from now. She shows me how Nik Nik and Esther are ruling 175, and that Earth 255 me had a child and named it after the mother she doesn't remember enough to resent. In the dark she reaches out to me, because no one is lost. It is not a testament to affection for me, but a fact of her existence. She finds us in the in-between places, cradling individuals in the same way she cradles the whole world.

My dead grow quiet in my chest, content now that I've brought them back to a place they know. The scientists would say this is all expected, that the pressure in my chest was just the toll traversing took on my most concentrated bones, and that my dreams are the same as the hallucinations in the hatch because they are both just the mind trying to process what it doesn't understand. And there is a world where they are right, and a world where they are wrong, and I don't need to know which this is.

I've been back for a month when she finds me like a miracle. I recognize her at first sight, though she lingers near the shop's entrance and only slowly makes her way to me. She bends over the vendor's creations as if she's interested in purchasing them. And maybe she is. Maybe she doesn't even notice me. It's not unheard of for Wileyites to get their thrills buying from downtown directly instead of waiting for a bazaar. She doesn't seem to have seen me yet anyway.

But of course she has. Of course she knew I was in this room just as I knew the moment she walked up to the door. We are planets in orbit, pulling at each other as surely as gravity.

She picks up a knickknack, a mudcroc made of local ash and clay, carrying the colors of Ashtown as if we need reminding.

"You're hard to find," she says, bringing the trinket to me.

I wonder if she thought I was dead. It's been time enough for Adam to have had me killed. There's also the matter of my possibly dying/

possibly not dying, given what Adam said about the serum. I wasn't looking at Dell's face when he said it, so I don't know if she believed him or not.

She doesn't look worried. She looks good. She's wearing all white, a color I've never seen on her. It makes her glow, and the Ashtown sun has pinkened her cheeks something lovely. She looks young, nervous.

"I may or may not have given Adam Bosch a terminal illness. I don't think he'll kill me, but it's best if I lay low."

She raises an eyebrow. "That does explain the shift. He's taken on a team of apprentices, and switched the company's gears from profit-making to community outreach."

"Lot of buildings going up with his name on them, I'm guessing?" She nods.

He's dying, and with the time he has left he will ensure he lives forever.

"How is it working there?"

"I don't know. Eldridge had become . . . unstable. I thought it best if I spent a little time focusing on family assets for now."

Moving money around is not the kind of thing I'm sure she'd want to do, but it's also always an option for an heir like Dell. She has a security that not even Adam Bosch could claim, wealth generations back growing fat on itself. Soon, they'll want her to marry. Sooner still, they'll want her to have a child.

I clear my throat and pick up the mudcroc. "Cash or barter?"

"Barter."

Dell slides over a jewelry box and takes the mudcroc without giving me time to assess it. I don't call her back, because I'm sure she's covered, but when I open it I wish I had.

In the box is Dell's jade earring, the third she had no use for, but it's been fixed onto a necklace. Instead of a platinum chain like most of Dell's jewelry, this chain is black as night and catches the light red like Ashtown stone.

I FIND MYSELF standing in a garden on the eightieth floor, where other versions of her have always found me. She approved my day pass, but this means nothing until she turns the corner. And there is a world where I wait forever, because she decides not to come. Where I go home, and try to make peace with a contentment I realize will never be true joy. And there is a world where I die old and unsatisfied, and there is a world where I die young, because Adam Bosch's rage escalates with his symptoms, or where he wasn't lying about the serum and my heart slows to a stop in my sleep just as I've finally gotten everything I want.

But there is also a world, and maybe there is only one, where a Wileyite girl comes into this garden and takes my hand. Where she reminds me there's more than one type of visa, where we buy an apartment on the edge, because I still work in Ashtown and because that is where half of our children will be from. Where I am always too rough and she is always too proper and it is a tension that keeps us interested far longer than lust.

It is only one world in infinite universes where this impossible happiness exists, but that is what makes it so valuable.

ACKNOWLEDGMENTS

I have put this off for longer than is healthy for either my or my editor's stress level. I always put off things I do not know how to do, and I do not know how to write an acknowledgment. I know how to be grateful, but my gratitude is a sloppy, spilled-over thing, nothing elegant enough for text. So bear with me as I gush.

Who else can I thank first but you, Cameron McClure? Who, when I decided to scrap the first project I'd worked on, the one in which you'd already invested so much time, said, "I signed up for a career, not just a book." And whose response to my every wild idea is, "I can sell that."

I would not have written this book without Patrick Rosal, a trickster mentor for the undercommons. You taught me Amiri Baraka's name and gave me permission to exist in a way that is unpalatable to others, and to write within the academy in a style and genre that it would only ever view as grit. More than that, you taught me what an honor it actually is to be viewed as grit, especially in a machine that's going to eat you anyway.

I am endlessly grateful to my whole heart, my where-ever-you-are-is home, Cherita Harrell, who pays her debts and *sees* her friends, and to all of the women writers who held me up in my MFA cohort:

Nina, Deena, Shelby, Katy, Caroline, Emily, and other kind faces I am sure I am forgetting. Also, an honorable mention for the men: Alex, Brock, and Kevin.

I have been taught writing by so many generous people, this seems a fitting place to re-create that lineage. To Tim Adell, who will not remember me, but who teaches creative writing at his community college in a way that makes us all believe we can do something beyond wither in the desert. To Susan Straight, Laila Lalami, and all the faculty at UC Riverside's creative writing program that encouraged me. And most of all the students I met there, my best, longest friends, the Breakfast Club: Joaquin Magos, Garrett Marak, and of course, of course, of course, Adam Kolvas. Knowing you guys has forever changed the shape of my life, and I am so lucky to have met you (but I'm still not getting a friendship tattoo). I *will* also thank Rutgers-Camden's MFA program and the Ralph Bunche Fellowship, because they paid me money and that is what you do when institutions pay you money, but I *want* to thank the living, breathing humans Lisa Zeidner, whose passion even about my mistakes made me feel valued, and Paul Lisicky, whose gentle mode of teaching was a calm port in the storm of my life.

And to my current institutional home, Vanderbilt University's Graduate English department, who signed up for a level-headed, serious literature scholar and ended up with a science-fiction writer in crisis, the way one sometimes rescues a cat that turns out to be pregnant. I am so grateful to the faculty and students (especially my cohort—Tori, Gigi, Katelyn, Josh, and Huntley), who have made this strange discipline and stranger town feel like home. Special shout out to Jay "Grandpapa" Clayton, for sharing my enthusiasm about robots, but also about theory and nineteenth-century literature. I absolutely can't leave a paragraph about Vanderbilt without mentioning Wesley Boyko. Thank you for always fighting with me like an equal, even when I was so new and knew so little. Thank you for twelve-hour days in the library researching and two-in-the-morning nights in your freezing apartment reading poetry. Thank you for being one consistent thing at a time when my academic, publishing, and personal lives were simultaneously in upheaval. Thank you because if I look up from my laptop you'll be sitting across from me at Fido, and somewhere along the line I have come to rely on that.

Thank you to my editors: Sarah Peed, for rolling with the punches, and Angeline Rodriguez, who was kind and encouraging even after she no longer needed to be.

Finally, and always, this book is for the Sisters Johnson, and for Ellie, Scarlett, Indigo, Emily, Emerald, and all that will come after.

Kya

ABOUT THE AUTHOR

Micaiah Johnson was raised in California's Mojave Desert surrounded by trees named Joshua and women who told stories. She received her bachelor of arts in creative writing from the University of California, Riverside, and her master of fine arts in fiction from Rutgers-Camden. She now studies American literature at Vanderbilt University, where she focuses on critical race theory and automatons.